W9-COX-428

The Blue House
Panda Books

Cheng Naishan was born in Shanghai in 1946. She graduated from the English Department of Shanghai's Education Institute and taught as an English teacher in one of Shanghai's middle schools.

In 1979 her first work, "The Song Mother Taught Me to Sing", was published in *Shanghai Literature* and she has so far published dozens of short stories.

In 1982, a collection of her stories, *The Death of the Swan*, was published by the Jiangsu People's Press. In September 1983 she joined the Shanghai Writers Association. She has been a professional writer since 1985.

In the winter of 1990, she went to Hong Kong and settled down there. She's now a member of the Hong Kong Writers Council.

The Blue House

Cheng Naishan

Panda Books

First Edition 2005

ISBN 7-119-03359-X

©Foreign Languages Press, Beijing, China, 2005

Published by Foreign Languages Press

24 Baiwanzhuang Road, Beijing 100037, China

Website: http://www.flp.com.cn

E-mail Address: info@flp.com.cn

sales@flp.com.cn

Distributed by China International Book Trading Corporation

35 Chegongzhuang Xilu, Beijing 100044, China

P.O. Box 399, Beijing, China

Printed in the People's Republic of China

CONTENTS

CONTENTS

Editors' Note

WHEN the Cultural Revolution came to an end in 1976, especially after 1978 when China adopted the policy of reform and opening to the outside world, one tidal wave of creative writing after another has washed over the face of Chinese literature. Chinese women writers have added their indelible inscriptions to this New Age Literature. Their works present a good cross-section of life in China. Among these writers are Shen Rong, Wang Anyi, Zhang Jie, Cheng Naishan, Tie Ning, Lu Xing'er, Chi Li, Zhang Xin, Fang Fang, Chi Zijian, and Bi Shumin, to name only a few.

The late 1970s and the early 1980s was a period of literary renaissance, thanks to the relaxed political climate and growing democracy in China. Many women writers emerged, dealing with all kinds of subject matters and attracting widespread attention. The school of "wound literature" took shape, which mainly focuses on people's lives during and after the Cultural Revolution. Shen Rong's "At Middle Age" raises the problems of middle-aged professionals, who enter the new age with marks left on them by the Cultural Revolution and who have to divide their time between career and family and more often than not neglect

one or the other. Cheng Naishan, perceptive, objective, penetrating, and compassionate, captivates her readers with stories
about the lives and loves, the destinies and the emotional entan-
glements of the industrial and business families of China's
metropolis, a class which has weathered political vicissitudes before and during the Cultural Revolution. "The Blue House," her
representative work, is one such story describing the turmoil going through the Gu family, the former steel giant in Shanghai
who owned the Blue House.

Women writers were truthful spokesmen for the youth who
suffered during the Cultural Revolution. Problems of the young
people of the time were frankly dealt with, such as their disrupted education; lack of interesting employment; the difficulties
met with by boys and girls sent from town to the countryside;
the low incomes and overcrowding which threaten to break up
young couples' marriages; their mental confusion after the turbulent years in which traditions were thrown overboard and bu-
reaucracy, nepotism and corruption were rampant. Zhang Jie's
"Love Must Not Be Forgotten" had aroused considerable interest
as well as much controversy. Boldly unconventional, idealistic
and intensely romantic, the story sheds interesting light on the
changes in the attitude to love in socialist China, still strongly
influenced by feudal ideas about marriage at the time.

While reform was still dawning on the Chinese horizon,
Zhang Jie captured the historic social changes of this mood of
reform in her important novel, "Leaden Wings." First published
in 1981 and an instant bestseller, the story has as its central
theme the modernization of industry. The publication of this
book aroused further controversy. Exposing various abuses and
man-made obstacles to modernization, it came under fire for

"attacking socialism." But many readers welcomed it as painting a truthful picture of modern Chinese society of the time.

In the mid-1980s, seeking out and examining the roots of Chinese culture became the dominant trend, hence the term "root literature." Leading this trend was Wang Anyi's novella "Xiaobao Village," which dissects the rights and wrongs of traditional moral values by portraying what happens behind closed doors in a tiny village that is generally extolled as a paragon of humanity and justice. The author's rich choice of language and her profound grasp of the cultural life and nature of people in a small village, places "Xiaobao Village" on a par with Ah Cheng's "The Chess Master" and Han Shaogong's "Father."

Wang Anyi, who represents the writers whose formal education was disrupted by the Cultural Revolution knows from firsthand experience the problems of young people who have returned from communes to the cities. In her stories, a sense of humanism appears. She is not one simply to condemn or write off the 10 years of her generation lost because of the Cultural Revolution. In her creative world, authentic human feelings live through the traumatic days of the Cultural Revolution. They are perpetuated along with—perhaps in tandem with—the old class relations, with all their old prejudices, suspicions, and tolerances, too. Wang Anyi analyzes China with an imagination that seems nourished by both pre-revolutionary and post-revolutionary culture. Her stories are alive with such tensions and contrasts. Her stories "Lapse of Time" and "The Destination" have won literary prizes in China.

In the late 1980s, Neo-realism came in vogue in Chinese fiction, of which Chi Li, author of "Trials and Tribulations," and Fang Fang, who wrote "Landscape," are both hailed as founding members.

Chi Li is an active writer on the Chinese literary scene. Her stories, like the above-mentioned "Trials and Tribulations" and "Apart from Love," mostly focus on the female world, their love and marriage, though her attitude has nothing to do with feminism. The detailed and earthy descriptions conjure up a vivid picture of life in the late 1980s.

Fang Fang began by writing humorous stories, which are full of caustic and witty remarks. She then turned to stories about magic in which her characters summon up wind and rain like spirits. But she later changed her style again. She is sort of unpredictable, constantly surprising readers and critics because she does not confine herself to a certain style. One of the most popular female writers in present-day China, she is best known for her stories about urban life, with characters ranging from intellectuals to laborers. Her "Landscape" depicts the relationships between an illiterate docker and his nine children, and the hardships they endure in a raw struggle to survive.

During the transitional 1990s, New Age Literature came to an end. The transformation of social and economic patterns in China has given rise to multiple literary patterns with writers of various pursuits locked in a keenly contested competition. The principle of literature has changed from serving life to serving man's existence, and from presenting people's aspirations for life and the historical destiny of collectives to depicting ordinary people's existence in this world. Works by women writers started to describe the petty vexations of people working to earn and survive in the mundane world. Neo-realism, first appearing in the late 1980s and represented by Chi Li and Fang Fang, has developed to a new height. Chi Li's relatively recent stories, "To and Fro" and "Life Show," have presented a vivid, realistic picture of the life of women in the fast-changing Chinese society. Bi Shumin, a doctor-turned woman writer, focuses on specific social and e-conomic phenomena, revealing the contradictions in modern society and the true nature of man in the face of the social and e-conomic reforms in China. But her works don't just stop there. Her novella "An Appointment with Death" and full-length novel *The Red Prescription* aim for a broader philosophical meaning beyond the superficial implications of subjects like hospice care, life and death, drug use and rehabilitation.

Today, China's relaxed political climate and growing democracy have resulted in more truthful writing and a wider range of themes. Love, social injustice, the value of the individual, humanism and other subjects formerly taboo are being fearlessly tackled by women writers—often with an unabashed display of emotion.

As editors, we hope that this series of women writers' works, compiled and published by Foreign Languages Press, will open a door to the world of Chinese women writers and to the everyday life of ordinary Chinese, for our readers who are interested in Chinese literature and China as well.

The Blue House

1

"DUE to the war in Europe in 1914, there was virtually no pig iron available for importation. Mr Gu Fuxiang had a large stockpile of pig iron, and by selling off the hoarded material at the suddenly skyrocketing prices, the distinguished Mr Gu Fuxiang became one of the richest industrialists in Shanghai overnight... Mr Gu had three sons. The eldest, Gu Hongzhi, following his father's instructions, went to America to study economics in order to further develop the family business. The second son, Gu Hongfei, became so dissatisfied with his family that he ran a notice in the newspaper publicly disowning his father. Gu Hongji, the third son, is currently pursuing studies at Xuhui College, where he is reportedly majoring in metallurgy... After the war with Japan, the Gu family's Huachang Steel Plant continued to expand and prosper, and today the Gu clan is considered the 'Steel Giant' of southeast Asia... The Gu estate is located in the French Concession, and the Gu mansion was designed by the German architect Burger. The exterior of the building is covered with blue tiling, and the interior is equally impressive, with the washrooms and kitchen fitted out with

American and British imported equipment. It is known in Shanghai as the 'Blue House'."

The library was closing, and Gu Chuanhui had to tear himself reluctantly from the yellowed 1946 edition of *A Narrative History of Shanghai Commerce*. Several lines in particular stayed with him even after he closed the book: "The second son, Gu Hongfei, became so dissatisfied with his family that he ran a notice in the newspaper publicly disowning his father." Intense feelings of anger and self-pity welled up within. By pure chance he had discovered that he himself was a descendent of this famous family. And "The second son, Gu Hongfei," was his very own father! To think that he had never heard a thing about this illustrious and once influential clan to which he belonged. Father had never said a word about it all these years. Incredible! But all the book could offer was those few lines, far from satisfactory.

He walked out of the municipal library and into the never-ceasing noise and ever-pressing crowds of Nanjing Road. "The second son, Gu Hongfei ... disowning his father." The words trailed behind him like a ghost as he walked out of the building. For the first time in twenty-seven years he was unhappy with his family, with himself.

Chuanhui was born on the ninth day of the first lunar month, a most auspicious day, so it was said—the birthday of the Jade Emperor himself! He was indeed blessed with good luck; there was no denying that. His parents had worked hard all their lives and were the epitome of cautiousness; they had adroitly dodged one political movement after another and had managed to live in relative peace in spite of the "storm of class struggle" that raged around them. And although his father had been criticized some during the "cultural revolution" (he now realized that it must have been connected to the fame of the Gu clan), his home suffered nothing compared to others; many families had been smashed or exiled. His family had been left intact and mostly at peace, and Chuanhui had to admit his good fortune. Moreover, being an only child he was spared the physical and mental anguish of those sent to the countryside during those nightmarish years; according to the policy an only child was given a menial government job near home. Menial government jobs—selling wheat cakes or sweeping the streets—were hardly the best jobs in the world, but at that time people's expectations were not high, and just the chance to stay in your home town would have made most people happy. But when word came that the boy would be given work at a cooked meat store, his middle school teacher father and nurse mother were far from content. The neighbours good-naturedly reminded the distressed parents that the pay was not all that bad, and besides, such a well-placed son might help them all get hold of some hard to come by food items; but the couple could find nothing to laugh at in the situation. It was not that the parents looked down on such a profession; it was just that they were afraid that after a few months the boy would turn into someone as slippery and ambitionless as those greasy youths in the store. Even in the days of Zhang Tiesheng's blank test paper, * the parents had made their son fill

---

* Zhang Tiesheng: During the "cultural revolution" this young man turned in an empty sheet of paper for his college entrance exam and later wrote an essay explaining that he was too busy making revolution to learn anything academic.

a page with calligraphy and study at least a few lines of English each night. Until he had been officially assigned his job, there had seemed to be some hope, but once stuck in a cooked meat store what kind of future could he possibly have? But any man who shares his birthday with the Jade Emperor has got a lucky star higher than the sky itself! After he had worked at the cooked meat store only two months, the college entrance examinations were reinstituted. Thanks to the solicitous coaching of his parents during those difficult times, Chuanhui had become an excellent student, and so with little effort he was able to bid farewell to the store and enter university.

After college he was assigned to the instrument and metre factory. The sight of him sitting there in his laboratory looking stylish in his white lab coat brought immense relief to the parents who had worried so much about him.

Life had indeed been good to him, and he was even endowed with each of his parents better physical features. He had the high forehead, tall stature, and strong, handsome features of his father, and from his mother he inherited thick eyebrows that shadowed sharp and lively eyes. A peaceful and cultured family life gave him a quick mind and sensitive soul. Simply put, he was a very likeable young man. If you had to find a fault, you could say his forehead was a little too shiny and a bit delicate looking or maybe that his complexion was a little too fair for that of a man. Perhaps he lacked the strength of character one hoped to find in a man. But that would be nitpicking. No one who knew him was bothered in the least by any minor frailty, and all the girls found him adorable. While he was still in middle school, the neighbours used to joke with his mother, "Boys are much sought after these days. Good boys are hard to find you know, and a fellow as well-mannered and well-behaved as your son can take his pick when the time comes to find a girl! Girls'll be fighting over him!" The words were true enough. The "Unite the majority!" slogan came around in the early 70s, and intellectuals were denounced. Yet, they were like "stinking bean curd". Stinking, maybe, but good to eat. By then the capitalist families had lost their attraction. High ranking cadres' families were out of reach to most marriageable youths, and besides, the way politics was swinging back and forth, they were not the best investment for a sound future. As for the families of the "Five Reds"*, they were just a bit too crude. So an intellectual family with sound finances suddenly became the ideal for the average citizen looking for a spouse.

All this could not help but give Chuanhui a sense of superiority. He moved with ease and confidence in public, especially with other young people. And he was equally confident—actually coldly calculating—when it came to romance. He held off till his last year of college before making any commitments, then finally made his move on an attractive girl with the latest hairstyle from the foreign language department. Her clothes were always stylish and never old-fashioned. She could swim, play tennis, and play the piano expertly. She was just the kind of girl he was looking for, but she was strangely indifferent to Chuanhui's attention. Finally, she rejected him altogether. Not long after he found out that every weekend the girl was met at the school gate by a short, stumpy fellow built something like a gourd who would whisk her away on his motorbike. This gourd had nothing

---

* Five Reds: workers, peasants, soldiers, students, and pedlars.

on Chuanhui as far as he could tell. He was more than a little shocked when he found out that this gourd's father was a big shop owner who handed his son 50,000 yuan the moment the policy of refunding businessmen was carried out. This defeat in his first romantic campaign punched a large hole in his ego, but he learned the lesson that circumstances can change rapidly for anyone, and that his time as "The Most Favoured One Under Heaven" had drawn to a close.

Circumstances can change dramatically, and so can people. Take Xiao Zhu, a fellow that did odd jobs around Chuanhui's lab, for example. The boy had spent five difficult years labouring in the countryside before finally returning to the city to take his mother's job when she retired. It was said that Xiao Zhu's father had jumped aboard a ship years ago and had not been heard of since. His mother had worked hard for years to eke out an existence for herself and her only son. Having a poor family and low-level job had left the boy with a deep inferiority complex, and everyone who saw him felt sorry for him. He could hardly whack up the courage to speak to the young men his age, much less girls. But a person's fate can often turn round overnight; the mysterious missing father was found. He had a business in West Germany, and Xiao Zhu was able to contact him. At that point Xiao Zhu's personality changed completely. The change was even more dramatic when the father came to Shanghai last year and bought Xiao Zhu a new apartment out at the Overseas Chinese Development. He suddenly became obnoxious and arrogant and spent the day roaring back and forth on his new Suzuki motorcycle, beeping his infernal horn till the heavens were about to split. He was well equipped electronically: an electronic watch, an electric lighter, an electronic calculator, even an electronic mosquito killer. Even Chuanhui, who had seen most of the newest gadgets around, was impressed. Xiao Zhu was haughty to everyone except Chuanhui, who at one time had been his teacher. Before his change of luck Xiao Zhu had enrolled in night school hoping that a diploma from the college program would give him a chance to escape his job of "boiling water and sweeping floors", and he had asked Chuanhui to help him with his English. "With a penniless family like mine and such a miserable job, I'll never find a woman that'll marry me," he had once said to Chuanhui in a rare moment of candour. But that was then, and this was now. He no longer attended the night school, and he was continually absent from work with one excuse or another. Such is life. Xiao Zhu now had so many girls to choose from that it made his head spin. Even if he had been illiterate it wouldn't have had an adverse effect on who was available to him. There were some men in the department who had graduated from college in '67, '68, and even in '65 and never got married for a variety of reasons: no housing, responsibility for older parents, no gas, no bathroom... It always boiled down to a matter of pure economics. The girls were just like lazy cats in a kitchen; they went wherever there was some heat. This fact chilled Chuanhui and eroded what little "self-confidence" he had.

Chuanhui could not find a single young lady that caught his fancy. All the girls at the factory dressed and acted as if they had all been made from the same mould—every one of them had long straight hair and wore the same style trousers, and the same high heels. If the fad this year was sheepskin hunting jackets, then everyone wore sheepskin hunting jackets. If the latest rage was to wear a sweater without a jacket, then the factory swarmed with girls sporting their colourful sweaters. It got to the point where he could hardly even distinguish between the girls in his own lab from a distance, let alone anyone else. "No individuality," he despaired privately. But a young woman that had recently joined the drafting department caught his attention before he ever saw her. The name on a blueprint enchanted him immediately: Bai Hong, "White Rainbow". Bai Hong. What a beautiful, poetic name. He liked poetry. He could remember vividly the words of a poem he had once read: "Before the teardrop can be wiped away, oh heart, you leap again at the thought of sweet reunion..." It was a poem only teenagers could like, and he did not know why those lines had fascinated him so, but he recalled perfectly the poet's name above the poem: Bai Hong. The lovely signature on the draft was identical to the one he remembered. The brief introduction at the bottom of the poem stated simply, "Bai Hong, female, age twenty-six, draftswoman." His heart raced inexplicably. He was confident that the girl was as beautiful as her poem. He was dying to meet the girl, but he was a college graduate and held a respectable position at his unit; he could not just march up to her like some of the other young guys. He kept his ear tuned for any information on her and found out she was indeed the amateur poetess and had recently transferred back to Shanghai. He looked for a chance to put a face to this name. His chance came one day in the dining hall as he noticed a leader from the trade union leading a girl around the tables looking for an empty seat. The older man directed the girl to a seat right across from Chuanhui and said to him, "This is Bai Hong, our factory's gifted scholar and beautiful lady." The girl smiled warmly at Chuanhui and sat down. So this was the Bai Hong of the poem, and exactly like he had pictured her: quiet, gentle, beautiful, and almost child-like.

"You write poetry, what a gifted person... Why, for a young girl to write what you have is simply incredible," he blurted with obvious admiration.

"You like poetry too? Most people don't, you know. That's the part of the books they skip over." She was genuinely happy that he enjoyed poetry.

"But you can't measure creativity and genius by popularity. Listen to these words: 'Before the teardrop can be wiped away, oh heart, you leap again at the thought of sweet reunion...' They succinctly express a profound philosophy in a few, short, melodious lines..." He broke off suddenly, afraid that she would think he was trying to ingratiate himself with her.

But she just smiled back encouragingly, thrilled that someone could actually quote one of her poems. "We poets have the fewest readers of any writers. Novelists have throngs of readers, while poets are lucky to get a dozen," she said, unable to hold back a laugh.

"That's not true." Chuanhui responded, doggedly continuing his defence of poetry. "A novel is like a painting; the colour, the scenery, everything is there for the reader to enjoy. But a poem is like a wisp of smoke, no, a sky full of clouds that keep floating by; the reader can visualize his own images using his imagination... Recently I read the words to an American song that goes 'Raindrops keep fallin' on my head'. The direct translation of that sounds pretty awkward in Chinese." Again he stopped himself. Who did he think he was sitting here with the poetess Bai Hong explaining poetry to her? He felt like the proverbial fool who wanted to show off his skill with the axe in

front of the master carpenter Lu Ban. But Bai Hong's attentive-
ness encouraged him to finish his thought. "The words are about
a man who has lost his love. 'Raindrops keep fallin' on my
head, but that doesn't mean my eyes will soon be turning
red...' Sorry, I guess my translation is not so hot either," he
mumbled feeling awkward.

"No, you're right," she offered quickly trying to help. "The
direct translation has no poetic flavour. You have to know the
original to appreciate a foreign song or poem. That's why I keep
studying French and English."

This girl is really something else, he thought. While all the
other girls he knew could not do much more than dress up, this
one could write poetry and read French and English. What a
girl. He looked around and realized for the first time that they
were the only two left sitting at the table. She smiled sweetly,
quickly finished her bowl of rice, then got up and left smiling a
farewell.

From that moment on he hoped to meet her again at the dining hall, but with several thousand workers at the plant, his
chances were fairly slim. As much as he hated doing it, he was
forced to look up the fellow from the trade union who had first
introduced her to him in the dining hall. Bai Hong worked with
him doing propaganda for the trade union, so he should be able
to help.

"I suppose she is pretty busy lately."

"Who is 'she'?"

"The poetess from the Drafting Department."

"Now how would I know?"

"It can't have been easy, publishing all those poems."

"I guess everybody has a hobby."

"She's really pretty."

"Pretty?" The man shrugged his shoulders. "Haven't you ever noticed those ugly pock-marks around her nose? She reckons she had chicken pox when she was a kid."

Pock-marks? What pock-marks? Anyway Chuanhui was not about to let the conversation stop there and replied quickly, "She's a sweet woman."

"Now how would you know that? You've met her, what, once?"

"You've obviously never read her poems."

"I understand." The propaganda worker had seen these symptoms before. He reached in a drawer and pulled out a movie ticket and handed it to Chuanhui. "Tomorrow evening at six at the Great Shanghai Cinema. The union has the place rented."

Chuanhui took the ticket in confusion.

"You nitwit, the ticket for the seat beside you will conveniently be given to her. You could at least thank me."

A nitwit indeed. He had always considered himself pretty clever and quite self-sufficient, but ever since he had met this Bai Hong he had become a near idiot. By the time he walked up to the movie theatre to sit beside her for the first time, he was totally drained of what little self-confidence he had had. He was like a bumbling fool not knowing where to put his arms or legs, and he was terrorized at the thought of accidently touching hers. He plopped himself down beside her and after a long while he was able to get out the memorized words, "Working on a great, new piece, I suppose?" The timing could hardly have been worse. The girl pouted her lip in a slight smile and nodded toward the screen to signal that he should be quiet during the movie.

That was the first of several times that the union arranged for them to sit together at the movies, and she certainly should have realized that it was more than coincidence. Of course, he could have taken a little more initiative himself; wasn't he the great romancer? But he dared not act too rashly for fear of scaring her off. Bai Hong was nothing like that girl in college he had first fallen in love with. Bai Hong was her own woman with her own outlook in life. That was easy enough to see just by reading the words of her poem: "Before the teardrop can be wiped away, oh heart, you leap again at the thought of sweet reunion...." What insight into human emotions! Was not life itself made up of so many farewells and reunions? She was so superior; maybe he wasn't good enough for her. He knew for sure he was not the "Most Favoured One Under Heaven" any more; just having a college degree made him nothing special! And girls looked down on anyone who earned a paltry 58.50 yuan a month. In a big place like Shanghai there were multitudes of rich sons looking for a wife; how could he ever compete with them? If that sounded like a low attitude, well, that was the way most girls saw things. Of course Bai Hong was not like most girls, but, he reminded himself, she was still a girl!

Chuanhui was pushed by the flood of pedestrians to the department store window.

From morning till late at night Nanjing Road was teeming with a torrent of people as if the entire Chinese population were all here. Such an immense mob of moving people frightened him; he rarely ventured out into this "jungle". Nevertheless he was about to muscle his way through the wall of people and cross the street to the Peace Cinema. The union had given him tickets for the movie *Midnight* that would be showing at six, and Bai Hong would be there!

But he would wait until the torrent of people ebbed a little, he thought, and he might as well kill some time checking out the Sanyo products in the shop window before heading for the cinema. The various VCRs and colour televisions on display were only samples. Anyone could buy them of course, but sincere inquiries about them were rare; the price would scare most people off immediately. It was no wonder Xiao Zhu acted like he owned the town; that stereo his father had brought him was worth a small fortune. The thought made him sigh deeply, and those words echoed through his mind again: "The second son, Gu Hongfei ... ran a notice in the newspaper publicly disowning his father." Yes, if things had been just a little different, he could buy all these gadgets on display without batting an eyelid; he was, after all, the third generation of the "Steel Giant Gu family". What made him angrier still was that somewhere the rest of the third generation Gu family was living a life quite different to his own, witness Xiao Zhu.

When Chuanhui bumped into Xiao Zhu that night the young man was dressed like a real overseas Chinese. He had not been to work for three days.

"Hey, where are you headed? Out to interview some prospective brides?" he teased Xiao Zhu.

"No, none of that for me right now. Too many girls to choose from. I get confused just thinking about it. I'm on my way to a Youth Association do."

Youth Association do! Chuanhui laughed. Before, Xiao Zhu was not even interested in attending the department parties;

now here he was running off to these Youth Association deals.

"You don't know what's happening, my friend." Xiao Zhu took a long draw on his cigarette then looked up into the sky. "You could say these Y. A. things are the Consultative Conference of Shanghai's young people, the place where all the high class types meet. I personally belong to the association's Group Two, which is comprised of sons and daughters of overseas Chinese, compatriots from Hongkong and Taiwan and well-known personages. We're a cut or two above those snobby high-ranking cadres' kids that come." Xiao Zhu waved his hand in contempt with those last few words.

"You mean... you count as a son of the United Front?" Chuanhui could hardly believe it; this boy was not the same person he had known just a year before.

"Naturally. Dad is doing some business with Nanjing. But people with my kind of background at the Y. A. are only small fries; most of the group is made up of children of big industrialists and businessmen. You know, the Dalong Factory's Yan family, the Guo family of the Wing On Company, the Gu clan of the Huachang Steel Plant. Oh yes, that reminds me, are you related to the Gu clan who owned the Huachang Steel Plant? Ever hear of the 'Blue House' on the other side of town? It was the old residence of the Gu clan, and the government has recently decided to return the place to its original owners. That's your 'old home', isn't it?"

"What are you talking about? There must be at least half a million people in Shanghai with the surname Gu; you talk like you saw me walking out of the Blue House yesterday." Chuanhui sighed even as he spoke; he would never be related to that splendid mansion unless there was a miracle.

"There's a guy in my Y. A. group named Chuanye," Xiao Zhu said in a grave tone. "Not only is his name similar to yours, but he was born in Wuxi too. Strangest of all is the resemblance; I saw him from a distance one night and was certain it was you. His grandfather was the boss of the Huachang Steel Plant. He asked me over to his place last week, and I'm not kidding, that Blue House is like something out of the movies. Talk about extravagant decor! I guess the only thing they are missing is their own limousine. And to think you may turn out to be one of them. Stranger things have happened. Look at me. It was just a stroke of luck that I found my dad."

Chuanhui found his excitement increasing as he listened to Xiao Zhu's speculation, even though he kept repeating: "You're making this up." His words hitting home, Xiao Zhu beamed with joy and smacked his lips. "Hey, this could be your big break. I'll do what I can to find out." With that he jumped on his motorcycle, cranked the throttle, and soon disappeared into the stream of bikes and cars. Behind him wafted the pungent odour of foreign cologne, no doubt a gift from his father. Xiao Zhu. He had once been a refreshingly frank and earnest fellow, but a little money had turned him into someone so...intolerably arrogant. Well, that kind of change of character would never happen to Chuanhui. But he would not have a change of luck like that anyway.

That night at the dinner table Chuanhui decided to tell what he had heard that day. He figured they would all get a laugh out of it, and besides, talking it over with his parents he was sure he would feel better about everything. Even as he talked, he could not help feeling a little envious of this cousin he had never met. He was totally unprepared for his father's response. He dropped his chopsticks to the table and said to his wife, "That has to be my little brother's boy."

Mother smiled and acted as if she was not interested, and said incongruously: "Number Three must be happy living in that place. It's a big house for just the three of them. I'll bet even the mayor's house pales in comparison. Their boy must be of marrying age by now; any woman who married him would have no financial worries." Chuanhui was not sure why his mother looked resentfully at him as she said that. Feeling just as resentful, he blurted out, "Aren't we part of the famous 'Steel Giant Gu family'?"

The father took a quick bite of food and looked at Chuanhui as if he was making much out of nothing. "This is an old story. But ask anyone over fifty about your grandfather. They all know. Your granddad used to carry galvanized plating through the streets of Shanghai when he was young, and through some sleazy operations and blatant cheating made himself into a millionaire. Sure, he started the Huachang Steel Plant. And do you know what he was known as in the steel trade? 'Gu the Devil.'"

"Dad, did you ever live in that Blue House?" Chuanhui leaned forward and could hear his own voice tremble as he spoke those last two words. It was as if the words "Blue House" cast a spell over him. In his mind the Blue House was a paradise of unparalleled splendour, pleasure, and wealth.

Leaning back in his chair, the father gazed back into a past, a past he rarely thought of. Deep emotions were flooding him; Chuanhui could tell. And why not? It is impossible for most people to think of their childhood without such feelings of nostalgia. Sure, his youthful years had not been happy, but the thought of his old home still held him, just like that talkative and loving nanny of his childhood who had literally tied him to her apron strings. This was the first time he had really talked with his son about his family and that house. During the "cultural revolution" he was afraid that he would be accused of "waiting to get back his corrupt wealth", so he had kept his mouth shut about it all. Even before the "cultural revolution" he had not been proud of the unsavoury past of the "parasites of society", and he had not told his little boy anything for fear that he would blab it around the neighbourhood and ruin his father's reputation. He had long ago cast those days from his mind, but to forget one's past is not an easy matter. As soon as his son had mentioned the house, feelings toward his old home overwhelmed him. It was like an old jug of wine had been uncorked, and the fragrance alone intoxicated him.

"It was a German-style home with a huge garden in front, and the porch around it was nearly as big as the house itself. When you opened a window the fragrance from the flowers...." Just then the father began coughing; the neighbours below them had just started their coal stove, and a thick cloud of black smoke was pouring in through their window. Wiping his nose with a handkerchief, the father continued: "That architect was brilliant. The house had twenty-nine rooms in it, and they were arranged in a most ingenious yet logical manner. The rooms were arranged in sets of three, and each set was connected to the adjoining sets. The sets could be joined or separated according to need. I heard the other day that the Architectural Department of Tongji University visited; it is one of the most famous houses in Shanghai."

Chuanhui was enthralled by his father's words. He was like a

little boy hearing a fairy tale of "... jewels and gold and treasures untold, hidden in a mountain cave, far, far away."

"If it was so nice, why don't you move into that place again?
Why do we have to keep living in this dump without cooking gas
or even our own bathroom? Why can't we move into there? Isn't
the house returned to the family according to that refunding policy? Why don't we have anything to do with them?" Chuanhui
asked earnestly.

The father's dreamy and gentle expression dropped into a dismal sneer. "What is so bewitching about the words 'Blue
House'? What's so bad about this place? We've got twenty-five
square metres to ourselves with a southern exposure. Why, I
have colleagues with three generations living in rooms smaller
than this..."

Another billow of black smoke poured in through the window, and they heard the neighbours complaining, "These no-
good coal bricks are making someone rich and me angry. It'll be
midnight before we'll get supper cooked on them!" The father
slammed the window shut then mumbled as he fought with the
window bolt, "This damn place, the windows all need to be replaced. The damn housing office only collects the rent; they
never fix a thing!"

"But, dad, I thought you just said this place was wonderful..." Chuanhui needled.

"Then why don't you just leave this 'dump' you just happened
to grow up in!" the father exploded. "Go look up your uncle and
your cousin, now they're rich again!" So the talk of the Blue
House stopped there. He had not even found out what had happened between his dad and granddad, but he decided there and
then to find out.

About that time the couple below started fighting, and the sound of objects bouncing off the wall sounded like a ping-pong game. Rather fond of intervening in these affairs, the respected "Mister Gu" trudged downstairs to try and calm the quarrelling couple down. Screaming and shouting could still be heard echoing up through the thin walls and floors. "How much money did you give me last month?" "Fifty yuan, wasn't it?" "How far will your measly fifty yuan get us? You try to run a household on that. You know how much simple vegetables cost now, do you?" Annoyed by the ruckus, Chuanhui covered his ears in utter vexation. This sort of thing wouldn't happen in the Blue House. "Culture and class are found only in the houses of the well-fed and well-dressed" the old saying went. That was for sure. The mother appeared from the kitchen with a steaming hot cup of coffee. The father always insisted on simple fare for every meal followed by a hot cup of coffee. Then for the first time Chuanhui wondered how his mother felt about the Blue House?

"Mum," Chuanhui said, "there's an old saying that 'A husband and wife in poverty suffer at every turn'. Do you think that's true?"

The mother thought carefully for a minute then said, "There are some things that cannot be answered with a simple 'true' or 'false'. I do know one thing, if poverty is balanced with spiritual wealth, then there's no suffering."

Under the soft glow of the ceiling light his mother looked very youthful. Because of her fair complexion and trim figure, she always looked much younger than she really was. For a while when he was a teenager he was ashamed to be seen walking with his mother. Teenagers often go through that stage. She had been a beautiful girl in her younger years. The wedding picture that hung on the wall above her bed was proof enough of that. When he was just a bawling baby his mother's beautiful face had been imprinted in his mind. During the "cultural revoluting" it was classified as part of the "Four Olds"* and had been thrown in the coal-burner. He remembered how his mother had clutched the photo and cried before it was burnt, and how a well-intentioned auntie from next door grabbed the picture from her and tossed it into the fire saying, "It's only a photograph; haven't you seen people throwing genuine treasures into the garbage cans? This kind of thing will only cause you trouble." It was only now, at twenty-seven years of age, that Chuanhui realized how much a picture of her youth must have meant to his mother and why she had cried when it was burnt. But the mystery of the Blue House made Chuanhui acutely aware that there was still a part of his own mother's life about which he knew absolutely nothing.

"Mum," Chuanhui said finally, "let's skip the philosophy. If you had choice between living in the Blue House or here, which would you choose?"

The mother stayed calm as if she had pondered the question a hundred times already.

"I've never lived in the Blue House; your father and I have lived in this room all our married life. Although conditions are far from satisfactory here, I would not like the Blue House because it is not our own. What I would really like to have is a nice three-bedroom apartment, and not one of those with concrete floors. One room for us, one for you to get married in, and the other room we could use for anything we wanted. They would

---

* Four Olds: old ideas, culture, habits and customs.

not have to be big rooms, just big enough for us to put some things..." She interrupted herself with a girlish timid giggle, then added, "I guess I've been wishing for that apartment since the day we were married."

"But how did you get stuck with a place like this?" Chuanhui could not help but whine. There was better housing to be found in Shanghai; just across the street there was a row of apartments that were much better than their own. Housing was not such a problem then and there was no housing office to restrict you either.

Irritated and doting, the mother looked at her son. The boy still did not understand. "This was what we could afford."

"But Grandfather was the 'Steel Giant', wasn't he?"

"That was his money," his mother answered flatly, "not ours."

Now you're thinking like a foreigner, Chuanhui thought to himself. He had to be honest with himself: he might normally think in those terms himself, but facing the reality of the situation...

"Of course we always hoped to move into something better when our salary went up," his mother sighed. "That was why we were quite content when we moved in here. This was a place that we could call our own; and we could do anything we liked here. The day we moved in this place we never thought that we would be spending the rest of our lives here."

Father came back up the stairs followed by some bald fellow obviously in his forties. Chuanhui knew him. In the 50s he had been the class monitor of one of his dad's primary school classes, and he was one of his father's favourite students as well. Just the week before a leading scientific journal had announced, "Lu

Dawei is one of China's most outstanding young scientists..."
But in their home the outstanding young scientist remained the
timid schoolboy that they had known years before. After greeting Chuanhui's mother he pulled some elegantly wrapped candy
from a coat pocket and bashfully handed it to his former teacher. "These are my wedding candies, Teacher Gu."

"What?" his father said in a tone of both surprise and joy. "Is
it all settled?"

Mother could hardly control herself. "Wonderful, just wonderful! Your mother must be relieved! Now she can rest easy in
her old age."

The young scientist found a seat on a stool and sat so respectfully bolt upright that Chuanhui felt tired just looking at him.

"My goodness, you work fast," the father joked. "Just a few
months ago you told me you hadn't got a girlfriend yet, and now
you're getting married!"

"I hope you won't be so secretive when your wife is pregnant," the mother added gleefully.

The poor young scientist's face was turning crimson. "Actually we work in the same lab, but the idea never occurred to either
of us at first. We had both been trying to find a partner for
quite a while, but both of us kept getting turned down or disappointed. We started talking to each other, and before we knew
it we decided that, well, why go looking all over the place?
So...that's how it happened."

"Housing?" Mother always linked happiness with housing.

"They assigned me an apartment last month on Wanping
Street."

"Marvelous, in a convenient part of the city," Mother said
with a note of envy.

"But...we've given it to someone else."

Mother's mouth dropped in shock, and even Chuanhui thought he had heard wrong.

"It's like this: next month I'm going to America to do some research for two years, and my wife will be leaving soon for Holland to study for three years. Leaving behind an empty apartment to collect dust while so many comrades are in need of housing simply doesn't make sense, so we let someone else have it. I'll probably get a new four-bedroom apartment when I come back, so why buy furniture now and have to move it all over the place when we return?"

"Oh, that's a good idea," Mother sighed in relief. "Where will your new apartment be?"

"Uh, they haven't built it yet, but I've heard it will be near our institute... Anyway, there is no rush." The scientist remained sitting straight as a calligrapher's brush without the slightest sign of fatigue.

"You've got everything," Father said softly, "A good profession, love, a home."

"Really!" the scientist beamed back in agreement.

The gaunt and balding fellow sitting before him presented an almost comical figure, but Chuanhui could not laugh. The man had paid dearly for the three things his father mentioned. His thoughts flew back to the Blue House. He would solve the mystery. Was it not the rage in foreign countries to "find one's roots"? Would not inquiring about one's family be interesting? Besides, he was a Gu; he had that right.

The scientist got up to leave and, realizing that it would be the last time he would see his teacher for quite a while, he nearly choked with emotion as he bowed and bid him farewell. The fellow then turned to Chuanhui and said with unfeigned envy, "You are lucky to have such a man for your father."

Chuanhui understood what he meant. Rumour had it that Lu's father had been an opium addict and had pulled his family with him into unimagined poverty. When Lu Dawei was young, it was Chuanhui's father that had paid for the books and magazines that had enabled him to study. Compared with him Chuanhui had been pretty lucky. But everything is relative: compared with someone else, say this cousin and his parents, could he still be considered so fortunate? The thought frightened him, and he quickly pushed it out of his mind...

By the time Chuanhui arrived at the Peace Cinema, the movie had already started. He groped his way down the aisle of the darkened theatre looking for his seat, all the while stepping on toes and feeling clumsy. Late again. He blamed that impossible mob of people that crammed the sidewalks; he blamed the impassable stream of bikes and cars and trucks that chocked the streets. He blamed them all, and he was getting madder by the second just thinking of them. "Over here!" a voice whispered to him. It was Bai Hong. Strange; her words instantly calmed his spirit.

"I was reading over some material in the library and lost track of the time. I'm sorry," he whispered to her. Now that was stupid, he thought as soon as the words had left his lips. This was just a union-organized movie, not a date. No need for "I'm sorry". Self-conscious and embarrassed, he scratched his palms and wriggled in his seat. It was quite a while before he could settle down and really get into the movie.

This evening's feature was the movie *Midnight*. He watched

as the character Wu Sunfu pulled into the main gate of his lavish estate and slowly drove up a driveway bordered with flower beds. The car stopped and the only sound was the car door opening. Out stepped cocky Wu Sunfu in patent leather shoes and a three-piece suit. He strode up the steps and into the luxurious mansion he called home. Chuanhui guessed from his age that he was his grandfather's peer. Ah, Grandfather! A grandfather as celebrated and illustrious as Wu Sunfu. Actually Chuanhui had met his own grandfather once.

It had happened on a rainy night in the early years of the "cultural revolution". It was a vague, cloudy memory. They were eating supper when there was a careful knock on the door. Father opened the door and then stepped outside to talk with someone in a low, nervous voice. Finally Father stepped back in the room with a thin and pallid old man. This old man, a total stranger to young Chuanhui, was soaking wet and so weak that Father had to support him by the arm as they entered the apartment. Mother set Chuanhui in front of the old man and told her son to call him "Grandfather". Chuanhui managed to say it once then quickly hid behind his mother's dress. Chuanhui remembered the look on the old man's face, a look of fear, insecurity, and hopelessness. The old man asked his mother, "His sister, how old would she be now?" "Twenty," Mother replied simply. Then she began to cry. Chuanhui knew that he had had an older sister who had died of pneumonia when she was three years old. He could not remember the rest of that evening; he only remembered that he curled up with his mother on his little bed, Father slept on the floor, and Grandfather slept in the double bed. Just before he fell asleep, Mother told him that from that day on he was to be a good little boy because Grandfather was going to be living with them. The next day he ran straight home after school. He would no longer be lonely while his parents were at work; now Grandfather would be there. But from down the alley he could see a crowd of people clustering around the entrance to the house where he lived in and an ambulance waiting outside. Grandfather had had a stroke, and he died two days later. Of course, for little Chuanhui there was no mourning; after going to the crematorium the entire affair was over for him. Grandfather had disappeared from his life as quickly as he had appeared, and all that was left now was a short and hazy memory of him. At the end of his life, why had Grandfather sought out father? To be reconciled? Forgiven? Who had abandoned whom, really?

"Oh Grandfather, when you first set eyes on your grandson, your own flesh and blood, what were your thoughts? Did you kiss me?" Chuanhui asked as he stared up at the close-up of Wu Sunfu on the screen.

"All that scheming and fretting for a few lousy dollars!" Bai Hong sighed. Chuanhui shivered; could it be that this bright and insightful girl had gazed into the depths of his heart? He glanced over at her nervously and was relieved to see that she was simply commenting on the plot of the movie. The lights on the screen reflected off the girl's face, sometimes revealing the brightness, sometimes the depth of those beautiful eyes.

Admittedly there was truth in the old cliché that money cannot buy happiness. But he also believed that money could get things done and could be put to good use. Take Xiao Zhu for example. Housing was probably one of the most common problems for people in Shanghai, but with a little money from his father, Xiao Zhu had got himself a nice apartment, hadn't he? And look at Father's favourite student. He had no money to get decent housing, and when he actually got an apartment, already a balding man, he threw it away to someone else. Practice is the test of truth, but there are some words that cannot be put to the test.

At the end of the movie Chuanhui could feel Bai Hong gently tugging at his shirt sleeve. "There will be a poetry reading at the Children's Palace next Tuesday, and I. . . I will be reciting one of my latest works."

He was so flabbergasted that he did not immediately take the ticket she held out to him. Most girls nowadays were fickle, changeful, even deceptive, but here was Bai Hong taking the risk of openly showing him her feelings. He was grateful for her honesty.

"Take the ticket!" she said, bravely and coquettishly, her eyes laughing at him.

Those eyes that had been so distant suddenly seemed so close. And although he also saw clearly for the first time the few small pock-marks around her cute nose, he concluded that her face reflected both beauty and intelligence. She was the poetess Bai Hong he had always imagined.

"Where can we go. . . go for a walk? It's still early," he said struggling to formulate an invitation.

"Half the factory is here, and you want to go for a walk?" she said as she disappeared into the crowd.

Chuanhui put the ticket carefully away and stood there feeling uncontrollable happiness. He strolled out on to the crowded sidewalk and could not help peeking at his reflection in a shop window. Not bad. Well built and dressed in good taste. Even he felt good about himself just then. Were it not for that illustrious surname of his, he might have felt completely happy with what he saw in that reflection.

Not many people ventured out on winter nights, and as he rounded the corner into the alleyway, the only sound that could be heard was the "thud, thud" of his leather shoes on the pavement. It was an oldfashioned lane lined with storied houses, each with double-panelled doors opening on to a countyard. All the old buildings here were solidly built and could easily last another hundred years. The problem was that they were too close together; you could even hear your neighbour across the lane sneeze. And there was not a single tree or clump of grass to be found in the neighbourhood. Red brick walls were the only scenery for as far as the eye could see. "Oh Dad," Chuanhui could not help thinking, "although I've always seen you shuffling around the room as if you were the happiest man on earth, I can't help wondering what your thoughts were when you first descended to this social level, when you first walked down these narrow streets. When the early brightness of the morning brought the smell of burning coal bricks and the cry of the garbage man to bring out your night-soil, what did you think then?"

A young boy arriving home late raced past Chuanhui whistling as he ran. Stopping at a doorway he looked up and intoned the silly words, "Open sesame!" No sooner had the words left his mouth than the window above him opened and down flew the key to the door.

"Open sesame!" and the entrance to the cave filled with marvelous treasures will open before you. What a beautiful fairy tale! Chuanhui believed he now stood before that treasure-filled cavern; but, for the moment at least, he did not know the magic words to gain entrance.

2

The Jinjiang Club! For Chuanhui it was like another world! He had often ridden his bicycle past this elegant French-style building on the corner of the secluded and quiet Maoming Road, and he had heard that it was the French Club before Liberation. He had never even thought of entering into this exclusive club before, but now Xiao Zhu had arranged for him to meet his cousin here. "Can ... I ... go in?" he asked Xiao Zhu as they met at the door, his insecurity all too evident. Xiao Zhu laughed heartily. "Can you go in? Of course you can. Nowadays anyone who can cough up the money can come in, so why not you?" Xiao Zhu's casual remark cut deep, and Chuanhui could feel his face flushing. For some reason he was feeling more and more like a bumpkin and misfit these days.

Chuanhui followed Xiao Zhu into the soft light of a large dining room. The hall had few people, most of them big-nosed, blond-headed foreigners, and the air was thick with the odour of perfume.

"This is the slack time of the tourist season, so the Consultative Conference opened it to the public—at twenty yuan per person. That includes a Western meal. In a few days it'll be Christmas, and we're going to have an all-night party. A Christmas tree, dance, the clock chiming. I tell you, it is almost like the West," Xiao Zhu explained in a tone of authority.

Twenty yuan a ticket! That was nearly half a month's salary. Xiao Zhu used to receive less than that for his winter subsidy, and he had to go through a mile of red tape to get that much. Times had indeed changed!

"Would you like something to drink?" someone asked the two in perfect Mandarin. Chuanhui turned around to face a formally dressed male attendant in a bow tie. Chuanhui was only a guest here and did not feel like he could take any initiative. He looked over to Xiao Zhu, who took time to light a cigarette before saying, "Any mineral water? Small bottles?" He was an old hand at this sort of thing. "Two bottles, please."

Across the way from them were a young couple, dressed like overseas Chinese. "See those two?" Xiao Zhu whispered in his ear nodding towards the pair.

"You mean those two overseas Chinese?"

"Overseas nothing, they're not the real goods! They're the grandkids of a couple of big names. The guy's grandfather owned the Da'an Company, and she's a descendent of the Fenghua Cotton Mill's boss..."

The couple became aware that they were being scrutinized and shot a look of contempt at the two men. Chuanhui had to give them credit; they were both tastefully dressed, especially the girl with her leather boots and black checkered dress. They were certainly a cut above the "amateur overseas Chinese" he often saw on the streets. There was no doubt about it, the people here were a breed apart, quite different from the people in his own neighbourhood. And his cousin was one of this kind. How would this cousin treat him when they met? Would he look down on him? Greet him with open arms? Just act indifferent? His anxiety was mounting. Chuanhui had gone to see the Blue House just a few days before. It had weathered the years amazingly well. Although the blue tiles were now a bit worn, the building had maintained its grandeur and unique style. The gentle sounds of a piano had come drifting through the blinds of the second-story windows, and Chuanhui had wondered how he would be received if he walked up to the front door and rang the bell.

"Look, here he comes," Xiao Zhu said nodding to the main entrance hall. Chuanhui would have immediately recognized the young man in the Western suit as his cousin without the help of Xiao Zhu; it was almost like watching himself in a mirror.

"Are you Chuanhui?" Chuanye's hearty and cheerful voice gave Chuanhui a good first impression. "I could tell by that high forehead and your height that you were one of the Gu clan. We lost contact with a lot of kin during those ten years."

The hall was centrally heated and warm, so Chuanye took off his overcoat and jacket. Beneath he wore a V-neck sweater and a starched, well-ironed shirt. Chuanhui regretted that he had merely put on his new wool jacket and forgotten to change the multi-coloured sweater his mother had knitted him from old yarn. Moreover, his shirt was badly wrinkled. He decided to leave the overcoat on; better to roast than to have anyone see his clothes. Fortunately a waiter came by just then offering coffee and ice cream. Coffee he was familiar with; Mother had brought out cups of steaming coffee after every evening meal, but coffee in a place like this was a whole different experience. And he was thrown off-balance by this cousin he was meeting for the first time. He was treating Chuanhui with genuine brotherly affection. That was new to Chuanhui, and he was deeply touched by it.

Chuanye was the son of the Gu family's heir apparent, Gu Hongji. The eldest son, Gu Hongzhi, had left China early on to study and start a career and family, while the second son, Hongfei, had broken all relations with the family. This left only Gu Hongji to carry on, and Chuanye was his only son, the sole heir of the Blue House. There were two daughters, but of course Chuanye counted as the only direct male descendent that was really a part of the family. Grandfather Gu had spoiled the child and placed all his hopes on him—that through Chuanye the glory and wealth of the Gu family would live on at the Blue House. Chuanye never understood what that meant when he was growing up, but now he knew he was like the crown prince of England: someday he would become king of the Blue House. He realized his superiority and flaunted it from time to time. There were more than a few people in Shanghai worth over a million yuan, and people who owned exotic and extravagant old houses were not so rare either, but to have both and to be the only heir of one of the great industrialists of the past, that was exceptional indeed. What family didn't have at least a few brothers to share the loot amongst? That sort of thing often led to family infighting but was something Chuanye had never had to worry about.

Chuanye was no ordinary citizen, and to prove it he was very fussy about whom he called a friend. His old colleagues from the factory were automatically excluded, that went without saying, and unless a person came from a prestigious and wealthy family they were not considered either. Even in a place as big as Shanghai that eliminated all but a few, and those types were always so busy with their own pursuits that it was not easy for them to get together often. That left Chuanye lonely most of the time, and his life was, in his own words, a bit of a drag. At first he had kept himself amused with cassette recorders and had a copy of every cassette that had ever circulated through Shanghai, but then the motorcycle craze came and he went for motorbikes in a big way. He had five different motorcycles within three months and came close to killing himself on the last one. His mother cried and carried on till he finally quit riding them altogether. His infatuation with cameras lasted a little more than a month. He had bought a 1,600-yuan Rolleiflex camera and started out by taking pictures of girls, then of the family's lazy cat, and finally of anything he saw, and he still had a drawer full of rolls of still-life shots that had never been developed due to his waning interest. But what was so surprising about that? One young man in a big place like the Blue House. It was a lonely existence. Both his sisters had homes and families of their own. When things had been tough, a high-ranking cadre's son got infatuated with the elder sister, who was quite a lady. Back then there were few young men of influential, prestigious families, so the sister had to condescend to marry this kid of some army big shot. Chuanye had not got on well with his brother-in-law from the beginning and constantly referred to him as a "bumpkin" behind his back, even though Chuanye himself actually knew very little about the finer things of life. Chuanye never knew what to talk about when they were together; they had nothing in common. And perhaps also it was that the offspring of a capitalist and that of a Communist Party member were just natural enemies and should never have got married. Heaven knows how the young couple got along. The younger sister married one of those more-Western-than-the-Westerners-type Hongkong Chinese with British citizenship, but this brother-in-law seemed to look down on Chuanye and would always joke that he was a "tyrant and evil capitalist". Anyway, Chuanye hardly ever saw him. For

Chuanye to find a "buddy" matching him both in economic and social position was not easy. Sure, there was always Xiao Zhu, who hovered around him like an imperial bodyguard. Xiao Zhu had some credentials; being the son of a wealthy West German entrepreneur counted for something, and so the son of the Steel Giant could tolerate his presence. But the boy was a nouveau riche, dull and unattractive; not much fun at all.

When a cousin cropped up all of a sudden, Chuanye was quite tickled. After all, he had nothing to fear from him; years before his father had renounced any right to the throne. Besides, none of the bigwigs in the business world would deny that Chuanye was the legitimate successor to the Gu estate; why else were they sending their daughters to catch him? Now he was observing his cousin with curiosity; what did he think of him?

So after listening with intense interest to Chuanhui retelling the description of the Gu clan in *A Narrative History of Shanghai Commerce*, Chuanye launched into a mockery of his uncle, Gu Hongfei. His tone was as condescending as his words were tactless.

"What I can't figure is why your old man fell out with Grandfather. Was principle worth more than money to him? There's just no comparison. My older sister was a fool too, publicly denouncing Mum and Dad in the first part of the 'cultural revolution'. She even signed up to go to Heilongjiang to work in the countryside. Fortunately, after Liberation nobody advertized that in the newspapers any more, and our neighbourhood committee knew nothing about it; otherwise, especially with no mother and father, how could she have ever got residence status to return to Shanghai? If Mum and Dad hadn't sent her money and things, she would have starved to death up there."

Chuanhui was not angry with him for talking about his father like that. He felt the same way; what his father had done was downright foolish, and his father had not left Chuanhui any room to manoeuver either: he couldn't even be a wealthy grandson.

"Tell me something about Grandfather," Chuanhui pleaded.

"Granddad? A strange old bird. You know how stingy he was? If someone found an unhusked kernel of rice in their food he would not allow them to spit it out. He wouldn't even spit it out himself."

"You mean...you had to eat husk and all?"

"And choke to death? No, you could take the husk off, but you still had to eat that half-cooked kernel. But I have to say he never made me do things like that. I was too little, he'd always say. He adored me."

The words galled Chuanhui. If his father had not left the Blue House, perhaps he would have shared some of Grandfather's affection.

"When I was little, Granddad would always tell me that, if it hadn't been for the Liberation, he would have got me a plant to manage."

"You mean to run?"

"Sure. I've always liked the idea of business. There's always risks, but it's exciting work. Some entrepreneur Dad was: he never cut a deal in his life. All he did was sit back after Liberation and get the fixed interest from the government on the assets they took over. What a man Granddad was—from tin peddler to steel magnate—what an accomplishment!"

"I saw Grandfather once!" Chuanhui interjected. "He came to our home in 1966."

"That could be. I remember the fellow who led the search-and-seize mission on our home drew a line on the floor with a piece of chalk and said anyone who wanted to be counted with the bloodsucking types such as Granddad should stand to the left of the line and everyone else to the right. That line of class distinction looked a lot like a game kids play, but this was no game. I was just a little boy, so I naturally followed Mum and Dad to the right side of the line. That must have been about the time Dad put up a big character poster at the Huachang Plant announcing he had 'turned his axe against one he had wrongly sided with' and cut all relations with his father. It was more than Granddad could bear." Chuanye casually pulled a chair over and put his feet up as he talked. He was incredibly casual about the whole thing. Chuanhui was amazed that his cousin could talk about this in such a relaxed, even amused, fashion. For his aunt and uncle to be so heartless towards the man who had earned the Blue House for them seemed incredibly ruthless.

Chuanye smiled knowingly. "Yes, it used to shock me, too, but after I had been around a little I didn't blame them. Granddad had pulled some pretty cruel tricks himself! Did you know that there was originally a partner in the Huachang Plant? Granddad squeezed him out and seized the entire plant for himself. That's life."

Chuanhui remained silent, a cold chill running down his spine. Although Chuanye's facts and logic seemed faultless, there was something wrong. When his aunt and uncle had run Grandfather out of the house, had not his own parents taken him in? What kind of people were these relatives? Ever since he was a boy his parents had taught him to be honest and kind to others, to always try to get along. "Life is like a poem, and love is what makes it rhyme. Where there is no love, there is no rhyme." Bai Hong had said that once. Then he remembered the poetry reading at the Children's Palace that night, the ticket that Bai Hong had given him, and he hurriedly excused himself. But Chuanye grabbed his arm. "Look, forget it. Let's just forget the past. Hey, when can you come over to my place, let Dad see his nephew. . ."

Chuanye's invitation hit the mark. Chuanhui sensed that this was a critical point in their relationship, and the invitation was important, so he sat back down. Bai Hong was a reasonable girl, she would forgive him if she knew the circumstances.

"Grandfather is dead now, and besides, the fact that he went to your father's house when he was dying proves that the two were reconciled. So everything's settled, isn't it? Everybody talks about 'looking ahead' these days, right? The bad old days are behind us. Interestingly, we of the younger generation are actually patching up relations for our elders," Chuanye said earnestly.

Chuanye could not say exactly what had prompted him to say what he had just said. Maybe he wanted to settle the important issue of the Gu clan's rightful successor, or maybe he was simply bored. Whatever it was, he was egged on by the envy and admiration that shone in his cousin's eyes.

Gu Chuanye. He was thirty-two, had never been in business and had never married. He had the strength of an ox but nowhere to use it. He had worked in a neighbourhood garment factory for 1.10 yuan a day with no sick pay or vacations, stooping over a sewing machine eight hours a day six days a week double-stitching mountains of cotton underwear. It was exhausting, tedious work, and looking back on it now, Chuanye was amazed that he had actually survived eight years and three months in that miserable sweat shop. It had been a wretched life, waiting all morning for the lunch bell to ring and spending all afternoon watching the clock move its cruelly slow arms toward quitting time. He lived for his one day off a week. The evening before that cherished day, or more accurately the afternoon before, was filled with the joyful anticipation of the following day of blissful rest. He could sleep as late as he wished, enjoy a leisurely meal rather than running down the street to work while gulping down his breakfast. His spirits sank with the evening sun—as he would be bending over a sewing machine for another six days. That was how those eight years and three months had dragged out. Then the government passed a law returning the capital of former businesses to their former owners, and he had received more money than he could spend in a lifetime. Even his father had said, "It's not like before Liberation now; there are no opium and gambling dens and no kidnappers, so there is no threat to our family's wealth." Chuanye quit his job as soon as the family got the money; he was not about to waste another precious day of his youth in that wretched factory. At first he thought of throwing himself into preparation for the college entrance exams, but he was not the kind to knuckle down to study with so much money and freedom all at once. His first few days away from work had simply been heaven. No more would he have to scramble out of bed; now the heavy curtains were closed to keep out the early morning light and street noise, and he could just stay in bed with his Walkman and listen to music. No longer would the company clock rule his life; he could arrange his own life and pleasures just as he wished. That was not exactly the kind of disciplined life-style that would get him into college, but Chuanye was not about to get himself tied down again anyway! Being locked up in a classroom for six days a week was not his idea of a good time.

But within a year he had become completely bored with life. Everyday was just the same as the next; it was worse than being at the factory. At least at the shop, no matter how bad things got, there were always rumours to listen to, customers to look over, and, of course, always the day off to look forward to. It was a curious place with a charm that was hard to put in words. Naturally, wild horses would never drag him back to that place now. That was no work for any man; abroad, it was done by robots.

To combat his chronic boredom, he was constantly seeking new friends, new foreign gadgets to play with, and new restaurants and hotels ... to visit provided they had previously been exclusively for foreigners of course. Some people suggested that he marry, but he rejected the idea out of hand. Life was boring enough without having to look at the same face every day for the rest of your life!

So now he was making the most of the opportunity to play the part of the world-wise aristocrat to someone new.

After supper Chuanye took Chuanhui on a tour of the club's billiard hall, bar, and gift shop. At the gift shop they ran into the two young people Chuanhui had looked at in the dining hall. Chuanye slapped the fellow's back, and the two chatted like they were old acquaintances.

"Well, well, if it isn't old Chuanye. Today we had a new French pastry called 'lemon chiffon'. Have you tried it yet?"

"I had some last week at the Longbai Hotel. I didn't think it was that great."

Chuanhui could not tell if they were talking like friends or flaunting their extravagant tastes to each other.

"I'd like to introduce you to my cousin, Chuanhui."

The two young people lit up and smiled cordially at Chuanhui as if they had totally forgotten the belligerent sneer they had cast at him in the dining hall. Chuanhui was amazed; the name of his grandfather seemed to hold all the magical power of an Aladdin's lamp.

The longer he followed Chuanye around, the more Chuanhui felt a sense of inferiority. When they walked into the recreation room, Chuanhui saw a long, shiny teak-wood aisle with gutters and ten wooden posts about the size of wine bottles standing in a "V" formation at the other end. Chuanye handed him a melon-sized ball and grinned, "Let's play a game!"

"I, I, don't know how," Chuanhui mumbled, shrinking back in fear.

Chuanye grabbed the ball, struck a pose as he took careful aim, then expertly hurled the ball down the aisle. The ball crashed into the wooden posts, knocking down every last one. The brilliant performance won an ovation from a group of tourists standing behind them, and Chuanye basked in the fleeting glory of the moment. It was the kind of experience he lived for. Chuanhui had seen this game in a foreign movie once, but what was it called? He was afraid to ask lest his cousin or Xiao Zhu laugh at his ignorance. What little self-confidence and self respect he once had simply crumbled in the face of these children of the rich and famous!

As they walked back through the gift shop, an exquisite little gold ring caught his eye. Thirty-five yuan, that was not expensive. Certainly cheaper than you could buy a ring from outside, and its workmanship was better, but the shop demanded Foreign Exchange Certificates, and where would Chuanhui get FEC? It was a beautiful ring, if someday he could slip one like it on to Bai Hong's finger. Someday, he thought, he would dress her just as elegantly as that girl he saw in the dining hall. He could not keep his eyes off the gold ring, and Chuanye read his thoughts.

"You want to buy that? No FEC, I suppose. Here, let me change some with you." Chuanye whipped out thirty-five yuan FEC and eagerly handed it to his cousin. Chuanye gloated over the chance to condescendingly help his cousin.

Chuanhui did not know what to do. In all his twenty-seven years he had never bought anything without consulting his parents first, much less an expensive gift like this. Besides, he had always given all his pay to his mother to take care of. He had just got paid today; how would he ever explain to her that he blew it all without asking her consent first? But to appear tight-fisted before his new friends would be mortifying! So buy it, he thought. May be in future, thirty or forty yuan would seen nothing to him either. He steeled himself and handed over the money, and picked up the glistening gold ring.

It was ten o'clock by the time he got home, and Mother was already asleep. He had heard something about her having to perform a major operation today, so she had probably come home exhausted. Father sat in front of the black and white nine-inch TV, enthralled by a football match. Chuanhui could never understand how his father could watch, much less enjoy, a football game on that tiny screen. One never knew where the ball was half the time. A colour TV set where the ball was really white and the grass green ... that was the only way to watch a football game. But he was in no mood to harp on that issue tonight, not with the gold ring in his pocket pricking his hand like an upset hedgehog. You see Dad, I got this... How could he bring it up?

"Say Dad, there's this game," he started, explaining what he had seen that night. "What's it called?"

Sure enough, Father knew all about the sport. "It's called 'bowling'. Where in the world did you find a place that had that old game? Kids today are always digging up all our old pastimes."

"Bowling," Chuanhui repeated. That was something new on him. He could hold his own in tennis and was even familiar with baseball, but even he had never heard of bowling.

"I used to be pretty good at it," continued the father turning away from the TV, anxious to talk about something from his younger days.

"I've never seen you playing it." Chuanhui felt that even after living with his father for twenty-seven years, he hardly knew the man.

"I suppose you young folks have just rediscovered it. How much does it cost to play? A bowling alley takes up plenty of space and requires special equipment. The hardwood alley must be springy but durable. Most people can never afford to play the game; how did you get to see it?"

"I ... I have an old classmate who works at the Jinjiang Club. He let me in this evening to look around." He lied, trying not to give away any hint that he had been out meeting long-lost relatives. Father would go mad if he found out, he reasoned. But there was still the ring. He would have to explain that sooner or later. He might as well face the storm now, he thought, and gritting his teeth, he pulled from his pocket the tiny box with the ring. "I bought this ring at the gift shop."

Father sat there wide-eyed and at a loss for words, and even Mother pulled on a nightgown and appeared, speechless with shock. Chuanhui might have pulled out a bomb from his pocket for the effect it caused. He stood there silently resigned to the wrath he expected, but when he opened his mouth he felt an unexpected sense of self-confidence and calm.

"I've met this girl. Have you ever heard of the poetry journal *A Hundred Flowers*? Well, she's a poet. Her poems get published in every issue, and this evening she was invited to recite some of her works at the Children's Palace. I ... I like her a lot." He spoke with the boldness of one who knows he is right, yet inside a pang of guilt pierced his heart. She had been waiting for him that night. The first date she had asked him to, and he had stood her up. Tonight at the recital she would have been looking into the faces of the audience, looking for him.

"It must have cost a bomb! You picked up ostentation pretty quick didn't you? You only earn 58 yuan a month. How could you do it?" Dad exploded, just as Chuanhui had expected. Here was the son of the wealthy Steel Giant ranting and raving over a measly 35 yuan.

"I'll tell you right now that a girl you can buy with a ring isn't worth having," Father added coldly.

"Curse me all you want," Chuanhui fired back, enraged by his father's last words, "but don't you ever insult her again!"

Father realized his last comment was unkind and wrong, but would not back down, trying to maintain his fatherly authority. "Ask your mother, just ask her. When we were young the stores were filled with jade and diamonds. Did your mother ever ask me for a ring?"

The mother glared viciously at her husband then turned to Chuanhui and said tenderly, "You've already bought it, so why don't you give it to me for safe keeping, and some Sunday you can invite this young lady over for dinner..."

"It's ... it's a little too early for that," Chuanhui replied nervously. Since the trip to the Jinjiang Club his sense of inferiority had all but overwhelmed him. Certainly a girl like Bai Hong would have a long list of admirers. Who knew what would happen? He didn't want to push her; if he acted too rashly he might blow everything.

"I'm no prize catch, you know," Chuanhui spoke sadly, "I don't know if she would even consider me."

"What do you mean you're no prize catch? You're a college graduate, a scientist, you'll be getting promoted to assistant engineer in a couple of years, you come from a small family, there are no complications..." Father went on counting on his fingers as if tallying up the family assets.

"Oh dad, those don't count for anything these days. Now if I lived in the Blue House, that would be another matter altogether!" he blurted out in a tearful voice, venting all the frustration, indignation, and resentment that had been boiling within him for the last few days.

"Are you still dreaming about the Blue House?" Father was shocked almost beyond words. "Forget it! You've no future there."

"Maybe not. But what kind of future do I have in this dump with curtains to divide our tiny room? If I can't get a piece of the Blue House then I can't get it, but one thing's for sure, no one'll sing my praises like they did Du Yunyun". *

"Just shut your mouth!" Gu Hongfei would not stand for that kind of talk in his house; the boy was speaking like one of those young yobs that hung out on the corner. "Let me tell you something else. If I had chosen to stay in the Blue House we might never have survived the 'cultural revolution'."

"Sure, and those who did stay have it a hundred times better now," Chuanhui answered sourly.

"And can you guarantee that there won't be another 'cultural revolution'?" Father defended himself doggedly.

The son impatiently lay down on his bed and pulled the quilt over himself. "They say the world is going to burn up some day, and do you stay up nights worrying about that, too?" he thought to himself. He did not bother saying it out loud, though. For one thing he did not feel like debating with an old man who knew so little about the world. And anyway, he was tired out. Old people have such weird ideas; like they always seem to think just the opposite to young people. Was this the so-called "generation gap" everyone was talking about? His father must never have seen it, but he had. When promotion time came around at the plant, people would fight like animals to claw themselves up a grade, even threaten suicide. But here was his father, neither a Party member nor a leading cadre, acting like his father's estate meant nothing to him. Just who was he trying to impress, anyway!

His mother's hands moved around the edge of his quilt, tuck-

---

* Du Yunyun: Shortly after the "cultural revolution" this young woman received a large sum of money from overseas relatives, and she turned it over to the government as an act of patriotism.

ing it in. He wanted to take those hands and kiss them, but in the end he just pretended he was asleep. There comes a time in a person's life when he desperately needs the consolation and love of another, but a mother's hand is not able to supply that need. He was a man now, and he needed a new life style. He needed some freedom and independence. He envied the young foreigners he had heard about who left home when they were twenty. He had outgrown the tiny cubicle of a bedroom with its curtains for walls.

A north wind whistled outside. It was on such nights, nestled in his clean and sun-dried quilt, that Chuanhui had always experienced the true meaning of the word "home". But tonight was different. By the dim light coming through the windows he looked around at the 25 square metres of floor space divided by curtains identical to those on the windows, and for the first time in his life he felt he was living in miserable poverty! That ancient nine-inch TV, with mother's hand-decorated cover on it, would probably be rejected by the second-hand shops. The wooden floor had been mopped till the boards were bare. That kitchen cupboard—it must have had paint on it at one time— ought to be in the kitchen, but with eight families using the same kitchen that was hardly possible. What a dilapidated old place, this home of the Steel Giant Gu Fuxiang's son and grandson! How dare he invite Bai Hong here? They had to be kidding.

"Are you feeling OK, Fen?"

Hongfei had felt his wife sigh beside him and was worried. His wife had serious heart problems—angina pectoris the doctor called it—and he was always on the alert at night. As they aged the husband had grown to love and appreciate his wife more. The truth was there was a latent and growing fear within him that he would part company with her some day. Both of them were past retirement age, but both their work units implored them to continue working. It was no wonder; a teacher with ability and a nurse with rich experience were invaluable assets to their units. Once he had pleaded like a child with his wife that they quit their jobs and take it easy for a few years. After about three days he realized that that kind of life was not really paradise after all. He read the morning and evening papers from cover to cover and was still bored to death. Worse still, his wife started getting crabby and picking on him, so both of them decided to go back to work. "You're destined to be a working man," he would often chide himself thereafter.

"I was just thinking," his wife said. "Maybe it wouldn't be such a bad idea to make contact with your family again."

"That's out of the question! We don't need their damned money!" Hongfei barked back.

"Who's talking about money? We're getting old and poor. Chuanhui has no brothers or sisters or even cousins to visit. It will be hard on him when we die, and he's left alone." Her husband had misjudged her motives, and it hurt her feelings.

"What are you worrying about? He won't stay a bachelor forever." It was a father's place not to budge on these things.

"Some of what Chuanhui says makes sense." The wife bit her lip then muttered to herself, "Without money and an apartment it'll be hard for him to find himself a wife."

"You over-protect him. A young man has to learn to stand on his own two feet. He's got a steady job; what's the big worry? Why, when I left home, I didn't get a penny from my family, and I was two years younger than he is now. Dad was thirteen when he came to Shanghai, and he was only a poor tinsmith's apprentice then, wasn't he? No one has it easy when they start out."

"But that was different. We had our difficulties then, and young people like our son have their own difficulties now. Chuanhui wants to get married, but, finding somewhere for him will be a real problem. When you left home, you could always find some place to stay, even if it was a dump. But if Chuanhui struck out on his own now, he'd have to sleep on the streets. How many girls would be willing to move into a place like this with a flimsy curtain to partition the room? Our room is not small in size, so to get a new flat will be harder than going to heaven. You can't blame Chuanhui for complaining."

"Don't be so pessimistic. Look at Lu Dawei. Everything turned out okay for him, didn't it?"

Bringing up Lu Dawei was a mistake. He could feel his wife's back stiffen at the sound of that name, and she replied irritably, "Sure, and look what it cost him. He went bald before he could find a woman. I'd die a nervous wreck if our son had to go through that."

Hongfei had to admit there was some truth in his wife's words. He put on his strongest tone of authority, "Look at you. I left the Blue House with nothing but a suitcase and one change of clothes, and you married me."

"And I must have been the only girl under heaven foolish enough to do it." The thought of those days flashed warmly in her heart, and her reply was coyness itself.

"You mean you regret marrying me?" Hongfei asked, teasing.

"Too late to regret anything, old man," she smiled warmly,

lovingly countering her husband's taunt. But her sentimental feelings passed quickly. "In the beginning I really believed that this room was only ours temporarily, that someday we would have a place even nicer than the Blue House, and that hope kept me alive. Our economic situation did improve a bit, sure, but our home... Looks like we'll be here till we die. If I knew back then what I know now, I would have insisted that we claim at least one room of the Blue House. For Chuanhui."

From the other side of the curtain could be heard the low and steady snore of their son. You had to envy young people; no matter what happened they could fall asleep and face things refreshed the next day. Tomorrow; it always held bright promises for them. But this old couple was past that time now. It would be a long and mostly sleepless night, as usual.

"At age sixty nothing said angers you," the old saying went. Hongfei tried to put himself in his son's shoes and rehearsed to himself what his son had said that night.

If his son could get some money and a piece of the old home he could catch a girl in no time. What were young people after these days? He was not so old that he could not know things like that. Just what made a modern home? Let's see, oh yes, a decent set of furniture, a fair-sized refrigerator, a colour television, a stereo, and most importantly an apartment; this was standard fare for a newlywed couple these days. He had to admit that young teachers had it rough, and their requests were not unreasonable. It was not like they were squandering their money away on frivolities or asking for a world cruise; everything they wanted could be had for about five thousand yuan. But if they had to depend on their own meagre salaries, they would have to save and scrape a lifetime to accumulate that much. However that was no excuse for them not to work and struggle for their material improvement, and it certainly did not give them the right to go begging from everyone they knew just to fill their own money bags. He simply could not stand the thought of his son grovelling at the feet of an uncle for a few crumbs just so he could find a wife. And what disgrace it would bring upon him, his father! Had not he done everything within his power to fulfill the duties of a father these thirty odd years? Should he go looking to anyone else for help? No! His son would just have to realize that you do not always get everything you want in life. In fact, if the truth were known, life was one long, tiresome struggle punctuated occassionally with mostly unnoticeable and always fleeting successes. Had that not been his experience for over sixty years? Had he himself not dreamed of becoming a famous jockey, of becoming rich, of building a house that would be the envy of his father? But he was not like his son; the thought of depending on others for his own success had never crossed his mind. He would be a self-made man or nothing!

"Go look up your little brother," his wife continued.

"Go begging?" he fumed. Did she still not under stand him?

"Not begging. Just get what is coming to our son."

It seemed that the older she got the more her thoughts were only for her son.

"You're saying ... I haven't done enough for Chuanhui?" he said, his feelings hurt.

"No..." She knew she had bruised his pride and was sorry, but for her son's sake she pressed on: "It's just he needs to get some housing, or he'll never find a wife. It's the only way." Her words trailed off into a pitiful whimper.

The Blue House, the Blue House, always the Blue House. Oh

Fen, when we first met you loved me because I had given up the Blue House; who would have imagined that so many years later the only thing we would quarrel about would be returning to that place, Hongfei groaned to himself.

Naturally he was ashamed of the fact that he had not provided a better home for his wife and family, but had he not done his best? They said the growth ringson a tree reflect the kind of years a tree has weathered; wide rings indicate a good year with plenty of rain and a thin ring indicates a year of drought. Life was like that. There were good times and bad, and the marks those experiences left on a person were what made a person the individual he was. You could not get rid of the marks, and there was no need to apologize for them. Anyway, he felt he had done a decent enough job coping with the lot fate had handed him. Of course, this was the kind of accomplishment only he could appreciate. No, he had not shaken the world, nor had he become a millionaire like his father; he had simply spent his life toiling at the blackboard with the quiet patience of a water buffalo. Among his many former students there were many scientists or top government officials; of course, a few had gone on to be street spivs, and the vast majority had simply turned into average citizens not so very different from himself. Through all the years he had kept struggling—struggling for the sake of his loved ones, struggling for their future. But it was not the kind of struggle that one could sit down and share with one's son. It was not an exciting tale.

He remembered well the year the Blue House was completed, when he was just nine years old. Dragging him by the hand from one room to the next, his mother had followed her husband through a tour of the Blue House. Mother just kept saying "Incredible! How marvellous! It's more than I deserve!" His mother had been born into a poor family, and her husband had been an apprentice under her father. The old man had seen that Gu Fuxiang was a bright lad, so he gave his seventeen-year-old daughter to him to marry. Although Hongfei's mother was illiterate, she was a woman of fathomless common sense and virtue. They said that when Gu Fuxiang was first starting in business, he invested the 500 yuan he had borrowed at usurious interest on a pile of totally useless and unmarketable pig iron. When it became obvious that he had spent his last coin on a pile of waste that nobody wanted, he nearly went mad and promised to drown himself in the Huangpu River. One night when he didn't return home, his wife gathered their new born baby in her arms and ran through the dark streets to the edge of the river. Sure enough, there was Gu Fuxiang, pacing the river bank about to throw himself in the water. His wife walked up to him and boxed his ears, and screamed, "You spineless excuse for a man! You want to kill yourself and make me and your son suffer for the mess you yourself got yourself into?" Gu Fuxiang followed his wife home like a whipped puppy dog. Six months later war broke out in Europe, and with all pig iron imports suddenly cut off, that useless pile of scrap suddenly turned gold, and Gu Fuxiang was sitting on top of it. After that abrupt turn of events, Mr Gu liked to tell people, "If my wife had not 'boxed my ears' that night, I wouldn't be standing here today. That's heaven giving a cornered man a way out!"

But heaven can be unjust as well, to the point of hounding a person to death.

The family became one of the richest and most powerful in Shanghai and was able to move into that mansion called the Blue

House. To prove that his social status was on a par with any of the other wealthy clans, the nearly illiterate Gu Fuxiang reluctantly filled his home with ancient artwork and paintings, even buying the most expensive imported silverware and cut glass. But the old tinsmith knew that behind his back people still ridiculed him as being just another bumpkin that happened to have got rich fast. The upper class were always mentioning their fathers and ancestors with their official titles and ranks. Not Gu Fuxiang. His father and his grandfather and his grandfather's grandfather had been poor peasants near Wuxi for as long as records had been kept. But fortunately he had two sons, and ignoring the tears and wails of their mother, Gu Fuxiang put the two of them in a strict Catholic boarding school, the Xuhui School. Gu Fuxiang had never heard the old saying of the French salons, "It takes three generations to produce a man of class and culture," but he realized that such an austere step was necessary to spare his children the stigma he hated so much. He also knew that there was something else that kept him from enjoying the status he craved: his wife. She could not do anything; she could not dance or play the piano, and she looked and dressed like a cabbage seller. You could almost smell the earth of Wuxi on her. The boys would have to be kept away from her lest she infect them with her rustic ways.

After they moved into the Blue House, the two boys often saw their father venting his anger on their mother; it was as if he had forgotten about the time she "boxed his ears" and saved his life. The mother was forced to stay hidden in a room on the third floor lest she embarrass her husband in front of his friends. Poor Mother, a prisoner in that beautiful mansion, not even permitted to cook or see her own family, and worst of all not allowed to see her two boys. The two lordly young men marching off to school in their stiff uniforms and polished shoes looked more like paper soldiers than the two little boys who had snuggled up to her as she sang them nursery rhymes. And she was becoming just as strange to them.

By then the powerful Gu Fuxiang could easily have had any number of concubines running about the house, but he did not. It was a cruel and ruthless world in which he lived, and he had to weigh the future repercussions of everything he did. Women? He could buy or rent as many as he wished; what he really lacked was that social position for his family, being on the top rung on the social ladder ... and that could not be bought. He could do nothing about the plebian blood in his veins given him by his humble parents, but his other regret—having married an uncouth tinsmith's daughter—was something he could do something about.

So one weekend when Hongfei and his brother returned home from boarding school, the servants informed them that their mother had left. Father had given her a large sum of money, bought her a home in a small town far from Shanghai, asked a lawyer to finalize the divorce, and thus permanently cut all ties with the wife of his youth, the woman who had "boxed his ears" and saved his life. When the boys asked their father where he had sent their mother, he replied curtly, "Just carry on as if she were dead." It took everything within the eleven-year-old Hongfei to stop himself from throwing himself against his father. It was the first time that he could remember feeling hatred and disgust for his father.

Not long afterwards Gu Fuxiang found a new wife, someone who could help him gain the social recognition he craved. She was the daughter of a high-ranking official who had served in Europe during the Northern Warlords Period. She was thirty years old and had never married, and she brought with her the fine tastes and social connections her new husband needed. She was the mother of the youngest son, Hongji.

Raised in Europe, the new mistress turned the Blue House into a whole new world. She patiently instructed Gu Fuxiang in Western table manners, dressed him in Western suits, and even taught him to waltz and tango. Before long she had the hall of the Blue House filled with ladies and gentlemen of the highest distinction coming to make social calls. But what she could never do was give the two elder boys a mother's love, especially after she had had one of her own. The Blue House was no longer a home to the boys; it was more like an overnight stop, a place to stay for the shortest time possible. When he was old enough, little Hongfei dreamed of leaving this place, going to find his mother, and bringing her back to live with them! One night father came charging into the boys' room. The two boys had been sitting there gazing at their mother's picture, tears trickling down their cheeks. The father stood there for a moment, gently wiping away the dust from the picture, then, looking around the room as if he had lost something, he announced abruptly, "Your mother ... is dead."

The boys simply stood there in perfect silence, their dark stares boring holes into their father. To this day Hongfei remembers how the hatred for his father had surpassed the grief for his mother! The father must have felt something; he turned on his heels and his stooped back, normally straight as an arrow, quivered.

"She took things too seriously. I told her I didn't care if she remarried. I gave her a nice house, money. How could I know she would ... hang herself? Everything was done ... for you boys, so you could have a family to be proud of!"

"Mother killed herself," Hongfei said interrupting his father, "because there was no one there to box her ears!"

His father spun around like he had been hit with an electric charge, and Hongfei could see his father's face twitch uncontrollably. The man's eyes narrowed in intense hatred as he glowered at his son, then he stomped out of the room, slamming the door behind him. From that day on Father could not look at Hongfei without the same venomous look. Every thread of natural love between father and son had been severed.

Hongfei graduated from middle school when he was eighteen, and he excitedly discussed with his classmates his plans to study at Nankai University. But his father would hear nothing of it. "What? You want to be an employee all your life? Even if you became an engineer, you'd starve without a boss." His father had his career all mapped out for him. He would become a lawyer and open his own firm. He would be his own boss, father said. The old man had spent a considerable amount of money hiring a lawyer to dissolve his first marriage and arrange the legal aspects of pushing his partner out of the way in the Huachang Steel Plant; and he was sure to need a lawyer many times more in the future. Number One Son had followed his father's orders and was studying economics in the U. S. With one son in economics and the other in law, Gu Fuxiang was sure that the Gu clan's future could only be bright.

The only problem was that Hongfei hated the thought of studying law; it was natural science that he enjoyed. But the tyrant of the Blue House wielded limitless power in his domain, and that included the aspirations of his son. The father's selfish ambitions had driven him to cut off his first wife, and he was not above manipulating his son. His son's youth was his to exploit.

"Please respect my wishes, dad, I'm a man now."

"Fart on your damn wishes!" Father could still display the old tinsmith in him, but of course only when the new mother was not around. "I raised you and fed you these last eighteen years, so don't go spouting off this new-fangled 'my wishes' stuff. You act like your damned dead mother, and you deserve to be as poor as her."

Hongfei's face darkened and sparks of hatred flew from his eyes. "You curse Mother like that again and...."

Father never dared bring up the subject of Mother after that. The boy was an adult now and nearly a head taller than him. Moreover, due to his strict upbringing at the boarding school, the boy had an air of stately reserve and confidence—something that people called "class"—and even his father was a bit intimidated by him. However, as the old man reminded himself, he was still his father, still the king of the Blue House, and he knew just how to take down his headstrong boy.

"You want to go to Nankai, I can't stop you. I'll respect your wishes. But don't expect any help from me."

Young and helpless, Hongfei could only go to the train station to see his classmates off while he stayed behind. "Don't worry about it," his classmates said trying to console him, "You'll enjoy studying law as much as you would engineering." But the words only made it more painfully clear than ever to him: he was a slave to his father's ambition. He could make no choices for himself. Some of his classmates would go on to be businessmen, some would get higher degrees in education, some would join the army (the war with Japan had just broken out). Many would face incredible hardships, but at least they would all have the freedom to choose their own paths. Hongfei, on the other hand, would spend the next few years being chauffered to the University of Shanghai to listen to the classes and read the books he personally deplored ... and all for no other reason than that that was his father's plan!

Young Gu Hongfei was a well-known figure in his university, and he was especially popular with his classmates. He himself knew, however, that his popularity was due in a large part to the fact that he came from a wealthy and well-connected family and from the famed Blue House. His home had a billiard room and tennis court, and Hongfei's friends loved to go there to enjoy these novel games. That was just fine with his father; Hongfei's classmates were all children of other rich and powerful Shanghai families, and for his son to mingle with such an elite crowd made the father immensey happy. Gu Fuxiang had now shed the old stigma of being a "nouveau riche" and had become a legitimate member of the upper class. In a desperate attempt to forget his present and past miseries, Hongfei indulged himself in every passing fancy and thrill that money could buy. Had things gone on the way they were, the rift between father and son might even have shrunk, or at least not widened into a gaping chasm. But that was not to be.

One day Hongfei drove to Hangzhou with his friends and on the way back rolled the car, broke his wrist and was knocked unconscious. As soon as his father found out, he had his son transferred to the famous French Hospital—not out of love for his son, but simply to demonstrate the wealth of the Gu family.

Delirious, young Hongfei saw his mother at his side, felt her lovingly caress his forehead just as she had when he had been ill as a child. But this was no dream, this tender stroking was real, it was Mum! Then, focusing his eyes on the figure hovering above him, he realized a beautiful young nurse was taking his pulse... It was Fen, and that was how a woman's love was reintroduced into his life.

His father never came to see him in the hospital, but his new mother visited every other day. She was so polite that it made him feel uncomfortable, as if he were lying on a bed of nails. He could never feel at ease with her.

One day after one such visit, Fen expressed curiosity about the way mother and son behaved. "Why do you and your mother act like strangers, Mr Gu?"

"She's not my mother; my mother is dead." Hongfei was suddenly overcome by a desire to unload his frustrations, and he began to tell the young nurse all about his lonely youth and the one great regret in his life—that he had never been able to retrieve his mother from the "cold palace" of exile to which his father had sent her like some disfavoured concubine.

Fen herself had grown up in an orphanage with no known relatives to look after her, and at eighteen she had had to strike out on her own. She could sympathize with her patient and thereafter took even greater pains to look after him. They fell in love. His father had his stepmother find an appropriate girlfriend for him as soon as he was out of the hospital, so he severed his relations with his father, as often happened in that era.

Gu Fuxiang had never sustained a loss in business or in his own cherished ambitions. However, this son of his threatened to change all that. "Just what do you want in life? Your problem is you don't know how good you've got it. This Blue House is second to none in Shanghai, and the Huachang Steel Plant is known all over Asia. They say it's easy to start a business, hard to keep it going. I've fed you and given you anything you've wanted all your life. I've never asked you to develop the business; the only thing I ask you to do is keep the Blue House and keep Huachang..." The Blue House again, always the Blue House. That 100,000-dollar pile of bricks that had cost Mamma her life, Hongfei his youth, and now his father was asking him to pay for it with his first love, the only woman he ever loved!

"All right, I can see I've wasted my money raising you. If you ever bring that tramp of a girlfriend to my house I will disown you as my son. Forever."

The old man was a firm believer in the power of money.

"If that's the way it is," said Hongfei, "then I'm leaving."

"Don't ever come crawling back here whining for Daddy to help you!" Father roared as his son walked out.

"The next time I set foot in the Blue House I'll be ten times richer than you ever dreamed of being!" Hongfei had vowed to his father. And if he could not become a multi-millionaire, he said to himself, nothing on earth could make him set foot in that place again. He had challenged his father, cried out against the injustice done to his mother and liberated himself from the suffocating grasp of the Blue House!

That had been forty years ago. That was the day he had begun to face the world alone. Before he had always looked enviously at those who lived independently, and from that day on he would learn what it really meant to stand on one's own two feet. He would learn the pain and the hardship that were the cost of such a life.

Fen would not let him drop out of school. "You've only got two more years left; it would be a waste to quit now. Don't worry, your fiancée may not have a rich dowry to give you, but she does have two hands. I'll support you till you get your degree."

As it was pretty clear that his son was head over heels for this young nurse Gu Fuxiang became desperate and wrote the boy a letter implying that if he would just marry the daughter of his plant's chairman of the board, he could still secretly marry this girlfriend of his and keep her at the Blue House as the family nurse. Hongfei was furious when he read the letter, and to insure that his father would never again attempt to interfere in his personal life, he asked a lawyer to draw up papers so that he could legally and permanently sever all relations with the Gu family!

Now penniless and with no ties to his father, Hongfei's social status in Shanghai plummeted to unplumbed depths overnight. All his friends disowned him, though that hardly mattered, as all his time was consumed in his studies anyway. To help ease the load on Fen, he worked part-time as a primary school teacher. After graduation he started looking for a job, but it was like running into a brick wall. He had no letters of recommendation, no powerful family to pull strings, just a fresh diploma. Not a law firm in Shanghai would give him the time of day. He tried asking the fathers of some of his classmates for help, but each one said in their polite and tactful way that they did not want to get in the crossfire of a family dispute, especially if the mighty Gu Fuxiang was involved. Some even tried to persuade him to give up and go back to his father; but whenever he heard those words, he simply turned on his heels and walked away. From morning till late at night he was out looking for a job until final-

ly—suffering from both physical fatigue and mental frustration—he collapsed from exhaustion.

"This society is just a graveyard; one guy has no more feeling
for the next than one corpse has for another...I can't stand it!"
Hongfei said, looking up at Fen with bloodshot eyes.

Fen just smiled. "You aren't the rich young buck you used to
be, you know. You think people are still going to hand you
favours and pat you on the back every time you ask for something? You want to know how I had to struggle to get my first
job? If you let such a little thing defeat you, how are you ever
going to go on to bigger and better things?" She reprimanded
him gently as she laid steaming towels on his sore back. Strange;
the pain suddenly disappeared, and he was not sure whether it
was that sweet, soothing voice that had healed him or the hot
towels.

"I'll go out again tomorrow. There must be a rice bowl for Gu
Hongfei somewhere!" he vowed, raising clenched fists into the
air as if he were taking on fate itself.

He never found that job as a lawyer, but he did find a private
middle school that needed a teacher. The salary was not high,
but at least now he could afford to get married. When he found
this room with a southern exposure and 25 square metres of living space in the old building, he felt it was a good enough place
to start out; little did he know he would be living there to this
day. The place was a little shabby, and the neighbourhood was
not the best in Shanghai, but it was all they could afford at the
time.

"Don't give up, Fen! Some day I'll build you a big Western-
style house!" he would often tell her. It pained him deeply to
bring his new bride to such a place. But at least it was his own

place. If only he could bring Mother back!

In 1946 they had a baby, a beautiful baby girl. Their little home seemed more precious, more filled with warmth and love than ever. But just as the birds of the air often have their little nests wrecked, so their home would suffer an unexpected tragedy. Their two-year-old daughter contracted the dreaded disease of that time, acute pneumonia. Back then, penicillin was nearly impossible to find, and even supposing you did find any, it took gold or U.S. dollars to buy it. Where would a poor teacher come up with that? The little girl's condition got worse and worse until there seemed to be no hope left. Finally Hongfei picked up a phone to call his father.

"Who is it?" his father's cold and haughty voice asked.

Hongfei held the receiver with trembling hands, then placed it back on the hook. When he returned home, his daughter had already died.

Never had he imagined that life could be so cruel, so ruthless!

He grew up fast after that. He felt as though his teeth had been punched in, but he learned to swallow both teeth and blood. After he left the Blue House, he knew what it meant to be a real man, to face life on his own. Now he bore not only his own grief over his darling daughter's death, but also the responsibility for a broken-hearted wife. The weight of it all began to show in the deep furrows on his high forehead.

But leaving the Blue House had brought him rewards as well.

He had become a middle school teacher. No one has ever got rich pushing chalk, and being called "Mr Teacher" had never been one of his aspirations in life, but since he was determined to do his job well, he worked tirelessly. After all, he had a family to support, and he was going to hold on to this rice bowl with both hands. Moreover, he had read "The Last Words of Sun Yat-sen" and been moved to tears by it. He was only an insignificant school teacher now, but he could not forget the words of this great man who challenged all men to make the world a better place. The more he worked with children the more he appreciated their innocence and simplicity. He grew to truly love his job. After teaching for over forty years, he had earned the respect and admiration of all the teachers in the area, and not long ago he had had the honour of being elected a representative to the district people's congress. It was a prestigious post that payed absolutely nothing, but he nevertheless spent his every spare moment investigating this school's lack of funds or that school's dispute with a neighbouring factory over pollution. His own son thought his dedication to the task was absurd, and one day cried, "The Great Representative doesn't even get to sit in a car. He has to spend his days running around catching buses!" Hongfei wanted to slap his son for making such a remark. Young people today were so cynical, so smart-mouthed. It was enough to make you sick.

Hongfei had long since learned his place in life and had never sought an official post. Now people looked up to him and had given him a responsibility, he was not about to let them down. Not in the least. It was a big country, and everyone had to do their part. If everyone expected the top leaders to do everything, how would anything get done? The Blue House had more than ten servants, but only one of them was an overseer.

"Chinese intellectuals are a pitiful lot. They've obediently done what they've been told for the last thirty years, and still been heckled and harrassed every step of the way..." Chuanhui watched his father run from meeting to meeting till his feet were swollen and his voice was hoarse. The whole thing was ridiculous, and he could not help but tell his father so. "Why all the sweat, dad? Just muddle through for a year or two then give the chore to someone else. It's not worth your time."

Young people were always talking like this, saying the first thing that came into their heads. The words shocked Hongfei; he himself could never talk like that. The last thirty years of political campaigns had taught him to be cautious almost to the point of cowardice. Be that as it may, he deplored the thought of "muddling through" anything; those words were simply not in his vocabulary. Whatever he was asked to do, he did with all his heart.

It was a policy that had served him well. It had brought him steadiness of purpose and the respect of all those around him. What was more, it had brought him peace of mind.

That was just the way he was. That was part of his character, part of the growth rings in Hongfei's life. Good years and bad years, prosperous times and the lean ones, these were his growth rings making him different from anyone else in the world. All these things made up the person of Hongfei, his individuality; and no one, not his son, not his father, could ever take that identity from him.

His son had been raised in a different era than himself, and obviously the lad faced many difficulties that he himself had never experienced. Perhaps he had no right to interfere in the boy's life, just as his father had had no right to interfere in his when he was young!

Hongfei rolled out of bed and draped a jacket over his back. He picked up the tiny box and lifted the gold ring to examine it more carefully. This ring was different in quality and style from rings he had seen in the past, but it had good workmanship. That was just like people. Times can change, but the virtues by which men are judged—industry, frugality, independence— these standards never change. He could not agree with the young people, his son included, who regarded the meticulous work style and frugality he had cultivated over the years as stagnation or backwardness. And he could not agree that this was a manifestation of a "generation gap" either.

Nor would he ever break the oath he had made in his youth and go begging at the gates of his brother's house just so his son could find some housing and hook a wife. Never!

He gently nudged Fen. He wanted so much to share these thoughts with her. He had become used to discussing everything with Fen and was equally accustomed to her support. But Fen did not respond this time. She was fast asleep.

Hongfei sighed deeply, and staring into the darkness, he began to count his growth rings. At the thought of every one a deeper sense of peace came over him until finally he fell into a restful sleep.

Fen lay in bed listening to the sound of breathing coming from her husband and son. She could not sleep. Like all mothers, she was worried about her son finding a wife. She was not like the petty women in the market, but the weight of public opinion did affect her nonetheless. Once during the mid-day break an administrative cadre came around talking about a girl he knew. She was a pretty young woman, he said, bright, and a graduate of the foreign languages school. The ideal girl. Fen naturally mentioned the prospects of her own son as a match, but the cadre, who was always bragging how he had been "forced into working all my childhood" and "went begging with my father when I was three" simply gave her a condescending smile and said, "I'm afraid the young man must have adequate housing and some relatives overseas." Fen was offended, not for herself, but for her son. Her boy was as good as anyone in Shanghai. When she reported this injustice to her husband, he just laughed at her childishness. "Why even bother with that type of person? They're not worth getting upset about." But she was upset and stayed angry for several days.

What her son had said that evening had made her regret many things. No, she did not regret having married Hongfei, but she did regret that they had so easily given up all the rights to an inheritance. On the other hand, if Hongfei had remained the carefree dandy of Shanghai, she would probably have rejected his love. She had met a lot of rich young men when she was working at the missionary hospital, and more than one of them had made some romantic overtures to her. Marrying a rich young man was the dream of every nurse there, every one except her. She did not trust those unrealiable playboys, not even Hongfei. In fact she had kept putting off any answer to his proposals and would probably never have agreed to marry him, but then Hongfei broke off all relations with his father, and things changed. If a man was willing to give up everything, every ounce of gold and even his own family for her, wasn't he worth her love? Ironically, it was the lack of these things that kept her son from finding a woman. Ah, life. It was just like trying to make a dress out of a small piece of fabric: If you make it long enough on one end you'll be short on the other.

That young lady Chuanhui had mentioned tonight; just what kind of a girl was she? Can write poetry, that says something for her, but she must have her sights set high when it comes to men.

Of course, if Chuanhui was living in the Blue House that problem would be solved. Mum was not against young people standing on their own two feet; it was just that with her son making a measly 58 yuan a month, he would be an old man before he could save enough to leave that room they shared. If Chuanhui hung on to his unbreakable iron rice bowl, independent or not independent, he would need to come into a big fortune to alter his living conditions.

3

By a stroke of great luck he bumped into Bai Hong just as he was going into the dining hall. For several days Chuanhui had wanted to look her up and explain why he had not been at the poetry recital, but he was never quite able to find the opportunity. Of course, he could have simply gone to her office, but there would be too many spying eyes and flapping ears there. Chuanhui was not about to give those silly rumour-mongers any more to blab about over their tea and lunch.

"Really sorry," Chuanhui stammered. "Something came up the other night, and I couldn't get away..." He debated whether he should explain everything to her, then decided that it was best to keep things under wraps until anything definite happened. But there was another reason too, one that crept out of the darker corners of his mind, and that he despised even as he entertained it: he did not wish to open to Bai Hong the world of affluence that he had just discovered. That would be a serious threat to him right now. "When everything works out, I'll explain it to you, just wait a while..."

"Fine," she said, flashing him a forgiving smile. "All young people with a bit of ambition have got big plans mapped out. I bet you're trying to get into a master's degree course, right? Why are you blushing? OK, OK, I won't ask any more questions." She smiled grandly then continued, "I have a secret of my own, but I don't want to mention anything about it either till things are more settled. By the way, I'll be off work for three months for advanced training. Give me your home address so we can keep in touch. Here," she said, handing him her address book.

Home address? His mind raced. What would she think if she ever saw that pigeon hole they called home?

"Hurry up!" she urged.

"Why don't you just give me your address? That way if anything comes up I can just run over to your place."

"My goodness," she answered, "Don't you have any manners? You can't just go around asking a girl for her address." She spoke with an air of righteous indignation, but her reddening face betrayed her embarrassment. Someone was calling for her now, and Chuanhui did not want to offend her any more by stalling, so he quickly scribbled down his address and hoped the worst would not happen. She put the address book away and smiled at him again, then gracefully excused herself and disappeared into the crowd. Ah, Bai Hong, you do everything with so much poise, tact, and sweetness! She was everything one could ask for in a girl. "I'll do everything within my power to make you happy," he said, looking into the space where she had been standing.

Who should sneak up behind him just then but Xiao Zhu.

"Aha! So that's the girl you bought the ring for? Don't do anything rash, Chuanhui. Nowadays guys like to play the field a bit before choosing a girl. Don't just slobber over the first vanilla cake you see. There might be a nice chocolate one right behind it!"

"Shut up, you!" Chuanhui snapped angrily, shoving Xiao Zhu back three steps. He had changed from mild to monstrous in a twinkling.

"Hey, don't get uptight; just joking." Surprisingly, Xiao Zhu did not appear upset and even managed a quiet snicker.

Chuanhui had suddenly lost his appetite, and he stormed away from the dining hall, viciously kicking any stone that happened to be in his path. He was not sure why he was so angry. He had become awfully moody lately, even he had to admit it. He had not studied English for over half a month and had not touched the translation he was supposed to be doing for a science magazine. He had just spent hours with motor-mouth Xiao Zhu trying to find his "roots". It was all Father's fault, damn it. If he had just been smarter when he was young, life would be so much simpler now!

The Zhonghua Hospital, Shanghai, High-Ranking Cadre's Ward.

Because of her skill and experience, Fen was often lent to the various hospitals around the city that cared for high officials. As chance would have it, today she was working in the former French Hospital, where her husband had been rushed after rolling his car. She could still remember the room: the third room on the right. Her feelings got the best of her, and while the patients were taking their noon nap, she made for the porch in a sentimental mood.

"... Your old man takes ginseng, does he? That stuff does

marvels."

"...Last year Xiao Liu gave us a bunch of it. Someone told me recently caterpillar fungus is the best there is..."

The sound of the two women's voices drifted from the French window she was passing. Fen resisted the temptation to go and investigate and turned her attention towards the garden. A new building had gobbled up a lot of space that used to be garden; the bench where she and Hongfei used to sit was long gone, and the pool had been filled in. She could not help but feel a little melancholy as she noted all the changes.

"Has your son been assigned his job yet?" Fen could hear the conversation clearly from where she stood.

"Old Li arranged for him to be a teacher in his university, but the boy wanted to work at the Academy of Social Sciences. They don't have to work in the office every day. He could take it easy some of the time."

Fen could hear the women's voices. Even the clicking of their knitting needles could be heard in the midday quiet. It sounded to her like both women were used to lives of ease and had husbands with no small clout. Their chit-chat droned on.

"And, ah, may I ask if your son has a girlfriend?"

It seemed that women always have that question on their minds.

"That goofy kid of mine, the only girls he looks at now belong to that dance troupe. And what do they have to offer besides good looks? They come from no-name families, they're usually poor, and they have no culture whatsoever. Disgraceful. What about your daughter, Xiaojun? Married yet?"

"Oh yes. She married the son of a former industrialist. Her father-in-law studied in England and is now a foreign trade representative for the government. He works for the motherland just like us, you know; we're not about to make a fuss about his class background. He wants the children to go to America to study. The family will pay the way, of course. They will be helping to build the four modernizations with the training..."

Fen was becoming more aggravated with every word she heard. So what was the big deal? She could have trotted out her son Chuanhui on an equal footing: Grandson of the Huachang Steel Giant who built the magnificent Blue House, a college grad, soon-to-be assistant engineer... What? Envious of these snobs? She couldn't care less about their social status or power. Just a girl for her son, that's all she was concerned about. Who cared if she was penniless? That was immaterial. From her motherly point of view, any girl with one good eye and a brain would fall head over heels for her son. Why he was just like the White Horse Prince of the fairy tales: he was everything a girl dreamed of. But not girls nowadays. If a guy didn't have an a-partment, forget it.

A gust of wind lifted the white gauze of the French window, and she was reminded of her wedding veil. They had had no money, but Hongfei had stubbornly insisted they invite several good friends for tea in a small restaurant at the Jinjiang Hotel. An old maid missionary from the orphanage, Laura, personally put the makeup on the new bride. As the elderly American kissed Fen on the forehead she burst into tears. "How I envy you," she sobbed. "I have never in my life been loved by a man like you are."

Those words had sent ripples of joy through Fen's soul. Those words were worth more than the Blue House, more than ten Blue Houses.

Hongfei appeared in a rented tuxedo to take her to the ceremony, and he looked every bit the wealthy young aristocrat: tall, broad-shouldered, every inch of him was born for attire like this. Suddenly, Fen was afraid.

"You've given up everything for me; don't you regret it?" Fen whispered timidly through her wedding veil, "You still have time to change your mind...."

Hongfei answered her question with a warm embrace. "And if you regret marrying a pauper like myself, there's still time for you to change your mind...."

The couple would repeat those lines many times throughout their married life. The words became used as the ultimate sign of affection between them as well as each one's trump card during any argument. That was why Hongfei had asked "You mean you regret marrying me?" that evening, and although he had meant no harm by it, she was hurt by it all the same.

"Love? Ha! That's just the creation of those lazy, no-good novelists. I don't believe in it. I hope you can help my son." The woman's voice suddenly grew angry and demanding. "That kid has got to listen to me this time. Do the best you can. A businesswoman, an intellectual, either one would suit him fine. Of course, if the girl had some relatives overseas, that would be even better. Appearance means everything nowadays, you know...."

"As a matter of fact I have one in mind. The only problem is she's a little old, thirty-one. Her father belongs to the Families of Overseas Chinese Association, and the family used to have large business holdings. Very well-known...."

"A bride three years older is worth a brick of gold, they say. No problem there," the woman replied crisply.

The two women's arrogant prattle rankled with Fen. It was her time to check the old cadre's blood pressure, so she walked out of hearing distance of the ladies towards her ward. The old cadre was in the field of law. He ought to know something about inheritance laws, so she might as well ask him. Just casually, of course.

A stylishly dressed man and woman stopped Fen in the hall.

"Doctor, about my father's condition..." The man must have been the cadre's son.

"Well, we're pretty optimistic. He should live another couple years if he gets the proper care," Fen said encouragingly.

"Come on," the woman whispered excitedly to her husband as she pulled him away. "Daddy's by himself now so let's make our move. Now remember, you've got to get him to write down his will now; we don't live here, and we'll miss out on a small fortune if you don't. Everyone will want a share, and we don't want to have to scramble for what few coins fall through their fingers." The woman's face revealed an urgency that verged on panic. At least that was what Fen saw.

Fen rushed ahead of them and blocked the door. "Look, under no circumstances can you..." To force a man dying of cancer to write out his will was as cruel an act as she had ever seen in all her career as a nurse.

The young man pushed Fen out of the way as if to say: "Mind you own business!"

Fen went to her office and slumped down at her desk. Inheritance, inheritance: it seemed that was all anyone talked about these days, and even she was getting sucked into the whirlpool.

She heard footsteps and turned around to see the young couple walk down the hall. They were walking away from her, so it was impossible to read the expression on their faces to tell if their mission had been successful.

She got up, tiptoed over to the old cadre's room and peeked in to see the old gentleman sitting up against his pillows. She slipped in quietly and tucked in his quilt. Society did not think highly of high-ranking cadres, but here was a seventy-year-old man with one arm missing and the rest of his body riddled with bullet wounds and cancer, and Fen could not help but feel a deep sense of sorrow and sympathy for this person entrusted to her care.

"Lately I can't help thinking of the *All's Well Song* out of *A Dream of Red Mansions* * ," the cadre said looking at Fen with a feeble smile. His voice was weak but steady, quiet yet penetrating. Only a person with a wealth of life's experience behind him and the knowledge of impending death before him could speak like that.

Fen decided not to ask the old man any questions about inheritance laws; the guilt that now stabbed a finger at her own heart would not permit her.

A peasant's basket full of winter bamboo shoots caught Fen's attention as she made her way through the crowded market. Hongfei still acted like the spoiled rich kid in some ways; he refused to eat fatty meat and loved fresh cooked vegetables. The old man of the house had been grumpy since their little dispute the other night. A dish of bamboo shoots cooked with black fungus would change that.

---

* *All's Well Song*: A satire on the devious motives and hypocrisy of ancient Chinese family relations.

"Two eighty," the peasant said looking at the scales, without a blink.

Fen was shocked. She quickly pulled some of the sprouts out of the scales and asked the peasant to weigh it again. A dish tastes better when there is less of it anyway.

Walking down the street, Fen brooded over the injustice done to her son. With the cost of everything going up, it was hard enough to make ends meet on a hundred yuan a month; how could a young man on his salary be expected to survive? What really baffled her was how so many young people seemed to have money to blow on their every whim. Her husband would only smoke the cheap Flying Horse Brand, but many young men smoked the fancy filter cigarettes. It was hard to understand.

As soon as Fen stepped into the kitchen on the ground floor, a neighbour yelled to her, "Hey, Chuanhui's mother, you have company. Your guest has been waiting here for half an hour." Fen looked up to see the old woman smile and wink surreptitiously at her, and before she could get an explanation, she heard someone call down the stairs in a sweet voice, "Auntie Gu!" What? A young lady!

"I'm ... I'm a colleague of Chuanhui's." The girl blushed at her own words. Fen understood and quickly took the girl to their room.

"Oh, what beautiful China pinks!" The young woman was drawn immediately to the flowers sitting on the chest of drawers. Fen loved flowers herself and had preferred to go without getting new clothes for a couple of years rather than miss buying flowers. They had to be cut flowers too. "Where did you manage to buy them in this cold weather?" the girl asked enthusiastically.

"You like them? Here, they're yours." Fen liked the girl instantly; she was outgoing, unpretentious, and she loved flowers. Any girl who loves flowers has a kind heart. At least that was how Fen saw it.

The girl pulled a form out of her knapsack. "The Municipal Scientists' Association is offering an evening course in French. I heard Chuanhui was wanting to study French, so I signed him up for the course. It wasn't easy, I can tell you," the girl laughed, pleased with her work. She also pulled out a blue ticket and explained, "This is for a concert this Saturday. Beethoven's ninth. I was going to just send it to him, but I was afraid it might get lost in the post, so I decided to bring it over myself."

The girl noticed some snapshots of Chuanhui under the glass covering the desk. They were pictures of him when he was a child, and she began studying them intently. Fen stepped alongside the girl and explained each photo.

"That was when he was two. His father took him to the bathhouse. He slipped and ... oh look, you can see the little bandage on him. Here he is at five, going to kindergarten. He hated going. Look how he screwed up his face when his dad took the picture. Here he's got his little red scarf on; proud as a peacock...."

Fen discovered that she adored this girl she had just met a few minutes before, for the simple reason that she listened with great relish to Fen's every detail about Chuanhui. Fen had waited all her life for the chance to talk about her wonderful son, Chuanhui. Her husband had once said to her, "Fen, how is it that all you want to talk about from dawn till dusk is that son of ours? Has it ever occurred to you that people are not as interested in him as you are? There's only one other person alive that would enjoy that kind of talk and would listen to it a hundred times over." "Who?" asked Fen, bewildered. "Your future daughter-in-law," her husband replied.

And here she stood. The girl had wanted to stay longer, until Chuanhui came home, but Fen could not control herself and said the last thing she should have said: "We only have one room here. But Chuanhui is going to do something about it when the time comes. There is always a way to get a place, and if not, we can get the housing management to brick up a partition..." The girl's face turned red, and she began making excuses to go before Fen had even finished her sentence. Fen wanted to kick herself for being an old fool and scaring the girl off.

"What's your name?" Fen just now thought to ask.

"Bai Hong." The words were just audible as the girl disappeared down the stairwell.

Bai Hong, White Rainbow—a pleasant name—just like the girl herself. The girl was only average in appearance, but women judge other women by what is on the inside, not the outside. Women (especially mothers-in-law) judge a girl by her conduct, temperament, and character. Bai Hong met with Fen's approval in every respect. Moreover, Fen could see in Bai Hong a reflection of herself a long time ago, when she herself was young.

When Bai Hong reached the alleyway, she realized she had forgotten the China pinks. A pity, but there was no way she could go back and face that embarrassing situation again. Why had Chuanhui never thought of bringing her flowers when there were such nice ones at home? Now that would make her happy. Men were pretty dense that way. Not that she had never had suitors who would have done almost anything to curry favour with her; it was just that they had never really loved her for what she was. They wanted her only for what her family could offer them.

Her father was an assistant commander in the army. Being from a high-status family was always a hindrance to a girl looking for true love. There were always boys interested in her, but the older she got the more she realized that it was her family background that attracted them. She had fallen in love with a young man once, the son of her father's old war buddy. She naively believed that since both of them were from the same social level, class status was not an issue with him. She was wrong. The fellow was transferred to Shanghai before she was, fell in love with a ballerina and quickly dumped Bai Hong. The move did not surprise most people—the guy had as much social clout as one could get—why should he bother marrying a plain girl like Bai Hong when there were plenty of gorgeous ones to pick from? A few people tried to comfort her with, "You'll get over it. Anyway, what does the daughter of an assistant commander have to worry about? There will be others." Those words added insult to injury. Granted, she was not the most beautiful girl in the world, and some young guys looked at those pockmarks around her nose as if they were some sort of fatal wound. But there was something beautiful inside her, she thought. How else could she produce those poems? She recalled a lesson in her high school geometry class when the teacher was explaining a hexahedron: "This solid figure has six plane surfaces, and each plane surface has a corresponding face on the opposite side of the figure." Sensitive and bright, Bai Hong was destined to become a poet. The geometric figure was like herself, she thought: since the divine force of the universe had created her, these must also be a corresponding "him". Though she was not physically beautiful, though her face was marred by those hateful little scars ... she was determined to find "him". And to find what it really meant to love and to be loved, she transferred out of the unit where everyone knew her family background. She got a job at a factory and changed her name. Now she was Bai Hong. Here she awaited her White Horse Prince.

And here she met Chuanhui. He was gentle and refined, and those timid eyes of his followed her every move. No man had ever looked at her like that before. They said timid eyes were a sure sign of love! She was happy beyond words; she had won a man's love because of what she was, not because of who she was related to.

Chuanhui was a high-minded young man, prudent, and showed self-restraint. She liked that. That was the way a man should be, not like those guys who went around flirting and fussing over anything in a skirt! She really had waited for him that night of the poetry recital. When he did not show up, she had been disappointed of course, but not angry. What kept him from coming, he would not say then. She had heard the factory's technicians had been given a new task, and she assumed he was in on it. He was the ambitious type who did not want to lose face and would keep quiet until the task was successfully completed. But yesterday she ran into someone from the Technical Department who said Chuanhui had not signed up for the new project. Well then Chuanhui must have had bigger things in mind. Word had it that the bureau was going to send four people to France to do some research. They were choosing from college graduates and promising scientists under thirty who spoke decent English and understood French; secondly they considered the field of work of the candidates. Chuanhui had to be busy with that. Or could it be that he was holding out to give her a really big surprise? She quietly vowed that she would translate several new foreign poems before the end of the year: that would make him proud of her!

It was just an ordinary home he lived in. The narrow stair-case, the crowded little kitchen shared by several families with its coal stoves looked like something out of the movie *The Crow and the Sparrow* about old Shanghai. But it was such a neat and tidy little place, and everyone was so nice. It was hard to be-lieve that such refined and noble people lived in such a simple setting. And his mother was such an adorable person. They were just like that bunch of gorgeous China pinks in the simple glass bowl: all they required was sunlight and water to grow and blos-som. A fancy setting was not necessary; all their attractiveness was from within.

She had peeked around the curtains that partitioned the room. That must be his bed with the clean, well-ironed, cross-stitched sheet on it. How did a 1.8-metre tall man like him sleep in such a small bed? She blushed. Beneath the glass cover on his desk was a ticket, the ticket to her poetry recital! That silly Chuan-hui, why was he so worried about missing that night? He must really love her! A guitar and tennis racket hung above his bed on the wall. Chuanhui still had a college boy's pastimes. She was happy to have had the chance to see parts of his life that she had not seen before.

If his mother had not embarrassed her like that, she would have loved to stay there longer and listen to her telling stories about her son. She loved every detail, every word. To her it was like the most beautiful poetry in the world. And she had fallen instantly in love with that simple but elegant home, especially that little world behind the curtain. Because that was where he lived.

The dark curtain of winter's night fell early; by five-thirty the trees were lifting their stark branches out to clutch the scattered evening stars. The bitter wind stung Bai Hong's cheeks as she quickened her pace. Only half an hour until her night class began. She always had a packed schedule, and that was the way she liked it. It made life full and meaningful. She also believed it was the only way to find one's niche in society, as well as win the respect of others. Her father's position provided power, and her family provided wealth, but if she depended on those things she would end up like her sister-in-law, sitting around and eating up their fortune. One had to stand on one's own two feet to be happy in life.

What luck! She could see Chuanhui walking stoop-shouldered towards her down the street. What had he been doing these last few days? He must have something on his mind; he never used to walk like that. He had always carried himself erect and walked with an easy and confident stride. He was wearing himself thin with his work. That was not wise.

"What? Don't you ever give your mind a rest?" she asked pretending to scold him.

Chuanhui was startled, then grinned as he saw it was Bai Hong. He was feeling overwhelmed with care and was glad to have someone to talk to. He asked Bai Hong to walk with him for a while, but she gracefully declined. "I have to catch an evening class." But to soothe him a bit, she added with a tone of feigned vanity and fuss, "When you take me to the concert next week, I'll be expecting flowers, China pinks to be exact, just like the ones your mother has."

She had gone to his house? Oh no, he thought. She had seen that dark, creaky stairwell, the room partitioned by a sheet, the worn-out wooden floor... His mood plummeted to new depths.

Bai Hong perceived the young man's thoughts and feelings. Her heart broke for the long-faced man before her. Couldn't Chuanhui see how she felt about him? She reached up, straightened his scarf for him and looked into his eyes. "Don't you forget, now. The concert's at six o'clock next Saturday. I'll be waiting for you."

He felt like a little boy who has just been comforted by his mother, and he had to fight back the tears. Those few words had touched him in a far greater way than any of her poems had, and all he could do was clutch her tiny cold hands.

"Really, I'll be waiting for you," she whispered again, then pulling her hands free, she took off down the street. Class would begin soon.

He stood there dumbfounded for several minutes. Why, he asked himself, did he feel so miserable? He should feel proud and happy. A girl was in love with him. In those few words "I'll be waiting for you" he had heard trust, hope and love!

Bai Hong's figure had disappeared quickly in the dark night shadows of the street. She did everything in a hurry. It was as if she were always running through life with never a rest. The poor girl. He ought to build her a palace, and then with his own two hands make her a throne to sit on. There on her throne she could relax. Relax.

A brand new motorcycle was parked by the back door of the courtyard. Who around here would have a guest with that kind of money? Chuanhui wondered. Not many in this dead-end, forgotten alleyway. Just as Chuanhui pushed open the door to his home, he heard an exuberant and friendly voice call out, "Is that you, Chuanhui? It's cold out, come and have some hot tea. One look at you says you're a Gu. You could pass for the brother of my son, Chuanye. Goodness, Chuanhui and Chuanye: the two remaining male Gus on the mainland, and the future of our clan!"

The visitor was Chuanye's father, his own uncle. He really was family, that was clear by his warm and chummy tone. Chuanhui scrutinized his uncle as they sat sipping tea. He was a tall and well-built man, and the new ski jacket he was wearing made him look even larger. On his large and well-fed face he sported a pair of sunscreen glasses. The ski-jacket looked nicer on him than on most of the young guys on the street. Just one look at uncle's bearing and clothes told you he belonged to the élite group of people around town with capital and property, Chuanhui mused.

"I've got to run now. I've been waiting here for quite a while just to have a look at this nephew of mine." As the uncle grabbed his hat and said his good-byes, Chuanhui felt overwhelmed with emotion. "I was just telling your folks, I want you come to our place this Saturday night for supper. That will be your grandfather's birthday, and we want to have a little memorial service for him."

For Grandfather! We're going home! Chuanhui had finally hit it lucky, he had found the magic words to open the door to that cave of riches.

Chuanhui's mother refilled her guest's cup again and said excitedly, "Father took things too seriously. If he could have borne the brunt a little he wouldn't have had to die. If he could only see his grandson now, a college graduate and a scientist, he would be bursting with pride and joy." Fen was becoming more animated with every word, but she suddenly stopped when she saw her husband's look of great displeasure. She also noticed that her brother-in-law was not the least bit interested in what she was saying.

The guest insisted that he could not drink the tea that had just been poured for him and gave a final farewell. Long after he had gone, the room was still filled with that air of class Chuanhui had sensed at the Jinjiang Club.

"Memorial service, bowing in respect to Father, what's he trying to prove? That's the same heartless son who threw Father out of his own home on to the streets," Hongfei muttered as he watched his brother disappear into the darkness.

They were eleven year apart and were actually only half brothers, sons of the same father. Their relationship had never been close, and now, after not seeing each other for thirty-odd years, it was virtually nonexistent. Hongfei had always felt closer to his older brother who had gone to America. They had suffered together, and even now Hongfei still missed him. With every passing political movement of the past, the correspondence with his brother in the U.S. had grown more and more infrequent, until finally it had ceased altogether. But he loved that brother, even dreamed about him! There had never been much brotherly affection between him and this younger brother. Before the "cultural revolution" Hongfei had kept track of his half-brother's career through the newspaper. He had become chief engineer and director representing the private ownership of the Huachang Steel Plant, had been appointed a member of the Municipal Consultative Conference and was often asked to attend important social functions. The country thought highly of him, inviting him to various social activities. Then in 1966 he had to pay the price for his forty years of high living. He was branded a "bloodsucking devil" and became a scapegoat for his father, suffering through dozens of "struggle meetings", being thrown out of the Blue House and given a tiny room to live in. Yes, the "cultural revolution" had been a turbulent time, and just as was planned, it "touched the soul of every person", from the pure-hearted and well-behaved like Hongfei to the high and mighty like his half-brother. No one escaped. During the height of the Red Terror, the youngest son had thrown his 78-year-old father into the streets in an attempt to save his own skin, but even that act could not gain him mercy. And when the son he had cherished most swung the axe against him, the father had been cut to the heart. When the old man finally died, Hongfei felt it was only right to inform this brother whom he had not seen for thirty years. But when he arrived at the Huachang Plant, his little brother had waved his hands and said emphatically that he had cut all relations with his father. "He's no kin of mine." To prove his innocence, the brother had asked one of the rebel leaders of the factory to witness the renouncement. Hongfei had had a long list of grievances against his father, and he thought he could never love him again, but when he saw the physical and emotional suffering the old man was going through in his last hours, all his childhood love for his father had returned. When his father, in his moment of despair and agony, came to his son's home, Hongfei was able to forgive him. Hongfei and Fen took care of the funeral, even though that left them open as targets of the big character posters and "search and confiscate" raids on their home. The act had brought Hongfei the consolation that he and his father had been reconciled, and that he had given his father warmth on his last day. Funny: without the cares of wealth and the Blue House, he was a warm and kind old man who sought only the love of his son and grandson. That night, when little Chuanhui was sound asleep, the old man had feebly bent over and softly kissed the grandchild whom he had just seen for the first time. Hongfei could never remember his father ever showing that kind of affection to him or his brother.

"Hongji drove me out of the house!" Father had said that night when Hongfei opened the door. "Don't worry, I won't bother you long. All I ask ... all I ask is that you take this Parker pen and sell it to buy a train ticket for me to get to Wuxi..." It was raining torrents that night, and the father had reached into his wet pocket to pull out the pen. The old man was soaked to the bone. Never in his wildest dreams had Hongfei ever imagined that his father would come to his home. The last time they had parted company was thirty years before. Hongfei was so shocked that he did not think to ask his father how he had found out where he lived. Although his father's face was haggard, it still gave away his sense of self-importance and his devil-may-care attitude; but his body could not hide the fatigue and pain, and he shivered uncontrollably. He was old and spent, ready to give out like a candle in the wind, and it would have been hard for anyone not to feel pity at such a sight. Hongfei helped his father inside, while Fen made him a steaming bowl of rice porridge.

Rain spattered against the window as the three generations of Gus huddled around the table. Forgotten for the moment were the chaos and upheavals of the present and the long separation of the past. The father had taken off his wet coat, and beneath it was a worn-out sweater and a filthy shirt. If only Father had been content with being a tinsmith, he would never have had to experience such calamity. How unpredictable life is!

"Dad, you can live here! You've got no kin left in Wuxi: who would take you in?" Fen asked gently. She had felt sorry for her father-in-law ever since her husband had told her about his mother's death. The man was totally broken, physically and e-motionally, and approaching his end; seeing his son and daugh-ter-in-law, he was overcome with remorse and could think of nothing to say. After the cremation the younger brother refused to come to pay his respects to his father's remains. Hongfei kept the small ash box in his home for a while. It was as if the ashes of the bloodsucking devil carried a fatal epidemic disease—even the crematorium refused to accept the remains for burial. China must have been the only place on earth where the dead had to account for their class status! By 1973 things had cooled down a little, and Hongfei was able to buy a small cemetery plot in Suzhou to bury his father. The younger brother never did ask him about his father's resting place.

"Poor Uncle had it tough from the beginning, being branded a capitalist and all. Nothing he could do," Chuanhui said, blindly defending his uncle.

"He's made a sincere effort to look us up; we can't be too hard on him," Fen chirped. "We don't want to appear vindic-tive, do we? Let's let bygones be bygones. They're promoting better relations with Taiwan these days. I do think you two brothers could learn something and be a little more friendly to-wards each other too." Fen hoped her little joke about Taiwan would help lighten the atmosphere; she did not want her hus-band to make a big issue out of the invitation. His brother had offered him a chance to change his mind without losing face, and he was still so stubborn. Had he lived through the "cultural revolution" without learning anything?

"Younger brother was always the crafty kind. I can't believe he's changed," Hongfei muttered.

Couldn't Fen see through that rascal? "I had the toughest time of all the brothers," he had just been saying as he sat at their table. "I had to carry Father's burden on my shoulders alone." It was as if he had been the scapegoat for all three brothers. Funny how he never mentioned that he alone had benefited from their father's riches and the Blue House these last few years. He also forgot to mention how Fen had helped him out of a tight spot some years before. One day in the early seventies he had appeared at Fen's hospital dressed in a factory uniform and pretending to be a worker. He went to Fen's ward and begged her to give his daughter a medical deferment so that she would not have to work in the countryside. Although her own son would not need to go to the countryside like most young people after schooling, she knew what a mother felt when she had to see her children sent there. What parent would not do the same under the circumstances? She saw his plight and gave in. Fen never told her husband about it; a fellow as straight as he was might spill it all, and then they would all have been in trouble. Just after the fall of Lin Biao, Hongji showed up again at Fen's ward. The factory clothes were replaced with the faded uniform of an old army officer. His hair was turning white, and he was a little potbellied, and he let on to be from a rather important army unit of that time. This time he asked Fen to help him get hold of a rare traditional medicine, gastrodia tuber.

"...My daughter married the son of a former assistant commander. The guy has had a tough time, and he's a physical mess right now. They say his case will be redressed soon, but we need to keep him alive long enough," he explained to Fen.

Plenty of old cadres had been beaten up during those terrible years, and she had heard that even the revered General Zhu De had suffered. Relief was in sight for this old soldier if he could just stay alive a little while longer. Fen got him the medicine. It was not the kind of favour one could broadcast, and in fact Fen had never told anyone about it. Besides, Fen was not the kind of person that wanted to be repaid for her favours. She never saw her brother-in-law again until today. This time he came dressed like a Hongkong tourist, and that rusty old bicycle was replaced with a brand new Suzuki. What a fellow; his clothes changed with the political climate. On the other hand, someone who was too frank, whose principles were too inflexible, always suffered for it. Why did her husband have to be that way? Yet she loved him for it, even if it did anger her at times. Life is so difficult sometimes.

Her husband's mood improved as he pulled three books out of a bag. "I bought a few books for Lu Dawei that he'll need in America. I've spent the last two weeks running all over town trying to find..." He looked around and saw that no one was paying any attention to him. His wife was busy fishing through an old trunk, and Chuanhui was totally engrossed with the blue concert ticket he held in one hand. He coughed and left the sentence unfinished, then went back to work carefully wrapping the books and adding a few beautifully written lines of English on the wrapping. He never did anything halfway.

"Aha, here it is!" his wife said as she pulled out a dark-grey herringbone overcoat from the trunk. Hongfei had worn it during his college days, but he had long since grown too fat to wear it and it had been stored away for years. She handed it to her son to try on, and sure enough it fitted perfectly.

"Classic clothes like this coat never go out of style. Just take it to get cleaned and pressed, and you'll be the best dressed man in town. Now our son will go back there in style!" Fen announced, looking with pride at Chuanhui.

"You're not really planning on going?" Her husband appeared surprised.

"Why not?" mother and son responded defensively.

Hongfei swallowed his first response. He had never been good at defending himself, but he had strong feelings about the Blue House and could not justify returning there now. A torrent of thoughts rushed through his mind: the death of his mother and daughter, the years of hardships and the independence that had created the growth rings that made him what he was. There were some hurts that could be forgiven but never forgotten.

Fen showed her son the label on the coat. "You won't find a coat of this quality any more," she said, bubbling with excitement. "The really great tailors all retired long ago. See here, it was custom-made by a French clothes store on the ' Rue Molière', as they used to call it back then. Your dad wore nothing but the best in those days."

Considering the situation, the timing, and his own feelings just then, Fen could not have chosen more inappropriate words, Hongfei sighed to himself. And he suddenly felt very lonely. He had been feeling lonely a lot lately, ever since talk of the Blue House had intruded into their lives.

They had just finished eating supper when a voice called from downstairs. "Old Gu! Old Gu!" Was everyone in Shanghai coming to visit them tonight? It turned out to be the headmaster of Hongfei's school and several of his colleagues.

"Congratulations," the headmaster said, puffing as he climbed the stairs. Everyone who climbed up that steep and narrow staircase needed half an hour just to regain their breath. "You've just been appointed a member of the Municipal Consultative Conference! We just got word from the district Bureau of Education."

"That..." Hongfei fruitlessly groped for words. Members of the Municipal People's Congress or the Consultative Conference seemed as far from Hongfei as the stars in the sky. Sure, the Consultative Conference was just one step above the district committee on which he served, but it was quite a step. "But I'm a nobody!" Hongfei finally managed to blurt out. True, as far as anyone could remember, Conference deputies had always been chosen for their outstanding contributions to society, their part in the United Front, or being VIPs or the children of VIPs. Hongfei could not see how he qualified for the post.

"A nobody? What about that?" the principal said, pointing to Hongfei's Thirty Years of Teaching Certificate hanging on the wall. "And this," he continued, touching the package of books with Lu Dawei's name written on it. "And how many years have you been working your tail off as teacher responsible for the class? You deserve the position if anyone does."

"And what kind of benefits does he get out of this new post?" Chuanhui asked sarcastically. "Does he get a car and chauffeur?"

"How dare you talk like that!" Fen had never raised her voice to her son before now, but Chuanhui's total disrespect for his father's many years of hard work was more than she could take.

"We should be happy just to have the honour. This is society's way of... expressing its appreciation to your father." A large knot formed in her throat as she said those last words. She was proud of her husband. Until now she had always thought that she was the only person on earth that appreciated his uprightness and his career. For years he had toiled as silently and tirelessly as an ox in the fields, and only she had seen it. He was an upright man, stubborn in his ways but faithful to his principles and content to be a nameless teacher with a thankless job. But he was no ordinary man to her; she respected and admired him, and she would never stand for anyone putting him down, including her son. Most of the other nurses her age at the hospital had husbands who were scholars or scientists, and she was certainly the only one there whose husband earned less than she did with his ordinary middle-school teacher's salary, but she had never thought less of him because of it. He could have had it all—power, position, money—but he had given it all up for her. In her heart he was as good a man as could be found, and now, at last, society had begun to recognize that fact.

Hongfei looked into his wife's eyes. It was she who had stood by him all these years and who knew more than anyone else about the growth rings of his life. As for his son ... well, they were flesh and blood, but they were also a generation and a world apart.

"Young people these days," Hongfei said sadly looking at his son, "How is it they think so much of material gain and so little about the things that really count?" He turned to the old principal and asked, "How... will they ever learn?"

"Maybe if everyone was rich they'd see material things for what they're really worth," the principal replied pensively as he ran his fingers through his thinning white hair.

"They're poor in character as well as materially!" Fen added sympathetically.

"You think so?" Chuanhui turned away to examine his own heart. He was ashamed of that wisecrack he had just made. In all fairness, he had to admit he was far better off both financially and emotionally than most people his age, but the last few days he had felt so tormented; it was as if some demon had jumped into his heart and was raising havoc there. He had changed! The news of his father being appointed to the Consultative Conference would have thrilled him beyond words at one time, but now, for some reason, he was not thrilled at all. Maybe it was because he had heard so much about Conference deputies recently. They were all real top dogs, but his father was just... just an old middle school teacher. His father could never compare with them... Chuanhui felt really ashamed at having made the comparison! Damn that demon!

"Congratulations, dad!" Chuanhui spoke up, disgusted with himself.

"Don't tell anyone about this," Father said firmly. The old teacher still felt he was unworthy of the position and was afraid that there might have been some mistake.

Chuanhui was not going to say anything. First of all, the news was not official yet, and anyway, he was far more interested in something else these days: the Steel Giant's mansion, the Blue House.

"Times have certainly changed," Hongfei said to his wife that night. "Used to be someone like me would never dream of great accomplishments. Success was just staying out of harm's way.

There's hope for China yet, Fen. Of course, I could never talk to Chuanhui like this; he'd say I was moralizing again! I'm so lucky to have you, Fen. You always understand me."

"Please forgive me," Fen said contritely. "I've been giving you a hard time these last few days. But I was just thinking of Chuanhui. And Bai Hong."

"Bai Hong?"

"The girl Chuanhui likes. She stopped by today. She's a fine young lady. I'd hate to see her have to live in this room with us and nothing but a curtain to separate us... Forgive me: I am a mother, you know." Fen could say no more. She buried her head in the pillow to muffle her sobs.

Hongfei spoke gently to console his wife: "Everything will work out, you'll see. Chuanhui will have it better than Lu Dawei did, I know he will!"

"Then Saturday night... are we going to visit your brother?" Fen whimpered, finding her own question a bit strange.

"Yes," her husband replied with confidence. "And we'll go there as a proud and decent family. We'll go to see the old place, not to beg for alms. I vowed once that I wouldn't return to that house until I was a hundred times wealthier than Father. Well, maybe I've finally made it..." Fen could feel her husband smile in satisfaction. She could also feel her own face flush red. She was glad it was dark in the room.

On the other side of the curtain, Chuanhui was fast asleep, dreaming. It was a touching sight: they were in the immaculately decorated Blue House, and Grandfather was standing there and embracing them all lovingly!

4

The Blue House lived up to its reputation. Although it was not perhaps as lavish as Wu Sunfu's mansion in the movie *Midnight* , it was everything that Chuanhui had imagined. A Sanyo electric heater in the corner kept the room warm and free from the dirt and odour of burning coal, steaming cups of hot coffee sat on the coffee table, and a new Hitachi stereo set was playing soothing music. "Comfortable" and "tasteful" were the two words that summed up everything in sight. Once his longing to set foot in the Blue House was realized, the desire to possess had come to the fore. Chuanhui's mood fluctuated between contentment at finally finding his "roots" and frustration over what to do next. One thing was sure: he did not want to go back to that ramshackle room with curtains for walls. Even Hongfei seemed softened by the cozy atmosphere; holding his wife in his arms he floated around the room dancing a light-hearted waltz.

Fen looked around her at the beautiful parlour as she clung to her husband. It was hard to believe that such extravagance and luxury had survived the thirty years since Liberation. Except for the modern furniture filling the room, there was hardly any indication that the owner of this mansion had been the victim of countless vicious political campaigns. Fen watched her sister-in-law shuttle back and forth from the kitchen to the living room. It was a Gu family tradition that the mistress of the household personally attended to serving respected guests tea. The custom had been initiated by their "modern" mother. Fen's sister-in-law made delicious lemon tarts, and her husband bragged that she could make over forty kinds of Western desserts. Fen had heard that she had a degree in economics from the Jinling Women's

College, but she had spent the last four decades holed up inside the Blue House making pastries. That seemed... Fen sneaked a glance at her hostess, wishing with all her heart that she could see beyond the grace and charm and into her heart. Wasn't she lonely? How did she kill time when she wasn't making lemon tarts? At the same time the hostess shot a curious look towards Fen. She simply could not understand this sister-in-law of hers. How could she have lived all those years outside the Blue House? Wasn't she jealous? The two women's eyes met, and Fen could instantly perceive a deep suspicion in her hostess's eyes. Did her sister-in-law really think she coveted her precious home? Fen was hurt by the unspoken accusation, but at the same time a peace came over her as she realized that all her anxieties had been unfounded. She could never humiliate her husband and herself by begging these people to help Chuanhui, much less drag the whole family into litigation over the inheritance. That was not like her, and if it had been, she would never have married a man like Hongfei.

"Hey uncle, you can really dance!" Chuanye was standing to one side admiring Hongfei's moves.

"Your uncle does a very orthodox step," Hongji answered his son, "not like you youngsters who twist your hips and flap your arms. His dance is a real performance. Do you remember that White Russian dance teacher, Hongfei? Looks like he knew what he was doing; you still don't miss a step. He came over once a week to give you and Hongzhi lessons, didn't he? Five U. S. dollars a lesson. Five dollars back then was worth something!"

Five U.S. dollars, that was ten yuan Renminbi! What a generous, free-spending man this Steel Giant must have been! My own grandfather! Chuanhui could hardly contain himself.

Chuanye just snorted in disapproval. What was so special about a Russki? He knew one guy whose family used to employ Englishmen as their tutors. And what was five dollars? He heard that people made that in an hour washing dishes in America.

Of course Hongfei remembered the White Russian. They paid him twenty dollars a month. That was a lot in those days... enough to buy several injections of penicillin. And if he had been able to get hold of that sum of money then, he could have saved his daughter; Fen and he would probably be holding a little grandchild by now! Hongfei sighed and suddenly felt very uncomfortable.

"Stop chomping and sucking that sweet, you big oaf," Hongji's daughter snarled at her husband, a sloppy-looking young man dressed in baggy army trousers. The immaculately dressed lady and her husband in army green were an incongruous pair.

"Seems we have to behave like foreigners even when we eat these days," the soldier retorted in disgust. There was something in the exchange that was more caustic than normal husband-and-wife disagreements.

Hongji turned and stared at his son-in-law. "You have a child who's almost at school age, and you two still scrap like a couple of school kids yourselves."

In just a few short minutes the warm and friendly atmosphere of the parlour had turned cold and hostile. But Hongji was an old hand at dealing with the complexities of social functions, and he quickly turned the conversation to something lighter.

"You said your son is about twenty-six or twenty-seven, didn't you, Hongfei? Got a girlfriend? I can help him out there. My son-in-law has a nice little sister; she'll be along in a little while. She's no great beauty, but she's very good-hearted. Quiet and gentle type. Her mother asked me to help find her someone. She works at..." Hongji turned to his daughter as if to ask for the details, but the daughter only waved him away impatiently. "How many times have I told you, father, those things are none of your business. Anyway, just because the family has a little power doesn't mean they have any class..."

The son-in-law naturally jumped in to defend his sister. "Hey, not so fast. If it weren't for my family your sister would never have got permission to go abroad!"

"Don't start fighting," Hongji said as he sat down and crossed his legs, then added with a smile, "What's so bad about it? A Westernized and a local family, that unites money with power. Nothing would be out of our reach!" Realizing that he was appearing too mercenary, Hongji changed the conversation back to the soldier's sister. "This girl is something else, I tell you. Just tonight, in spite of the cold, she went out to see the French conductor Perisson perform at the concert hall. How many girls do you know these days who can appreciate a symphony?"

The words jolted Chuanhui's memory; hadn't he made a date with Bai Hong to see the concert tonight? How could he have forgotten? The last few days he had been like a man possessed; the Blue House had consumed him and driven him, and any other commitment, like those China pinks he had promised Bai Hong, had been easily forgotten. It was only a few days ago that she had said to him with earnest expectation, "I'll be waiting for you!" He could remember her small, shivering hands in his. Damn you, Chuanhui, he cursed himself, how could you have forgotten?

When Hongji first broached the subject of a mate for Chuan-hui, Fen had been tempted to interrupt him and say that he already had a girlfriend, a truly good one who didn't care that he lived in a room with curtains for a partition and who stared at the old photographs of him as though she were memorizing them for eternity. But the more she heard her brother-in-law go on, the more disgusted she had become, especially with all the talk about "money and power". Treating love like some kind of business deal, how despicable! She decided not to mention the name of Bai Hong to them. She was not about to let the name of this pure and beautiful girl be stained by association with such indecency and greed.

"We could never hope to be related to this general. He may have power, but we have no money." Fen was irritated at her brother-in-law, and wanted to keep him in check.

But Hongji misread her intentions. He had never intended to introduce his nephew to anyone and had simply said it as a ploy to liven up the conversation. When he realized that he had stumbled on to something that was a taboo, he tried to make a joke out of it. "Ha, ha! Come on, with the two of you working, I can hardly imagine you're starving! Ha, ha!"

"We let our son decide these matters for himself. If he asks for advice, we give it to him, but nothing more." Hongfei spoke frankly and honestly, as was his habit.

"Right, right," Hongji said agreeably. "Fathers in the forties emphasized freedom and love more than anything, and you certainly lived up to those standards when you gave up the Blue House for the one you loved. Those principles are even more valued now in the eighties."

Chuanhui's heart missed a beat. Father had left the Blue

House for love. Well, fortunately that was all in the past. He slumped back in the sofa to relax a little, but the fierce struggle in his mind afforded little rest: should or should he not go to the concert to find Bai Hong? There was still time. But the demon was tormenting him again; in a few minutes they would begin the memorial ceremony for his grandfather and this ceremony would cement his status in the Gu clan. It was as serious as a baptism in the Christian faith: how could he miss it? He had been living for this moment for days. There would be time enough to take care of Bai Hong; he would pay her back a thousand fold. Soon.

"You're quite a workaholic, sister-in-law, continuing your work after retirement. Are you strong enough to keep it up?" Hongji's wife asked Fen. Her two snow-white, delicate hands had apparently been taken good care of.

"I'm in good enough shape. Just yesterday I assisted in major surgery, and I was on my feet for seven straight hours." Fen was proud of her physical stamina.

"Heavens!" The hostess seemed shocked. "You stood for seven hours?"

The woman had never gone to work a day in her life, and she had probably never even taken a trolley bus, so naturally she was surprised. But for Fen, seven hours on her feet was hardly anything novel. Many was the day she had spent at least that many hours in the operating room, with nothing for lunch except a cold bun wolfed down when there was a moment free. She was a nurse; they all worked like that.

"Why don't you just retire?"

"The hospital won't let me. There's a severe shortage of nurses right now, and there will be until a new crop are trained and in place." For the first time that evening Fen felt at ease and animated by the conversation and could not help feeling a sense of pride in herself. And why not? Her sister-in-law might not have to go to work every day or ride crowded trolley cars or wait for the night staff to come and relieve her from work, but she had no profession and nothing that she could contribute to society! What could be sadder?

"I suppose you get quite a bonus, right?" The sister-in-law could not understand.

"I get the same salary as before."

"It's not worth it, is it?"

Not worth it? Fen had never really thought about it like that.

"If we're good, we can take an examination to raise our professional status."

"You mean after you retire you still have to take examinations? And what about doctors? What kind of pension do they get after retirement?" It was as if she were listening to some strange tale.

Actually, Fen's pay was quite a bit higher than most doctors because of her high technical rank, but she had not taken those tests just for the raise. This pastry-maker would never... Why couldn't they talk about something more interesting? Sons! Mothers always love to talk about their sons!

"And where does your son work?" Fen asked politely.

"He stays at home."

"Ah, preparing for the college entrance exam?"

"What for? College graduates don't make much more than he did at his old factory job!"

"Well ... what does he do all day?"

"I won't let him go back to that factory; he might get hurt.

He stays in his room, playing the piano, reading a little English."

"And the future...?"

"We're looking for a suitable girl to take care of him. He's thirty-two now: he really needs a wife."

Fen was appalled. She looked over at the young man sitting beside her son and felt sorry for him. Her nephew was a good-looking and bright fellow; What a waste!

"Mum, you've burned the pastries!" the young man suddenly bellowed in displeasure. "And what's this, apple pie again?"

"That was all that they had at the fruit store I go to," the woman explained, but her son was in no forgiving mood and angrily threw the pie back on the tray. "Disgusting. Only a peasant could eat these things."

Fen nearly choked on the pastry in her mouth. How could her nephew be so rude!

A maid came in presently and announced that everything was ready for the memorial service. Everyone filed into a small parlour. In the centre of the room on a small table, a large photograph of Gu Fuxiang stared sternly at his descendents through the swirls of incense smoke.

Hongfei stepped before the picture of his father and bowed deeply. The photo before him showed a middle-aged man in a tie and was probably a blow-up of one taken before the "cultural revolution". There was a fierce look of pride and self-importance in those eyes; the man could never have imagined at the time the photo was taken that a few short years later it would be difficult to find any photograph of him! There was an exterior of toughness in the man's countenance, but it was only exterior, for when his riches and the Blue House vanished, he vanished likewise. He had been a capable and hard-working man, but not wise. He had become a slave to fame and wealth, both very unreliable masters. A person has to learn to be a master of his own destiny. As long as a person stands tall, nothing can destroy him.

The two daughters-in-law stepped up to the altar side by side and bowed. Fen could detect the sweet smell of perfume on her sister-in-law. Although the woman was at least ten years her junior, it seemed to Fen that she was standing beside something very old, like an antique that had just been pulled out of some old chest. It was the odor of mothballs. This woman in the traditional cotton coat and long painted fingernails reminded Fen of people living ages ago...

"Life is so empty. Death pays all debts!" uttered the woman, fighting back tears. Those words were not for the deceased, Fen decided; the woman was thinking of her own life. Of course, she was miserable. Locked up in this gilded cage day after day with nothing to look forward to, nothing to do. Of course life was empty. Never mind sister-in-law—she was in her fifties anyway—they should never, thought Fen, never, allow a strong young man like Chuanye to stay imprisoned in this place all his life. The Blue House was nothing more than a gorgeous tomb. Neither time nor air nor light entered its thick walls. Those who lived in it died of suffocation. It was the first time Fen had realized the fact so strongly.

"We're reunited now except for our older brother who ran off to the U.S. We haven't had a really intimate talk for years, all of us being so busy with ... our engineering work and business and all. We're all white-haired old men now, you know!" Hongji went on with feeling when the memorial ceremony was over. "You and Big Brother haven't written for quite a while, have you? He really misses you all, says he's been concerned about you ever since he left China. Communication with anyone overseas was taboo for quite a while, so I didn't tell you about him. Anyway, I got a letter from him last week, and he says he's coming next month. The Municipal Business and Commerce Committee has decided to officially vindicate Father of all wrongdoing, and they're going to have an official ceremony as soon as our brother returns. I've heard that XXX of the Consultative Conference will be there." Hongji's tone implied a more than casual relationship with the renowned deputy. He was fond of name dropping.

"Oh, I doubt he can come," Hongfei replied frankly. "I heard the other day he's going to Japan at the end of the month...."

Hongji was stunned by how well-informed his brother seemed to be. "How do youknow?" he asked, now genuinely curious. Hongfei just laughed and said, "Everbody knows what celebrities are up to." Actually, Hongfei had been down to the conference office a few days before to take care of some formalities to do with his recent admittance as a deputy and had met the man they were talking about. But he was not one to show off.

"Big Brother's letter says," Hongji continued with his usual fervour and confidence, "that he misses you and asks if you still live at your old address. He wants to write you...." That was true enough. Actually the letter had made Hongji very unhappy. He had long since forgotten he had such a brother as Hongfei, but it was obvious that Big Brother would still stand by him. At heart, at least, they remained inseparable. The two were, after all, brothers! And that did not bode well for Hongji's plans. Big

Brother was an overseas Chinese, and that was worth a lot these days. Gu Hongji had a lot of favours to ask him, and at this point he could not afford to offend this favoured big brother. Besides, there was another thing... "Big Brother would like to visit Father's tomb during his trip here, and of course it's up to the two of us to arrange the trip and take care of him. Let's go upstairs and leave this floor to the third generation Gu boys, eh?"

So things turned out better than Chuanhui had imagined, and he could not help thinking of his future here: every day after work he would pull out his own key to the front door and enter the Blue House, and after greeting his father and uncle in the parlour downstairs, he would go to his own set of rooms. The house had three floors; it was hard to say which floor his rooms would be on. And Bai Hong? Ah yes, she would be reclining on their large sofa awaiting his return from work. If they were in the mood, they could invite some friends over to dance or just chat and have some coffee and dessert. This paradise lacked nothing.

"Are you going to ask Uncle to help you get to America? I know I am," Chuanhui's cousin asked him.

He had never thought about going to America. His only dream until now had been getting into the Blue House and escaping the world's cares.

"Go to study, I suppose?" Chuanhui asked innocently.

"Study, nothing! I'm going to wash dishes!"

"You're kidding."

"Really," the cousin answered in all sincerity. "You can make four dollars an hour. That's 32 dollars for an eight-hour day. I can certainly live off that kind of money."

"What's so bad about your life here?" Chuanhui asked, looking puzzled. "You've got it good here. Few people in America have anything nearly as nice as the Blue House perhaps."

Chuanye started pacing impatiently back and forth in front of his cousin. "How is it that everyone starts moralizing the moment they mention this place? The Blue House, the Blue House, I tell you I'm suffocating in this place. I dream of doing great things, and those dreams can only come true in America."

Chuanhui, completely bewildered, stared at his cousin. How could this cousin who couldn't speak a word of English actually expect to go to America and be successful? What kind of life had he led to entertain such fantasies?

"Really," Chuanye continued with growing excitement, "all I need to do is get a big win at the horse races, and the rest will be easy. Or maybe I'll be an explorer and discover a gold mine or something... Anyway I've got to go and try my luck, just like Grandpa did when he came to Shanghai with nothing but a bedroll under his arm."

The wilder Chuanye's talk became, the more Chuanhui wanted to laugh. "You make it sound like everyone in America is a millionaire."

"That's not true, but like the old saying goes, 'The stairway to heaven is narrow and steep, but there are always a few who manage to chimb it.'"

Chuanhui was fast losing interest in the conversation, and he began thinking about Bai Hong. But it was already 9:30, and even if he left right now, the concert would be over.

Chuanye found it strange that his discourse on life in America had not captivated his cousin's attention, and he was bothered by the fact that Chuanhui was not giving him the kind of fawning respect he had given him when they first met. He was getting tired of him anyway. Then the thought of playing a little trick on his cousin popped into his mind.

Chuanye pointed cryptically upstairs then said mysteriously, "Above us the pot is beginning to boil, and the two parties shall soon begin to bargain."

Chuanhui was shocked. Bargain? What did he mean? It was a distasteful term, like people haggling over a pound of potatoes.

"You mean you don't know? That's why Dad asked you all to come here. Our elder uncle will be arriving next month and will want to see Grandfather's tomb, but Dad doesn't know where it is. Now how's he going to explain that? You know how overseas Chinese are: they're really into that 'filial piety' stuff..."

Hongji had been racking his brains for months over the problems involved with his brother's return to China. It had all looked so good at first; for a man with his wealth, receiving an overseas relative was like adding flowers to the brocade, making perfection better. But one needs to have insight at all times. If he had known years before that things were going to turn out as they did, he would never have abandoned his father. Not long after the "cultural revolution" he had renewed his correspondence with his overseas brother but had always talked about their father's death in vague terms. As a matter of fact, even if his father had survived the early political movements with all their struggle sessions and searches, he wouldn't have survived the later forced labour and confinement forced on capitalists. Not at the age of 78. It was unfair to pin all the blame on him, Hongji thought. When his brother arrived from the States, he would be asking more detailed questions about the death, but that did not worry Hongji; he was a smooth and fast talker.

Even the problem of the grave site could be taken care of. For about 3,000 yuan he could have a memorial tomb built for his father, and his brother would never dig up the coffin to see if the remains were really in there. The problem was that his Big Brother would be insisting on seeing Hongfei—his real brother— and Big Brother's relationship with Hongfei would be stronger than with him. Would Hongfei bring up how he had abandoned his father during the "cultural revolution"? Big Brother had gone to America when he was only twenty years old and would never understand how much Hongji had suffered during the movement. When the "cultural revolution" broke out in 1966, Hongji had been a little over forty, just the age one begins to enjoy one's life and work, but instead the movement broke like a storm on him! He had two daughters and a son; that alone was reason enough to denounce his father. He had to admit he and Big Brother had little in common. Big Brother was fifteen years older than him, and all he could remember about him was that he seemed an elegant young man of the world. He never saw him again after he left for the U.S. Big Brother's letters from America would have a "My regards to Youngest Brother" tacked on the end, but that was as far as their relationship went. Nevertheless, Hongji would set himself up as the official representative of the Gu clan on his brother's return, and he would seize the chance to ask his brother to be his financial sponsor, so he could visit America. It was something he had to see. But what would Big Brother think if he found out how things had really been between him and his father? Hongfei could ruin everything. He was struggling with the problem when his son first brought him the news about his nephew, Chuanhui. At first he had accused his son of looking for trouble; family lawsuits were common nowadays, and a person could lose a fortune. But forty years of living with his father had not been wasted on Hongji; he had learned the art of currying favour for personal gain, and he saw in this recent development the opportunity he needed. He would get chummy with this muddle-headed half-brother of his. Eventually Hongfei would relent and promise never to mention the unsavoury goings on in the past to Big Brother. They were a soft-hearted family. His sister-in-law had never asked for any favour in return for helping him get his daughter a medical exemption from going to the countryside, had she? If that older Chinese American brother stirred feelings of fear in him, then this impoverished brother who taught at school evoked nothing but contempt. His childhood impression of the middle brother was that of a cold and aloof young gentleman, but with a certain flashy style and a love for stylish clothes. Little Hongji had silently idolized him. Hongji could vividly remember the scene when Brother Hongfei had broken off with Father: Hongfei had spoken softly but with a clear and penetrating voice, while his father had sprayed him with spittle as he screamed and cursed in his face. Hongji was in that romantic mood of youth at the time, so he of course always sided silently with his brother. Besides, deep in his heart he had no respect for this father, who was really nothing more than a poor tinsmith. But his attitude towards Brother Hongfei changed over the years. When they received the wedding picture of Big Brother and an Irish girl, he began to realize that there was a chance that he alone would become heir to the Blue House and the steel plant. He was twenty-four when China was liberated, and he was every bit the cultured young gentleman he was expected to be. With his father's vast capital and his own ample ability, he was going to make a real name for himself in the business world. Travelling down a street once in a pedicab he happened to spot Brother Hongfei in a faded blue jacket carrying a vegetable basket in one hand. A man doing a woman's work! He quickly turned his head from the sight of his down-and-out brother. How could he have known then that a few years later the political winds would blow in a different direction. During the "cultural revolution" he would have gladly traded places with his brother; living on ten yuan a month he had nearly been forced to go begging! He had thought many times then of going to his brother and asking for help; he heard that his sister-in-law made over 100 yuan a month, and that was worth a million yuan to a capitalist in those days. But then his daughter married into a powerful family, and his life changed. The plant leaders treated him with a new-found respect, and he was given a salary of 150 yuan a month. Although that was only half his original salary, it was still considered big money then, and the raise had to be approved by the Municipal Revolutionary Committee. All that got him out of a tight spot, and he quickly discarded his plans to visit his brother. Times and needs were always changing. With his salary raised to over 400 a month, the Blue House put back in his name, and the frozen assets of the plant returned to him, he normally had no time or need to think of his unambitious and simple-minded brother; but now just this once he would have to get together with him and string him along a bit. Fortunately Brother Hongfei did not know how big a fortune his father had had—unless the old man had disclosed it just before he died—so all he had to do was give fim five or ten percent of the inheritance (better yet put it in the name of his nephew, Chuanhui, so his brother would not get too cocky), and he'd stay happy and quiet. And if by chance his brother's family got too greedy, he could take care of that... At any rate his lawyer friend had assured him that the Blue House would always remain in his hands because of what had happened in the past: not one square inch of floor space would ever have to be ceded!

Bargain! Chuanhui's mind throbbed with that word, and he was feeling as if this whole idea of "coming home" was just a bad joke.

"That kind of thing goes on all the time," his cousin commented, noting that Chuanhui was troubled. "People are all like that." His cousin was enjoying Chuanhui's obvious and growing dejection.

Forget it, Chuanhui convinced himself. As long as we can return to the clan, nothing else really matters!

Chuanye did not notice the change in Chuanhui's mood and continued his barrage. "That girl Dad just told you about is a homely thing that couldn't find a husband. Her father's an army big shot, and she really reckons herself. She spouts on all day long about spiritual things and she writes poetry! It's enough to make a guy puke!"

The doorbell rang, and the son-in-law got up to see who was there. Chuanye slumped deeply in the couch, and his shiny grey shoes almost touched the coffee table before him. "That must be her now. She comes around pretty often to borrow some of Dad's English magazines. The girl is really weird. She talks as if she's making a political report."

They could hear the girl's brother mildly reprimand her as she walked in. "It's too cold to be out for just a concert. Why couldn't you have watched the relay on TV?"

"A live concert is a whole lot different than a TV one, and anyway, I promised to meet a friend there," she said, unable to hide her disappointment. It was a clear, sweet voice, like that of a TV announcer. It was a gentle, soothing voice, and familiar ... Bai Hong!

Although completely taken by surprise, Chuanhui was thrilled to see her. But a moment later the joy turned to a feeling of guilt, and before he could think of a way to explain, she had walked into the living room. She was shocked to see Chuanhui, then a look of understanding came across her face. "You must have come here to borrow some books from Uncle Gu, right?"

"This is my cousin. Hey, you two know each other?" Chuanye jumped up from the sofa and looked at her then looked at him.

"Say, looks like you broke another date." Bai Hong's eyes sparkled with their usual joy and fun. There was not a hint of annoyance in her voice.

"I'm terribly sorry... I forgot..." He had meant to think of an excuse, but her gentle smile made it hard to lie.

"You show up here like Chen Jingrun, the absentminded professor," Bai Hong said, still happy.

"He's no Chen Jingrun. He came here to see his grandaddy's estate," Chuanye announced with relish, ignoring his cousin's eyes, that were pleading him to stop. He told everything, from how they first met at the Jinjiang Club to what had happened that same night. He watched with glee as Bai Hong's eyes grew sadder, and his cousin's eyes dropped lower and lower in disgrace and disgust with himself. It was like a child teasing a puppy or a kitten. He had guessed the two's relationship the moment their eyes had met. He had never loved anyone and was extremely jealous of anyone who had, so the cruel little game he was playing gave him a special thrill!

Chuanye's words gave a painfully accurate description of Chuanhui's "search for his roots".

"You mean this is the secret you were going to tell me someday?" Bai Hong asked, disappointed.

Having heard the objective description of his "search for his roots", even Chuanhui could see he'd turned into something despicable. He hung his head in shame.

"You mean this was why you didn't have time to hear my poetry or go to the concert?" Bai Hong's face turned ashen. She had played the fool, and now her anger eclipsed her embarrassment. She did not care who or how many people saw her as she tore into Chuanhui with rapid-fire accusations.

Chuanye realized that he had created an explosive situation and moved quickly to calm things down before they got totally out of hand. "Don't get all shook up over this. Chuanhui was just trying to get ahead; you've got nothing to lose by it! You can't live to be two hurdred, so why bother being stupidly honest."

"It's because I know I won't live to be two hundred that I cherish the things I have!" Bai Hong cried in a trembling yet proud voice, her eyes brimming with tears. Exactly what was that look in her eyes? Heartbreak? Hatred?

Chuanye sneaked off. He had not expected such a violent reaction. Only Chuanhui and Bai Hong were left in the room.

Comforted somehow by her own outburst, Bai Hong now calmly picked up a *Weekend* magazine from the coffee table and began to look through it with studied interest.

Chuanhui knew there was no use in trying to apologize or explain to her. She had too much self-dignity for that.

"I did it all for one reason... Because... I love you, and wanted to make you happy."

"You're no different than your cousin!" she answered coldly. "And you obviously don't understand me at all!"

That was for sure.

Chuanhui retreated to a dark corner of the room. You have lost her, something deep within him said, for ever.

In the room above, the "negotiations" started in earnest.

"Recently, several responsible people from the Department of the United Front have taken a deep interest in our father's case," Hongji commenced deliberately, blowing a ring of cigarette smoke. Hongfei was too honest a man to understand why this brother who had known and cared nothing about his father's death was suddenly taking such an interest, and he was afraid to find out. All that really mattered was that his father had died in peace and comforted by loved ones.

Just then Hongji brought up the crucial point, "Father is buried in Suzhou... at the foot of Lingyan or Tianping Mountain? We really need to fix a proper grave site; it would be a shame to leave him with such a shabby memorial..."

Shabby? What was he talking about? Hongfei was upset. Sure, Father's tomb was simple, a mound of yellow dirt with a concrete covering on top, but that was all they could do in those years. Moreover, Fen had gone to considerable trouble just to arrange getting that little bit of concrete. Things were not that easy then. Hongji misread his half-brother and thought he was ready to offer his side of the bargain.

"Father is dead now, and we brothers hold no grudge against each other. I accept your son Chuanhui as my nephew and am prepared to deposit 10,000 yuan in an account under his name... Of course, that's Father's money. You may not realize it, Hongfei, but our family was not nearly as rich as it was famous. Mother could never handle money, I'm afraid, and by the time of the 'cultural revolution', Father was nearly broke and..." Hongji spoke slowly as if to give his opponent time to think over the deal and make a reasonable offer.

Hongfei's cheeks turned a fiery red, and the muscles in his neck began to twitch uncontrollably. He arched his back then stood up to face his brother. He looked like a guard about to deal with an assault from the other side. "Father is buried at Lingyan Mountain, and there is no headstone, and maybe it's not the prettiest tomb there. But you know how tough things were at the time. If all you wanted was to know the location of the cemetery lot, you could have just called me at work and we would have arranged a time to take you there. There was no need for you to ask us over as guests or arrange this memorial service. You could have saved yourself a lot of trouble." He cut his brother off in mid-sentence because he did not want to hear any more of this disgusting deal. His little brother had certainly earned the inheritance to the Blue House; he was just like his father when it came to thinking that anything could be had if the price was right. Hongfei had suspected it all along, but he was still shocked when he heard it for himself.

Fen followed her husband down the stairs feeling ashamed of herself. He had been right all along. She slipped her arm around his waist as a sign that she was sorry. He understood.

It was an awkward situation for everyone when they all got downstairs. Hongji and his wife could handle almost any social situation, but they hardly knew where to turn now. Moreover,

Hongji was a nervous wreck wondering if this half-brother would really take him to the grave site as he had promised. When Big Brother arrived from America, he would really be put on the spot.

"I ... I'll take care of that thing for Chuanhui," Hongji said awkwardly.

"No, our Chuanhui doesn't need it. He's got his own work, his own salary," Fen answered back curtly. True, Fen thought, chances like this are few and far between, but she preferred that her son miss out now rather than turn into someone like his uncle who cared more for a few grubby dollars than for people.

"How much money is he making?" Hongji asked, unable to stifle a laugh. "He'll half starve living off that salary!"

"Other people have done it, and so can he," Fen said calmly.

"Fen, Chuanhui will have to decide that for himself. He's an adult," Hongfei said gently to his wife. Yes, he had to respect his son's independence. He would tell him everything and let him decide for himself.

Hongji and his wife looked on silently. So it was all up to their nephew, Chuanhui!

"The world belongs to the young," Hongji managed to say as he opened the door to the living room. He had regained his knack for keeping a conversation alive. "We've done all we could for them, haven't we, brother?"

A young lady warmly greeted them as they walked into the room, and Fen was delighted to see that it was Bai Hong. Across the parlour Chuanhui stood alone outside the French windows. What was the matter with the two of them? Were they just shy, or had they quarrelled?

"You know each other? This is the girl I was just talking about," Hongji said, happily turning the conversation in yet another direction.

"She's beautiful, not what I imagined a general's daughter to look like!" Fen's praise was sincere, but she was not about to let her in-laws know of Bai Hong's relationship with Chuanhui. She loved the girl too much for that! She would never want to see her hurt.

Hongfei strode over to the window. The cold and lonely light of the half moon drenched the garden and walkway outside, giving the stark trees and shrubs an eerie colour. It was on this very path that he had walked out of the Blue House and into the wide world, carrying with him a grief for the past and an excitement for the future.

"What person doesn't plan for their children's future? It was just that back then they planned too much, they tied our hands and feet together, and we couldn't stand it!" Hongfei said. "Father planned everything for me! School, work, even my wife, and I couldn't stand it..."

After returning to the Blue House and experiencing the "brotherly kindness" of his brother, he felt that he needed to tell these young people about his past. They needed to hear, these young folks with no experience in the world, especially this son of his who dreamed of returning to the Blue House to live. He called Chuanhui in.

"...In 1936, the King of England, Edward VIII, gave up his throne to marry the woman he loved. That left a deep impression on me. When I left the Blue House, I found true love myself, but I also found far more than that. Life is full of disappointments, frustrations, and heartaches, but it is these very things that give life depth and meaning. It's only people reaching my age who could understand that. I have no doubt life's trials will give you a chance to discover who you really are too..."

A wave of warmth and emotion flooded the room as Hongfei finished speaking, and even the indifferent and insensitive Chuanye stopped cracking melon seeds and bowed his head, lost in thought. Following Fen's eyes, Bai Hong looked out the window at the quiet path outside, awash with soft moonlight. She was thinking of the China pinks that grew in that simple glass bowl, and a poem began to take shape in her mind.

Hongji could not help but feel a little moved and envious at his brother's words. If he were to tell his children about his experience in life, what could he say? How to play cards, or do tango steps? Everything he had ever done seemed so vain and empty now, and hardly worth remembering. Other than inheriting this opulent Blue House and the family fortune, he had nothing to brag about. He had never even experienced falling in love; a matchmaker had shown his father a photograph of a girl, and his father had nodded his approval. He met her for supper once a week for the appropriate period of time, and then they were married, just like getting on a bus and getting off at a stop. Nothing worth remembering or to be considered about. He had to admit his life had never been full or meaningful.

"You've got the young folks spellbound!" Hongji said, hoping to break the spell. He had to say something now, or he would certainly lose face before the young people. "In a few years it will be your turn to talk about the old days here at the Blue House! This house was built to last—just look at those sturdy window frames. This place will be around to house the Gu clan for another four or five generations at the very least!"

"Young people... don't go in for a place this extravagant. It would cost them too much," Fen said solemnly.

"Property tax is a burden, that's for sure. Four hundred yuan a quarter," Hongji nodded in agreement.

"Four hundred yuan? No, that's not much. I meant something else."

With the memorial service over, the bargaining done, and the "return home" complete, even Hongji could not stifle a yawn—it had been hard work making the family reunion at least appear warmhearted—and he was tired.

Just as everyone was about to say their good-byes, the television that no one had been watching began to announce the last programme of the night, the evening news.

"...And now for the top stories of the day..." As the newscaster began to speak, everyone in the room became silent.

"The names of the newly appointed members of the Municipal People's Congress and the Municipal Political Consultative Conference have just been released. The names are as follows..."

Hongji could not have been more surprised when he heard the name of his brother, Hongfei, listed as a deputy of the Consultative Conference. In his mind his brother was nothing, a nobody. Someone with the same name? No, that was not possible. One look at his brother and sister-in-law told him that it was true. "Well, we Gus are really making it big, really making it big," Hongji said in genuine satisfaction. "One brother a Consultative Conference deputy and another a committee member of the Industry and Business Association..."

"You are what you are because you were born that way; I am what I am because I chose..." That quote of Beethoven ran through Hongfei's mind, but he dared not say it. He never tried to make others lose face.

After the evening news it was time to go. As they passed by those imposing large steel doors, Fen suddenly thought of something. "Chuanhui, you and Bai Hong go on ahead by yourselves."

"No," Bai Hong said quickly. "I can get home by myself. Thank you so much, auntie and uncle. Not long ago I thought that the only thing that was truly beautiful and lasting was poetry. But your life together is living poetry. I'll never forget you." Bai Hong reluctantly said good-bye to the two of them and then left. Fen wanted to press Chuanhui to catch up with her, but her husband stopped her. He had noticed that something was amiss between the two.

After Bai Hong was out of sight, Fen turned to Chuanhui and asked, "Were you two fighting?"

Chuanhui smiled painfully. He did not feel like describing the whole ugly thing to them. "We weren't fighting," he explained simply. "It's just that I don't deserve her."

"Because you don't have an apartment?" Fen asked incredulously.

"No, no. It's me. I don't deserve her." Chuanhui sighed deeply. A woman, a beautiful, artistic woman, had loved him, and he had lost her. And all because of the Blue House.

"You don't know how to take care of the things you love," his mother had often scolded him when he was little, but the words stung more now as he repeated them to himself.

Fen could see that her son was hurting deeply, but what could she do? Perhaps every young person had to go through this sort of thing and mature because of it. From what she could see, it was her son who was at fault here. Bai Hong was such a sweet girl, and she still owed her that bouquet of China pinks!

She quickened her husband's pace so that their son could be alone to think things out. This would be the worst time to bother him.

"You've seen the Blue House now," her husband said. "Do you like it?"

"It's luxurious!"

"You mean you think it's beautiful?" her husband asked, probing her feelings.

"Luxurious is luxurious, not beautiful!"

"Don't play games with me, Fen. Do you regret marrying me?"

Fen answered his question by warmly squeezing his hand. She thought back to just a few minutes before when the newscaster was announcing the names. Her sister-in-law had turned to her to see her reaction when Hongfei's name was called, no doubt expecting her to be jumping with joy. But Fen had remained quiet and still. A demonstration of joy wouldn't show her love for her husband.

Fen turned around and looked at the Blue House, and an old saying came to mind: whatever you do in life, don't look back. But there were times in life when it was good to look back for just a moment. The blue tiles glowed a deep blue in the moonlight. How would she just have remembered that magnificent wall and forgotten all that was within? Tonight she had discovered that everything in there had grown so old, so ancient. The Blue House was old and useless and would some day collapse. How could she ever allow her son to live there?

The bitter night wind cut to the marrow. Chuanhui pulled up

the collar of his heavy coat, but the chill continued to penetrate.

"Before the teardrop can be wiped away, Oh heart,
You leap again at the thought of sweet reunion...".

The lines to that poem crept up in his heart, and he heaved a troubled sigh.

Hongfei mistook his son's feelings, as fathers often do, and asked, "What's the matter? Disappointed? Chuanhui, do you know why they asked us to the Blue House? I've always said never ask for charity, because what you get will never really be yours. There will always be strings attached!"

"Please don't start, dad," Chuanhui pleaded.

"No, you're so young, there are some things I have to tell you." Father's resonant voice cut through the cold silence of the night. "The growth rings of a tree are determined by the environment in which the tree lives. Different environments create different trees. If your father had stayed in the Blue House, he would not have turned out to be the same man you know today. And you would not have turned out to be the same person you are today."

"And your mother would not have turned out to be the same person she is today," Fen felt compelled to add.

"Your uncle wanted to put 10,000 yuan in an account for you, but for some reason linked that with information about your grandfather's grave site. We'll always despise ourselves if we sell our principles. I told your uncle where Grandfather's grave was, but whether or not you accept the 10,000 yuan or not is up to you. You're a 27-year-old man. The account would be in your name alone, and your mother and I would never force our ideas..."

Ten thousand yuan! He could fit up a decent home with 5,000, and the other 5,000 could be stashed in the bank to earn interest. No more cares about money. This was the magic word to open up that cave of treasures he dreamed of. But why was he not happy? Could he really sink so low as to sell out now and hurt his parents? Who could he enjoy this vast sum of money with? Certainly not his parents, and Bai Hong—well, he would probably never see her again. Xiao Zhu, his cousin, and that gang? And where would he go to just shoot the breeze with his friends? The ritzy Dingxiang Gardens or Longbo Hotel? Never!

He stumbled ahead to catch up with his parents.

"I've always felt that young people should learn to keep their desires within the limits of reality," Chuanhui's father was saying. "Life is full of temptations; without a little self-control you're doomed."

Father was so right. He had pawned his own happiness in his search for a little economic security!

5

Chuanhui joined the stream of people pouring out of the factory gate at quitting time.

Several girls giggled and said hello to Chuanhui. The news of him being the grandson of the founder of the Huachang Steel Plant had spread throughout the factory as quickly as the news about Xiao Zhu finding his overseas father had. People would point at him and say, "Hey, there he is. That guy has all the luck." Some did not quite understand and would ask, "Why bother coming to work? You could live off the old man's money!" Girls were always looking for an excuse to stop and banter with him. He was happy, wasn't he? His wishes had all come true. His uncle opened an account for him; 10,000 yuan! But he had not touched the account yet. His other uncle was coming from America the following month and would bring him a gift. He would be able to get everything he wanted now, including his own room. With all the things that people craved for these days—a colour television, refrigerator, stereo—within his reach, he should be content at last, right? How he'd deluded himself!

While waiting for the bus to go home he browsed through the magazines on the newsstand. Finding this week's *Hundred Flowers* poetry weekly, he glanced down the list of authors in the table of contents as was his habit. Sure enough, there was Bai Hong's name. Her latest work was not her own poem but a translation of the lyrics to *Raindrops*. Ah yes, he thought to himself as he read the poem:

Raindrops keep fallin' on my head,
But that doesn't mean my eyes will soon be turning red,
Crying's not for me,
'Cause I'm never gonna stop the rain by complainin'.
Because I'm free, nothin's worryin' me.

He heard someone hurrying up the street and turned around to see who it was. Bai Hong. She was wearing a blue down coat and a durable pair of low-heeled shoes. Practical but attractive clothes, just like college girls wore. As she brushed by him, she nodded in recognition and kept on going. Then, a few steps past him, she turned around. Together they walked down the street.

"You got another piece published. I'm happy for you," Chuanhui said cordially. "You're a determined young lady. I mentioned the poem casually to you, and you found the poem and translated it."

"That's because I love poetry, and because I've done my share of crying." Then realizing he might have misunderstood, she added quickly, "A couple of years ago I had some real heartache. What happened?" she asked, pointing to the bandage around Chuanhui's hand.

"Our research group was doing some new experiments, and I cut myself on the lathe. I wasn't too familiar with that machine."

"You joined the research group?"

"Helping with new research is a good way to keep on top of things in your field."

"I've got to go. Listen, I hope you won't tell anyone about..."

"Don't worry, I'll never tell anyone about...us..."

"No, that's not what I meant." Bai Hong blushed. "I mean I hope you won't tell anyone about my family."

An old peasant lady was walking down the street towards them selling bouquets of flowers, fresh and delicate China pinks.

"Wait here a second." Chuanhui ran up to the old woman, bought a bunch of the flowers and handed them to Bai Hong. "Please accept these for my mother's sake. She always felt bad that she never gave you any of hers."

"Thank you," Bai Hong said, taking the flowers. "Goodbye."

Chuanhui wanted to call her back and ask her if she would ever sit beside him at the movies again, but he stopped himself. That would be like a child who had got in trouble asking his mother and father, "Do you still love me?" How childish!

He had lost Bai Hong. Even if he married a princess and was given the Blue House for his own, he would forever curse his own stupidity for losing her. Could he win her back? That was hard to say, but he still hoped...

The man who walked slowly and silently down the street was not the same man we met at the beginning of this story. He was no longer a carefree young fellow. He had grown up. And across that forehead that had always been so shiny there were now some wrinkles.

Translated by Jeff Book

The Poor Street

1

THE most annoying thing in the world must be having to wear clothes you dislike and having to put yourself in an environment you detest... Just because it was Monday, Wen Xixiu had had to steel herself to take the wire brush and straighten out her curls, whereas in fact she had only just had her hair tidied by the hairdresser that Saturday. That new style with the ends flicking up at the side of her face was really suited to her vivacious and easygoing nature. Also, that ivory-coloured woollen skirt was just the thing for this early autumn weather! With a bright red blouse to go with the skirt and the addition of a pair of high-heeled white shoes, which was what she had worn the day before, a Sunday, she looked both tasteful and elegant, so that she had laughed with pleasure as she looked at herself in the mirror. But at this hour, she was regretfully attired in a pair of trousers from the "cultural revolution" that were so baggy around the hips you could have got an old hen in there at the same time—with their standard six-inch legs, she knew how sloppy and common she looked, but what choice did she have? She resented being a teacher—in fact she still had to put up with lectures from her mother every day: don't run after buses, go slowly; don't get over-friendly with your colleagues, otherwise you'll be in a mess if there's ever another campaign; and you don't want to go provoking those hooliganish schoolboys; you don't know if they may have a sharp knife hidden on them... To listen to all these admonitions every day, you wouldn't think Wen Xixiu was an English teacher in charge of three classes about to graduate from lower middle school and a form mistress as well, but a schoolgirl herself off to school with her schoolbag tucked under her arm! She wouldn't have minded if it was just being a teacher; there were lots of women teachers in the middle school across from their home who wore highish heels and had curly hair, but the fact that Wen Xixiu stood out somewhat at the school where she worked was not so surprising since it was located on a poor street!

The Shanghai Pure Light Middle School, what a grand name! "Pure Light" indeed; it was only called that because the name of the street on which it stood was "Pure Light Street"! No use searching for it on the map of the area, because it isn't there. Too small and narrow, it would never dare show its face on the grand Shanghai map! In fact the municipal housing department should really go and take a look, as the houses there should have been razed by the bulldozers long ago. On the day Wen Xixiu reported for work it was almost unbelievable the way the whole street looked her up and down as if she was a foreigner, the girls in particular, who unashamedly scrutinized her hairstyle, skirt, even down to the high-heeled sandals she had got from the market on Wuyuan Street. And when she eventually found the Pure Light Middle School her heart sank even more. For underneath the school name plaque there proudly stood an uncovered chamber pot drying in the sun, which looked like the personal property of the owner of the little house that snuggled next to the school. So you see what kind of a workplace Wen Xixiu's was! Comparing teaching to gardening, her flower garden didn't even measure up to a tiny courtyard, and to put it even more plainly...it was a wasteland, a real wasteland.

"You've only just started work, so watch out a bit. Don't get yourself involved in disputes between the other teachers, and mind your own business as much as possible with those who don't work with you, but listen to the teacher who does, and if he says to go on home visits, then you'd better do a few. It's better to create a good impression when you've only just come..." Her mother never lost an opportunity to give her a few pieces of advice just as she was going out the door to work.

Well, it was easy enough for her mother to say "do a few home visits", but if she was to come to this poor street herself it wouldn't make any difference that she was a retired teacher; with her permed, dyed hair and gold-rimmed spectacles, she would no doubt feel the power of those eyes looking her up and down. This was the reason why so far Wen Xixiu had put off visiting her pupils' homes time and time again so that it had now become a psychological burden. Even wearing those baggy trousers with standard-measurement legs was no use. Firstly because she was a newcomer, secondly because she was young, and thirdly because she came from the classy district were reasons enough to cause her to be the celebrity of Pure Light Street!

The school was a good hour's bus ride from where she lived, but this hour's journey was like stepping from the First World into the Third World, the streets getting distinctly narrower, the buildings on each side less tall and the clothes poles stretching from each window closer together: socks, sheets, even brassieres and underpants brazenly swung in the breeze like multi-coloured flags on a steamship. When she stepped off the bus she could feel the "pollution" of the streets both with her eyes and in her throat, as she carefully skirted the piles of old iron that lay dozing by the warehouse year in year out, walked for ten minutes before turning right, and there was the street sign of Pure Light Street. How little it saw daylight, this street sign, because it was always decorated with shoes and mops etc. put there to dry, and Pure Light Middle School was that grey four-storey building which appeared to be craning its neck above the others.

Before coming to work here Wen Xixiu would never have believed that a town such as Shanghai that claimed to be one of the great metropolises of the Far East could have such a corner forgotten by the bustle!

The tiny, narrow streets full of schoolchildren going to school were lively and bustling with activity. The children looked her over with interest, talking in whispers about her, and in the distance she would hear them saying her nickname— "Coquette"— what could she do? She was born with a meek-looking face; it really was a mistake coming to work here. The best thing to do would be to give it up, and ever since the first day she had been racking her brains to find an opportunity for a transfer. At the moment all she could do, to use the popular street-talk of the schoolchildren around her, was to lump it!

"Morning, Xiao Wen."

That was Zhang Xianglin who worked with her going past with his bicycle. Next he would surely ask her if she'd done any home visits on Saturday. This Zhang Xianglin looked like he was completely ignorant of the Western custom of "ladies first",

and was determined to make Wen Xixiu toe the line. Sure e-
nough...

"Have you been to Chen Genmei's? She hasn't come to school
for three days now. You must find a spare moment to go today,
even if she's already back at school...."

In fact, if the pupils didn't come to school for three days,
they'd be back by the end of the month anyway! Did one have to
plead with them to come to school? But how could she say that?
After all, she was a form mistress!

A form mistress! Her mother had been a form mistress, and
when Spring Festival came round every available place to sit in
their house was filled with visitors, so that Wen Xixiu ran her
legs off making tea for her mother's pupils. It was even the same
during the "cultural revolution". On the day of her mother's retirement the pupils came, one set after another: pupils from the
fifties, sixties, seventies, and eighties... However, her mother
had been form mistress in that renowned No. 3 Middle School!
Those who graduated from there either went on to get master's
degrees or to study abroad, or at least became great doctors or
engineers, which could hardly be compared with her Pure Light
Middle School with the uncovered chamber pot drying in the sun
outside! In the past, every day before going to work, her mother used to spend a long time looking at herself critically in the
mirror: Were her shoes polished, did the collar of her blouse go
with the colour of her sweater, was her hair untidy...? She used
to say that standing on the teacher's platform was no different to
being on stage. But Wen Xixiu, who had a good sense of dress,
was obliged to step on to the platform in trousers as baggy as
flour sacks! Just because... she was a form mistress! A form
mistress! A form mistress on a poor street.

On her first day, the school principal had looked her over for a time, and had then taken two elastic bands out of a drawer and handed them to her:

"We don't allow the pupils to have hair trailing over their shoulders. Also... that collarless shirt you're wearing... the colour is indeed quite nice, but here we usually wear shirts with collars, besides which we are planning to put you in charge of the third year, you know. We teach our pupils to lead a simple life, and one should set an example... In other words, the teachers here are all very plain."

The school principal was indeed a perfect example: hair cut short and very neat, reminding Wen Xixiu of a paintbrush; black trousers faded with washing, and a patch on her collar— Wen Xixiu kept wondering how long it would take to wear something before you had to patch it, since clothes nowadays were of man-made fibre. Perhaps this was the poor-street style?

Afterwards, in order to "set a good example" to her pupils, she cut the hair she had worn long for so many years, pestered her mother to dig out a load of old clothes made by her elder sisters according to the requirements of the "cultural revolution" and did her best to fit in with her surroundings.

However, she gradually came to realize that it wasn't that school and street had no money, though they were indeed poor.... Of course, this belongs to a later story.

"Teacher Wen!" A number of boys pushed and shoved each other to stand in front of her. The just breaking voices sounded awkward and funny but betrayed a sincere greeting which moved Wen Xixiu, seeming as fresh as the air at dawn. To take back her words, although the schoolchildren weren't all that refined to look at, most of them were very frank, and they never asked questions about the teacher's study record or level, nor did they try to test her mettle by asking difficult questions like the kids in the city centre.

"Professor Wen!" Because his sister was a university student, Liu Guoliang liked to stand out from the others whenever possible, and show himself to be different. His peculiar form of address provoked laughter among the other students, which he seemed to take exception to: "What's so funny? At university they call all their teachers 'professor', my big sister says. And sometimes when they say it so fast you can only hear the 'prof'!"

"Professor Wen, Chen Genmei wants two more days off. Here's the letter," said Liu Guoliang.

Evidently she would have to go to Chen Genmei's house. It was now five days since she had been to school, and it would be unreasonable of Wen Xixiu not to pay any attention. But she hated going to the pupils' homes; she didn't like the way the residents of the poor street surveyed her critically from head to foot right in front of her face. If her colleague Zhang Xianglin had been willing to do these kinds of jobs instead of her it would've been all right. She hadn't anticipated that Zhang Xianglin, who looked refined enough, wouldn't have the least idea of chivalry.

She had heard that Zhang Xianglin had recently got a transfer from another school, only a term before she herself had arrived. At first this made her wonder: why on earth did someone who looked as intelligent and capable as Zhang Xianglin want to transfer to Pure Light School? Here none went on to higher education, and they didn't care about quality, so it must be that he hadn't known what a rotten school this was! But later all became clear. It must have been that he was anxious to have a change of scene, because he had just got divorced. A handsome divorcee: that was really food for thought. Particularly after her mother's warnings to beware, because "divorced men are no good", she felt him to be all the more mysterious, which was an abstruse state of mind that she couldn't account for.

On the day that they announced the staff allocation for the new term, she heard only that she was to work with a man named Zhang Xianglin. Zhang Xianglin, a name chosen in poor taste, and she was just trying to figure out if the person Zhang Xianglin would be as vulgar as his name when a tall, strong, handsome man with a flash of a dimple that appeared from time to time in the centre of a clean-shaven chin came up and introduced himself in the style of a Japanese, humorously bending his body: "Zhang Xianglin. Please forgive me. Single, live-in, go home at weekends. Need anything, welcome at any time!" When he spoke his eyes laughingly became two curving slits. Wen Xixiu liked him at once; working with a male teacher in the prime of life, her workload would be light indeed. Besides which, at first sight he looked quite interesting, and she hadn't expected that in this dull, grey street, among a crowd of drably dressed teachers, she would find such an attractive exception as this, and the prospect of working with him pleased her greatly. It was quite in line with Freudian sexology, not of course that this secondary reason could be brought frankly to the fore. It remained secret and subconscious.

Who would have thought that the enchanting dimple on his chin was all to no purpose! He didn't understand a woman's feelings one bit. He didn't show any consideration for Wen Xixiu! No wonder he was divorced.

To take this hateful visiting for example, although it was part of her duties as a form teacher, any intelligent person that was the least bit chivalrous would obviously help her out once they knew she was reluctant to go. She had tried to prompt him: "Can't you just get on your bike and go round for me? I'd have to go on my own two feet..." Who'd have thought this wouldn't move him in the slightest? "No, you're the form mistress. Go yourself!"

"Every time I go to and from work each day I have to pass those open doorways, and it really makes me panic!" Wen Xixiu pouted and looked sorry for herself, trying to win his sympathy.

"You'll get used to it when you've done it a few times!" He took no notice at all of her pitiful air, and slamming the school register shut with a bang, walked off and left her. She was so angry she longed to wave her fist at him behind his back. Who did he think he was? Cocky as anything just because he had a fascinating dimple on his chin!

The bell for the morning study period rang, when she met him again in the corridor.

"Oh, your hair..." he said approvingly, raising his eyebrows.

"What's up? Isn't it suitable?" she began to tense up.

"No, it's very beautiful," he said sincerely, surveying her with his head to one side.

From her reflection in the glass window, Wen Xixiu saw that the tips of her electrically permed hair that the steel comb couldn't after all control were sticking up again at the sides. Well, if she wasn't wearing these loose sack-like trousers, she'd surprise him even more. Maybe then she'd be able to get him under her thumb, and then he'd go off like a good boy on his bike and do her home visits!

"Don't go to the study period this morning." See, the flicks in her hair had had an effect. Zhang Xianglin was beginning to be solicitous. "I'll go."

"No..." Wen Xixiu decided to be polite.

"I'm going to give them an extra class. Thirty-six of them didn't pass their test yesterday!"

So it wasn't because of her hair! But his sense of duty moved her.

"The pupils in this run-down district aren't scholarship material anyway, so it's not much good giving them extra classes. In any case this school of ours only trains people for manual labour, and most of them will end up as replacements doing latrine cleaning or flatbread baking. They don't need to study geometry and trigonometry..." She seemed to be reassuring him, but in fact she was really reassuring herself; in the English test in her last lesson only two had passed out of the whole class, and she was ashamed to give the mark book in.

"Then... lucky for you, you weren't born here, born in this poor street. Precisely because of this, you should drink to your luck every day," he said scornfully, showing no mercy.

He was having a dig at her! In what way had she offended him? What she said had been aimed at the pupils. What was it to do with him? He went into the classroom, as usual with his head held high. His made-to-measure clothing did a good job of enhancing his well-proportioned physique, and although he was dressed very ordinarily, it could not be called "drab", and in fact it was rather loud. As a newcomer, she was sorry to have provoked anger. Didn't her mother keep advising her time and time again to do her best to get on with the staff?

2

Pure Light Street really was a poor street.

That bumpy road made of broken stones was not only the thoroughfare connecting with Shanghai's flourishing centre, but also the sole gutter of the residents on both sides of the road: washing-up water and water used to clean the chamber pots all got thrown here, and thus from morning till night the whole year round it was constantly wet and sticky.

The west end of the road led to an asphalted street, from where one could reach the heart of Shanghai—Nanjing Road—in an hour by bus, so that the road was labelled "The Second World" by the local youths, and Pure Light Street was jokingly known as "The Third World". The eastern extremity led to a murky, foul-smelling canal—an offshoot of Suzhou Creek— which after *Death on the Nile* was shown took on a name with a foreign flavour—the River Nile! It was said that the first generation to open up this street climbed the banks at this point, put their tents up and settled in. Soon afterwards, relatives helped relatives, friends brought in friends, the residents began to grow in number, and a street was formed. As numbers increased, the street extended and spread out further in all directions like a spider's web, becoming the labyrinthine web of closely woven alleys that it was today.

From the look of it, the entrance to Pure Light Street did not appear to be all that narrow and could fit the "Shanghai" limousine owned by an old overseas Chinese who had returned here after having made his fortune! But the road got narrower the further in you went, so that in the narrowest place it was not even possible to put up a large oilcloth umbrella. Which, you see, is why the inhabitants' doors and windows had become symbolic objects, so that even if there was no one in they could be left wide open without having to worry, because no burglar would dare to break in with people all around him. On the contrary, windows and doors shut during the daytime would attract the neighbours' suspicion; what were the occupants up to? Why were they being so secretive? So the relationship between the residents, although not without fights and squabbles, on the whole verified the saying: "If one family has a problem, ten thousand families come to help." This was the reason why some of the residents were not particularly eager to move into flats with gas and a bathroom, and always considered carefully before making the decision to move away.

Number 156 was where Chen Genmei lived, and the room was so crowded with guests that they were overflowing outside the door and into the rooms of the neighbours on either side. The guests were sipping tea and cracking melon seeds, talking and laughing. It was apparently a wedding celebration. And sure e-nough Chen Genmei's elder sister was getting married that day. In that tiny room not ten metres square, from thermos flask to high spittoon, television set to sewing machine, there really was everything you'd expect to find, turning it into a small department store!

"The new society is good indeed!" Chen Genmei's mother, a robust woman of fifty or so was saying feelingly to He Fugui's grandmother. "In the old days when we got married, we didn't have a trousseau. If you bought a few feet of foreign stuff and made something decent to wear, then that wasn't bad!"

He Fugui's grandmother nodded her head in agreement: "That's how it was when my eldest daughter got married! When was it ever like now, when young people can buy a whole set of furniture just like that for a thousand or a thousand five hundred without batting an eyelid...they really are in on their luck!"

Chen Genmei's mother gently caressed the smooth polished surface of the sewing machine with both barklike hands and laughed from the depths of her heart.

"Aunt Chen, it can't be easy for you with four daughters, each one better than the last. This time, once the wedding's over, you ought to make yourself a few decent clothes and get yourself something nice to eat..."

"No such luck. One of my daughters is still young!" Genmei's mother pouted her lips at Genmei with a mixture of fondness and disapproval: "Her do will have to be even better than the others, as she's the youngest."

"What year is your Genmei in?"

"Grade three, due to graduate this summer. That's really soon now. Just because of this little problem, I've carried on working full time instead of taking my retirement, so the supervisor of our food market has a grudge against me!"

"Could you bear to let your Genmei replace you in the food market? It's such hard work!"

"What's hard about it? You've only got to get up early, and there's nothing to do in the afternoons. The bonuses and wages aren't a cent less than in any other trade. They're substantial e-nough. So you see, as soon as our Genmei takes my place and starts to work, she'll be almost ready to get married. See them off one by one, then that's about it for this old body!"

At that moment Genmei was talking enthusiastically in the group of girls and hadn't heard a word of what her mother had said. Like most of the girls born in the Huaihe River area, Genmei was very pretty: her skin was white tinged with pink and her eyes black and clear, but the plucked eyebrows spoiled the natural purity of her youth. And that Hongkong-style knitted nylon dress with a bright red background and sapphire blue pattern imperceptibly made her look a few years older, so that she no longer looked like a schoolgirl but a worker who had already stepped into society. The girls around here lacked a sense of style and individual taste.

"One of the girls in our factory, her wedding was a real sight: twenty tables in the Jing'an Hotel, and in their new place, a colour TV, fridge, twintub washing machine, the lot. Looks like they won't have to worry about buying anything for the rest of their lives." One of the wedding guests put in.

"The bridegroom at the last wedding I went to was pretty well connected... He took every single one of the guests to his new house in taxis," someone else added, not to be outdone.

Genmei strained her neck to listen, heaving a sigh that she had to put up with another year behind a desk. Her not particularly stunning big sister, who had always been run-of-the-mill, had been the centre of attention all week, which had really made her envious. Today they were taking the trousseau to her new home, two days later they were having the feast; the climax was still to come! At this moment her sister was wearing a palace suit and bright red high-heeled shoes, her hair coal black and glossy, so that she was really a different person from normal. When her sister was at school, she had also been at the Pure Light Middle School, but because there was a lot to do in the house and she didn't have any nice clothes, Genmei's impression of her was one of sloppiness. But as soon as she went to the factory, her "costumes" had begun to improve. One pair of shoes after another, one item of clothing after another, and she had heard that they were all bought by boyfriends. You had to pick the ones with an income as boyfriends, as they were more liberal with their money. Those schoolboys, even Liu Guoliang who was usually given to indulging in exaggerations, apart from asking you to go to a film or buying you an ice cream, never did anything!

Her sister was showing off her wedding outfit to her friends, a bright red cheongsam trimmed with gold edging. Genmei was terribly envious! When would her turn to be in the limelight ever come? Last week she had gone with her sister to have her photograph taken in full wedding dress, and the white gauze dress looked so much like those worn by Western aristocrats that it made her want to put it on and have her picture taken too. After all it was only five yuan, so she hit up her brother-in-law for the money. Who would have thought that the photographic studio had a rule that you could only have your photo taken in wedding dress if you had a marriage certificate!

Her sister couldn't stop giggling, just as if she had already had too much to drink!

To call this street poor was quite unjust! The latest stereo sounds could be heard coming from almost all of the squat, crude houses, so that one was afraid those thin wooden partitions would collapse with the vibrations of heavy bass! Many of those gaping doors revealed a corner of a well-modernized room, with glass cabinets displaying all kinds of knick-knacks such as foreign dolls or a lighted standard lamp with a lampshade in georgette! But Wen Xixiu still felt that all this did nothing to dispel that sense of poverty that was hard to put your finger on.

At a little after four o'clock in the afternoon, perhaps a custom left over from the pioneers in saving on paraffin oil, business finished extremely early in these parts, and in the doorways of the houses on both sides quite a number of people had already got their evening dinner bowls and were shovelling up their food as they surveyed her with avid interest that was as great as that of her little nephew watching TV as he ate.

Wen Xixiu walked hurriedly, thinking only to avoid those eyes which made her feel so uneasy as they came to rest on her. However, the alleys that extended like a spider web had already confused her and made her lose her bearings.

"Whose house are you looking for?" said a voice from above her head, which turned out to be from the second floor—if it could be called the second floor, the window being only slightly higher than a person—out of which a woman combing her long waves was poking her head. "Genmei's house? Straight ahead and then turn the corner... next to the boiler room..."

The scratching sound of the comb coming into contact with the scalp made Wen Xixiu feel as if dandruff was falling into her hair and getting inside her collar. Therefore she didn't wait to find out the precise location but hurriedly set off and in her haste kicked over a small stool in the doorway.

"Professor Wen!" Liu Guoliang emerged from the place where the lane turned. "Whose house are you going to?"

What luck to meet a little guide.

"With this place of ours, if we had a war, we could go in for tunnel warfare!" Liu Guoliang said proudly as he led the way for his teacher. He was a young fellow who was both physically and mentally mature for his age. The pupils of grade three were not more than fifteen or sixteen, but his voice had already begun to deepen. "Once the enemy got in, they certainly couldn't get out again!" He suddenly perceived that his analogy was inappropriate and awkwardly scratched his head and laughed. The pupils in this class were even more charming outside school than in.

Liu Guoliang told his teacher that he had gone to the corner to wait for his sister. His elder sister and Genmei's had been good friends ever since they were small, but after his sister had got into a key middle school she had begun to drift apart from Genmei's sister, and after she entered university they saw even less of each other. As today was Genmei's sister's trousseau day, his mother had wanted her to come home at all costs to congratulate her friend.

"My sister doesn't want to come. She says she hates this sort of occasion. And my sister has a busy timetable. She doesn't usually even come home on Sundays."

"Your sister is right."

"But if she loses her old friends when she gets into university, that's not right either." Little brother had his own point of view.

"What does your sister study?"

"Radio." Liu Guoliang was very proud of his sister.

Not an easy matter. Everywhere the footprints of fighters can be seen, and the poor street was no exception!

Far away in the distance the entrance to Chen Genmei's house was a hive of activity, and even before Wen Xixiu reached the doorway a large rocket came flying out of the room with a boom, making her jump. But what startled her even more was Chen Genmei, her eyebrows plucked into thin lines. She had just come rushing all in a whirl out of the room, yelling with a voice loud enough to shake the heavens as if she wanted the whole world to know. "What? The limousine we ordered isn't here yet!"

All of a sudden she came face to face with her form mistress. She was a little disconcerted but certainly not alarmed. "Ma, teacher's here." She turned her head and called out, implying mother's virtual omnipresence.

"Oh, teacher's here." Genmei's mother came out from the inner room with a warm welcome, pulling over a chair and wiping the clean seat with her palm in a habitual gesture, then inviting Wen Xixiu to sit down. "Her sister's been busy with arrangements these last few days, and there's been a lot to do at home, so we let Genmei have a few days off to help out at home!"

Wen Xixiu was a little angry with this foolish mother. "Chen Genmei's marks are already bad enough, and so many lessons..."

"That..." The mother shot an alarmed look at the roomful of guests, and then, as if it was a secret, said in a low voice to Wen Xixiu: "To tell the truth, as you're her teacher, our Genmei isn't scholarship material, and I'm not placing any hopes on her. If she can replace me, that'll be fine. I hope you don't mind too much, teacher!"

At the last sentence Wen Xixiu didn't know whether to laugh or cry.

"No chance of any Number One Scholars* in this place..." Wen Xixiu stopped Chen Genmei's mother before she had finished speaking. "Didn't Liu Guoliang's sister get into university?"

---

* Number One Scholar in the Imperial Examination System.

"Oh, her." Chen Genmei's mother gave her a meaningful look. "Gets into university, looks down on this and turns her nose up at that, oh yes, doesn't even come to congratulate Genmei's sister on her trousseau day. Normally she gets her clothes made and her books bought every other day by her mother. That kind of student thinks she's an empress or something. We're not shelling out for the likes of her!"

Liu Guoliang very much minded other people deriding his sister in front of everyone, although it really was a bit much that she hadn't come back today of all days to congratulate her friend, as, extravagant or not, this was the custom of Pure Light Street! Glancing to make sure that the others didn't notice, he sneaked out quietly again to wait for his sister.

Chen Genmei's mother tugged at Wen Xixiu's sleeve and said in a low voice: "Frankly speaking, as long as girls from our kind of family can do a bit of needlework and read a few words, that's pretty well enough.... After all, we're not the sort of folk who live in those Western-style buildings."

The women all around with nothing to do but crack melon seeds and listen to gossip echoed their agreement, but Wen Xixiu could find nothing to say.

At that moment a small boy dashed into the room from outside. "The car's here, waiting at the intersection!"

Quick as lightning, Genmei's mother grabbed a packet of "Double Happiness" cigarettes and stuffed it into the small boy's hand. "Quick, give this to the driver, mind you call him 'uncle', and ask him to drive the car in."

"I've asked already, but he won't. He says the road's too narrow."

"Nonsense. The girl from ninety-six got married this year,

and didn't the car drive right up to the end of the alley? Go on, have a few more words with that driver." As she spoke, Genmei's mother pressed a second packet of "Peony" cigarettes into the boy's hand.

The limousine put the whole room in chaos in a moment, so that Wen Xixiu was forgotten. People were concerned merely with taking stock of the goods in the store-like array of the trousseau. She had no choice but to leave sullenly. As she passed Genmei, she couldn't stop herself saying softly in her ear: "Make the best of this last year at lower middle school. You can't just live for..." She had been about to say "getting married", but then decided this was too blunt, so changed it to "being a replacement worker"!

Chen Genmei, who was at that moment cautiously carrying a "555" brand desk clock, merely nodded her head vigorously, whereas in fact she just wanted to get rid of her teacher as quickly as possible, as at that moment all her thoughts were concentrated on that beautiful limousine already parked at the intersection. She was impatiently longing to step into the limousine under the gaze of the neighbours, wearing the beautiful dress that she had borrowed with difficulty... She had been looking forward to this day for ages!

Just as the planets all have their own orbits, Wen Xixiu felt completely out of place here. There was constantly some centrifugal force pushing her out. No matter how embarrassed and uncomfortable today's visit had made her feel, at any rate she could report it. Therefore, as if she had been relieved of a heavy burden, she let out a deep breath, and screened by the gradually fading light, she walked briskly towards the "Second World" through the curious stares that continued to fall on her person from both sides of the street.

"How was it? You didn't get lost, did you?" Zhang Xianglin's bicycle came gleaming out of another alley.

"Oh, I wasted over an hour going to Chen Genmei's house to see a trousseau!" She had meant to flare up at him, but for some reason her words as she uttered them had turned into a complaint and sounded a little like a...spoiled child.

The way he stood there laughing at you silently, how could you get angry with him?

"That's why you have to run over to their houses. Their lives are so completely different from yours! If you don't understand them, you'll never be able to do your job properly. I've just been to He Fugui's house to give him extra lessons, worrying for him while he didn't care a whit about his lessons. He only got twenty-three in the last Chinese test, and when I got there just now, he was busy making furniture with his dad."

What was so strange about that? If it had been the time when she had just arrived at Pure Light Middle School, Wen Xixiu might well have been surprised at this piece of news, but she was regretfully already used to this kind of thing. It was just the rhythm of life on the poor street.

"But they can't carry on like this!" He went on sighing and shaking his head.

"Liu Guoliang's sister's all right though. She's a university student, with a future." She thought of Liu Guoliang's elder sister; for a girl to have such high aspirations was a rare thing!

"But..." Zhang Xianglin pondered: "Did you know Liu Guoliang's family have it pretty hard? His father died in an industrial accident, and to keep his sister at university and in beautiful clothes, and even to let her go away on holiday at vacations, both mother and son have to unravel cotton half the night! D'you know how little you get for unravelling half a kilo of cotton?"

Wen Xixiu shook her head blankly.

"Sixty cents a half kilo, and a half kilo's a great big pile like this."

"Then why go to all that bother? I mean it's not like before Liberation, when you had to really dress up if you went to university." Wen Xixiu felt now that Liu Guoliang and his mother overspoilt this university student. Frankly speaking, what was so special about university students? Wasn't it just that they'd had a few extra years' study?

Zhang Xianglin chuckled. "You really should visit a few more of their houses! Find a spare moment to have a chat with Liu Guoliang's mother." He looked at her, his manner just as if he was looking at a nursery school infant. How he looked down on people! Although to tell the truth, when he wasn't being angry he was really quite amiable.

"Can you cook?" He ventured suddenly, gripping his handlebar.

"Cook? I don't know. Maybe..." she um-ed and uh-ed in reply. She had never done anything in the kitchen, so of course she did not know whether she could actually cook or not.

He couldn't help laughing seeing her blushing scarlet. This form mistress it appeared was even greener than the schoolgirls, with no experience in the world at all. No wonder she was even scared of going to their homes, putting it off time and time again. She was really still a child; he shouldn't have teased her in the morning. He hated this temper of his that wouldn't let people off. He had too much pride!

"You'll have to get over the obstacle of calling on their parents sooner or later. You mean you've never been to a slum area like this at your age? You might be interested to have a look; people can live anywhere!"

"Where's your home?" she asked with great interest. According to the custom of the Shanghainese, you could tell a person's financial situation and social standing from where they lived. She very much wanted to find out what kind of person this Zhang Xianglin who stood out among the hundred or so members of staff of the Pure Light Middle School was after all.

"Yueyang Road."

"Oh, nice place."

"I'm an exception. I live on the other side of the big wall."

Wen Xixiu blinked. She hadn't understood.

"Goodbye!" He got on his bicycle. When he had ridden a short way off he turned his head and looked at her. She was wholly engrossed in striding along the bumpy narrow road, her faded and baggy semi-old trousers and simple white shirt failing to disguise her characteristic coquettish air, lending her the comical appearance of a mischievous little girl dressed in grown-up clothing.

"Had a good look? Mind you don't get too carried away looking at girls. Careful you don't bump into a truck..." A bicycle came up right in front of him on the diminutively narrow street, almost colliding with him, and its rider savagely rebuked him.

But Zhang Xianglin was far from angry; he was well used to this kind of person, all bark but no bite. Who knew what unhappy event had just befallen him?

"If a girl's pretty of course you want to have a good look. Like animals in a zoo, those who look more attractive always have a larger audience, and all the more so with human beings!" he jocularly said in reply, and quickly pedalled his bike away.

Since he had first seen Wen Xixiu, her shy and naive air reminded him of the days when he and his wife, with whom he had just been through a divorce, had first met and fallen in love, and although his marriage had been a tragedy it was undeniable that those days had been a colourful and joyous chapter of his life.

Wen Xixiu really resembled his ex-wife, including that cautious nature that often needed someone to give her a push before she could get anything done. He very much enjoyed working with a teacher like her.

It was just when everyone was finishing work, and on the main traffic lanes the trams, buses, vans and cars piled up to form a long dragon as they were stopped by a red light. Through the wide open window in the crowded bus Wen Xixiu caught a glimpse of a van next to them piled high with quilts of all colours, which just happened to be Chen Genmei's sister's trouseau car. In the back seat, Chen Genmei was still protectively clutching the big "555" desk clock. Her face beaming with joy, she was talking to her sister, the bride-to-be.

Wen Xixiu stared perplexedly at the new bride. This person who was only one or two years older than herself, did she now feel happy and contented? When the excitement of being newly married had died down, would she still be made such a fuss of by the crowd like today? If getting married was the only way one could see one's own splendour, then... that was a bit too sad.

What Zhang Xianglin had said about "people being able to live anywhere" wasn't in the least untrue. Everyone lived according to their own habits. Only she disliked the rhythm and way of life of Pure Light Street, and if she hadn't seen it with her own eyes today she would have thought that kind of article criticizing "extravagant marriages" was a piece of air-to-air propaganda.

3

The pupils, who on the whole had heavy northern Jiangsu accents, just could not manage to pronounce correctly words containing the phonemes [k], [g], [t], or [d], instead making noises rather like puffed rice exploding, so that even English people couldn't have known it was English.

Wen Xixiu had corrected them repeatedly but to no avail, and she was beginning to despair. The students were also beginning to lose patience, in particular He Fugui, who deliberately read the word "vegetable" as "full up", causing roars of laughter.

"What are you playing at?" Wen Xixiu was angry.

"Don't understand, do I!" He Fugui was pretending to be ignorant.

"If you don't understand, you should listen properly and stop making trouble."

"In any case I'm not going to be a translator." His manner was completely "couldn't-care-less".

"Well! 'Be a translator'! You don't think that someone's going to ask you to be a translator on your thick northern Jiangsu accent alone? If you don't understand you might as well just close your mouth and have a rest and stop losing face and showing off. You may as well save your strength for when you get home to your carpentry, because that's all you'll end up doing," Wen Xixiu retorted sarcastically.

"Right, so you look down on people!" He Fugui flew into a rage.

"Teacher looks down on us northern Jiangsu people. What kind of attitude is that!" some people in the class said with open resentment. With these words, several dozen pairs of eyes fell on Wen Xixiu, and for a moment there was not a sound to be heard in the classroom. That silent reproachful gaze made Wen Xixiu feel extremely flustered, and she could hear the regular thudding of her heart.

Luckily the bell rang, and she made her escape from the classroom.

Sitting in the office, her thoughts were still full of what had just happened in class. That kind of look frightened her even more than those rough hoodlums who kept little sharp knives hidden in their pockets.

"What's up, have the students been making you angry again?" the teacher next to her asked sympathetically.

She gave a little noncommittal laugh.

Oh dear, nothing was at all like she had pictured before. At the outset the comrade in charge at the District Bureau of Education had informed her that due to social as well as historical factors, the pupils of Pure Light Middle School were a fairly special case. At the time she had said lightly that it didn't matter. She had just seen *The Village Teacher* and *My Teacher*, and the fragile girl-teacher in the first movie had even been able to control the drunken louts, so how was it that she couldn't even cope with a few schoolkids? Then, she had imagined herself reading beautiful poetry to her pupils, taking them to art exhibitions and to find out about nature. Well, her intentions had been wonderful anyway! Nothing was anything like as poetic as it had been described in the films. Finally she now realized that being a teacher not only consisted of cramming in all the knowledge contained in the textbook itself but also of dealing with the many hard problems that often arose in her everyday life.

"Professor Wen." Liu Guoliang lightly pushed open the door and came in. "Some of the words we learnt today, will you teach me how to read them once more?"

Painstakingly he read, but because of his habitual accent he still couldn't get the pronunciation. It was only then that Wen Xixiu realized that for reading English they really did have an inherent linguistic disability.

"Out of so many subjects, I feel the one I've got the least grasp of is English. It's so hard. As soon as I get home I've forgotten everything, and I haven't even got anyone to ask," Liu Guoliang grumbled. He was dressed very plainly, and even though this was a poor street you didn't see any of the other boys dressed like Liu Guoliang in grey drill with the cuffs worn threadbare. Nowadays even tracksuit tops with zip fasteners and running shoes had infiltrated this area from the "First World". Only the teachers remained dowdy, not brave enough to make any rash innovations in their style. But Liu Guoliang's clothes were not merely plain; they could only properly be described as shabby. When she thought that he also had to unravel cloth to help with family finances, Wen Xixiu's heart ached for him. She was too unfamiliar with this kind of life, or perhaps the expression "one wonders at what one has never experienced" could be aptly employed here.

"Do you unravel cotton every evening?" she asked, at the same time thinking of the children the same age as him in her alley at home, eating chocolate ice-creams every day even in the middle of winter.

"That's light work." He didn't seem to take any notice at all of his teacher's excessive concern. "You can get a whole pile done in a single evening."

"Life must be pretty hard with no father?" Wen Xixiu genuinely admired Liu Guoliang from the bottom of her heart.

"Yes, I'm the only male in the family, and Ma's health isn't too good either. As soon as my sister went to university, our family's expenses went up too. She has to have extra clothes and go off travelling." He had assumed the manner of head of the family. No wonder he came himself to the meeting for heads of the family at the beginning of term, saying that he was his own family head. Wen Xixiu had at first thought he was playing a joke on her, but afterwards Zhang Xianglin had solemnly invited him to take a seat with the others.

"Actually, there's nothing so awfully special about going to university. You really don't have to have new clothes and go travelling!" she said.

"Teacher, you don't understand!" Liu Guoliang said rather rudely. "If everyone goes travelling and she doesn't, and if everyone's dressed fashionably and only her clothes are unsophisticated, people will laugh. Especially at people like us from a dump like Pure Light Street."

"That's a bit too vain." Wen Xixiu shook her head disapprovingly.

"Teacher, you haven't been here long, and you don't understand," Liu Guoliang couldn't help shaking his head and saying.

"You don't understand..." Wen Xixiu really didn't understand. She recalled that when she was at university there had al-

so been a girl whose family lived in Zhabei District, an industrial workers' residential area in Shanghai, whose clothes and bedding were all brand new. Even her face cream was the very special kind mixed with powered pearls. But really, what was the
point? She had really looked down on that student.

Although Wen XiXiu had to make a two-hour-long trek to get
to work and back every day, and the workload was heavy in
comparison with most other middle schools, she was still fortunate. Only a third of her time each day belonged to this poor
street, the remaining two-thirds belonging to the more comfortable life of the materially rich "First World"!

Dead on a quarter to five she got ready to leave work.

Going past the sports pitch, she saw Zhang Xianglin playing
volleyball with He Fugui and the rest. He was wearing a white
T-shirt, which revealed the swarthy, strong muscles of his body.
His look of vitality made it hard to imagine that his personal life
had already suffered a major change of circumstance. She
stopped and watched him for a while over in the distance. Originally she had thought that he had no idea of how to be nice to
women, but now it looked like her judgment had been wrong.
He was very good at it, much better than those male college students, whom she referred to as sissies. He waved a greeting to
her, some of the boys waved too, and she acknowledged them
with a smile. Frankly speaking, although for this rotten teaching job she had to put on clothes she personally disliked, she still
felt that teaching was far more interesting than being a factory
worker. Every day was filled with new substance and new situa-
tions, and she came into contact with real live people, unlike in
a factory, every day dealing only with the immutable faces of
those inflexible spare parts and lathes. She would never stand it.

He Fugui coldly cast a sidelong glance at her from the sports pitch, and once again his expression was one she could not bear. If it had been during the "cultural revolution" he would certainly have struggled against her. Her heart gave a jump, and she felt extremely uncomfortable.

She dejectedly went off the sports pitch. Before she had come to register, she had been looking forward to the noble appeal of being a teacher. She had believed she would love children—she had already got to this age, and she had never hated anyone yet. She wanted the children to love her too! But as it turned out, compared with Zhang Xianglin, who was likewise in charge of a class, she seemed to be so isolated and superfluous here, and moreover she was rather at a loss. And at university she had been the best student in the class. But now she was in such a difficult position; only two of the students she taught had passed. The scene in class also constantly made her unsure whether to laugh or cry. If she could change her work unit she would definitely be able to do a better job than she could at present!

An hour's bus journey and she again returned to the First World from the Third World, and her unsteady heart seemed to settle down.

This had once been the British Concession, and on such a big piece of ground behind the iron gate they had built three three-storey apartment buildings in the English style, between each of which was a verdant stretch of green. Here, Wen Xixiu, like her grandparents before her, occupied a ten-metre-wide apartment. During the "cultural revolution", her parents had been determined to keep these rooms they loved after living in them for so many years, not hesitating to sell off the family's few bits and pieces and scraping a miserable sum out from between their teeth, and continuing to hand over their costly monthly rent of thirty-six yuan on time, thus managing to keep this comfortable accommodation.

Wen Xixiu ran up the stairs, and though her key was undoubtedly in her pocket raised both fists to drum on the door.

"Ma, is there anything to eat? I'm starving." She went in through the front door, crossed the hall, then entered the reception room, depositing as she went her handbag, that day's evening paper which she had just removed from the letter box and a bag of liqueur chocolates she had bought on the way back on the nearest available chairback, sofa and small tea table, and then, using one foot to help the other, en route took off the shoes that were splashed with mud from the poor quarter and crossed barefooted to the shoe cupboard to change into slippers, collapsing full length on to the sofa as she did so and resting both legs on the arm in complete abandonment. The first few minutes when she got home each day were her happiest moments.

From the wide-open door of her mother's room came the sound of two voices, one old and one young, reading English. This was her mother's pupil—the little fourth-year grandson of Professor Gao from downstairs was studying English with Wen Xixiu's mother. The Gao family were intent on training their younger generation in foreign languages, and starting from kindergarten this little boy had been coming here to learn English. He had already got through four volumes of Active English. There was a rumour that this year the Foreign Languages School was going to take in a small number of students from certain primary schools, and there was great hope for this small boy.

Out of professional habit, although Wen Xixiu had only been an English teacher for a month, she still twisted her head round and listened with great interest as the little boy and her mother expressively read a children's poem about a cat and mouse. Both the old and young voices read vividly and dramatically with plenty of enthusiasm, so that it sounded more like playing games than having a lesson. This... was really how a lesson shouldb be! Not like her, Wen Xixiu, sounding not at all like a lesson, more like hawkers on the corner of the street crying: "Ice-creams! Get your ice-creams here!"

The boy misplaced the stress on a word, and her mother only had to remind him with a gentle "Mm", and the boy promptly corrected himself.

How intelligent! It was only interesting to teach this kind of pupil. But Wen Xixiu's teaching was simply a waste of time. No matter how carefully she preparedher lessons, the mark book was still a sheet of red. The only one in the class who could count was Liu Guoliang, but his pronunciation did not come up to the Gao Family's grandson's by a long chalk. To say something one shouldn't, those pupils were just thick. Or perhaps the Creator had arranged it that way: some people were born to ascend the ladder through primary school, middle school, up to university, and another set of people were born to provide society with a labour force. When she was a child she had been very naive, and after hearing the report about "recalling past suffering and thinking of the source of present happiness" she had in deadly earnest asked her mother: now that China's been liberated, and everyone can get to university, who's going to sweep the roads? Afterwards the "cultural revolution" had come, and her big brother, who had been the first-prize winner in the district mathematics contest, had been sent to sell pickles in the food market. Now, of course, he had left the food market a long time ago and had passed the exam to go and study abroad on a state scholarship. Nevertheless, Chen Genmei was going to the food market for sure, unless she could into upper middle school, which would be a miracle. It seemed as if anyone who was born in the poor area was destined to have a rough deal!

Wen Xixiu raised her eyes towards the violet lampshade suspended from the ceiling, a feeling of good fortune suddenly welling up in her heart; if by bad luck she had been born in a little one-storey house on Pure Light Street, what would be her lot? A cold shiver ran down her spine. Maybe she really should drink to her own good luck.

The phone rang. It was her friend asking her to go and see a ballet!

On the poor street night fell a little earlier than on the other streets of this big city, and just after eight o'clock struck the whole street was already as silent as the grave. However, the edge of the "River Nile" was uncommonly lively; He Fugui's family was doing their carpentry there where there was lots of space, so they didn't need to worry about wood shavings and sawdust flying everywhere, and there was the free light from the handy street lamp as well.

He Fugui was just learning how to polish on the just-completed small glass cabinet.

"In the end it pays to do it yourself. Just go to the woodworks and get a bit of old wood and make it up, and you can reckon on thirty yuan. If you went to the furniture shop and bought one you'd spend nearly a hundred at least!" He Fugui's father said with satisfaction as he looked over the nearly completed small glass cabinet. "You can get two for the price of one. When it's finished go and ask for a couple of *maotai* bottles to put in, and then it's a wine cabinet. Get the wife to put toilet water or something on the top shelf and...."

"Let me put a model boat on the bottom shelf," He Fugui put in.

"Don't let your attention wander when you're doing something, little devil," the father rebuked his son affectionately, then suddenly thought of something: "Hey, have you done your lessons today?"

"Ages ago," He Fugui said expressionlessly, whereas in fact he hadn't opened his schoolbag at all after he had got home.

"In a few days go to the factory and pick up an old waterpipe, rub it down with sand paper and spray on some paint, and you've got the stand for a standard lamp..." Contentedly the father started to make plans again.

"Master He, you've now got a sofa and wine cabinet, if you get a standard lamp as well your place'll be really sophisticated," the neighbours teased him. "Aren't you afraid of bursting out of that place of yours that's only as big as a bit of dried beancurd?"

"That's not my affair. What's 'standing up' all about? It's the eighties now, and we ordinary folk should have a bit of ease and comfort too. To live like our old men with only a bed board and bench in their houses would lack self-respect! As for the room being small, I can't do anything about that. That's the country's self-respect." Master He's disapprobatory joke made everyone laugh.

Liu Guoliang had at some point or other also slipped out and was watching He Fugui's craftsmanship with admiration.

"You're really good, Ah Fu! I reckon you may as well just do this for a living later on."

"You're really smart, did your homework before slipping out to play a bit. Everyone knows you're planning to go to university. But here you are coming and blackmailing me to become a carpenter, so that I can do you a free job when you get married," He Fugui said half in jest and half seriously, tweaking Liu Guoliang's nose with a pair of greasy hands. "Hey, do us a favour, pal. I haven't copied out any of that foreign language homework 'Coquette' gave us today. Spare a moment tomorrow and lend it to me to copy, or you could just do it for me."

"You little devil, you really are the limit, wanting people even to do your homework for you. You've been so lazy you'll get maggots," Master He exclaimed, clipping his son on the head.

"Don't you want me to help you sand down that water pipe tomorrow? Where will I find the time?" his son protested. "Isn't it supposed to be for that lamp stand of yours?"

"The devil only knows you haven't done any of your lessons. You're not doing the lamp stand tomorrow any more; you'll do your lessons." Master He said, turning to face the neighbours and starting to complain. "These young louts today have it too easy at school: they don't seem to have any homework when they come home. Not like in our day, when the teacher used to beat the palm of your hand... All right, all right, anyway no one's expecting him to come top, otherwise see if I wouldn't beat the hell out of him!"

"Did you hear? My homework book's in my bag, and if I don't hand it in, 'Coquette' will have a go at me again on Monday. She doesn't care a bit about my reputation, and I can't swallow it. Must try and think of a way to put an end to her cockiness," He Fugui said, pressing close to Liu Guoling's ear.

It was the weekend, and also the day when Zhang Xianglin was in the habit of going home.

Zhang Xianglin's home was in the well-known compound in the West District, only he had to enter by the side door, because his home was behind the main block, where the apartments were lower and less roomy than those in front and were packed together like pigeon coops, originally forming the part of the compound where the carters, cooks and other servants had lived. After Liberation some of the tenants in the front had left the country, some had moved, and some were imprisoned, and on the other hand a fair number of high-ranking cadres had moved in, so that the original tenants had changed a great deal, whereas their cooks and servants, etc. went on living at the back as before. Most of them lived and worked here in peace and contentment, giving birth to the next generations, so that year in year out two completely different worlds existed side by side within the compound.

Zhang Xianglin's mother had been a maid to one of the families in the front, and his father had driven the family's three-wheeled cart. After Liberation the family went abroad, and his father began to pedal a three-wheeled delivery cart for the transport corps. His mother had continued to keep house for someone.

"How come you're late today? I've been saving a big fish head for you to eat when you came home!" said his mother, fondly regarding the son whom she saw only once a week. Her right hand immediately felt for her pocket, and she seemed to be about to say something, then stopped.

"Ma, have you got something to say to me?"

"Eat. Have something to eat first."

"Ma." Zhang Xianglin drew his mother's arm and led her over to sit on the edge of the bed. "Didn't I tell you a long time ago, Ma? If you've got something to say to me then say it, like when I was small. When..." he hesitated. "When I got married I said to you and Dad, I'm still your son. And even more so now I've...only got you now, Ma!"

At these words from the depths of her son's heart, the mother's eyes reddened again. She drew from her pocket a crumpled letter. "There's a letter from her. A photo of Qinqin."Qinqin, his daughter!

His daughter was wearing a red checked tartan skirt and knee-length woolen socks, and her long hair was loose; she was dressed just like a little foreign girl. On the back of the photograph was his ex-wife's handwriting. "Qinqin is seven now. She can already speak fluent English and everyone takes her for a Japanese girl." Her temperament hadn't changed; everything foreign was good, and she was even pleased that other people thought their daughter was Japanese. Admittedly being able to speak fluent English, was something to be pleased about, but did this mean that her Shanghainese would be forgotten forever?

He turned the photo over again and took a closer look at his daughter. Her appearance had not changed very much; she still looked the same as she had three years before when she left the country with her mother, only she had grown a little in size. In the last line his wife had written: "I already have the green card, so our daughter can hopefully get American citizenship!"

Falling in love, getting married, getting divorced, emigrating, becoming American citizens... His past seemed further and further away from him, to have vanished to a completely different world. Could it be because at the outset his and her origins were completely different, she in the south block and he in the servants' quarters? Put in the words of that new female teacher, he also belonged to a poor street!

He gave a wry smile and carefully placed his daughter's photograph inside his wallet.

Three years had passed in a flash. Would their daughter still remember her father? At the time when he had seen off mother and daughter at the airport he already had no feelings of sorrow at all at the departure of his ex-wife, who had become a stranger to him long ago, and could only sigh that he had wasted his love in vain. But his daughter, his own flesh and blood whom he cared for deeply, had really been difficult to part with, particularly when she had stepped on to the gangway and turned her head again and again towards his, calling out, "Goodbye, Daddy!" He had merely raised his hand and smiled an agonized smile, in the end not managing to get the word "goodbye" out, because he had already realized that he might never see his daughter again as long as he lived.

Before they decided to separate, he and his wife had given a lot of careful thought to who should have their daughter. He had strongly requested that she would live with him. However, his father-in-law's words had obliged him to think carefully, when he said: "With such an opportunity as this you really should let Qinqin go with her mother; if the situation changes again she won't be able to leave any more. And besides..." In fact his father-in-law didn't add anything further and merely smoked in silence. However, Zhang Xianglin already understood the meaning of his omitted words: Since he and his wife had already decided on a divorce, he would naturally have to move from his father-in-law's south building back to the rear building, where he had grown up. According to the legal clause, the court could allocate him one room, but it was out of the question for him to make such a demand, as he felt that would be blackmail. In that case Qinqin would also be obliged to move back to her grandmother's home in the rear building, which would be extremely awkward and distressing for her maternal grandparents living in the south building! For this reason the ideal solution had been to allow Qinqin to go far away with her mother! And besides, his wife's family had already felt regrets about this far-from-perfect marriage for a long time, and since it was now possible to put an end to it all, what was the point of leaving behind an appendage that caused pain?

Only... his daughter, his flesh and blood, his closest relative, had now gone from him forever. Like a little bird carrying a seed in its beak, when because of a single mistake, one illusion, one oversight, the seed drops out as soon as it opens its beak, but not on to the little bird's resting place, and it can only gaze with regret at the seed which has already sprouted and continue to search for a resting place of its own... but can it find one? When and where?

He noticed that his mother was watching him with tenderness. Because he did not want his mother to see he had so much on his mind, he affected to have an appetite and lifted the lid of the casserole dish: "Hey, this fish smells really good! Let's eat; I'm hungry!"

His mother said nothing but stretched out a hand and lightly touched her son's forehead, where three distinct lines had appeared.

"Ma!" He gently drew his mother's hand away, and just like when he was small and had been bullied by someone outside and came home to be comforted by his mother, he really wished he could bury his head in those hands that were red from being immersed in soapsuds all year round.

"Child, you can't be on your own for ever!" his mother said fondly, watching him anxiously. She knew that it wasn't enough for a man of over thirty to depend solely on his mother's love.

"What are you afraid of? Don't you know that in today's market there are more women than men!" he said jokingly.

"But your situation isn't ideal. For one thing, it'll be your second marriage, and we haven't got a place either... It's all the fault of us parents having no education...."

"Don't say that, Ma!" Zhang Xianglin gently clasped his mother to his breast. "I'll be grateful to you for ever for going short of clothes and food to bring me up, for sending me to senior middle school as I wanted and not making me go out and earn money as soon as possible. To this day I haven't forgotten how in the three years' famine* you saved your own food for me and my brother, who were still growing at the time... And besides, I will find someone to love me. Only we're still looking for each other..."

"Now you mention studying, I really do regret it a little. Maybe at the time we shouldn't have let you go to university..."
His mother's white-streaked hair softly brushed against his chin. He noticed with distress that the white hairs on the crown of his

---

* 1959-1961.

mother's head were so thin that her scalp clearly showed through. "By now your wages and bonus put together would certainly be more than you're getting at the moment, and you wouldn't have met that harbinger of ill fortune from the front building either."

Zhang Xianglin laughed, knowing what his mother meant. If he had not gone to university in the first place, he would have gone to work as soon as he was able and then taken as his wife a strong, hard-working woman, and they would have maintained their existence along the same groove in the rear building as their fathers' generation and thus enjoyed their days... No, thank goodness he had chosen another road. Perhaps he should admit that if he hadn't gone to university his marriage might not have been a tragedy. There was once a girl in the rear building who was both sincere and industrious, and who his mother and father had already secretly betrothed to become their future daughter-in-law, and maybe at one time she might have become his wife. However, knowledge had caused him to acquire new objects of pursuit where love was concerned, and he had fallen deeply in love with a different kind of girl, the sweet and innocent kind that was highly accomplished artistically, and this kind of girl more often than not lived in the south building. So he had fallen in love with Little Qin's mother in senior middle school. Because she dearly loved literature he had decided to take the exam for the Chinese department, and because she lived in the south building he had sworn to himself that he too would find a way of getting out of the back building... She didn't condescend to pay the slightest attention to him, but he had gone all out to get her to notice him; by the teacher reviewing one of his compositions and his poems being read at the literary meeting of the students' union, he had done all he could to attract her attention. Only now when he was a little older did he discover that this was just where the tragedy lay; his love bore the nature of a fierce challenge and of immature adolescent vanity, and just because it was so, when finally he had at long last spoken of her he had felt extremely uneasy, dicovering that he didn't even know her very well yet. And now he knew in his heart that their union had had nothing to do with his own glory, but that what she saw had merely been due to a certain splendour lent him by the "cultural revolution", which had been going on at the time. On the eve of his wedding his companions had joked with him: "Xianglin's moving to the south block of the big foreign building, but don't forget your friends from the back...." Although this had been said only in fun, it had still given him the guilty feeling that he was abandoning them...And when the splendour conferred on him by that stretch of history had receded, the tragedy had immediately followed.

A tragedy, a pure tragedy; however, however, those meetings after dusk, the waiting in the bitingly cold wind, the shy touching of hands...these were all filled with a bittersweet aftertaste. Who was it said it? A tragedy's better than no drama at all! Better to exceed the bounds and proceed than to follow the well-beaten track in ignorance, as even if you make a mess of it you will have had a taste of life! When he thought of those lively children of Pure Light Middle School, who were all either consciously or unconsciously following that well-worn path, he honestly felt sorry for them. They should come out and take a look at the real world!

"I feel relieved when you get home," his mother said.

He was very glad to be able to make his mother happy. A pity there was not enough room at home, as when his younger brother had got married he had nowhere to sleep, so was obliged to live at school and could not keep his mother company every day. His brother and sister-in-law were both very understanding, and knowing that he might have a private matter to talk over with his mother they took the child and squeezed in with his brother's father-in-law every Saturday. For this, Zhang Xianglin was very grateful to his sister-in-law, and the amity between the brothers depended on her completely.

"How's Little Niu been doing at school lately?" he asked. Little Niu was his nephew, and since his daughter had left him he had transferred his love entirely to Little Niu.

"His dad had to smack him the day before yesterday."

"Why? Did he fail?"

"No. He told us that on the pupils' registration form, he had changed his family home from Yancheng, Jiangsu to Ningbo, Zhejiang."

Zhang Xianglin's heart felt suddenly heavy, and he got up and crossed to the window. His field of vision was completely blocked by the twelve-storey main building, and all he could see was the back of that building, which, because it had not been whitewashed for a great many years—as this was the back, and the side nearest the road was whitewashed once every three or five years—appeared very ancient and dismal.

"But why did they hit him?" he said tenderly.

"Doesn't want to know his old ancestors any more. He deserved to be hit!" his mother said with directness. "We northern Jiangsu people, we may be poor, but we're proud!"

Although she said this, could one blame this child, who was only in his third year? He thought of the way He Fugui and his group had surged angrily into his office that day to complain about Wen Xixiu. "She looks down on us northern Jiangsu folk!" The group of pupils had dared to explicitly use the words "us northern Jiangsu folk", including Zhang Xianglin, though it was only that they lived on the so-called poor street, Pure Light Street. In spirit they were equal. And he could well understand his little nephew's plight, since his own childhood had also been spent in this same kind of misery. To think that the big court-yard alone divided two completely different worlds! This abnor-mal living arrangement had been the cause of a feeling of insu-perable pressure and humiliation during his own childhood years, and now this had been transferred to his little nephew! When on earth would it change once and for all?

"Don't blame him, Ma. He's too young to realize. When I was at middle school and people asked me where I lived, I would just point to the South Building, too shy to say I lived in the servants' block behind. Now I wouldn't be embarrassed about it," he said to his mother.

After dinner, he started to prepare his lessons. They were just about to begin Liang Qichao's "On the Youth of China", and he liked the text of this lesson very much: "Today's responsibility lies not with others but with us young people. If the nation's youth are wise, then the nation will be wise, if its youth are rich the nation will be rich, if its youth are strong the nation will be strong..." What a beautiful sentence! If only all his students could understand the expectations and love it held! He had heard that this time the training college was intending to use just this lesson for a public teaching session, and he would really like to have gone. Pure Light Middle School had never had a turn at a public teaching session, but there was no reason not to try.

His mother quietly cleared the dinner table and then took up a shoe sole and silently began to sew over where the light was bad. She was making the shoes for him, for although nowadays the fashion was all leather shoes and training shoes, she still insisted on making a pair of cloth shoes, as cotton shoes with cloth soles were warmer than cotton shoes with plastic soles, and besides, it would make him feel better to wear shoes made by his mother's own hands—there was someone who loved him! As his mother made stitch after stitch without thinking, under the lamplight her son was absorbed in his work, which made her feel really at ease in her heart—anyway, her son had not had a breakdown, and his life was very stable. It looked like it was a good thing after all to have a bit of learning!

In one of the small one-storey houses on Pure Light Street, Liu Guoliang and his mother sat opposite one another under the light unravelling cloth. The cotton they had unravelled was piled like a small mountain on the floor.

"You go to bed. You've had a tiring day," his mother said fondly to her son.

"You go instead. You have to go to work tomorrow. I'll finish off this little lot." Liu Guoliang began to whistle cheerfully as he spoke, as if the job was really interesting and enjoyable. In fact his neck, through having been bent over his work for such a long time, was aching like anything. But after his father's death he had already learnt to be patient. As his practised hands pulled at the yarn, his mother noticed that their backs were no longer plump and rounded but were now the hands of an adult with the muscles and bones showing through and with strong joints. It was only thanks to these hands of her son's that she could manage to get by.

"All right then, you finish off what's left, and I'll make use of the time to open the buttonholes on that patterned woollen coat of your sisters'. The weather's turning cold now. You never know when she'll need to wear it."

Liu Guoliang was silent. His sister had not been home now for three weeks. The times his sister came back were getting further and further apart, and now she basically only came back to fetch clothes. After she had gone to university her feelings for her family had seemed to grow more and more indifferent.

"Guoliang, yesterday when you phoned your sister, what did she say exactly? Did she say what time she'd probably be coming home?"

"She didn't say for definite. She's got a lot of classes at the moment, and they're going to have a mid-term exam." Liu Guoliang reassured his mother, at the same time lovingly watching as she painstakingly cock-stitched the buttonhole, one stitch after another. His sister had told him on the phone to think of a way to sell that piece of woollen cloth for her, because today that kind of clothing was out of fashion. Who would have thought her mother, fearing that his sister would have nothing to wear now the season was changing, would cut it out for her well in advance, and was now staying up late into the night to stitch the buttonholes for her... Liu Guoliang really didn't have the heart to tell his mother what his sister had said.

"Don't stay up too late, Ma," he urged his mother again.

"Won't be long now. There's only two more buttonholes to do." His mother adjusted her presbyopia glasses and placed the coat under the light to admire it. Satisfied, she said: "Your sister has a fair complexion, so this rust-red will look just right on her. It'll make her look even prettier."

His sister was pretty, looking at the photo there on the wall, taken on the boat when she went to Qingdao to spend the summer holiday last year. The sea breeze had ruffled her hair, and she was smiling straight at the lens. The school badge on her breast showed up as clearly as if it was the main focus of the camera.

The neighbours had said his sister's sitting the college entrance exam was like sitting for the Imperial Examination, which was not in the least untrue. He remembered how at the time she would only drink soup, refusing to eat anything, saying that drinking soup saved time as you didn't have to chew. This way of sitting a college entrance exam frightened Liu Guoliang, as it was sheer hardship. But his sister merely said it was called "redesigning herself". As her level of study increased, her speech became more and more incomprehensible. Now his sister didn't seem to want to talk to him at all any more, whereas before she had always treated him as a guardian.

And it was probably just because of this "redesigning herself" that her clothing and daily requirements were growing all the time. For her to go to university, their mother had pooled money right, left and centre to buy his sister a new set of bedclothes, but after two weeks she had brought back the red phoenix and rising sun design sheet, insisting on exchanging it for a plain white one. Their mother thought white sheets ugly—like ones they used in hospitals, and showed the dirt too—but his sister wouldn't hear of it, so mother made Liu Guoliang go to the store there and then to buy a white sheet to take to his sister. When Liu Guoliang got to his sister's dormitory, he saw

that of the six beds in the room not one had a patterned sheet
and that one was even covered with an embroidered bedspread.
There was a small embellishment on the wall beside each bunk;
on some it was a guitar, on some it was a tennis racket, and over
one bed four golden-haired foreign dolls hung in a row, said to
belong to the daughter of a famous actress. In the midst of all
this was his sister's bed, and although everything was brand
new, the bright red and green quilt and pillow cover did generally make it stand out.

"Those five are all from cadres', doctors' or actors' families..." his sister said to him, pointing enviously to each clean,
individualized bed.

Liu Guoliang understood his sister's words. He felt no resentment towards her. He also felt sorry for their mother. Oh dear,
if he were her elder brother and she his younger sister it would
be all right. He could go out to work and get even more clothes
for her, as he was the only male in the family.

Deep in the night, a new crescent moon hung way up in the
sky above the town, casting its clear, soft, light on the lattice
windows of the low houses on the poor street and also shedding
it gently on the white gauze windows of the English- and Span-
ish-style apartment buildings. After all, nature is impartial!

4

Wen Xixiu had a presentiment that whenever the classroom door
was surrounded by people, it meant something had occurred in
class.

This lesson happened to be her English lesson. Today was really her most tiring day: she left home at six-thirty in the morning to be on time for the early study period at seven-fifteen, fol-

lowed immediately by the early-morning exercises and then two lessons. She hadn't sat down to rest for a moment. Now when she saw in the distance the classroom doorway surrounded by people, she couldn't stop her heart from starting to thump.

Sure enough, the cheekily grinning boys by the door said to her, "Teacher, our classroom's turned into a ladies' toilet, so we won't go in." Wen Xixiu raised her eyes and looked and almost fainted. The sign saying "Class Three (4)" which used to be in the classroom doorway had been exchanged with the women's toilet sign opposite by some bright spark.

"What a low trick!" Wen Xixiu's face was white with anger. "Whoever took it down can put it back again. I don't have any appetite for taking lessons in a toilet!" However, the moment the words were out of her mouth she regretted them. The troublemaker certainly wouldn't come out obediently in front of everyone and own up, nor would these pupils take her sonorous but ineffectual reproof to heart. She'd fluffed it, and she had left herself no way out.

"What's this? No one's going to own up?" Making an effort to keep her dignity she repeated her sentence. Even she could perceive how feeble and incompetent were her words. At this moment, she really wished that a... if only one of those princes that could surmount all difficulties in fairy tales would come to her aid! She had already noticed the sly grin that meant "let's see how you cope" on the faces of He Fugui and the others. What was she to do?

"All of you go in the classroom."

It was Zhang Xianglin's quiet, stern voice. The group of grinning boys immediately sobered up and silently went into the classroom. Zhang Xianglin dragged over a desk, but before he could climb on to it He Fugui forestalled him, climbed up and took down the ladies' toilet sign, and then pulled the desk over to the doorway of the women's toilet opposite, at which point he turned his head and gazed at the classroom full of seated pupils and hesitated, and then Chen Genmei suddenly stood up, climbed onto the desk and took down the sign saying "Class Three (4)".

"After school, everybody stay behind in the classroom," Zhang Xianglin said syllable by syllable, so that you could tell he was not losing his temper but was extremely angry. Losing your temper is another thing from getting angry, and normally anger is more effective at making your opponent feel remorse—if the incident was provoked by your opponent. Instantaneously silence reigned in the classroom.

On this occasion he had helped Wen Xixiu out of an extremely difficult situation. A prince couldn't have done any better! Wen Xixiu turned her head back gratefully to look at him, not expecting to see his face livid with anger. It was as if she could feel the heart inside his solid body quivering faintly! She hadn't expected him to be so easily upset.

Because of the unusual occurrence, the lesson went extraordinarily smoothly. These perpetually incomprehensible school children!

After the lesson, Wen Xixiu hurried to Zhang Xianglin's office. "We have to think of a way to find out who thought up this rotten idea," she said.

"The problem's not to lay our finger on the culprit—after all we're not the Public Security Bureau—but to teach them how base and low this disgusting action is. How could they have thought of it!" He rapped the table in distress.

After school, the whole class obediently remained in the class-room to await their dressing down.

As their regular form teacher, Wen Xixiu began the lecture, starting with the "Five Stresses and the Four Beauties"* and go-ing on to Spiritual Civilization, with the students behaving themselves and listening. It was so quiet you could have heard a pin drop. But it was clear to Wen Xixiu that she herself had still failed, because there was Zhang Xianglin at the side "keeping the field down", thus echoing the idiom that "the fox borrows the tiger's terror".

"I'd like to tell you all my story..." Zhang Xianglin sat in a small corner of the first row of desks with his hands entwined, seeming to have forgotten that they were being kept in for a dressing down, and began to chat to them...

That was really a poor street too, although it was only sepa-rated from the big building in front by a courtyard. A long row of coal stoves stood like a line of soldiers in the very narrow pas-sageway outside the room doors, and the choking smell from the coal bricks could not be prevented from permeating the rooms through the cracks made by the doors which didn't fit, and as soon as he got inside he was obliged to take off his shoes and get on to the bed, because there honestly wasn't any space left over which could accommodate him. Therefore, all day long he was put out to pasture in the spacious courtyard below as if he were a sheep being put out to grass, and the ample outdoor activity had

---

* Stress on decorum, manners, hygiene, discipline and morals, and beautification of the mind, language, behaviour and environment.

made him strong and sturdy as a young ox.

There was only one table at home, used both for eating and as the place where mother chopped the vegetables and meat, as well as for keeping the bottles of oil and the salt pot on and being the only table for him to do his lessons at, so it was hard to prevent his exercise book from getting grubby with grease stains, in addition to which one time he had forgotten to put it away and his little brother had added beards to the two Young Pioneers on the cover. Hence one day the teacher had taken out his book and shown it to everyone: "Look, what a mess!"

His classmates roared with laughter. They laughed so much he couldn't lift his head up.

"He lives in the back building: of course it's dirty. Little northerner!"

A spoilt girl seated in front of him curled her lips contemptuously at him, mocking him. In fact not long before, a pretty lace blouse of hers had had ink spilled on it in several places by Zhang Xianglin as a prank.

Like an angry young lion, not even caring that he was in class, Zhang Xianglin leapt out from his desk and grabbed the girl: "You're clean: I'll make you clean." As he spoke he desperately hauled her off towards the waste paper basket behind the door. His classmates began to cry out in alarm, and even the teacher couldn't stop him.

That evening, the girl's mother brought her over to their home to complain. Her eyes on the girl's wrist, which was bruised black and blue, his mother apologized profusely to them over and over again.

Having complained for half the evening, the girl's mother still didn't seem to want to go, as if she wanted to wait and see

Zhang Xianglin get a good hiding.

"You should tell her off for shouting abuse at people too. If she calls me a little northerner from the back building again I'll hit her again." Zhang Xianglin did not give in.

"You do come from north of the river, don't you? Did she call you the wrong name?" The girl's mother was still aggressive.

Zhang Xianglin's mother had no need to bow down to her "betters" any more. After all they were now in the new society, and it was no longer like the past when she had been a meek and subservient maid.

"What's wrong with folk from north of the river? Aren't folk from north of the river people then?" his mother said indignantly.

"What's wrong with folk from north of the river? Just ask your son. Can he compare with my daughter in anything? Language? Arithmetic? Or nature, or geography? He only knows how to fight, swear, run wild... He's had no upbringing!" These few words of the small girl's mother's were like a sharp knife cruelly thrust into young Xianglin's heart.

As soon as the girl and her mother left, his mother picked up the fire-tongs they used to light the stove and beat him relentlessly. "You little bastard, showing me up! You little brat, bringing shame on me!"

His lower leg was mottled black and blue from the beating with the fire-tongs, but he gritted his teeth and did not cry out once, because he felt he deserved to be beaten, since he really had let his mother down. His mother grew weary of hitting him and laid the tongs aside. When she noticed that her son's body was covered in bruises and became aware of what she was doing, she hugged him and started to sob brokenheartedly.

"Don't cry, mamma. I'll bring you credit in the future," he said softly, bending over to his mother's ear and gently wiping away her tears with his fingers. His mother's tears grew more copious.

After that, he changed. When he did his homework he always first spread an old piece of newspaper out on the table to prevent the grease from dirtying his book. He never went to the courtyard to play any more and started to work hard. Because his parents were uneducated, it took him a long time. His father disliked him working so late at his lessons every day, as it used up the electric light, so he took a small wooden stool and read by the light of the street lamp.

He set the spoiled girl's marks as a target and caught up mark by mark.

At last came a day, like the launching of a manmade satellite, when the teacher held up a neat, clean exam paper with full marks in front of the whole class. "Look, the only one with full marks in the whole class. Guess who it is? Zhang Xianglin!"

For a moment the eyes of the whole class swept over him, including those of that girl classmate. He felt good and pleased with himself and stuck his chest out a few degrees higher than usual.

"Ma, I was the only one in the whole class who got full marks. I came top of the class. That girl can't give herself airs any more." When he got back he stuffed the exam paper happily under his mother's nose.

As she proudly admired this piece of paper, of which she couldn't read a word, his mother heard him mocking that girl and rapped him lightly over the head: "Don't laugh at people. Everyone messes things up!"

From then on he found that excellent marks won him prestige more easily than fists or his voice. When he graduated from primary school his marks were the most outstanding in the whole class. He passed the exam to get into a key middle school, whereas that girl didn't get in because she was three points short. She had wept with bitter disappointment. He had felt bad, as if he had usurped her place. In '65 he was accepted by the Chinese department of the prestigious Fudan University! This shook the whole of the back building and his pals lifted him up high and let off firecrackers, so that the inhabitants of the front building all pushed open their windows and peered into the courtyard, which was just what they hoped: look then, we've turned out a university student here too. Although all these lads were themselves factory apprentices, the way they were sincerely happy for him and congratulating him did not have the slightest jealousy or sourness to it. Well, that was the nature of people like them from northern Jiangsu; boorish sometimes to the extent of seeming to be unreasonable, but this was the inevitable result of a long sojourn at the bottom, and their nature was really as pure as a crystal!

Although his father, as before, still went to pedal the three-wheel delivery cart each day, and his mother still went and washed clothes for people in turn, the look the neighbours from the front building gave them when they met was now another story! "Hey, Mother Zhang, your son's really got somewhere!" "Sister Zhang, you're so farsighted!" Thus the old couple both now felt they could hold their heads up high.

"...So that was how I went to register at university with my things in a simple bundle tucked under my arm. I felt simply drowned by a kind of intoxicating happiness: This was my sunrise, the new starting point of my life. I really wanted to raise my arm and shout: live for ever!"

Wen Xixiu, sitting in an empty seat in the back row, was utterly and absolutely entranced by his story. This was the first time she had looked at him closely face on, as before she had never dared to look straight into his eyes. His eyes held a compelling, luminous light, which now appeared to be that fierce fighting spirit and self-confident nature. He couldn't bear other people to look down on him! That type of temperament was fierce like that and irrepressible, just as the radiation from light and heat was fierce and could not be deflected. No wonder the few times when she had mentioned the children of this poor street disdainfully he had been sarcastic and derided her like that!

"... When I went to register at university, I wrote the words 'Yancheng, Jiangsu' in very large letters in the column headed place of origin. Although I'd never been there once, that barren land raised my parents, my grandparents, my ancestors... Although some people in this society look down on our native land, I wanted to do credit to our ancestors and seal the lips of that vulgar group of people, but we ourselves... must also do our best to put right the moral darkness, backwardness and ignorance left us by history, because times have changed!"

He Fugui twisted his body awkwardly in his seat, as if someone had touched a sore spot. Strange: normally he didn't let people make him unhappy, but this time, noiselessly tracing the grooves in the desk with a finger nail, he felt extremely ill at ease.

"Teacher, when your marks were lowest, how many subjects did you fail?" someone timidly ventured. As soon as he had finished speaking, everyone present laughed out loud, and the atmosphere began to get more lively.

"Me? When they were lowest, I didn't pass either Chinese or arithmetic. There was one time in the third year when I even forgot an exam as I was playing football, and when I reached the school, my back bare and dripping with sweat, everyone had finished. So that year I got two duck's eggs* in Chinese and arithmetic!"

"But you caught up again?"

"I did!"

"Teacher's brought credit to us folk from northern Jiangsu."
Liu Guoliang was the first to start clapping.

"No, we shouldn't make divisions between races," Zhang Xianglin said jocularly, "only, we must all move up, and then move up again. We are just about to have a lesson on Liang Qichao's *On the Youth of China*, and we can't just blunder along aimlessly. We can't...! We only live in this world once, so we should live as though we're really alive..."

The more he talked the more serious he got. His deep, unfathomable eyes rested on the pupils' faces in turn as if wanting them to reply one by one, and he even made no exception of Wen Xixiu, resting his eyes on her face too. Wen Xixiu hastily dropped her eyes. From the changing of the signs, she had thought only of catching the troublemaker, which more precisely speaking was no more than giving vent to her anger. But this was what real education was all about—this was education through and through. It was true: why was it so necessary to know who did it? As long as the culprit was stirred by this

---

* Duck's egg: a failing grade, from the resemblance of a "zero" to an egg.

speech...

Wen Xixiu sat in the empty seat in the last row listening spell-bound with her chin cupped in her hand. She had not in the least expected that he came from a poor street too. No wonder he had said he grew up behind the big wall!

She was not at all unfamiliar with boys who messed around all day in the alleys like sheep put out to pasture. When she was small she had been most afraid of the boys that lived in the back alley garages, who were also tanned all over, looking with their eyes wide open for ways to pick quarrels with the timid girls from the front alley all day long, deliberately kicking their miniature footballs in their direction and creasing over with laughter if they left a big mark on their clothes... so it turned out that he used to be like that too... She could almost picture how he had dragged that poor little girl off towards the rubbish pile: she laughed!

He laughed too: confident, pleased, the dimple on his chin making a deep hollow; this was the smile of a winner! He had escaped! He was a man, and men had to do as he had done. She discovered she now had a completely new understanding of him, and she was very surprised, even a little panicky!

"Wait a minute." Before Zhang Xianglin could dismiss the class, Wen Xixiu stood up. "In the English class, I humiliated He Fugui, which...was hateful, low, and...snobbish, just like the girl's mother Teacher Zhang just told us about!" Right, hadn't she always despised snobbery above all else? When had she herself also become tainted by this snobbish attitude? That's how people are: extremely sensitive to other people's faults, but completely unaware of their own. "If there's anything you don't understand, please feel free to come and find me. I'll be in the office. We can start from the phonetic alphabet..."

She spoke more and more softly, her manner becoming increasingly diffident and awkward, not at all like a form teacher but like a pupil owning up in front of the teacher. The strange thing was, the whole class sat in solemn silence, not one person laughed, and He Fugui's face had flushed red.

Zhang Xianglin felt very surprised. He had not anticipated that the normally timid Wen Xixiu who liked to beat about the bush could be as candid as this. Looking at her approvingly he began to clap, and the pupils joined in too. The clapping grew louder and louder, but Wen Xixiu only became shier.

When they had finished, it was already half past five, and it would be half past six before she got home. The workload here was too much; if you wanted to deal with a class matter, you were obliged to carry on until this hour. On the other hand, Wen Xixiu felt very much at ease, particularly as when He Fugui passed by her he had tugged awkwardly at the brim of his cap, and said in pidgin English: "Good—bye, tea—cher."

Really, why was it so necessary to catch the offender, as long as everything could be satisfactorily settled?

"You're really straightforward and honest with people, Xiao Wen," Zhang Xianglin said with emotion. "I'm not nearly so bold as to dare to admit my mistakes in front of the students. I've got too much pride!"

"But what happened in the English class was my fault," she said earnestly, staring with large, limpid eyes.

"Like crystal!" murmured Zhang Xianglin faintly.

He had discovered that she really did ressemble his wife when he had been passionately in love with her, only Wen Xixiu had a bit more gumption than she had.

She didn't know why he had to praise her like this for such a small thing: "You're trying to urge me not to feel dejected by this affair with that rotten sign, aren't you? Let me tell you, I forgot about it ages ago!" With that, she gave him an innocent look, then turned around and flew gracefully down the stair-case.

A few lines of poetry suddenly formed themselves in Zhang Xianglin's heart: "... Placing both my hands on your head, I wish that you will always be as pure and as lovely..."

He couldn't help turning his head, and caught another glimpse of her figure. "Looking at women again. But beautiful women are really worth looking at!" he said to himself, as if trying to find an excuse.

5

Downstairs in Professor Gao's guest room were seated Professor Gao and his wife, Wen Xixiu and her mother, as well as a tall and slim young man wearing gold-rimmed spectacles.

"This student is really one of the best I've had in the past few years. He's due to graduate this summer, and I'm planning on keeping him on as my assistant." Professor Gao's tone was full of appreciation as he introduced the shy young man, at the same time winking at him continually as a hint that he should open his mouth and say a few words. Hence the young man, blushing, opened his mouth:

"Wen... Teacher Wen, which school do you teach at? Oh, such a long way away! Do you find the students there rather hard to teach?"

Obviously, this was a matchmaking session. Because they were unfamiliar with each other the atmosphere seemed a little oppressive and dull, and awkward silences where none knew what to say kept occurring.

"Do you still remember Doctor Qiu who used to be at Tongren Hospital? That's his grandfather. Remember that time when Doctor Qiu was constantly at your house treating your father?"

As matchmaker, the professor's wife was trying to dig up old friendships and connections in order to make the scene more friendly.

"Oh, so you're Doctor Qiu's grandson! Doctor Qiu is a really first-rate lung specialist! Well then, we're old family friends." Wen Xixiu's mother was delighted by the discovery of this new connection and already seemed to be completely satisfied with this hardworking research student who had already made great achievements.

Wen Xixiu sat in silence on the sofa, not from shyness but from sheer embarrassment... Could love really come about like this?

The young man was giving an account of his family circumstances to her mother as if reciting a curriculum vitae, and the preoccupied Wen Xixiu only disjointedly heard him say... three people in his family, live on the third floor, the first and second floors being still occupied by other people... From the way he talked, with "my mother says..." at every breath, he seemed like Wen Xixiu to have to endure a warning lecture from his mother every time he went out the door, as well as being a great big child who lost confidence when away from his mother, although he was four years her senior!

The more the older generation on both sides talked, the more congenial it seemed to get, but the two young people just got more and more embarrassed. Wen Xixiu couldn't sit there any longer, so she got up and took her leave.

At the end of the passage her mother couldn't restrain herself any longer and asked: "How about it? I think he's pretty suitable, very decent and hard working too. The conditions at his home seem to be on a par with our family as well, and we're old family friends..."

"Money again, conditions again, it's so vulgar." Wen Xixiu stopped her mother short, sick to death of it all.

"Little devil, only you're so high and mighty." Her mother was a little angry now. "You've got everything all set up, so naturally you don't have to bother about money. Marry you off into that poor street of yours, and every morning you'd have to get up and scrub the chamber pot and carry water. I wouldn't be surprised if you cried all day long. Let's see you get high andmighty again!"

"We just see each other once, and we hardly even say anything, and you want to fix it up. Not me..."

"Don't be an idiot. Your mother's not an old feudalist. If he seems suitable, you may as well see him for a while. I've already invited him home for a meal the day after tomorrow. Stop pouting. Have I ever interfered with your ordinary male friends? But when you're thinking about a marriage partner you have to be a bit more cautious, a bit more thorough. You even have to consider vulgar matters, to put it more plainly."

"All right, then!" Wen Xixiu had always been her mother's obedient daughter; she felt the young research student wasn't bad either, and she had no particular reason to refuse to have anything to do with him. After all, she was no longer a child, and although she had a number of friends of the opposite sex, at heart she knew that if you were choosing a husband you had to

consider the other person's academic background and family circumstances, and on these two points today's young man was
highly suitable. She knew also that in today's society there was
an excess of girls, and it wasn't terribly easy to come across an
ideal partner who was basically suited to her. She ought to asso-
ciate with him, let them get to know each other, then following
the natural course of things she would move into that spacious,
comfortable room in his house, and she wouldn't have to worry
about anything or exert herself over anything, nor would she
lack any kind of comfort, just like when she lived with her
mother! Wasn't this how it was with her elder sister and elder
brother? Of course, their family wouldn't have a huge wedding
reception or a great big dowry show, remembering that her sister-in-law's dowry had come specially in the evening for fear
that other people would see and think it too ostentatious. But
the outcome, wasn't the outcome all the same—merely having a
family? Hadn't she already decided that if it was only for that,
then she'd rather stay single!

She had read lots of love stories, and she realized that life and
novels were two completely different things, but she still
thought: wait, hang on a bit! Since she knew there was such a
poor street, and such a man, who had been through so much and
escaped from the poor street, and who in addition wanted to
pull those children who were still there out by hook or by
crook... Why had he wanted to separate from his wife? Was it
due to lack of understanding? No love? Or because of a misun-
derstanding? He... didn't he feel lonely? She found that her
thoughts had got carried away.

"When I get married later on, whatever happens I want to

marry into a better class district, into a rich family. Look how hard it is for my sister, having to worry about debts as soon as she gets married, so boring." By the light of the street lamp, Chen Genmei was expertly crocheting the handiwork in her hands.

"You can't talk like that. At any rate your sister had her moment. She went in a car. Isn't everything you do just for appearances anyway?" The other girl feigned worldliness: "As much as you whole-heartedly want to marry into the posh district, would people from the posh district want you to marry into their family? There are girls in the posh area too."

"I am going to marry into a good area," Genmei said determinedly, "and have a colour TV at home, and a fridge, and loads of beautiful clothes..." she put down the handiwork she was holding and enumerated in a trembling voice as if making a prayer and pleading with the gods, her manner completely serious.

"And you'll want air-conditioning, a car..." The girl-friend mocked her, but in the end she even let out a sigh herself: "We're both dreaming!"

"Hey, last time in the office I heard another teacher saying that 'Coquette's' house is just like that, posh as anything," Genmei said, as if recalling something.

"That's for sure. I've counted: from the beginning of the term up until now, she's worn twelve different shirts, five sweaters... and the style of her shirt collars are all different from ours."

"Go and borrow a pattern from her and we'll make one too. I want to make a shirt, but I can never find a good pattern," someone said seriously.

"Go yourself. You go and borrow one." The other simply refused.

Then Genmei asked with considerable interest: "What d'you say? If 'Coquette' was choosing a boyfriend, what kind would she pick?"

"She'd do her best to pick a good one of course!" The tone of the response was now a little sour. "She'd pick one of those with a great big foreign place, a colour TV and a washing machine..."

"If 'Coquette' set out her dowry it'd be bound to be as long as Nanjing Road.."

"Bound to!"

This was by the side of the "River Nile", which was the world of the poor street's middle school students.

These middle school students had reached the age where they should be having a social life of their own, but in their homes the size of a square of dried beancurd where there was no longer any room for their bodies that grew taller every day, how could there be any talk of providing them with a place to get together? Young workers with an income could go and sit in the cafés in the town centre or hang out in the cinema, but these middle school students with little money in their pockets could only meet in this place where it didn't cost any money. Although the smell wafting up from the river's surface was not particularly pleasant, and when autumn came around it was a little cool when the wind blew, this was their world.

Here you didn't hear the adults' curses, and you had no fear of some private discussion being interrupted by them. Also you could talk about some topic that you couldn't talk about openly at school to your heart's content, so it was pleasant enough. To tell the truth, despite the fact that these school children were still affectionately called "little devil" and "little rascal" by their elders at home, they were in fact growing up and becoming more mature hour by hour. If the girls' conversation had been overheard by their parents, it would have been surprising if they didn't get a good box round the ears.

"Seriously speaking, Genmei, I heard you've got a boyfriend now. Is it true?" One of her female companions surreptitiously gave Genmei a nudge with her elbow.

"Come on, out with it, who is it? That He Fugui from your class?" As she spoke she pouted her lips slightly in the direction of the crowd of boys.

"Oh, I'm not interested in those schoolboys." Genmei curled her lips contemptuously. "They've got no style at all, and they're stingy with their money. If I look for someone it'll be the sort with a job. They've got loads of style."

"Everyone says you're with He Fugui." Her girlfriend wouldn't let her off. "Otherwise, how come you were willing to help him take off that women's toilet sign?"

Genmei assumed a forthright manner. "What about it? Wouldn't he have felt awkward going over to the women's toilet in front of so many people? I was only giving him a hand."

"But really, when you fixed 'Coquette' that time, you did go over the top rather."

"Although, Teacher Zhang was right." Chen Genmei seemed not to want to pursue the subject further. "We shouldn't keep doing pointless things which make people laugh at us northern Jiangsu folk!"

"And your teacher didn't pursue the matter any more afterwards?"

"No."

"That's the ticket!" the girls said, their thumbs held up in approval.

In the ordinary course of events the topics of conversation among the boys were more extensive and profound than those of the girls.

"I recently got hold of a copy of *Anna Karenina*. It's good." Liu Guoliang patted the fat volume, showing off again.

"Oh, I saw it on TV. It's as boring as anything. That Anna's a fool. She's got such good conditions at home, her house is as big as anything, her husband knows what he's doing, and she has to go and kill herself. Honestly!" He Fugui took the book in Liu Guoliang's hands, and placed it underneath his own bottom.

"Don't keep talking rubbish, making us northern Jiangsu folk lose face. It's a world-famous book!"

"I don't care if it's famous or not. In any case if I get married, I won't pick a nut-case like that woman!"

"Thick-o! Don't you think about whether she'll want to marry you or not?" Liu Guoliang threw a fistful of sand at him to taunt him. "Just because you had the guts to take down a women's toilet sign?"

"All right, if she doesn't want to marry me she can marry you," He Fugui retorted sarcastically.

"Not necessarily. I'm going to learn from our Teacher Zhang and get into university later on, so maybe I'll get a decent wife." At first Liu Guoliang's tone had been one of jest, but by the end he was deadly serious.

"All right. I've never heard that Teacher Zhang was still a bachelor. I heard he's divorced."

"That's no matter," Liu Guoliang said. "I admire him. He reminds me a bit of the Japanese film actor Takakura Ken. Anyway, I'm not resigned to being stranded here all my life, beside this 'River Nile'...."

These words touched everyone's heart, so that for a moment no one made a sound, and there was only the lapping sound of the river water gently beating against the embankment and in the distance a steam whistle sounding on a boat once, then again.

"F..." He Fugui swore savagely. On the other hand, when they swore they really didn't mean what they said. Vulgar language had lost its original obscene meaning to them ages ago, and it represented nothing more than an emotion, an exclamation expressing feeling. "Who doesn't want to bring credit to their parents. But why do I have to be thick, thick! In the last English test it was another duck egg!"

"This time I got eighty-two, ten points more than last time." Liu Guoliang studied the stars in the canopy of the heavens. "Another ten points next time, ninety-two, then get into a key upper middle school, university. I...mean to do it!"

"You little b... you've really started indulging in wishful thinking." He Fugui regarded him enviously.

Someone pulled out some cigarettes. "Come on, come on, what's the point in just talking? Anyway no-one here's going to go shooting their mouth off sneaking, so take one each. Real men not smoking are worse-looking than girls with beards."

Liu Guoliang surreptitiously stole a glance over toward the nearby group of girls, then deliberately raising his voice, said: "Come on, give me one."

Although he had begun to smoke a long time ago, he actually

hadn't smoked much, and therefore after taking his first puff he was choked by the smoke. In fact he didn't really like the taste of that choking cigarette smoke, and he smoked only because of an unwritten rule: that smoking is a sign of maturity.

"Ho, it's pretty lively around here."

Without giving them a chance to think about throwing away the cigarettes they were holding, Teacher Zhang's large hand had already come to rest on He Fugui's shoulder. Teacher Zhang was wearing a sheep-skin jacket and looked even more casual and at ease than in the classroom.

"Give us a light." Teacher Zhang drew the cigarette from between He Fugui's fingers and lit his own, then passed the cigarette back to him, but He Fugui naturally wouldn't put out his hand and take it, so he threw the cigarette into the "River Nile". He then pulled out a few fruit sweets from his pocket and passed them out to the boys, who had quietly thrown their cigarettes away a long time ago. "Fruit sweets are more suitable for you," he said.

From the group of girls the sound of laughter erupted, as the boys unwrapped their sweets in embarrassment...

"Come over here, all the pupils in class Three (4). Come over here all together." With practice, Zhang Xianglin indicated that they should dress the ranks. "Next week the district's holding a public teaching session, and I'd like to try and give our class a chance..."

The students broke into a clamour of surprise and self-derision.

"Oh! Counting on us alone? Aren't you afraid we'll make an exhibition of ourselves for you?" said He Fugui, raising his head above the group of people.

"Who's responsible for that kind of hopeless talk? Who is it?" Zhang Xianglin said in a stern voice, a little angry. "Why do you look down on yourselves like that? Everyone stand to attention and listen. For this public teaching session we haven't any other objectives, and you don't all have to pretend to look like exceptional students. We'll have the lesson in the way we normally have it. Since other schools can have a turn, our Pure Light Middle School must naturally have a go too... Isn't that right?"

"Right!" the students replied mechanically, uncertainly.

Zhang Xianglin was not satisfied with this kind of reply.

"I mean, apart from swapping toilet signs and that kind of thing—forgive me for raking up your faults—can we or can we not do something serious to win other people's good opinion?"

The students scratched their heads in embarrassment.

"How about it? Can we or can't we?" Zhang Xianglin pressed them further.

"We can!"

This time the sound was loud enough.

"D'you know Liang Qichao? Let me tell you..."

Someone came and told Liu Guoliang to go home. It turned out his sister had returned.

"Sir, what's 'redesigning oneself'? Liu Guoliang's always going on about it lately," asked He Fugui.

Well... what the standardized explanation should be, Zhang Xianglin couldn't say for sure either. In fact everyone could put forward their own explanation of those two words.

"As I understand it, redesigning oneself means striving to make oneself perfect, enriched, complete..."

"Well, I reckon Liu Guoliang's sister's 'redesigning herself' is making her more and more hard to take. She doesn't even want to come home much any more," said He Fugui.

Zhang Xianglin rambled on: "It's true that redesigning one-self is the way to become a useful person, but it can't become a kind of gamble or stake! You, children of the back streets, the gunfire of the Communist Party made your elders stand up polit-ically, but to stand up spiritually and culturally, you've only got yourselves to rely on!"

He noticed that what he was saying was getting too profound, and that the students could only blink in bewilderment.

"For example," he lit a cigarette, and the blue smoke curling upward made him crinkle his eyes slightly. The effect was so full of poise that the boys nearly died of envy! "Starting from to-morrow, supposing you see... let's say Teacher Wen, coming past carrying something like the small blackboard for hanging charts on, d'you think you boys could consider going up to give her a hand? She would certainly be really pleased. That's the way life is, to redesign yourself you don't necessarily have to go to university. Some things that to us are just things as small as the effort involved in raising a hand can bring a lot of happiness and convenience to people, and it will leave a good impression of you on the other person... Life has many opportunities such as this. It's just that we often let them slip by!"

Drawing on his cigarette, Zhang Xianglin weighed his words carefully. In front of those pairs of devout and trusting eyes thirsting for knowledge Zhang Xianglin had a more and more prominent feeling that as an 'old' form master, his abilities were not equal to his ambition in his job. However, this should be considered a good thing, the very sign that each generation is better than the last!

The lights in the houses on the banks of the "River Nile" went out one by one; night had already fallen. It is in the constant alternation between day and night that children are quietly growing up and becoming adult, when young hearts are wide open to society and to life, and one would wish to sprinkle a little more sweet dew, a little less mud into their hearts!

6

Saturday afternoon was the most relaxing day for Wen Xixiu; however it was also the most stressful day, as recently a social benefit manual labour session had been added every Saturday afternoon, and this afternoon as luck would have it Zhang Xianglin was also going to the training college to prepare lessons in a group, so she would have to shoulder the burden of Grade Three (4) on her own.

For this session of manual labour, her class was allocated to a Chinese traditional medicine factory. As far as the pupils in this class were concerned, manual work was much more fun than sitting in a classroom, as when you were doing manual work you could move about, talk to each other and laugh, mess around and cause a rumpus. When they had their lessons as usual, some of them would think up all kinds of excuses such as head or stomach aches, and ask to be let off, but when it came to manual work even the most mischievous He Fugui wouldn't miss it for anything. Manual work was so enjoyable; in summer there were cold drinks, and in winter they could shower in the factory's washroom, so they certainly didn't want to let the opportunity slip by. But their form teacher Wen Xixiu earnestly wished the trouble makers would in fact absent themselves from the manual work. Just think, at normal times fifty school children shut in a classroom were like cats on hot bricks, so as soon as you let them loose on this two-storey factory it was like letting monkeys loose in Monkey King's domain on the Flower and Fruit Mountain. Busily dividing them into small groups on her own as well as rushing here, there and everywhere to "superintend" their labour discipline took over an hour, by which time her lips were dry and cracked from her exertions and her back ached.

There was a telephone call for her in the janitor's room, from that recent acquaintance, the graduate student. It looked as if their relationship had already reached the "second act", the first act being the introduction and getting to know each other, the second act dating, the third act marriage, and then the fourth act...and then the curtain falls! It really was a cushy and flat road, a road laid by her mother!

As expected, it was the graduate student asking her to go to the theatre. He also told her he was doing his best to get her a transfer to the city centre. Only, she must first write a report listing her problems. Getting a transfer for an "alternate scholar" who luxuriated in clover as he did was a very troublesome affair. Or maybe to serve women was a man's vocation then? I mean, even the princes in children's fairy stories, if they want to win a princess, have to surmount certain difficulties! So in that case no wonder that law-abiding graduate student also had to run around for her as much as he could!

"...You'd better make the problems fairly specific, no good just writing that it's a long way away," the graduate student warned her over the phone. "Make your argument pretty substantial."

Evidently sticky problems that were hard to solve could hasten one to maturity. The graduate student's voice now sounded much more cool-headed and experienced.

The sentence "make your argument fairly substantial" still had a kind of bookish ring to it though. If she had to give arguments, well, Wen Xixiu had plenty. Just look, through the window she saw a few of the boys laughing and joking as they stood on a three-wheeled cart. These kids, what would happen if they ran into someone or fell off and injured themselves? Also, every inch of the pharmaceutical factory was packed with crates of medicinal herbs. What if this gang of little devils were to hide in some corner to have a smoke and start a fire? What a nuisance... However, sticky, troublesome matters could make people mature. Moreover, the life here was novel, very different from what she was used to... Only it really was too exhausting, and—what displeased her most—she also had to wear a set of clothes she didn't like. Nice-looking clothes could only be worn inside one's outer garments. And now she wanted more and more to wear something a bit prettier. She fervently hoped that Zhang Xianglin could look once more at the slight flick-ups at the ends of her hair with his head on one side in the way that he had once done in the doorway of the corridor... She would so much like him to see how she looked on Sundays, at least not wearing this set of clothes she disliked.

She honestly both wanted to transfer and did not want to transfer. She was constantly running into this kind of situation where it was impossible to make a prompt decision. What should she do? If only she could ask her mother once more, but regrettably she was already past that age!

"Wham!" The three-wheeled cart crashed into the wall, and the mischief-makers on it were almost shaken off, scaring Wen

Xixiu into a cold sweat all over! In a hoarse voice she called out
to them loudly to go back to their own work positions.

"Have a little rest, Teacher." Even the old man in the
janitor's room seeing the hoarse-throated Wen Xixiu dripping
with sweat became a little soft-hearted. He pulled a chair across
for her. "Sit down for a while. How can you be a match for
those lively young monkeys all on your own?"

He had hardly finished speaking when an old worker came
over, all of a fluster.

"Oh, Teacher, I don't know which one it was, but one of the
pupils has drunk a bottle of syrup for making up tonic from our
storeroom!"

Wen Xixiu's head gave a buzz. So something had happened
after all. She had been prepared for them to come to blows,
prepared for them to recklessly ride the three-wheeled delivery
cart, and had even been prepared for them to cause a fire
through smoking. She just hadn't been ready for them to drink
syrup on the sly! You really couldn't guard against everything!

"I'll come immediately." Apologetically she gave the fuming
worker a flattering smile.

The old worker related it furiously to the other workers:
"Drunk just a few mouthfuls of acanthopanax syrup, and ruined
the entire bottle! This set of little devils . . . a few dozen yuan a
bottle too. It's going to have to be paid for!"

"This teacher's too soft. She can't stand up to them."

"The teachers in the last couple of classes were a different
kettle of fish. They only had to glare and the pupils didn't dare
move a muscle. . ."

The workers' sympathetic and well-meaning derision made
Wen Xixiu's face flush red and then white when she heard it. In

her mind she made a rapid calculation: there were six pupils allocated to the storeroom, two girls and four boys. Should she interrogate them all...? That wouldn't work. Supposing they didn't own up? Wasn't the "changing toilet signs affair" a good lesson? This set of pupils was smart. If there was no proof, they would never easily own up. What should she do? Unwittingly her eyes fell on the shiny jet-black telephone, and she dialled the number of the training college.

"Mm?" When a deep voice came from the receiver, she felt extremely tired, so tired that she could no longer stand up.

"Me, Wen Xixiu. Something's happened in the class. Come over quickly." She collapsed on to a chair.

"Don't worry, I'll leave now."

The other party hung up, but Wen Xixiu still clutched the receiver tightly. She fervently wished that Zhang Xianglin had told her at once over the phone how to deal with this bunch of greedy devils.

The six "suspects" assigned to the storeroom planted themselves like candles in front of Wen Xixiu's desk. No matter how Wen Xixiu went about admonishing them and "trying to get them to confess by explaining the Party's policy", they simply were not going to open their mouths.

The door was pushed open with a bang, and a worried-looking Zhang Xianglin entered.

"I just received a phone-call from the pharmaceutical factory—the workers have processed that bottle of syrup, and it contains an anti-cancer drug that's extremely poisonous. Those who drank it quickly come with me to the hospital for an enema and to get an antidote..."

Hardly had he finished speaking, and before Wen Xixiu could clear her head, Chen Genmei had already given a cry of "Oh Mother...I must... Let my Ma go with me!"

Almost simultaneously, He Fugui's face changed colour. "I ... drank some too!"

At this moment Zhang Xianglin waved his hand to dismiss the other four students, keeping the two of them behind. "OK. As for the antidote, you can pay ten yuan each. I asked at the factory. One bottle of syrup is twenty yuan."

Wen Xixiu was struck dumb. She felt surprise at Zhang Xianglin's remarkable ability in solving the problem, but his method of solving it made her furious; it was sheer trickery, sheer deception.

"Go back and be honest with your parents, and bring the reparation tomorrow. Is this medicine to be taken indiscriminately? If it really was a poisonous drug, then what would you do?"

Zhang Xianglin was in the process of reprimanding the two outrageous students, when he suddenly felt a raw, dissatisfied gaze settle on his back, a gaze that was cold in a way that froze right through to his heart. He turned his head to look. The eyes were Wen Xixiu's.

Wen Xixiu was leaning next to the door, scrutinizing him as if he were a stranger.

"What's wrong? Can it be the way I've handled it?" he asked himself quietly.

"How could you...!" Wen Xixiu's eyes were still staring at him, just as innocent and guiltless as his daughter's. Maybe she...was right?

First he sent He Fugui and Chen Genmei away, then turned

towards Wen Xixiu rubbing his hands together uneasily and said, "Just now I went to the factory to find out the situation. They were furious and demanded that the loss be made up. If we didn't catch them quickly it would have given a bad impression."

"Didn't you say that school isn't the Public Security Bureau...?" Wen Xixiu noticed that he needed a shave; the formerly clean-shaven chin was now covered with stubble, so that the elusive dimple was completely hidden.

"This kind of matter is external. It can't be compared to the matter last time of hanging up the women's toilet sign. That was an internal affair. External affairs have to be settled as soon as possible."

"But... isn't that tricking people?" Wen Xixiu never usually spoke loudly, but this time, because she was furious and indignant, she involuntarily raised her voice too, and her face was a vivid red. "A teacher yourself, yet you deceive people... make fun of people..."

"Did you drop down from the moon or just come back from abroad? Can you really not know that sometimes... we have to use our brains before we can accomplish something?"

"But how can we make the pupils believe what we say afterwards then?"

"That..." All at once he stopped short, and that inexplicable anger rose up. "What d'you want me to do? Anyway you can't have the nerve to say to the people from the factory, 'Sorry, I can't find out; I'll make up the loss!'"

"If there's honestly no other way, that's all you can do. They ought to know too that we teachers aren't supernatural beings either. Anyway, we shouldn't be unscrupulous!"

Zhang Xianglin lost patience: "You know, all you need is a

bright red scarf* fastened around your neck! If you're so clever, then don't go calling me up over the phone." He had hardly finished when he suddenly felt that the last sentence had been too sharp! But the words were already out. He merely saw Wen Xixiu give him a hurt look, push open the door and leave, her eyes brimming with tears. On the other side of the office door, He Fugui and Chen Genmei were still standing there, not having left.

"Teacher Wen!" Chen Genmei glanced nervously at their form teacher, who was in the process of wiping her tears.

"Don't tell the other pupils that I...cried." Wen Xixiu pulled out a handkerchief and wiped away her tears, then left hurriedly.

Chen Genmei and He Fugui looked at each other, speechless. They had never expected that Wen Xixiu would be candid like that, that she would ask that of them without covering up. Even less had they expected that the two form teachers would quarrel with each other on top of it all.

"Really it doesn't matter. Everyone cries sometimes," said He Fugui sympathetically in the direction of the receding figure of their teacher.

"What happened today was all started by you." Chen Genmei gave him a poisonous stare.

"It was you who said that plain hot water was too insipid and tasteless, that it would be good if we had a cup of malt extract and milk to put in..."

"Did I make you put syrup in? I didn't make you put syrup in either!" Chen Genmei yelled at him.

---

* As worn by young pioneers.

"All right, let's go!" With a heavy heart He Fugui looked at the tightly closed office door. "Otherwise Teacher Zhang's bound to come out too!"

Zhang Xianglin was smoking dispiritedly. He could not work out why his temper was as bad as that today either.

He suddenly thought of when his daughter had been two, and to test her affection for him he had done something as preposterous as playing a trick on her. He had said to his daughter, "Daddy's going to die!" Then he had lain down on the wooden floor without flinching a muscle, and his daughter had pulled him and pushed him in fright while he contained his laughter and didn't so much as utter a sound, and not until his daughter burst out crying had he suddenly leapt up from the floor. "Good girl, daddy was fooling you." His daughter had fixed her tearful eyes on him, regarding him both with joy and fury at once. Those eyes were so clear they were like crystals, and he had been deeply sorry: he should not have deceived a child's heart that was so very like crystal.

Yes, right from when Wen Xixiu had started to protest against his fooling the pupils he had felt himself to be wrong, and his anger was in fact directed against himself, honestly, just against himself. He hated the fact that on this point he was actually inferior to a youthful woman teacher who had not yet cast off the innocence of childhood!

In the evening it began to rain. With a raincoat wrapped around him Zhang Xianglin was walking along the extremely narrow street. The whole street was as still as could be, and there was only the sound of the rain splashing on the ground. It just happened to be the time of the broadcasting station's stereo programme, and from inside one low lattice window came wafting Schubert's *The Trout*.

In the clear, clear river water,

A little trout was swimming...

Because of the stillness of the night, the sound of the "Trout" song floated clearly on to the street:

...But the fisherman would not wait for long,

Wasting time.

So he made the river water turbid,

And fished the little trout out of the water.

Below Zhang Xianglin's thick, bushy eyebrows, his eyes began to grow coldly solemn.

Getting heavier every second, the raindrops beat on the eaves, beat on the window lattice. On the opposite side of the road the door of one solitary little house was opened, and a not very tall but sturdy figure came out.

"Teacher Zhang!" It turned out to be Liu Guoliang. "Whose house are you going to so late?"

"I...did something wrong. Now I'm on my way to find He Fugui and Chen Genmei to apologize." Zhang Xianglin drew in a deep breath.

"What was it?" The teacher's serious tone left Liu Guoliang dumbstruck.

...My heart full of stirring emotion,

I looked on as the trout was deceived...

The formerly bright, lively rhythm now became roused and angry, then changed into a variation. Zhang Xianglin broke into a remorseful smile.

"I tricked them...," he said, and then stretched out a hand

and clapped Liu Guoliang on the shoulder. "Where are you off to on such a rainy day?"

"I'm going to meet my sister. It's Saturday today, and she's gone to see a film. She's scared to come home alone in the evening and got me to go and meet her. She didn't even take an umbrella." Liu Guoliang gave a wave of a pale yellow nylon folding umbrella under his arm. He himself held an ancient, black cloth umbrella peppered with little holes.

"You make a good guardian! Your dad really can be easy in his grave." Zhang Xianglin looked approvingly at Liu Guoliang's face, which already had a considerable air of a mature man about it, and whose contours had already begun to coarsen. "How old will you be this year?"

"Sixteen." As he spoke he couldn't help straightening himself up a little.

"Teacher," he hesitated a moment, then immediately trusting, said, "My sister has a boyfriend!" Under the lamplight, the expression on his face seemed so gratified that it was a little coy. But there was really no call for him to be shy about it.

"Thank you for telling me."

"Thank you?" Liu Guoliang was very surprised.

"That means you trust me!" To tell the truth, the pupils' trust makes a teacher happier than anything.

"Ma and me are both really pleased. Sister's boyfriend's a first-rate student, in the same class as her. Dad had always hoped our family would produce a generation of intellectuals. That's who my sister went to the cinema with this evening."

"Then is there any need for you to go to the bus station to meet your sister? Or d'you want to play gooseberry?" Zhang Xianglin joked with him.

"They haven't known each other long... He's a professor's son, and she doesn't want him to know she lives here..."

He understood. A vague sense of anxiety constricted Zhang Xianglin's heart. And why? Maybe he understood this only too well! Hadn't his own marriage resulted in a tragedy? He had been too naive in the beginning. He had previously thought that that formidable "cultural revolution", almighty, had already closed up the gap between rich and poor, the chasm between the back building and the south building in front! His ex-wife had lived in the south building, only it had now been reduced to one room. His mother had continued to wash clothes for her family, not for money, just because she felt sorry for them. Faced with a basin of dirty washing, his mother-in-law, who couldn't even wash a handkerchief, was simply at her wits' end! Then they had fallen in love, and when her family was reinstated according to policy in '76 they had been married. He had gone to the south building as a live-in son-in-law. Not until he had been with her family from dawn till dusk did he come to feel that it seemed so out of tune, out of step; his parents-in-law didn't welcome visits from his companions of the back building, afraid that they would dirty their mosaic floor. When his wife's friends came for a visit, he could never get a word in edgeways. He didn't understand the makes of cassette-players and cameras, he couldn't play the piano or talk expertly about music... As far as his deprived childhood was concerned, these things were all very costly treats, and he had never had the experience... Consequently innumerable, subtle rifts had caused the bridge to collapse, and his marriage to her was finally destroyed. That chasm was not easy to close!

Far away in the distance, at the entrance to the alley, was the slim figure of a girl.

"Oh dear, my sister's here. It's my fault for talking so much I forgot the time." Liu Guoliang hastily went to meet her. Opening the beautiful pale yellow flowery umbrella with a "whoosh", he seemed to have raised a halo above his sister's head.

"You're so late coming!" His sister grumbled at him.

Although the night was black and heavy with rain, the shapes of the brother and sister were still sharply outlined due to the excessive contrast between the two umbrellas. This outstanding disharmony again evoked Zhang Xianglin's unaccountable anxiety and inquietude of a little while ago.

The paths of fighters are winding, and he hoped that on the day of their success they would not abandon that which was most lovable, just as he Zhang Xianglin, who reckoned himself completely mature and utterly capable, had today found through Wen Xixiu, whom he had all along looked on as a child, that he had abandoned something extremely precious; the sincerity that cannot tolerate the least falsehood!

"I bless you and hope that you will always be beautifully pure and gentle."

He said it to himself.

In the rain the air was really fresh and cool, really clean! He took a very deep breath and suddenly felt as if his heart had passed through a filter and grown peaceful and younger!

7

Because it was Sunday, Wen Xixiu took pains to dress herself up; the ends of her hair at the sides were flicked up again, and a pale mauve polo-neck sweater set off a woollen shirt with alternate grey and mauve checks. Wen Xixiu very much liked wearing skirts. Truthfully speaking, why was it absolutely necessary to wear those baggy, sack-like trousers to be compatible with the status of a teacher of the people? She loved wearing skirts, she thought skirts could best reveal a person's figure.

Beginning at some uncertain time the graduate student had punctually been coming to her room every Sunday afternoon to report. Between him and her the worry of accommodation and money that most young people getting married faced did not exist, therefore there was no need to make any effort, only to sit and chat leisurely, drinking cups of coffee, and then wait for the day...just as a train running along its rails stops station by station... Really, they lacked nothing at all; the only thing missing was...love.

Since they sat together, it was necessary to find a topic of conversation. So Wen Xixiu told him about the syrup incident, at the same time also telling him how surprised and let down she had been by Zhang Xianglin's way of handling the incident.

"Well I never!" Really, their profession were as different as chalk and cheese. The graduate student rubbed his hands together, his reaction exactly as if he had just heard a passage of comic talk by Yao Mushuang or Zhou Baichun. *

"...I've always admired him very much. I didn't expect that he could fool the students like that, too." Wen Xixiu lowered her voice to the level of a soliloquy, giving up the hope that she would receive the response "how can he fool the students like that?" from the graduate student.

"Well I never!" At a loss for what to say, the graduate student went on rubbing his hands together.

---

* Yao Mushuang and Zhou Baichun are famous Shanghai comedians.

"Carrying on like that, he'll lose the pupils' good impression of him. The pupils used to love him so much!"

Fully aware that her interlocutor would not understand her feelings, she still went on talking as if to herself. She had to talk about it.

"Aunty, there's a visitor," said her little niece mysteriously, pushing open the door. "It looks like a stranger. He hasn't been here before!"

"Hello!" Zhang Xianglin stood in the doorway. Maybe because he was coming on a visit, it looked as if he had smartened himself up: he'd had a haircut and a shave. A light cream-coloured sweater and a coffee-coloured corduroy jacket made him look casual and amiable, as well as...very handsome!

"What's up? Do I look all right?" Feeling that she was looking him up and down, he laughed with embarrassment. "You don't look bad yourself today. Hey, if we two form teachers went into class dressed like this tomorrow, what kind of reaction d'you say we'd get?"

With a chuckle Wen Xixiu started to laugh, and at once felt much more relaxed and at ease. "The students would certainly take up for a bride and groom!" Not until she had finished speaking did she realize that she had said something utterly foolish and disgraceful, and she immediately felt herself blush red.

"You have a lot of style, really!" he said sincerely, completely ignoring her *faux pas*.

"Do you really think so?" she raised her eyes and asked him excitedly, an innocent, happy expression on her face, which again made him recall those clear eyes of his daughter's. To deceive other people in front of her was a sheer blasphemy of purity!

"Believe me, from now on I will never again tell falsehoods in order to deceive other people." At this point he noticed that Wen Xixiu had lowered her head and was laughing with embarrassment. When he saw her laughing, he was very happy. This signified that the ill feeling between them had already disappeared. Even he himself did not understand why he was so afraid of a lack of understanding existing between himself and her.

Wen Xixiu sat genteelly on a dressing table stool. He really could not imagine that this was the person who yesterday had yelled at him like an angry little cat: "How could you...?" Just as every kind of life has its own flavour, so was this elegantly furnished room permeated with a flavour he had once been wholly familiar with; the kind of subtle, honeyed flavour that was both pervasively warm and comfortable. He too had once sat quietly thus to one side, appreciating his wife's not over-brilliant skill on the piano, only no matter how much effort he made, he simply had not been able to adapt himself to this rhythm of life...

"In the 'purifying the class ranks movement', my big brother and a very good girlfriend of his were deceived by people in exactly the same way. The workers' propaganda team said to my big brother, 'She exposed you a long time ago,' and my big brother thought it was true and all at once 'confessed' everything, almost ruining his girlfriend... How can people deceive others like that? As soon as you said that yesterday I thought of the 'cultural revolution'. Now there are people telling lies all over the place and trying to put one over, I can't bear it. But you... Playing a trick on those innocent children, it wasn't like you!"

Zhang Xianglin smoked in silence. Through the spiralling smoke Wen Xixiu's face had a perplexed look of beauty. This girl made him feel both familiar and unfamiliar. What was familiar was that she had many points in common with his ex-wife which that kind of girl who lived a life of ease always had, such as a soft gentleness, quietness, kindness, the inability to tell a single lie all her life, and a lack of the audacity to look society's cold and harsh realities in the face... But she was also very different from her, in that underneath her meek exterior there was an unflagging spirit.

Wen Xixiu suddenly remembered that she ought to introduce the graduate student to him, but she discovered that the graduate student had at some point or another left. She was very sorry.

"Can... you play something for me?" Zhang Xianglin indicated the piano.

"What d'you want to listen to?" Wen Xixiu opened the music. "D'you want to hear *The Maiden's Prayer*?"

"Can you play Schubert's *The Trout*?" Hence the strains of a lively, sprightly melody began to sound:

In the clear, clear river water,
A little trout is swimming...
As long as the river is clear as clear.
It's no good thinking you'll catch him, fisherman...

Inside was the sweet-sounding, moving music; outside were the clumps of trees entangled in a green light: everything was so tranquil, glorious and rich.

How long it was since Zhang Xianglin had so quietly and peacefully spent a Sunday! Who said he could not adapt to this rhythm of life? Everyone should lead a better life. People need plenty of room to move about, a good education, as well as music... The tragedy of his life did not lie in the fact that he could not follow a comfortable rhythm of life, but in that between them there had been a lack of understanding!

"I heard... you're thinking of getting a transfer?" asked Zhang Xianglin at the end of one song, his eyes fixed on his cigarette end.

"It... has been in my mind. It's too far to travel, and besides.... I haven't the ability. I'm of too feeble a disposition. I can't cope with them!" she said haltingly, dropping her head awkwardly as if she had done something she shouldn't.

"Could you not be so hasty... about going, maybe? There are lots of teachers in the town centre. It wouldn't make much odds if you made one more or one less, but on this poor street of ours we're too short of teachers. Indeed the pupils really need you. Yesterday evening I went to Chen Genmei's house, and d'you know what a few of the girls were doing? They were making clothes, and the shirt style was one that you had worn. They were embarrassed to ask you if they could borrow it, so they drew a pattern of your collar and sleeves from memory..."

"Oh!" Wen Xixiu was both shy and surprised, as those were merely a couple of shirts that couldn't be more ordinary.

"I've always thought that a teacher's work is not only on the blackboard, but also in your shirts, your coats, right down to your hair. Through your own persona, you present to the students a really good and fine world! So you see, yesterday, what a bastard of a thing I did." He discovered that he had been a little coarse and inclined his head, embarrassed. "On this poor street, if even we want to avoid them, who else is there worthy

for them to imitate, to worship? In my childhood, it was my
teacher who was the first hero I looked up to! Because I lived on
a poor street too! My teacher was the first cultured person I
came into contact with." He took a stride towards Wen Xixiu,
and stretched out his hand sincerely. "What you possess is precisely what I've already lost; and what I have just happens to be
what you lack, so we can work very well together! Help me!"

In the twenty-three dream-like years of Wen Xixiu's experience, this was the first time someone had sincerely said to her
like that, "Help me!" Moreover this was a tall, strong man who
was older than her and who had a more profound experience
than she did. Not until this moment did she really feel that she
was no longer a child who needed her mother's constant advice
on everything, but a teacher. She was very grateful to Zhang
Xianglin for making her come to sense this!

Sundays for the pupils of Pure Light Street just meant lolling
about on the edge of the "River Nile" the whole day.

Chen Genmei had dressed herself up very finely: the so-called
"dressing-up" was just releasing her plait and letting her hair
hang loose over her shoulders, after which she had put on that
newly-sewn shirt and grabbed a handful of melon seeds, which
she cracked as she went along until she reached the bank of the
"River Nile". After her sister's wedding the excitement at home
had soon died down, and the limelight of going in the car and
accompanying the bride under the watching eyes of the crowd
was also now in the past, so that all of a sudden life had become
desolate, really boring. On top of that, yesterday the "syrup"
incident had occurred. At first she had been really scared, but
then they had been kidded by Teacher Zhang, and the anger she

had felt... Of course, the teacher had already paid a call and apologized, so her anger was appeased. But to have to pay out ten yuan as compensation made her really simmer with rage. She decided to go and ask He Fugui and see what he had done about it, see if he was really going to cough up the ten yuan compensation.

As she passed the gaping front door of Liu Guoliang's house, he was engrossed in reading aloud the text of *On the Youth of China*, which Teacher Zhang had asked everyone to prepare in advance for the public teaching session. He did indeed take the teacher's words to heart!

"You're so studious, I'm sure you'll get into university later on," she mocked Liu Guoliang. Here everyone was a close neighbour, so between the girls and boys there was no strict division like in other schools.

"It was Teacher Zhang who assigned it. When the time comes we simply can't make an exhibition of Teacher Zhang. He's so good to us! Yesterday he came to call on you so late too. Said it was to apologize."

Chen Genmei didn't want him to bring up that unfortunate "syrup" incident again, so she picked up a piece of cloth that was to hand and began to unravel it expertly, deliberately dropping the subject. "Everyone's saying your sister has a new boyfriend. Lives in the posh area, right? Everyone's saying your sister's got lots of ability; first she goes to university, then she finds a posh boyfriend, and then she'll fly out of this poor nest of ours with a 'whoosh'...."

"Stop prattling on foolishly. The thing's only just got off the ground!" said Liu Guoliang guardedly.

"So people are also saying that Liu Guoliang's going all out to go to university! That he must be wanting to fly away too!"

"Get lost!" Liu Guoliang was angry now and drove Genmei out.

He sat down again at the table, when an earsplitting laugh outside penetrated the room. Today was Sunday, and those of the neighbours that went to work were all at home and were playing cards outside. One of them had already clipped three clothes pegs to one ear. *

To tell the truth, Liu Guoliang had got his heart set on going to university, but his thoughts hadn't got as carried away as Genmei had said, and he wanted merely to live like Teacher Zhang.

He Fugui had again set out his carpentry work by the side of the "River Nile".

"Hey, what are you knocking up now?" Chen Genmei asked him.

"A dowry for you." He Fugui waved the plane he held at her.

"Get lost." Chen Genmei scattered a handful of melon seed shells in his direction. Because they had not had much in the way of discipline or upbringing, the girls here were mostly rude and skittish. "What are you making?"

"A chalk box for 'Coquette', with this bit of broken wood. Look, it's got two levels. The top's for putting chalk in, and in the bottom there's a little drawer for the blackborad rubber. Haven't you seen? She uses a metal cigarette box to put the chalk in. She doesn't smoke, so where'd she get the cigarette box?"

"Don't be an idiot. She doesn't smoke, but can't a person's boyfriend smoke?" Chen Genmei assumed the air of an expert.

---

* The loser of a game get a clothes peg clipped to his ear.

"It doesn't show, as 'Coquette's' normally got such a spoiled look, but yesterday when she started arguing with Teacher Zhang, she was really competent. You wouldn't think she'd stick her neck out for us."

By now, the "Coquette" that they uttered with every breath had in fact already become a term of affection, although even they themselves hadn't realized this yet.

"Hey, have we really got to pay that ten yuan compensation?" asked Chen Genmei exploratively.

"Aren't you prepared to pay it yet? Have you got the nerve? 'Coquette' argued with Old Zhang on our behalf, and Old Zhang braved the rain to come and apologize to us... If you don't acknowledge it now you can't be human."

"True. I'm stuck on those two form teachers of ours, even though they're not fierce."

To make someone afraid is very easy, but to make someone trust and love you with esteem however is very difficult!

"Genmei, come over here!"

Someone called her from a long way away. It was a young apprentice who had just taken over his father's job at a factory. He took out a pair of pretty hairgrips and flaunted them before Chen Genmei. "Look, Hongkong goods. I got someone to buy them in Shenzhen."

Chen Genmei's eyes lit up as she went to grab the pair of hairgrips.

"But I can't give them to you for nothing. Come with me to the cinema tonight."

"Then.... you have to give me the hairgrips first."

"Okay, take them then. Remember, the film's at 7:30 in the evening!"

Chen Genmei took the hairgrips, grinned from ear to ear and ran off home as quick as lightning. In the few hours that were left of this Sunday she now had something to do—she could admire the hairgrips over and over again in front of the mirror.

The next day was Monday, and Wen Xixiu was again desperately combing the ends of her hair at the side of her face with the steel wire comb, but this time the perm had really taken, so that whatever she did the hair at the side of her face just would not permit itself to be tamed. She couldn't help but look at her image in the mirror and suddenly thought—wasn't this in pretty good taste too? Hadn't Zhang Xianglin just been saying that a teacher's job wasn't merely on the blackboard, but also in shirts, coats, hair... She really ought to teach this group of schoolgirls how to dress. Look at Chen Genmei, quite a pretty, charming face yet with the eyebrows plucked so narrow, and a sapphire blue shirt collar outside a bright red sweater. She really ought to teach them. She remembered a jacket-style coat just made last week—that would be really suitable for these schoolgirls to wear. So she took the jacket out of the wardrobe and put it into her shoulder bag, intending to lend it to them the next day to copy, so as to avoid interfering with their concentration during the lesson.

Her mother entered softly. She began to inquire about how things were progressing between her and the graduate student.

Very evenly, very smoothly, very easily... she didn't even know how she should reply. In any case she could expect that in the event that she did spend her life with him, it would feel just like when she had played "families" as a child, with everything there already. However, she was already past the age of playing "families".

"That one who came today, he's that form teacher of yours, isn't he?" Her mother looked at her anxiously. "Beware of him! Divorced men are worst of all!"

Wen Xixiu perplexedly gave her mother a sidelong glance, her heart filled with a curious emotion which she could not positively identify as either alarm or uneasiness.

"He's really great, Ma. He's the only one who talks to me on an equal basis and in an equal manner, and he begged me to help him too. He makes me feel that I'm not a giggling young girl any more!"

The mother saw for the first time that the look in her daughter's eyes and her facial expression both betrayed a feeling of self-confidence. Without saying anything further she withdrew softly. Being a cultured person herself, her mother knew when it was time to speak and when it was time to let her daughter think for herself. Her daughter was grown up and could not get through every juncture in life clutching mamma's apron strings!

Wen Xixiu admired herself in the mirror. At last she had let him see her looking her best, and she was very happy. She switched on the cassette player as she went, and a vibrant and unaffected female voice rang out:

Ah...
You're twenty-seven, I'm only thirteen,
I'm too young to love you,
But...
Wait for me.
I will grow up!

It was a popular American tune that had just come out, and

she softly hummed along, turning the cassette over time and time again and humming along over and over again...

8

Just as if a bomb had been dropped on Pure Light Street, in the Pure Light Middle School, Liu Guoliang's elder sister had attempted suicide! She had taken an overdose of sleeping pills, but luckily the students in her dormitory had discovered her early and she had been brought back to life.

"But why did she do it? She's got really good looks, and she got into university too. Although her boyfriend didn't want her any more it's not worth killing yourself for!" asked Wen Xixiu of Zhang Xianglin on the way back from their trip to the hospital to make inquiries.

Despite much thought she remained puzzled over this problem. Suicide seemed so absurd, so much out of keeping with the new trends of the eighties. To be sure there were many deficiences, but life, life was so glorious!

"Precisely because she's pretty and got into university she projected for herself a bridge leading to happiness, but the bridge had no piers, hence it collapsed... I'm now a little worried about Liu Guoliang—he can't project for himself the same kind of single-plank bridge with no supports too..."

"That girl's too vain," said Wen Xixiu.

"Don't blame her too much. How can she compare with you? You have no lack of either talent or substance, but only of...a knight in shining armour. Sorry for being so blunt! That little narrow street won't give those girls who were born on the poor street very much, therefore those so-called 'grabbers' who are often condemned by society are in fact all born and bred in the poor streets; they receive little, so they demand more! So you see, life is sometimes cruel like that, and it seems as if even highmindedness has to be bought with money! For them, of course they can only stake all their future hopes and happiness on that unknown husband..."

While he was talking they had already reached the school gateway. The main building of the school was as black as a cavern, the time to stop work having past long ago. Zhang Xianglin suggested that she go up to his dormitory for a while and have a bite to eat and then go to see Liu Guoliang, as although he had always considered himself to be the patron saint of his family, he was after all only a sixteen-year-old child!

This was the first time Wen Xixiu had been in a man's room, and she was rather embarrassed. The tiny room was very neat and tidy, and on the writing desk beside the window stood a photograph of a sweet, chubby little girl.

"What a pretty little girl!"

"My daughter."

"Abroad?"

"She left with her mother."

"Don't you miss her?"

"Yes!"

"Then, you miss her mother?" she asked gently, affecting to be casual but feeling her voice tremble.

"Sometimes I miss her too." He fiddled with a fountain pen in his hand so that he could conceal the look of desolation in his eyes.

To tell the truth, he really did sometimes miss his ex-wife. Before, when he was able to see her, he felt as if he had no sense of regret towards her, but now when he was sure that he might never see her again in his life, he did actually miss her sometimes—he only missed her charms. That's just how unpredictable people are!

"But why... did you split up?" To pry into other people's secrets is nothing but an extremely unrefined kind of curiosity, but for some unknown reason Wen Xixiu desperately wanted to know... She played casually with the frame of his daughter's photo, deliberately demonstrating that she was merely actuated by curiosity.

"There are many factors there. Perhaps, to some extent, for the same reason as Liu Guoliang's sister's tragic love affair—a chasm, the chasm that exists between poor streets and rich streets!"

"But this is the new society, after Liberation!" she cried out rebelliously.

"But China's history goes back five thousand years, and New China has only been established thirty-five years."

"You mean that there's no way to close this chasm in our generation?" asked Wen Xixiu almost despairingly.

"Why can't it be filled and evened out? It depends on us—you and me—on the hands, spirits as well as love of everyone living in the poor streets and the rich streets...."

Wen Xixiu's eyes lit up, then she dropped her head and carefully studied the photograph of his daughter, trying her hardest to figure out from it what her mother had looked like. A long time passed before she said, "Then... did you love each other?"

"Well... I ought to say that we did love each other, only at that time neither of us understood love. My loving her, in the end, boils down to loving myself. A kind of vanity, a kind of intense manifestation of self. I was very vain when I was young.

Once I felt my name was too vulgar and I wanted to go and change it in secret."

"In the event why didn't you change it?" She actually did feel his name was a little vulgar, and inappropriate to the exactitude of his demeanour.

"My mother wouldn't let me. When she heard I wanted to change my name she gave me a good hiding."

"How old were you then?"

"Already at university."

To think of him being such a grown-up son and still being beaten she tittered with laughter. He however didn't laugh but strolled over to the window. His dormitory was on the fourth floor, and it was the highest building in the vicinity; beneath the window the roofs of the squat houses stretched row upon row, and the lights of the boats on the "River Nile" twinkled in response to the starry bright night sky. Although it was a crowded and inadequate world, it still did its best to breed life, to emit the intense joy of living. The people here still lived with a staunch optimism. People, when you leave here, you must not forget it!

Abruptly he turned round: "Has what I've been saying bored you?" He himself did not know why he had to tell her so much. He had always detested people asking about his broken marriage, and he didn't want his suffering to serve as the subject matter of people's after-dinner chats. "That's precisely my temperament, just paying attention to what I'm saying myself. Maybe you didn't want to listen, you're too young!"

"No, wait for me! I will grow up!" she said hurriedly.

He stared at her in amazement, and she shyly lowered her head. Both of them felt uneasy and awkward about what they had each said and what they each felt.

Zhang Xianglin felt it was necessary to close this extremely taboo topic of conversation, because she was too young, too simple, too guileless, too incapable of pretence, so that although it was a long time since he had had this kind of conversation which was able to console him he had to stop it—he could not ignore the more than ten years chasm between their respective ages!

"Tomorrow you must go and seek out Chen Genmei. I heard she's got a boyfriend. This kind of matter is more appropriately settled by you women teachers than by me..."

This put Wen Xixiu in a very awkward situation. In handling that kind of... "love" between adolescent boys and girls her experience was limited. Even she wanted to find someone for advice.

"I'm... afraid I can't." A red flush suffused her neck. "How...should I go about it?"

"It's just like at first when you were frightened of doing home visits. Once you've battled your way through the first time it will be all right," he said.

Wen Xixiu began to wonder how in the first place she had dared so unhesitatingly to write in the wish to go to the Teacher Training College. You had to have such a lot of guts to be a teacher! To be a teacher on a poor street you had to have even more guts.

Winding poor street, for ever wet and overcast. At only just after seven there was already not a sound to be heard on the street. There was only the sound of the alternate rise and fall of Zhang Xianglin's and Wen Xixiu's steps. Two long and slender shadows fell on the road surface paved with broken stones.

"Your hairstyle looks really nice. You ought to get up on to the platform wearing what you had on that day at home," he said.

"How could I?" She laughed.

"Why not? People all like to look at beautiful images. I'll write a report to the head and suggest we run a 'beauty course', specially aimed at the girls, teach them how to match tones, select clothing material and styles suited to their own personalities, how to be a real...woman! One of the principal lecturers should be you."

"Oh, no, I can't." Wen Xixiu waved her hand several times.

"You can. You should make them enjoy life's happiness a little more too!" he said sincerely. "Okay?"

"Mm." She nodded. She decided to change the baggy, sack-like trousers the following day.

Wen Xixiu inserted her hands into the pockets of her coat and touched a small piece of paper. She recalled that it was the phone number of the comrade in charge of personnel in the Education Bureau in some district or other. The graduate student had discreetly handed it to her and she had stuffed it automatically into her pocket....

"We'll go to Liu Guoliang's house first, then to Chen Genmei's...." said Zhang Xianglin. "It's not too late is it? You'll be too late going home."

"It doesn't matter," she said, at the same time crumpling the piece of paper into a ball inside her pocket—there were too many things that needed doing here. If she wanted to grow up, then she'd have to manage a few more things!

She carefully rounded the small puddles full of bumps and hollows, her steps quick and hurried. The dim light of a lamp clear-

ly outlined her attractive, natural figure. No, she was completely dissimilar to that former wife of his made of sweet dough.

"The poor street will make her mature very quickly." Zhang
Xianglin gazed at her beautiful profile approvingly.

What a good-for-nothing, staring at her again. But, to say the
same thing over again, a beautiful flower and a lovable little an-
imal can both make people stop and linger, let alone a beautiful
spirit of the universe—a human being!

Translated by Frances McDonald

Hong Taitai

EVERYBODY called her Hong Taitai. * Fifty years ago that name was celebrated throughout Shanghai society. A party marking a baby's first month of life, a wedding banquet or a birthday all fell short of perfection if Hong Taitai was not in attendance. There was a period after 1949 when the words "Hong Taitai" seemed redolent of mothballs, as if they had been shaken from a camphorwood chest. But within the circle of the few rich families in Shanghai, for example, they still carried a good deal of weight right up until the "great proletarian cultural revolution" of the 1960s. In Shanghai, one had one's own little circle of happiness. And no matter how the storms raged outside, as long as one had three meals a day and stuck to one's own affairs, and thanks to the government policy of buying out the bourgeoisie, one could rest assured of eating at the Park Hotel today, the "Maison Rouge" or Jade Buddha Temple tomorrow. No one would interfere. It was a very active period for Hong Taitai.

---

* Taitai is the traditional term for Mrs or wife, which fell into disuse after 1949 as being considered a very bourgeois title and was severely discouraged during the "cultural revolution." The Chinese term is retained here, rather than replaced with the English "Mrs" to call attention to this connotation, which the term "Mrs" lacks.

The managers of both the public and private sections of the big restaurants and hotels all knew her; she was a very warm person. If Hong Taitai came forward to do the honours for a banquet on some special occasion, it would be reasonably priced but ample. And the food would be something special, quite out of the ordinary.

My first impression of her dates from my tenth birthday.

I was the ninth child in the family, nicknamed "Jiujiu", or "Little Ninth". My parents were in America. When they left they had been afraid that I was too small to make such a long trip and would be in the way. Then the situation had changed, unexpectedly and so greatly, and I was left behind in Shanghai for good to live with my eldest brother and his wife. My brother was 21 years older than I and often joked that he could have fathered a child my age. He did spoil me as if I were his own daughter. Fatherliness in an eldest brother has always been the Chinese way.

The day of my tenth birthday they did things up a bit on my account, though it was nothing more than noodles and a few dishes. In those days my brother and sister-in-law were rather careful of appearances. They couldn't have competed with Hong Taitai at any rate; she was the wife of a bourgeois. Brother and his wife, no matter what, were subject to their work units, and they had to be careful. So they did no more than invite the brothers and sisters still in Shanghai over for an ordinary family dinner.

We had just sat down—we hadn't even got around to pouring the wine—when there was a knock at the door, and a voice, vivacious and sweet, was heard, "I've come to beg a bowl of birthday noodles."

"It's Hong Taitai!" My sister-in-law gasped, startled, and pushing back her chair she fled into her room to change her dress.

"That's how thoughtful she is." My brother hastened to open the door; sisters and sisters-in-law busied themselves getting an extra bowl and chopsticks, bustling and rushing about. Thinking back on it now, this Hong Taitai's entrance into my life was strangely like that of the domineering Wang Xifeng in *A Dream of Red Mansions*, who always announced her arrival on the scene with some arresting remark like: "So sorry I'm late welcoming visitors from afar!" The exact words were different, but the effect was the same. Her voice was so confident and hearty; she had an air of being completely at home.

"Hong Taitai!" The family stood to greet her.

"Ah, I made it on time," Hong Taitai said, removing her white kid gloves. She wore a square of checked wool on her head, the ends so long they fluttered with her every movement, adding immensely to her charm. When she took off her full-length cashmere coat, she was wearing a claret-coloured *qipao* * underneath, a phoenix embroidered in gold thread down the front, dazzling in its brilliance. In the 1950s such elegance had become a rare sight for anyone, let alone a child such as myself who had as yet seen nothing of the world. This sudden manifestation of such a gorgeously-dressed beauty took my breath away.

She sat down next to me and pressed a red envelope into my hand. There was a shining golden character glued to the envelope—longevity—but because it was in the traditional, complicated form, it took me a moment to recognize it. At that time

---

* Traditional high-necked, close-fitting Chinese dress.

such red envelopes, used for giving presents of money to children on special occasions, were no longer on sale. Hong Taitai said she had glued it together herself of red paper; the character was also her own handiwork.

"Hong Taitai, really, you shouldn't put yourself out of pocket over Jiujiu's birthday. She's a child." My sister-in-law had changed and come back out, and though she was much younger than Hong Taitai, she looked faded beside her. The only thing one noticed in that whole room was that brilliant combination of red and gold: dazzling, but pleasingly so!

"Mr Hong and I are old friends of your parents. I went to see Jiujiu at the hospital the day she was born. She was so alert and bright-eyed, such personality, not like most babies. When the nurse brought you in you were as pink as a glutinous rice dumpling." She described it vividly, and I was enthralled.

"At first your parents planned to come for you after a while, but now look... They must miss you terribly. I pity you that your mother isn't here. So though I pay no attention when one of your brothers or sisters has a birthday, Jiujiu is different; I have to come to celebrate your tenth birthday, to stand in for your mother and raise a glass to you, wishing you long life!" Her words warmed my heart.

After the meal, my brothers and sisters put on some music, *A Rose for You*, a Xinjiang folk song quite popular at the time, and the brothers and brothers-in-law all surged toward Hong Taitai. But she frowned, and with a graceful flick of the hand in which she held a cigarette, said, "Put on Bing Crosby. We old folks like the old songs." When that bewitching voice was heard, she laid aside her cigarette and began, tripping lightly, to dance. As she danced, the side slits in that claret *qipao* rose

and fell, now hiding, now revealing her graceful legs. I really
hoped I might grow up a bit faster and be all that she was: full
of life, charming, beautiful.

When all the guests had gone, I took out the red envelope she
had given me and counted: forty yuan! Forty yuan in those
days!

"A grand gesture. Mr Hong is the only one who could afford
her," Sister-in-law said, pouting her lower lip. "What a memory
she has. How could she remember Jiujiu's birthday, let alone
that it was her tenth!"*

"That's her stock-in-trade." Having said that, Brother added
sympathetically, "Her lot is a hard one, too. If she'd been born
into a good family and got an education, she'd certainly have
done well, an intelligent person like that."

Only later did I find out that Mr Hong was in the raw silk
business and when Mrs Hong took up with him, he was already
quite successful. He had a wife and family, but he rented a small
house in the western district of Shanghai and lived there with
Hong Taitai. She it was he took everywhere with him, thus in
everybody's mind, she was "Hong Taitai". But there was talk,
both out in the open and on the sly, some of it not very compli-
mentary. As for the true facts of Hong Taitai's background, no
one was able to find out. Even the Hong's housemaid, Aju,
knew only that one night, carrying a white leather bag, she had
arrived with Mr Hong and had been there ever since. It was said
that Hong Taitai was a good cook, and Mr Hong had grown
pink and stout under her care. Almost overnight she became

---

* According to Chinese custom, birthdays marking a full decade are the most important.

well known; Mei Lanfang* and Zhou Xuan** both were guests in the Hong family parlour. For a time, the house was filled with important guests every day. It seemed that this Hong Taitai had "arrived" in society the same way—a white leather bag in hand. And with her arrival, Mr Hong's business expanded.

My second meeting with Hong Taitai occurred while I was in senior middle school, at Mr Hong's memorial service. Elder Brother was the natural representative of our family and took me along on the strength of my having been the recipient of Mr Hong's forty-yuan birthday gift. The service was held at the International Funeral Home. There were leading comrades from both the Chinese People's Political Consultative Conference and the Association of Industry and Commerce present. As we entered, I saw Hong Taitai dressed in a black taffeta *qipao* with close-fitting sleeves, wearing a pair of the black leather pointed-toe shoes that were extremely popular in the sixties. Though there were indications that she was putting on weight, her graceful waist made her appear as lovely as ever. She walked composedly among those who had come to pay their condolences, greeting those who ought to be greeted, nodding to those who needed nodding to. The grief weighing on her made her seem even more dignified and noble. On the hairnet holding the thick tresses was a spray of pure white orchids, giving her a very refined air. As soon as her glance fell on us, she hurried to greet us.

"Jiujiu, you've become a young lady." Her gentle voice dispelled the dread I felt in this venue of eternal parting. "You're

* A Beijing opera star.
** A popular film star.

the next generation. Wear a yellow flower." * Her soft white hand fastened the yellow bloom to my blouse. She began to speak of all Mr Hong's good qualities, and as she spoke she grew sad and dabbed at the tears in the corners of her eyes with a linen handkerchief. By comparison with the main wife, weeping and wailing to one side, she appeared to be more highly bred, more worthy of the title Mrs. Yet in the end it was mere similitude, for when the formalities began, she conscientiously peeled off to one side, a mourner who knew her place.

"Hong Taitai will suffer now! This is really difficult for her!" The other mourners commented surreptitiously among themselves.

"Yes, Mr Hong was a man among men. But was he willing to entrust the family property to Hong Taitai? Naturally, it was safer with his wife. With him gone, Hong Taitai is left with nothing, not even a last word. It's hard for her."

Hearing such talk, looking at the lovely black-garbed Hong Taitai, I thought of Chen Bailu in Cao Yu's play *Sunrise*.

Once Mr Hong died, we saw little of Hong Taitai. In the adults' eyes, she was, after all, a woman of uncertain past!

In a twinkling, I was twenty years old. The celebration was still a family affair. Recalling the gaiety of ten years ago, I couldn't help thinking of Hong Taitai. I accused Elder Brother of being a snob, but he said I was naive. As we locked horns, there was a soft knocking at the door. It was Hong Taitai's maid, Aju, a woman about thirty years old from Shaoxing. She was carrying a red-lacquered tray, which held a specially prepared duck. Attached to the duck was a glittering gold *shou*

---

* Flowers, real or artificial, are worn as symbols of mourning.

character—longevity—exactly like the one I had received ten years before.

"Hong Taitai's indisposed, so she sent me to convey her best wishes to Jiujiu. She prepared the duck herself," Aju rattled off as instructed. One could see she had learned it off by heart before she came. Everyone asked after Hong Taitai, and Aju stammered, "The house has been let out. Hong Taitai has a second-floor room with a balcony and a room on the first floor for me and the kitchen. It's enough for the two of us; it's fine, just fine. Goodbye now." With that she made her escape.

Everybody began to inspect the duck. It lacked nothing in appearance, fragrance or flavour. It was then the three hard years of natural calamities. A duck such as this one would cost at least ten yuan on the black market. At the same time that we were saying what a crime it was to eat Hong Taitai's food, we were all scrutinizing the duck. It was lean. It was quite possible that it was one Aju had stood in line all night to buy, in which case it wouldn't have cost much more than two yuan. Since it had been personally cooked and sent over specially, it seemed to be worth much more than that. But the gift was small after all, so she didn't appear in person. "She's a very capable woman!" everyone agreed.

Not long after, the tempest* blew up in 1966, and people could hardly fend for themselves, much less worry about Hong Taitai.

Two years passed, and things became relatively quiet. I happened to be walking by Hong Taitai's one day, and looking up at her balcony without thinking, I suddenly discovered the old fa-

---

* The "cultural revolution".

miliar curtain fabric. Spurred by this, I headed upstairs. A young man wearing a work overall with "work safely" printed on it barred my way and asked in a rough manner, "Who are you? Who are you looking for?" "I'm looking for Hong Taitai," I stammered out. I regretted that as soon as it was out. To call someone "taitai" in those days was to invite criticism.

Unexpectedly, he sang out, "Hong Taitai, someone to see you," and led me upstairs.

"Jiujiu!" Hong Taitai welcomed me with surprise and pleasure and wiped away tears, moved. How rare in those days, a genuine sigh and embrace. I leaned against her bosom and cried.

The room was still furnished with French-style furniture. The mirror was covered with pictures of leaders, the best method of protecting mirrors in those days. Aju brought tea, and I had just said, "Thank you, Aju," when Hong Taitai corrected me softly, "Call her Sister Aju. I've adopted her." That guy on the stairs was Aju's husband.

Hong Taitai was wearing a blue Chinese-style cotton jacket. With her hair cut short, in revolutionary fashion, she looked much like someone who would be principal of an elementary school.

"Thanks to their moving in with me, no one dares bother me. The house was ransacked till there was not even one yuan left and I was half-dead myself. As I was crying over it, Aju came and said we should bring her man to live with us; he was a worker and no one would dare bully me then. I said I didn't want to involve them in my troubles, but she said, 'Anyway I'm a servant. Even if worst came to worst I'd still be a servant. I'm not afraid.' I'm so grateful to Aju and her family!"

"Hong taitai," Sister Aju cut her short, embarrassed.

"I've told you before, don't call me Hong Taitai. Call me mother."

"Ah," Aju laughed ingenuously. "I can't do it. I'm not used to it."

"I get only 18 yuan a month for living expenses, so I have to depend on the two of them to take care of me, and they have two children of their own." Hong Taitai sighed deeply. "Ai, how could I have come to this! If I had only gone out to work earlier on, I wouldn't have got into this predicament, no income at all!"

Hong Taitai kept me on to dinner. She hadn't been able to break that habit. With Aju, her husband and their two lovely, innocent daughters, plus Hong Taitai and myself, there were six gathered round the square table. It was a home-style meal of two dishes and a soup with an additional plate of scrambled eggs in my honour. The bluish glow of the eight-watt fluorescent tube shone gently on us. Hong Taitai now and again put some food into the children's bowls with her chopsticks, very grandmotherly. I thought I heard them call her "Nanna", and I found it very strange. "They mean mother's mother," Hong Taitai explained. "I like them to call me that." The children, seeing their opportunity, purposely raised a chorus of "Nanna", and Hong Taitai beamed. I sensed that she had never before laughed so contentedly. Her son-in-law stolidly scooped in his food without saying a word. But when I was taking my leave he dashed ahead turning on the stairway lights all the way down. "My son-in-law hasn't any education; he's a bit rough, but he's a very good man," Hong Taitai told me softly. "There's no need to be afraid of him."

When I got back and told my brother and sister-in-law what

had happened, they expressed great admiration for Hong Taitai. "That Hong Taitai, she can take the bad with the good. What an incredibly capable woman!"

Later I got married. Tied down to housework and child, I hardly made the effort to see my brother and sister-in-law, let alone Hong Taitai.

In 1982, my parents made their first visit back to Shanghai from the US. All the old friends gathered, and of course Hong Taitai was invited as well. During the "cultural revolution" many of them had lost touch with each other, and they were glad to renew relationships, but though it grew quite late, Hong Taitai still didn't appear.

"Where's Hong Taitai? We're waiting for her reappearance in society."

"Ah, didn't you know, she's a famous slowpoke."

Just as we were really growing anxious, she arrived, accompanied by Aju. She was wearing a downy mohair coat over a close-fitting black satin jacket, and though her hair was raven black, you could tell it had been dyed. Yes, she had aged some, but she was as graceful and refined as ever. The company rose to greet her, but she pushed Aju forward, "My adopted daughter."

When it came time to eat, no place had been set for Aju.

"Aju, go out and have a bowl of noodles and come back for Hong Taitai in two hours," we suggested.

"Just squeeze together a bit," said Hong Taitai, pulling Aju to the table and asked the waiter to bring another bowl and chopsticks. The others were rather startled; the atmosphere grew somewhat embarrassed. Though society as a whole had changed, such circles still clung to iron-clad rules. Before all the hot dishes had been served, Hong Taitai got up to leave, saying she had something to do.

The gathering fell to discussing her.

"How could she take a servant into the family? She must be crazy!"

"Well, it's not so surprising. Her own background is more or less the same."

"That's what happens when one lives with servants. You become petty and overlook etiquette."

These dreadful comments, served up with the food and drink, dropped airily from their mouths. I hastily gathered up my child and left.

A few days ago, a woman friend of mine moved by chance to a place in Hong Taitai's lane, and I dropped by to see her, since I was in the neighbourhood.

She welcomed me happily, "Jiujiu's come!" Her silver hair made her look kinder than ever. She said she no longer dyed it. "I'm getting old, and it doesn't turn out well anymore," she said, patting her hair. Sister Aju politely brought tea and sweets for me.

"Jiujiu thinks of me. Of the old crowd, you're the only one who thinks of coming to see me. How big is your son now?"

"Ten." As I said it, I remembered my own tenth birthday and told her how struck I had been by her beauty.

She smiled wanly. "That's past."

She told me that in the beginning a few old friends still came to see her. Now everything was back to normal after the "cultural revolution". There were even mahjongg parties and dancing, but she was done with it all, because her stiff old legs couldn't manage it now.

"Actually it's all a waste of money and time. Aju is so busy. I can't do much to help her, but I can knit a few sweaters, to thank her for being so good to me. They're extremely frugal themselves, but they know my delicate appetite, and there's always one dish especially for me at each meal. There aren't many daughters—even natural-born ones—like that." She touched my sleeve, speaking emotionally, while her hands never ceased their work on the small sweater she was knitting.

"Mother Hong, what are you making?" A passing neighbour stopped in.

"My granddaughter's having her baby any day now. I'm knitting it a little sweater."

"Well! The fourth generation! You're very lucky, Mother Hong!"

"Yes, I am," Hong Taitai replied contentedly, and she smiled.

Translated by Janice Wickeri

Gong Chun's Teapot

OLD folk in Shanghai used to say, "It's better to marry a maid-servant from a big house than the daughter of a small family." Why? Because a maidservant in a big house was bound to have manners and would know how to please. Certainly, any man who married one could expect to be well looked after; and then, there were her savings to consider, and the handsome dowry her mistress would in all likelihood contribute—in keeping with the extravagant habits of the rich. There were, in short, powerful reasons for a fortune hunter to keep his eye on such young ladies.

Xiuzhen came from the countryside of Zhejiang and had grown up in a family that bred silkworms for a living. Though the region as a whole was considered wealthy, families in the countryside were poor, and the killing of baby girls—considered an unnecessary burden—was common. Indeed, since Xiuzhen had an elder brother, she herself had very nearly been killed at birth, and it was only the intervention of her grandmother, who had argued that "we might as well keep her as she can help in the kitchen and take care of her brothers," that had prevented her being drowned in the water-hole. Throughout her life, whenever she made a mess, Xiuzhen was rebuked with the words, "You good-for-nothing! We should have killed you then and there!"

After Xiuzhen had come three younger brothers and two sisters. The two girls were promptly killed in the water-hole, which made Xiuzhen value her life even more. She was careful never to slack in her chores: cooking, looking after her brothers, feeding the silkworms, or clearing up after them.

Almost every household in the area made their living breeding silkworms, and at an early age Xiuzhen was taught by her mother and grandmother to fluff floss. Her grandmother, when in a good mood, used to say, "If you can sew and fluff floss you will always be able to make money if you need to, even after you get married. People say 'what one's parents make is good, what one's husband makes is better, but what one makes oneself is best of all.'" But whenever she spoke of marriage she looked sad, a fact which left Xiuzhen with the lasting impression that marriage meant suffering, and she became inexplicably anxious any time anyone discussed it.

The combination of fear and a lack of self-confidence made Xiuzhen quite ugly: her hair was yellow and straggling; her heavily-lidded eyes set unaturally far apart. But her teeth were straight and white.

In spite of the day-to-day hardships suffered by the family, life dragged on. One baby was born after another, and occasionally a glimmer of hope illuminated their otherwise drab existence.

One of the families in the village had made quite a lot of money from breeding silkworms and had established a silk flossing business in town. They flourished and eventually expanded their business to Shanghai.

Another family had saved every penny they could in order to pay for their son to be educated in Hangzhou. By an amazing stroke of good fortune, the son met a foreign missionary who paid for his schooling and even paid for him to continue his studies abroad. Now the son was a boss in Nanjing and had built a house for his parents back in the countryside.

Was having daughters pointless? It was hard to say. One little girl, regularly beaten by her stepmother, used to always be heard crying in the middle of the night. Her shrieks were loud enough to bring the house down and made the hair on the back of people's necks stand on end, which only inflamed the stepmother further. After a while the crying could no longer be heard and it was said that the girl was sold in Suzhou. Several years later a rich-looking lady, attended by a bevy of servants, came to the village dressed in an expensive fur coat that even the proprietress of the silk factory wouldn't have been able to afford. She stopped in front of the stepmother's house, and after presenting her with a handful of silver dollars and several yards of foreign-made fabric, she said, with the utmost display of courtesy, "I'm grateful to you for having sent me out to see the world." Nobody knew if she was being sarcastic or sincere. In any event, the stepmother died several days later—of rage, according to local gossip. Not long afterwards, the lady took all her brothers and sisters away from the countryside.

Too many stories and too many hopes. However, whatever their dreams, the villagers maintained that money should be made morally.

Once, the silk store at the end of the street where Xiuzhen often went window-shopping, was levelled to the ground in a fire. Yet for some strange reason the grocery store and tea-house on

either side of it remained intact. People said that the owner of
the silk store was not from the area, that his native village had
been hit by a flood, that he had made a hair-raising escape on a
door-plank, and that he had then seen a dead woman floating in
the river gripping a jewelry box. The man had pulled the corpse
out and wrenched the box from her grip. This, they declared,
was filthy money, and held that even if he didn't believe in retribution he should at least have given the corpse a decent burial. But he had merely kicked the body back into the river. Sub-
sequently he had used the money to open a silk store, and now it
had been raised to the ground.

If fortune was destined to knock at your door—or so the country people believed—you couldn't shut it out even if you wanted
to, and if it didn't come knocking, no amount of begging would
induce it. Born up by this philosophy the local people nevertheless hoped for miracles.

One day a stranger, somewhere in her mid-twenties, paid a
visit to Xiuzhen's neighbour. She was dressed in a pale serge
linen blouse, a full-length black silk skirt, dark stockings made
from foreign material and a pair of black canvass shoes. If it
hadn't been for the pair of darting eyes which flashed out from
beneath her fringe and her animated voice, she might well have
passed for a local student.

Her name was Sister Hu and she was rumoured to work in
Shanghai. In any event her white, delicate hands showed that
she was not a labourer.

"The house in which I work is extremely large," she said, ad-
dressing the group assembled in the neighbour's house. "The
cook just does the cooking; the cleaner only cleans and the
babysitter just takes care of the baby. I myself work for the mis-

tress, looking after her wardrobe and keeping her company."

"How fascinating!" thought Xiuzhen. She had always had to hold her little brother in one arm while simultaneously feeding the stove and the silkworms with the other.

"My mistress has asked me to find a servant-girl," continued Sister Hu, "of about the age of sixteen or seventeen. The trouble is such girls are hard to come by in this area. What happened? Were they all killed at birth? The work in the house is easy, even an old woman could do it. All the girl would have to do would be to fluff floss and sew. The mistress doesn't trust employment agencies—they don't know who they are recommending—which is why she insists on finding an honest girl from the countryside. The salary is three silver dollars a month plus room and board and two pieces of jewelry a year—one at the Mid-Autumn Festival and one at the Spring Festival."

"Isn't that the same as a service girl?" someone asked hesitantly.

Sister Hu's mouth twitched for a moment and her eyes moved from one person to another before coming to rest on Xiuzhen, who suddenly felt as though she was burning even though the room was dark. Her heart beat faster.

"Shanghai is now quite modern," replied Sister Hu eventually, "and no one buys service girls any more. After you have worked for three years you can leave and get married. All you need to do is give notice beforehand. In addition, the mistress will give you a handsome dowry. I tell you, people in Shanghai would jump at such a chance. I've only come here because my mistress insists, and because I'm a kind person..."

In spite of her expensive clothes and her repetition of such tempting words as "fortune", "two pieces of jewelry a year", "handsome dowry", the country folk had their own set of values and no one was interested in taking up her offer. Here in the country, girls were only allowed to go elsewhere to work if the family had absolutely no alternative, or if a daughter was bullied by a stepmother. Otherwise they risked missing out on a marriage proposal and consequently sullying their parents' name. No amount of persuasion could make them to change their minds.

After she had popped the last smoked pea into her mouth, Sister Hu brushed the crumbs from her lap and said dryly, "I always give villagers first refusal, but it seems the girls here don't know much about the world. Oh, well, there are plenty of girls in town who will be more than willing to grasp the opportunity. How quickly the evenings draw in here. We'd better light the lamp. I will be leaving first thing in the morning."

The next morning, as the sun began to filter through the clouds and the sky began to clear after a night of drizzle, Sister Hu emerged from the house to find a small figure waiting for her motionlessly on the road. It was Xiuzhen.

By now her youngest brother had grown sufficiently that he no longer needed to be held in her arms. Her four other brothers spent their days working in the mulberry fields. As for cooking and looking after the silkworms, her mother and grandmother could handle that. Her brothers would be getting married sooner or later which meant a good deal of betrothal money would need to be found. Hadn't the woman said she would get three silver dollars a month? And the family would have one less mouth to feed. That made a big difference. So, after turning the matter over until well into the night, Xiuzhen's parents decided to let her go. However, a lingering sense of shame drove them to push her out of the house at the crack of dawn before anybody was up.

Though not dark, it was a desolate late autumn morning. The crops had been gathered, leaving the fields bare and fragrant. Xiuzhen was not sentimental, but as she sat in the boat and looked back at the desolate fields and saw the cooking smoke curling up from the direction of the village she couldn't stop the tears from rolling down her face.

2

Sister Hu hadn't lied.

The Hes had made their fortune in the tea business, and lived in a two-storey, foreign-style house close to the city temple. They adhered to the ancient tradition of keeping their shutters drawn at all times so as to avoid exhibiting their wealth. This made the place cool, even in summer.

The mistress' room was the second on the left on the upper floor. Though only in her thirties, she was chronically ill and spent more time in bed than out of it. Lack of sunshine had turned her face ashen. Her husband, however, was not unduly worried about her and only came in in the evenings to chat to her for a while after work. Her illness naturally prevented him ever staying the night, but as far as anyone knew he neither took a concubine nor a lover. This was his second marriage, his first wife having died some time ago.

The present mistress, it was said, came from a very wealthy family. She had been the only daughter and had proved so fastidious in choosing a husband that she had finally burned her boats and ended up as Mr He's second wife. Before he married her his business had been declining, but with the injection of funds she brought with her it once again began to boom.

Xiuzhen learned all this gradually from the servants and service girls who gossiped in the kitchen and on the stairs. At first she couldn't make head or tail of what they were saying and merely listened without asking questions. She was not of an inquisitive nature.

Xiuzhen's ugliness quickly gained her a foothold into the mistress' confidence, and the relationship was strengthened by Xiuzhen's hard work. The worktable she was given on which to fluff floss was placed close to the mistress' bedroom, in the corridor by the window. When the mood took her, and she was able to move about, the mistress would come and chat to Xiuzhen.

There were more than a dozen members of the family, including the children left by the first mistress and their wives and husbands. Each year their silk-padded clothes and quilts needed to be fluffed, and new ones made. When the work-load was heavy, Xiuzhen's fingers would often become bloodstained, but she worked uncomplainingly; she was used to it. If she had a query she would ask Sister Hu. Xiuzhen felt indebted to her. Here she didn't have to worry whether she would have enough to eat. At the sound of the bell she went down and ate with the rest of the servants. They sat at two tables and were given two dishes, plus a soup and an unlimited supply of rice. Xiuzhen had never dreamt that such a carefree life was possible.

But Sister Hu was sly, and when the mistress took a nap she would often ask Xiuzhen to take over her chores while she sneaked out. People said she had a lover.

The mistress' quarters faced south and consisted of two rooms—bedroom and living room, separated by an oak doorframe in which stood a lacquered screen. The bedroom was furnished simply, with little more than a bed and a three-piece padauk suite. The only signs of wealth were several liver-coloured teapots which were prominently displayed on a shelf in the living room. "Rich families even have fancy teapots," thought Xiuzhen.

The teapots had been part of the mistress' dowry. If the master wanted to show them to his friends he had to ask her permission first. The mistress had only one child—a daughter named Ye Qianling who was currently in her second year of primary school. She was spoilt, but nevertheless was affectionate towards Xiuzhen and the two developed a certain rapport. After school she would pester Xiuzhen to tell her stories about silkworms and when, the following spring, she was given some, Xiuzhen gave her an old basket to keep them in and taught her how to look after them. Seeing the two of them laughing and talking together, heads bent over the basket, the mistress decided to let Xiuzhen take care of the child and raised her salary a little to compensate.

Now Xiuzhen had other things to do besides fluffing floss. She took the child to and from school and looked after her every need. As a result she had more occasion to talk to the mistress and imperceptibly began to be favoured over Sister Hu. This made Xiuzhen uneasy, but Sister Hu couldn't care less. Her mind was on things that lay outside the house, in particular her boyfriend, a bank manager in the southern district of the city who frequently called for her to take her out. One day Sister Hu shyly told the mistress that she planned to get married.

"What a fool," thought Xiuzhen to herself. "You can't help at home, your parents won't feed you all your life, yet here you are fed with plenty of rice three times a day, nobody is forcibly kicking you out, so why get married?"

"We were not born to be service girls," said Sister Hu one day, sensing Xiuzhen's perplexity and pulling her aside to explain. "Why should we stay here for the rest of our lives? The best thing to do is to make as much money as we can while we can work and then find a good man to marry. After that our worries will be over."

The mistress, following the traditional practice in the house, gave Sister Hu a dowry befitting a personal maid, including four floss-padded quilts and a pair of gold bracelets weighing seven or eight ounces. The four quilts, of course, were made by Xiuzhen.

After Sister Hu left, Xiuzhen took her place. Her duties were light: looking after the mistress' clothes, brushing her hair and cleaning the teapots on the shelf in the living room.

"These have been handed down by our ancestors," said the mistress one day, obviously in the mood to chat. "They are at least two hundred years old and, like certain types of people, get better-looking with age if they are properly cared for."

"But they are so dingy and crude," said Xiuzhen disbelievingly. "The western china in the dining room is so much prettier."

"You don't understand," sighed the mistress. "They are valued precisely because their charm is hidden. They don't show off like the chinaware. Look how modest and unassuming they are; yet they are worth a fortune. People who like them show they have taste..."

Xiuzhen only half understood what was being said; but one thing was clear: people were not to show off like china but should emulate these dark pots—be worthy but modest.

She bore this in mind.

Working as an amah had considerable advantages over her previous position. Whenever she ran errands, for example, to her mistress' friends or relatives, she would return with a tip in her pocket. If someone came to the house to play mahjong Xiuzhen once again received a tip. And there were the bonuses handed out at the Spring and Mid-Autumn festivals. Xiuzhen was able to send home her monthly three dollar salary and save the remainder. As time went by her pay was increased even further and her savings grew proportionately. But no matter what she earned she continued to dress simply in coarse grey or black.

Even the mistress tried to persuade her to brighten herself up.

"You are young. Why not get yourself a bright, patterned dress?"

"I don't want to be like the western chinaware," answered Xiuzhen, and her reply made the mistress trust her even more. After all, she was a woman and the master often came up to see her. If she had a pretty girl beside her the whole time who could tell what might happen? Even if Sister Hu had wanted to stay, the mistress would have got rid of her sooner or later. A young woman as plain and honest as Xiuzhen was hard to come by.

Time flew past and before she knew it Xiuzhen had been living at the house for several years. The mistress' health was not getting any better. Then, in mid-November one year, the mistress' third stepdaughter prepared to get married and the mistress took personal responsibility for organizing her dowry. She sent someone to Suzhou for the famous embroidered silk bed covers and had Xiuzhen make sixteen silk padded quilts, and as many dresses. Xiuzhen had been working on them since the spring and as the mistress' health was so bad she had had the fluffing board brought into her living room so that she could supervise Xiuzhen from her bed.

"You are very generous," said Xiuzhen one day, while chatting with the mistress as she worked. "Your health is so delicate yet you still take care of the dowry personally. Her own mother could hardly have been more assiduous."

"She is a child of the Hes," sighed the mistress, "even if not born by me. She lost her mother when she was very young and has called me mother for over ten years. I must give her her due."

Xiuzhen knew the real reason for the mistress' care. Knowing that her illness was incurable and that she might not live to see Qianling's marriage, she was concerned that if the master married again no one would take care of Qianling's dowry. But a good deed now might be rewarded later by whoever took her place.

"Your kindness will be repaid," said Xiuzhen, pleasantly. Then she told the story of the silk store destroyed in a mysterious fire in her hometown. "I believe in retribution," she added earnestly. "No matter how secretively one does things, there is a God above who is watching us."

The mistress nodded approvingly, then fell silent.

One of the six amahs working for the second stepdaughter had married shortly before Sister Hu, but because her husband had gambled away all her savings she had eventually come back to the mistress begging to be allowed to work again. But by that time the second stepdaughter had married and there seemed to be no job available. The former amah begged and pleaded, saying she would be willing to work as a labourer, but the mistress awkwardly put her off, saying she would call her as soon as they needed help. Even as she said it she knew it wouldn't happen.

As Xiuzhen was walking the amah to the door, the latter suddenly glanced around her and seeing no one nearby, removed from her wrist a silver bracelet and pressed it into Xiuzhen's hand.

"Sister Xiuzhen," she said, her voice quivering, "the mistress trusts you. Please put in a word for me... I have a four-year-old child to feed..."

How could Xiuzhen accept the bracelet? She had gained the mistress' trust through hard work and she must be sensible. She shouldn't use her influence lightly. Besides, she was only on casual terms with this woman.

"I warned her before she got married," said the mistress as Xiuzhen slowly combed her hair. "You have to work even after you get married. At least here you get paid, and are provided with food and a roof over your head. Once you get married you work for nothing and may be treated badly into the bargain."

"True!" thought Xiuzhen. "Work here and you get paid. Work for a husband and you get nothing. Remember the humiliated expression on that amah's face as she was begging for help and count your blessings. If I were to give this up for marriage I'd be an idiot."

During festivals, Sister Hu came to visit the mistress. Married life agreed with her, and it was easy. One year later she had had a son. On the mistress' birthday she presented her with a piece of silverware. No wonder the mistress treated her differently than others, and offered her a seat and a cup of tea.

The third stepdaughter's wedding was an impressive affair. The mistress managed to be present at the banquet, but soon afterwards her health deteriorated sharply. This time the master really did become worried, and sent for doctors of Chinese and

Western medicine.

Xiuzhen was busy again; so was a seamstress working outside the mistress' chamber. They were making padded and unpadded funeral clothes in the hope that the ritual itself would expel the evil spirit from the mistress' body.

Before long winter arrived, and one pitch-black night, when even the stars were obliterated and a piercing wind howled outside, the mistress summoned Xiuzhen to her bed. Despite the fire which burned in the grate, the room was still cool. For the past few days the master had been coming up to keep the mistress company and had even put a bed up in the living room.

The mistress told Xiuzhen to light a hardly used oil lamp and its yellow rays, flickering across the ceiling and around the room, cast a melancholy glow over the surroundings. Handing Xiuzhen a bunch of keys, the mistress bid her open one of the padauk cabinets and take out a casket wrapped in silk.

"Be very careful with it," said the mistress in a trembling voice. "If you drop it I'll haunt you from beyond the grave until the day you die."

The master hurriedly stood up and took it from her, then laid it down and opened it. Inside was a dark brown tea-pot, roughly six or seven inches tall, which Xiuzhen had never seen displayed on the shelf. The master lifted the lid with extreme care and studied the pot closely. As he did so the mistress told Xiuzhen to brew the best tea they had. After she had done so, Xiuzhen made to leave the room, thinking that the master and mistress would wish to speak with each other alone. But the mistress stopped her. "You come and have a look too."

The master began pouring the tea into the pot. How strange! As the pot began to fill, it gradually turned from brown to green so that by the time it was full it looked like a piece of fine jade. Then the master slowly poured the tea out again and the pot reverted to its original colour.

"This is 'Gong Chun's Teapot'," explained the mistress. "It was made by Yixing's most famous sculptor, Gong Chun. Look how fine it is and how beautifully smooth. People say that he only ever made two. One is in the hands of Prince Li of Jingkou—apparently it cost him a fortune—the other is here, and has been handed down through our family for generations. There are many people who would like to get their hands on it." Then, laboriously supporting herself on her elbow, she said solemnly to the master: "You can dispose of anything in my dowry, including the various pots on the shelf, except this. This is to be part of Qianling's dowry and you are not to sell it to anyone for any price." Her voice trembled with excitement.

The master looked worried. "Trust me," he said, trying to make her lie down, "I will keep it for Qianling."

"No," responded the mistress firmly. "I want Xiuzhen to keep it. Fortune won't smile on you forever, you know, and once you're down on your luck you won't have the strength to keep it. 'A defeathered phoenix suffers more than a fowl.' Xiuzhen is plain and honest. I would feel safer if the teapot was in her hands. I'm dying. Think of the pot as having been buried with me once I'm gone. That way fortune-seekers will give up hope. Then, just before Qianling gets married, the two of you must give it to her."

"The mistress must be out of her mind," thought Xiuzhen. Then, aloud, she said soothingly, "You worry too much. You will recover..."

Stopping her with a gesture, the master bent down over the

mistress and said, "Don't worry. Not just this one, but all the teapots on the shelf will go to Qianling. I promise she will have her due. And we will give Xiuzhen this one right now."

Xiuzhen felt a chill run up her spine. "How can I keep such a priceless treasure?" she asked, hesitantly.

"Think of the kindness the mistress has shown you all these years," said the master, persuasively. "It wouldn't occur to burglars to look for it in your room."

After that, on the pretext of looking after the mistress, Xiuzhen moved out of the room she had shared with the other amahs and into one opposite the mistress'.

The mistress died at the beginning of spring, and was buried in the cemetery at Hongqiao. Her death temporarily threw the household into chaos, but thanks to the fact that Xiuzhen knew exactly how the mistress had run things—even down to the grocery stores she patronized—everything was under control by the time the new mistress arrived at the time of the Double Ninth Festival. The master was impressed by Xiuzhen's cool-headedness and relied on her ever more heavily, finally handing over to her the keys of the house. Xiuzhen tied the most important ones around her waist and carried them with her at all times. They jangled as she moved, sounding a warning to the other servants that she was approaching. Her position was cemented. Even the new mistress called her "Sister Xiuzhen".

3

Unlike her predecessor, who had devoted herself to managing household affairs, the new mistress was a modern woman who liked to socialize. During the first few days Xiuzhen had gone to her twice a day for instructions, but the new mistress couldn't be bothered with it; she preferred to leave everything to Xiuzhen.

Qianling moved into the dead mistress' quarters. Everything in the living room remained the same, including the various teapots still standing on the shelf. The new mistress loved cut glass, and wouldn't even deign to look at the dark earthen pottery-ware. Sometimes the master came alone to look at them and caress them.

One day Sister Hu came to visit. She sat down and began to chat. "You are running the house, I see. Behind those demure looks of yours is a cunning mind."

Sister Hu looked prettier than she had before marriage. Her eyes smiled out from under her long, well-plucked eyebrows. No wonder the bank manager loved her so much. As they talked, Xiuzhen continued to work, her hands moving rapidly over the floss she was fluffing for Qianling's winter clothes. These days she didn't have to worry about anyone else's clothes except hers. There was a seamstress from Huzhou who dealt with the rest in the back yard. Since Xiuzhen had taken over, no strangers were permitted inside the rooms.

"Heard from home recently?" asked Sister Hu, holding a cup of tea in one hand. Then, before Xiuzhen could answer, she began to lecture her as of old. "You still dress in that awful black and grey. Why don't you wear something bright for a change? You look like an old woman."

Xiuzhen looked at herself. Her black dress which she had worn throughout the summer was indeed faded. "It's true, I'm old." She smiled indifferently. Sister Hu calculated on her fingers. Xiuzhen was over twenty years old. In those days a woman in her twenties was not considered young.

"Surely you don't want to end your days here, do you?"

Xiuzhen's hands stopped moving, and it was a while before she replied: "I've managed to stick it out without a husband. I can support myself."

"But what for?" cried Sister Hu in exasperation. "Even Seventh Angel misses her lover. Why shouldn't you or I?" She leaned over and whispered something in Xiuzhen's ear, which instantly made Xiuzhen flush. "Silly girl," she snapped, then added, "in any case, it isn't all that easy to be supported by a husband unless you're lucky enough to find a bank manager like you did." Xiuzhen knew she would never have that sort of luck herself. She was ugly and awkward at pleasing men. Rich men had money. What they wanted from a wife was pleasure.

"Do you mean you would like to marry a bank manager?" asked Sister Hu, her interest immediately kindled. She sprang to her feet and smiled broadly.

"What are you looking at me like that for?" asked Xiuzhen, though she knew what Sister Hu was thinking. She pretended to be confused until finally Sister Hu burst out, "There's someone in this very building who has asked me to make a match with you: Tailor Long. He works for the new mistress and has had his eye on you for ages. He had already asked a number of people to approach you before finally coming to me for help."

Xiuzhen's heart missed a beat. She knew very few men in Shanghai other than the master, the driver, the doorman and the cook, and the last thing she had expected was that someone might fall in love with her.

"Tailor Long is starting up his own business; he's found premises in Ximo Street..." continued Sister Hu, beginning to outline an attractive scenario, just as she had done that day she came to the countryside in search of a servant-girl.

Tailor Long was not unknown to Xiuzhen. The new mistress, who loved fashionable clothes but didn't trust the seamstress to make them for her, had hired him to design and make her garments. He was in his thirties, fair-skinned and quiet. Each time he passed Xiuzhen he smiled and called her "Sister Xiuzhen".

He was a gentle fellow. No matter how demanding the new mistress was during her fittings, he always smiled good humouredly and, with his mouth full of pins, made the required adjustments. Xiuzhen used to worry that he might swallow one. For some reason he had become forgetful recently, always leaving something behind. Once he forgot to take his material away and had to return the next day to pick it up. As usual, Xiuzhen brewed him some tea which he drank in silence. Xiuzhen always felt awkward with him.

"He must have forgotten these things on purpose in order to have an excuse to approach me," thought Xiuzhen, her face burning.

"His clients are all wealthy," Sister Hu continued, "and as long as they continue to use him his business will be successful."

"But he must be in his thirties at least," said Xiuzhen, thoughtfully. "Has he ever been married before?"

"How can you be so fastidious," sighed Sister Hu. "You aren't exactly young yourself! I had to marry a widower too: it seems that's the best we can hope to get—unless your parents have arranged a marriage back home for you." She looked sad for a moment, then clearing her throat, added, "Think of it this way: you are no longer young, and marriage is not like wine, which gets better as it matures. It's time for me to go now. I have to get back to cook for my husband."

Xiuzhen didn't move. She was lost in thought. A man had

fallen in love with her! If she wanted to she could marry and have children. Suddenly, the memory of how her mother had killed her new-born baby sisters in the well, using a broom-stick to pin the struggling infants down, rose before her eyes. The broom-stick was to prevent them floating to the surface... Xiuzhen broke out into a cold sweat.

She remained motionless for a long time, staring blankly into space, until finally she heard Qianling calling for her. She was going to a birthday party and wanted to wear her silk blouse with lace trimming and her red coat. If Xiuzhen wasn't around she could never find anything.

As if by arrangement, Tailor Long came two days later to give the mistress a fitting. He normally kept up a lively patter of conversation during these sessions but today he was silent. Even the mistress noticed and asked why he was so quiet.

After the fitting, when the mistress had stepped out to get some buttons, Tailor Long grasped his chance. "Did Sister Hu speak to you?" he asked, nervously. Then, seeing that Xiuzhen was not annoyed, he added, "I have other skills too, you know. You won't go wrong if you marry me..."

"What nonsense!" said Xiuzhen coyly, pretending to be irritated.

That evening, Xiuzhen turned down Qianling's bed and prepared a hot water bottle for her. Just as she was about to retire to her own room Qianling came in clutching her stomach and collapsed onto the bed. Xiuzhen knew immediately that she had her period. This happened every time: the poor girl suffered terrible pains and inevitably ended up staining her underwear and sheets. Xiuzhen hurriedly placed the hot water bottle on Qianling's stomach, cushioned her with a thick towel and brewed her a bowl of hot motherwort juice. Not until Qianling had drunk the juice and fallen asleep did Xiuzhen put out the light and leave.

"How terrifying to be a teenager without having a mother nearby," thought Xiuzhen. "Nobody can offer the kind of comfort a mother can at such times. If I go, who will bring her a hot water bottle?" Xiuzhen's eyes fell on an old suitcase at the end of her bed. Inside it was the precious teapot. She had vowed to the dead mistress that she would keep it until Qianling got married.

"You can't go wrong if you marry me." Tailor Long's face flashed before her eyes. She hadn't noticed until today that his skin was pockmarked. Didn't people say that nine pockmarked men out of ten are sly dogs? And how sinister his smile seemed today, in spite of his normally honest appearance. Xiuzhen was troubled.

A week later Sister Hu returned for an answer, and when Xiuzhen declined, she was taken aback.

"Where else are you going to find such an honest, good-natured and skilful man like him? Don't be stupid and consign yourself to this place for the rest of your life. You won't be letting the dead mistress down. Besides, Qianling will get married sooner or later, and suppose she doesn't appreciate your loyalty? You are just an amah, let's face it, and she is the spoilt daughter of a rich family."

On this last point at least, Sister Hu was right. As Qianling had grown older she had become absorbed in her own affairs and no longer hung around Xiuzhen as she had when she was a little girl. Sometimes she even found Xiuzhen's presence irritating. Once, after Xiuzhen had run her a bath and urged her a couple of times to get in before the water got cold, Qianling had flared up and smashed a glass.

"But I promised. How can I quit before Qianling gets married?"

"Have you really made up your mind then? What if he doesn't have the patience to wait?" Sister Hu sighed and took her leave.

Two days later Tailor Long came to deliver a new overcoat for the mistress. After examining it critically she went out to get some money to pay him and Xiuzhen was left alone with him. Averting his eyes, he asked, "Don't you think I'm good enough for you?"

Xiuzhen looked at him out of the corner of her eye, and he slowly turned his face towards her. Xiuzhen felt a twinge of guilt at the pain in his gentle eyes.

"It's not that..." Her lips quivered. But before she could go on, the mistress returned. She didn't know whether he had heard what she said. Tailor Long took his money and left, his white robe shimmering briefly in the dark corridor before disappearing from sight.

After that he never came back. "He's gotten fancy since he opened his own shop," complained the mistress, "I've sent for him three times but he refuses to come."

Autumn was over and winter followed hard on its heels. Shanghai was plunged into turmoil when the Japanese invaders began bombarding the city. Then Japanese troops occupied the concessions; rice and cooking oil were rationed; a pregnant woman was trampled and killed as a mad crowd struggled to get food... But inside the walls of the He residence life went on as usual. The only change was that because of gasoline shortages, the master, mistress and children no longer rode in cars. They switched instead to bicycles and tricycles. The Japanese occupation made little difference to their lives. The mistress kept busy entertaining her friends or being entertained, and dancing. Outside, people queued up for rice. But the Hes had plenty, and to prevent it getting mouldy Xiuzhen would send a few servants to air it whenever the weather was fine.

Time elevates people to positions of power, and before she knew it Xiuzhen had become the most senior amah in the house. More keys were hung around her waistband, even those to the granary. The bronzewares that were used for offering up sacrifices to the ancestors were also in her safe keeping. She had gained a little weight and a sharp temper, often scolding the other servants in the imperious tone of a mistress. "You stupid creatures, never observing the rules..." But her dresses were still black or grey.

A young servant-girl who worked in the kitchen became friendly with the young milkman and they met every morning at the back door. Nobody minded: who had not had some kind of romance like that when they were young? But one day Xiuzhen caught sight of them—the tall young man, neatly dressed in livery, and much more attractive than Tailor Long, leaning against the wall with one hand in his pocket whispering into the girl's ear. The girl seemed almost to be in a trance. Xiuzhen remembered that she had once captured a man's heart too, but she had refused him. After that he had stopped taking the mistress' orders. Xiuzhen wondered why she had refused.

The girl began to giggle, and the sound pricked Xiuzhen's ears like needles. She couldn't stand it. Rushing down the stairs like a tornado, she began to shout furiously: "How can you be so indiscreet in broad daylight. You are ruining the master's reputation and threatening your own!" Her voice was so loud it was enough to wake up half the neighbourhood.

That evening, as the mistress dressed for a dinner engagement, Xiuzhen related a spiced up version of the episode with the milkman.

"People are getting worse, mistress, and things outside are bad. The master is busy and you are so lenient. A big house like this would be seriously affected if ever a trouble-maker managed to wheedle his way inside. The cook told me that a family in Xiaoshadu got robbed and that the inside man was none other than the maid's lover. Aren't we at risk of ushering the wolf into room?"

Alarmed, the mistress immediately gave the girl her wages and sacked her. After that the servants lived in fear, and Xiuzhen became even more imperious.

Sister Hu came again, this time heavily pregnant. She looked old and haggard and her usually fine complexion had gone. The Japanese army had bombed her husband's property; her savings had all but been used up and life as an expectant mother was proving hard.

"You know times are hard, yet you still go and get pregnant again," chided Xiuzhen, shaking her head and looking at Sister Hu's belly. She felt fortunate in not having entered the dead end of marriage herself.

For a while Sister Hu was lost for words. Then she chuckled. "Just try it and then see if you feel the same," she said. "You will probably want seven or eight babies before you feel satisfied."

"How people change," reflected Xiuzhen. She thought back to the time when Sister Hu had come to her native village dressed in a black serge blouse and a silk skirt. No young lady, from however rich a family, could have been more impressive. And after she had got married, she had become even more attractive, and her gift to the old mistress of a silver ornament seemed to complete the picture. No wonder the old mistress had treated her with such respect, offering her tea and a seat. What other reason could there have been?

The dead mistress had said that a defeathered phoenix suffered more than a fowl. One look at Sister Hu seemed to bear that statement out. Her head was bent and she looked much older than her age. How frightening to be poor. Xiuzhen's heart contracted. Sister Hu continued to pour out her troubles and Xiuzhen gradually began to wonder whether she hadn't come to borrow some money. Xiuzhen knew she owed Sister Hu a favour, and that she should try to help. But how could she? What if she kept returning for more?

Xiuzhen changed the subject. "Things are indeed hard! It seems that in wartime small families suffer the most. Only powerful men such as Mr He, who have well-protected houses, get by. But what's the use of crying about it? You must try to think of a way out."

Sister Hu threw out her arms in despair, and pointed at her protruding belly. "How can I at a time like this?"

Xiuzhen looked at her belly maliciously and her eyes glittered. An idea had occurred to her. "The mistress said the first daughter was looking for a wet nurse for her baby. She wants someone who is experienced."

"But what about my own baby?" said Sister Hu, painfully, "and my daughter."

Xiuzhen smiled coldly. "You brought all this on yourself. My mother killed three baby girls in a well."

"Don't frighten me, Xiuzhen!" Sister Hu's face turned ashen and her arms reached out instinctively to protect her belly while her teeth chattered uncontrollably.

"How can you be so muddle-headed?" thought Xiuzhen. "You used to be so smart." Then she turned to Sister Hu and said:

"What's the use of crying? You can send your baby to an orphanage."

"That's worse than killing it at birth. There she'd almost certainly have a long drawn-out death."

"Well, your crying upsets me. Die of hunger then, all of you. That way you can be permanently together."

Sister Hu wept harder. Xiuzhen's heart softened. She took out some paper notes, and gave them to Sister Hu. "Buy some food with this. Don't be so thin and pale. People will think you're sick. I'll talk to the mistress right now. If you can work as a wet nurse you'll have a few worry-free years. Don't be so stubborn."

Seeing it was late, and concerned that someone might see Sister Hu in such a poverty-stricken condition, Xiuzhen hurriedly ushered her out of a corner gate that hadn't been used for years. Its hinge was rusty, and when Xiuzhen finally managed to push it open she was shocked to see an old woman beggar lying motionless in the doorway.

Sister Hu left. Xiuzhen sighed in relief after she had bolted the gate.

Beyond the gate there seemed to be another world. Everything seems to revolve around money, Xiuzhen thought, no matter what. Look at the master. He has plenty of money so even the Japanese can do nothing to him.

Xiuzhen became obsessive about saving money. She loaned to other servants and charged a little interest. Her saving grew into gold bars. She didn't feel safe leaving them anywhere, not even inside the mistress' room; so she sewed them into her waist band and carried them with her at all times.

Sister Hu gave birth to a boy. She gave him away and wet-nursed the first daughter's baby. On New Year's day she held the baby in her arms and accompanied the first daughter to offer greetings to the master and mistress. As a mere wet nurse the mistress treated her like all the other servants and gave her the same amount of New Year money. No longer worried about food, her face had regained a little colour. Only her eyes looked sad.

Before half a year had gone by the baby she was breast-feeding fell ill. The doctor suspected the baby might have diphtheria. He gave Sister Hu an anti-lactation injection and made her take a blood test. The result showed that there was nothing wrong with her, but her milk was gone. The first daughter believed she hadn't nursed the baby properly. Sister Hu was sacked. Ashamed, she didn't come to Xiuzhen for help, and was never heard of again.

4

Qianling had grown into a pretty young woman. She had many boyfriends who often came either to listen to music or to take her out to a dance or movie. Match-makers came frequently too. The new mistress said she wanted nothing to do with Qianling's marriage. Soon the master accepted a marriage proposal from the Fans. The Fans were another established family in the Bund, probably wealthier than the Hes. The master was eager to make a connection with them. He planned to have an engagement ceremony first, and the wedding would be held later after Qianling had graduated from college. Qianling cried out in protest at this arranged marriage.

Xiuzhen looked forward to Qianling's graduation. She would then be able to present her with the teapot and would be finally relieved of her responsibility.

The day of the engagement banquet was set. On New Year's Eve a man came from the Fans to deliver New Year presents. Xiuzhen took the gifts and tipped him. But the man showed no inclination to leave. He began to chat. He told Xiuzhen he was connected with the dead mistress, and asked about Gong Chun's Teapot.

"People say the dead mistress' parents were extremely rich, and that as she was the only daughter much of their treasure was passed on to her. It is said that she had a magic teapot. When it has tea inside it turns from brown to green. Is that true?"

Xiuzhen grew suspicious. Qianling was not yet betrothed, and marriage was still a long way off. "I should by no means let the secret out," she thought. So she feigned ignorance and said, "We have several teapots on the shelf. I don't know if they change colours."

"Not those on the shelf," said the man, trying to draw her out. "Our master has seen them all. People say that the magic teapot was among the mistress' funeral objects. You were her amah—you must know."

Xiuzhen grew impatient. "Right. There was one among the objects, but I don't know if it's the one you are talking about. I'm an amah, not a detective. Why not go and ask our master? He is right now in his study upstairs."

The man, embarrassed, hurriedly took his leave.

Xiuzhen was worried: if the Fans wanted to get hold of the teapot through marriage, Qianling would have a hard time.

Several days later, before she had had a chance to tell the master about her doubts and put him on his guard, something happened to the ever-so-peaceful household—Qianling eloped.

On Christmas Eve Qianling usually left word that she would be back late. But this was neither a weekend nor a holiday, and at two o'clock in the morning she still hadn't returned. Xiuzhen finally grew so anxious that she went to tell the master and mistress.

The master immediately began dashing about, puffing and wheezing. Eventually he found a letter on Qianling's dressing table. He ran his eyes over it quickly, then collapsed into a sofa. With a wave of his hand he sighed in exasperation. "It's too late now. We can't get her back. Her ship left ten hours ago..."

The mistress turned on Xiuzhen. "You are supposed to take care of her and you failed in your duty. How come you know nothing about this, after all these years together? She left the letter yesterday morning and yet you didn't notice it until now..."

"She is no longer a little child," interjected the master, "how can one keep an eye on her all the time? Be quiet. This is a family matter anyway."

Ever since she had come to the house Xiuzhen had never been treated this way. She knew the rest of the servants were excited by her public disgrace, as were some of the young ladies who otherwise had little say about domestic matters. She felt her face burning. For the first time she experienced the bitterness of "being turned against by a friend".

That night, after shutting her door, she sorted out her belongings. She didn't have much in the way of luggage. All she really had were her savings. Gold bars, silver dollars, paper notes and jewelry were piled up on the table, gleaming under the light. She couldn't believe it was all hers, and wondered at her luck in acquiring such a fortune. The more she thought the more she worried, until finally she took a piece of cloth, made it into a bag, put her treasure inside and tied it around her waist.

As people said, "Never try to harm anyone; but always be on guard against them." One only needed to look at those amahs and young ladies who had taken such pleasure in her humiliation. If she were to fall, they would undoubtedly give her an additional kick. This was not her home anyway. Fortunately, by now her family in the countryside had remodelled their house with the money she had sent back, and all her brothers had got married. If she went back she would, she was sure, receive due respect.

But what about that teapot? Xiuzhen had taken it out of its casket and wrapped it in old clothes to make it less noticeable. She took it out. Covered with tea stains, the pot looked dull, as common as the one the doorman was using. How was it that it had been inherited as a priceless treasure? There was nothing special about it except that it changed colour. What was the use of that?

Out of curiosity she slowly poured some tea into the pot and watched it gradually change colour. Then she poured the tea out and the teapot changed back to dark brown. Xiuzhen was not impressed at all. After all, it was pottery, not jade.

If Qianling had known she was about to inherit this priceless item, would she still have eloped? Perhaps I should have dropped a hint? No, that would have been worse. If people had known she had it she would have been surrounded by swindlers.

Everybody in the house agreed that Qianling had probably run away with her boyfriend. If it was true, then disgraceful as it was, Qianling might have found true love. The young man had just taken her away, and clearly wasn't interested in her dowry or a connection with the Hes. He must have genuinely loved Qianling and perhaps she would be happy with him. If Xiuzhen had known this was going to happen, she would probably have agreed to Tailor Long's proposal and would by now have had a home of her own.

Before she knew it, it was dawn. "If only I could write like Qianling," she thought, "I would write a letter and leave too."

That day she approached the master. "I'm employed to look after Qianling. Now that she is gone, there seems no reason for me to stay. I would like to go back home."

The master fell silent for a while, then drew hard on his cigarette before saying, "Let's talk about this later. The mistress lost her temper and you must accept it. Mistresses often scold their amahs: there's nothing strange about it. Nevertheless, I apologize for her. If you are determined to go, please don't do it immediately. Give me some time. Besides, where am I going to keep that thing once you quit? I can't keep it in my room; people are in and out of it all the time. And..." He drew hard on his cigarette again. Xiuzhen noticed he looked emaciated and pale, his eyes blood-shot. It's not easy to make money, thought Xiuzhen.

"I haven't been doing very well recently," continued the master. "I may have problems. Keep the secret from everyone, including the mistress. If anyone ever comes for it, even if it's in my name, don't give it to them, unless I ask for it personally. You understand?"

He put his hand on her shoulder and gave it a gentle squeeze. Of course Xiuzhen understood what he meant by "the thing".

"Are you in trouble?" Xiuzhen was frightened.

"People say that luck changes every sixty years. It's likely the Hes will soon be out of it." The master gave a sigh and shook his head. Before he could go any further the mistress pushed open the door. Opening the heavy curtain, she asked: "Why do you have the curtains drawn when the sun is so bright?"

The mistress was modern. She didn't believe that by keeping the curtains drawn one could also keep one's fortune. She liked bright rooms. As the sun flooded into the room she suddenly noticed the sad looks on their faces. She started. "What's the matter with you two?"

Thanks to Xiuzhen's ugliness and her perpetual drab old clothes, the mistress was unperturbed by the otherwise suspicious sight of a man and a woman locked inside a dark room together.

The storm came from out of the blue.

The Japanese left, and just as everybody was expecting a peaceful life the master was taken away and jailed as an "economic traitor".

Friends stopped coming to the house and the mistress was the only one who tried desperately to get him out.

Xiuzhen decided to leave the teapot where it was. Then, one midnight, the mistress came to her room and bowed sadly before her. Scared, Xiuzhen jumped out of bed barefooted.

"Sister Xiuzhen, I've been doing everything possible to try to

get the master out. I have spoken to a middleman who has a-
greed to work on it if we give him an inherited teapot called
'Gong Chun's Teapot'. You have been in the house for many
years. Have you ever heard of it?"

Xiuzhen pressed her foot hard against the case under the bed.
She had pledged to take good care of this teapot; she couldn't
afford to make the slightest mistake. If she failed in this duty,
she firmly believed misfortune would overtake her. So no matter
what the mistress said, Xiuzhen stubbornly maintained she knew
of no others than those on the shelf.

"The teapot on the shelf made by Shi Dabin is certainly rare,"
said the mistress, beginning to sob, "but people claim we have
an inherited treasure that's much more valuable. Their price is
outrageous. How can I possibly satisfy them?"

"Why not ask the master?" said Xiuzhen hesitantly. "Maybe
he knows something about it."

"Him!" moaned the mistress through her teeth. "He's just
prepared to wait for a trial. At least he is being housed and fed,
and everyone in the family has somewhere to go except me! I'm
at the end of my tether. It seems that I'm going to have to steel
myself to abandoning him."

Within the next few days the mistress became a different person—eyes sunken, mouth sagging—she looked quite old.

The house was wrapped in deep silence, and Xiuzhen now
knew both desolation and loneliness. She felt hollow inside, as
though if it weren't for the gold bars around her waist she might
have floated into the air like a bubble blown by children.

Before long, soldiers trooped in the house. Everything was
confiscated as "enemy property". The gate was sealed, and the
Hes compelled to vacate the property at once.

The master was sentenced to eight years' imprisonment, as long as the Anti-Japanese War itself. If it hadn't been for the money he had spent, people said he might have got an even longer sentence.

Chaos reigned as everybody suddenly dispersed, like monkeys leaping from a falling tree. The mistress took her child back to her parents' family. The cook, doorman and amahs were gone too.

Xiuzhen had no place to go. Moreover, since she had rarely gone beyond the gates of the house she knew nothing of the world outside.

5

Xiuzhen's brother came to take her home.

She didn't have much luggage apart from a case and a bundle. With the money Xiuzhen had sent back, her family had prospered. Her brother, therefore, refrained from asking why her belongings were so few.

Once again she was on the road connecting the town with her home village. The soil here was fertile, and close to a water source. When a waterwheel was established, crops could survive even if serious droughts lasted for several months.

By the time she reached the village it was evening, and the Milky Way lay before her in the starry sky. Such a sight would have been inconceivable in Shanghai as there were too many buildings. Insects were chorusing their welcome. Xiuzhen felt a warm glow run through her.

Several days later, her mother took her aside and whispered confidentially: "The Zhous' son, who lives in a neighbouring area has been widowed for two years. He has heard about you and wants to offer you a marriage proposal. Yesterday he sent over a matchmaker. The Zhous are a big family, with a great deal of land and a dozen or more houses in town. It's because you have seen life in Shanghai and worked for the Hes that he is interested in you...."

Marriage again! You can avoid it for a while, but not for ever. To Xiuzhen, men seemed part of her lost youth. Even Tailor Long now seemed remote.

Xiuzhen felt the bars around her waist. "I don't need a man to support me, and I don't want to marry either!" She was firm, but her hoarse voice betrayed her emotion.

"Of course I'd like you to stay," said her mother in a low voice, putting a hand on her shoulder, "but you have brothers and sisters-in-law. Right now everybody is being kind to you, but once your savings have run out..."

"Don't worry about me," retorted Xiuzhen, stamping her foot, "I'll live by myself! Just think of me as having been killed in the well at birth!"

A long silence followed, then a heavy sigh. Tears rose to Xiuzhen's eyes. Her mother knew she had given in.

Xiuzhen insisted on preparing her dowry herself. She tucked the bag with all her savings in the bottom of a case, together with Gong Chun's Teapot which was wrapped safely and securely. Then she fastened the key to her waistband. She insisted that a second marriage should have no fanfare, and personally fluffed silk floss for two dowry quilts. The Zhous were happy to get a thrifty new mistress.

The Zhous, like all landlords, had considerable prestige in the countryside. The walls of their house were high and painted; the entrance was impressive, carved with unicorns and lions. Even though this was Mr Zhou's second marriage, the bedroom was furnished with brand-new mahogany furniture. A red mosquito net, embroidered with golden flowers, hung over the bed, which was piled high with red and green quilts and a thick fox fur blanket. The house was filled with happiness. "All this is transient and unreliable," thought Xiuzhen. "I won't be like Sister Hu and Sixth Amah, who handed over their savings and became dependent on men. Even the Hes, once so prosperous, are now in decline. How can a landlord family like the Zhous be secure forever?

Her husband was an easy-going fellow, fifteen years her senior. He smoked opium, and so did the children left by the first mistress. At their age, children in the Hes had graduated from college and begun to work in an office. But the Zhous' children merely lay in bed puffing away their days. It seemed they were twenty years behind the Hes.

Even as second mistress Xiuzhen couldn't bear to see this. "Why not send them to school or to work in Shanghai while they are young," she asked her husband. "Otherwise they will end up good-for-nothings."

Mr Zhou was unperturbed. He had plenty of estates and businesses in town, and several hundred acres of land. Smoking opium was not, he argued, as vicious as gambling. Moreover, wars were going on outside. Some of his relatives had gone to study in Shanghai and Hangzhou, and somehow they had all become communists. One had even been killed. The children were no trouble at home, and all they cost him was a little opium.

"It has been a republic for many years," Xiuzhen rebuked, "not all students in Shanghai become communists. . ."

"What does schooling get you anyway? Mr He had schooling.

He studied abroad. But look where it got him. He became a traitor and lost his family!" responded her husband dryly, between puffs.

Xiuzhen had a son. She named him Baiqi, and made up her mind to send him to a school in Shanghai when he grew up. She believed the Zhous would decline sooner or later, and even thought she could hear the sound of the roof creaking.

She took out some of her savings and asked her brother to keep an eye on land prices. She meant to buy some property for herself and her son. She was lucky: the price was dropping drastically. She didn't know, however, that because of the wars, people were anxious to sell land and make off with the money.

To Xiuzhen land was more secure than her gold bars and cumbersome teapot. One could always lose out in a trade, but never with land. Land gave forth crops every year.

Though Xiuzhen was a mistress, she still dressed in blue or grey. Her husband was content with this—cosmetics and clothes cost so much.

There was a tall man in the village who lived by begging and doing odd jobs. At night he slept in the village temple. Nobody knew where he came from and he was often insulted by the Zhous' servants when he came to the door. Servants could often be more arrogant than masters. One day it happened within Xiuzhen's earshot. She immediately hushed the servant. Since the Hes' decline she had lost confidence in everything. If even a family as prosperous as the Hes could fall into decline, who could say who wouldn't be reduced to beggary one day? Might as well do a few good deeds while she could? As she bent down to fill him a large bowl of rice, she felt the gold bars pressing into her waist. She gave the man the food, and told him to come again whenever he was hungry.

That evening she took off the bag. Her waist was bruised. She knew she was getting old. Gritting her teeth she fastened the bag back again. When she had first arrived at the Zhous she had, for a while, kept the bag locked in her case; but feeling it to be unsafe she had soon carried it with her again. Fortunately, her husband seldom came to bother her, content to curl up like a shrimp with his opium.

The gold bars filled with mixed feeling, reminding her as they did of her missed youth.

After a great deal of effort, Sister Hu in Shanghai had managed to get hold of Xiuzhen's address, and wrote enclosing a photo. She told Xiuzhen that she was an amah with a foreign family, working during the day and coming home in the evening like any other worker. From the letter Xiuzhen guessed Sister Hu was no longer with the bank proprietor. The photo, evidently taken in a photo shop, showed Sister Hu dressed in a *qipao* dress holding a woolen overcoat over her arm. Xiuzhen couldn't tell if it was borrowed for the purposes of the picture. Xiuzhen knew that working for foreigners paid well; but the work was more demanding. She remembered the amah in the foreign family next door to the Hes, who always had to get down on her knees to clean the floor.

She held the picture up to the light for a closer look. Sister Hu seemed to have put on weight; her curled hair had grown down to her shoulders; her eyebrows were neatly trimmed—the very image of a Shanghai woman.

Xiuzhen was not beset with worries—material or otherwise; nevertheless she was envious of Sister Hu. Nothing was more comforting than a regular income.

Sure enough, the Zhous' days ended.

The Communist Party came to power and immediately forbad the smoking of opium and the maintenance of concubines. Women were organized to learn reading and writing at night schools, and the Zhous' children were forced to work. Good, Xiuzhen thought. If the Communist Party had come ten years earlier she wouldn't be illiterate now. But when she learnt that the Communist Party had annulled title deeds for land, she began to worry about the fields she had bought with her silver dollars.

One morning there was a loud knocking at the Zhous' gate. When it was opened a martial-looking man strode in, followed by a couple of young men. Xiuzhen's husband was lying in bed in the inner chamber suffering withdrawal symptoms from the lack of opium and stress brought about by the recent changes.

"Tell your husband that at the sounding of a gong tomorrow morning he's to go to a meeting in the primary school," the man shouted. Xiuzhen was scared, and lowered her head. After a while she asked tentatively, "He is sick in bed. Can I go instead?"

"Can't you understand my words?" The man's voice became more threatening. "Raise your head and listen: he must go even if he is sick!"

Xiuzhen slowly raised her head, then started in surprise. The man was none other than the beggar, who had not been around for some time. He was dressed in a yellow uniform and had a pistol at his belt. His fierce glare made Xiuzhen's legs quake.

"Remember, tell your husband to go to the meeting. Understand? What are you still standing there for? Get away!" He kicked at Xiuzhen's leg, simultaneously shooting a meaningful look into her eyes. Xiuzhen understood. Her heart began to beat wildly.

The moment the men had disappeared, Xiuzhen picked up her son and started towards the gate, telling her husband she was going for his medicine. On the threshold she stopped, having remembered that damned thing! She dared not leave it behind to be destroyed. In her mind's eye she saw the fire that had destroyed the silk store in town. She clenched her teeth and hurried back. She took the teapot out from under the old clothes, but where was she to put it? She pondered for a while before placing it inside a battered old basket. Repeating her story to the others that she was going for her husband's prescription and some loquat juice for Baiqi's cough, she pressed the child against her and left, carrying the basket under her arm.

She had always been considered a dutiful wife, and had been kind to everybody; so no one was suspicious as they saw her hurry away carrying her baby and a basket. They knew her husband had become very ill after his opium supply had been cut.

Her son's feet prodded her belly as she walked, but the weight at her waist kept her spirits up.

The rice had grown excellently this year, and the ears were already turning gold. Too bad she couldn't take the fields with her. It began to drizzle, but Xiuzhen didn't notice. The golden ears of rice bent under the weight of the rain, piercing her heart as they swayed.

She felt that she was not walking, but drifting along on clouds. She put one foot mechanically in front of the other until eventually she crossed the bridge that led to her parents' home. By the time she arrived the sun had already dipped behind the horizon. She put down the child in front of her elder brother, kowtowed three times, grabbed a few changes of clothes which she tied into a bundle, and left.

The drizzle turned to rain, soaking her head and shoulders.

She was on the night boat to Shanghai. Inside the small cabin, no more than several metres across, a dozen or more passengers pressed up against each other—dozing, smoking or chatting. Nobody noticed Xiuzhen. From the rocking of the boat she knew she was getting farther and farther away from her home.

The teapot was securely wrapped in her bundle and her treasure was still fastened to her waist. Xiuzhen drew herself up laboriously. She lifted the oilcloth from the porthole and gazed out at the dark, foggy river. Even though it was night, the river was still busy. Every few minutes, ships laden with firewood or baskets sailed past.

Yet from fear and despair, hope slowly began to grow in her breast.

6

When Xiuzhen found Sister Hu's place it was two or three o'clock in the afternoon. Sister Hu was not there. "She's probably still at work," thought Xiuzhen. Nevertheless she was let in by a kind-hearted neighbour and was surprised to find a little girl, who couldn't have been more than five years old, locked inside. "How fertile Sister Hu is," thought Xiuzhen. "Is she still with that bank manager?" She looked about her, but found nothing that might belong to a man.

It was a room not much bigger than a chicken coop. The ceiling lay inches above her head, and the simple rooms reminded her of the servants' quarters near the Hes, which were for those servants working in the foreigners' block. The only difference was that most of the servants here had families. Rents in Shanghai were high. Servants couldn't possibly afford another place for their families. Fortunately, after the Liberation, their masters had become a little more tolerant.

Sister Hu didn't arrive home until eight o'clock in the evening. She looked in a better health than when Xiuzhen had last seen her, and though a bit older, her eyes were still bright.

Xiuzhen simply told her she had had a quarrel with the Zhous. She said she couldn't stay with her brothers and asked Sister Hu to find her a place to work as an amah.

"I came with nothing," said Xiuzhen bitterly, "and I have a child back in the countryside." She straightened her back painfully, her waist sore from the weight around it. "So long as they give me food and a place to sleep, I don't care about the pay."

Sister Hu rapidly put a meal together and served. The little girl pounced on her portion hungrily. No wonder—it was nine o'clock already.

"Poor little thing," said Sister Hu, looking at the girl sorrowfully. "Foreigners have dinner late, and they change plates for each course. It's always this late when I get off."

"How's your husband? And how about your sons?"

"I lost them all in wars," sighed Sister Hu.

After her husband's bank had been bombed, and she had given the infant to a foundling hospital and worked at the Hes as a wet nurse, her husband had taken his eldest son back to the countryside, where he had not been heard from since. There had been so many wars and skirmishes that Sister Hu didn't even know if they were still alive. After she had been dismissed from the Hes she had at first not known where to turn. Fortunately the driver in the house had taken pity on her, and after much effort found her this job, and these lodgings.

"He is the father of this little girl," said Sister Hu, pouting her lips at the hungry child. Then, half fondly and half reproachingly, she said, "Watch your table manners! Why do you have to eat in such a hurry? Nobody is going to take your food away." She turned to Xiuzhen. "I can't blame her, as I always come home this late. Probably when she gets a bit older she will be able to cook for herself."

Looking at this thin, pale little girl with delicate features, Xiuzhen was reminded of her son. Who was taking care of him right now? And he was two years younger than this girl! Suddenly she was seized by an irrational spite. She gave the girl's plait a sharp tug, and said, "A girl like this is killed at birth in the countryside. They try to struggle to surface so we use a broom to push them down."

"They still do this even now?" asked Sister Hu, doubtfully.

"Yes. People are still poor."

The little girl was speechless for a while, then burst into tears. Sister Hu, assuming Xiuzhen had been joking, hushed her daughter. "Silly girl, nobody's going to do that to you! Stop that noise!"

"Where's her dad?" No sooner had Xiuzhen asked the question than she regretted it. Sister Hu's face clouded over.

"My fate is harsh," she said woodenly, not even bothering to conceal her sadness.

The driver had been kind to her. When the master's family finally left, he had chauffeured them to the pier where they were met with a huge crowd of people, all bustling about in confusion. The master bid him take the suitcases on board, but before he could get off again chaos broke out on the ship and the ladder disappeared. Despite his frantic shouts nobody took any notice. He was gone with the ship.

Everyone in the world had their sorrows.

Before long Sister Hu found Xiuzhen a job as an amah for a doctor's family. The couple had two children and lived in an English-style two-roomed apartment.

Having worked at the Hes, she found the job relatively easy. When she had time, she fluffed silk floss to make padded clothes for the doctor's children.

Though the pay was poor and she had almost no extra money, for the first time in her life Xiuzhen felt genuinely happy. The couple treated her well and gave her a room between the kitchen and the rear stairs, one which had previously been locked all year round. She got herself a bed and later a soap box in which to keep her things.

Under Communist Party administration, Shanghai improved. Prices were stable. Xiuzhen no longer felt it necessary to rush to the bank each time she was paid to change it for silver dollars. She sent some of it home for her son's living expenses and left the rest in her employer's safe keeping. At the end of a year they gave her a bank certificate.

Several times her brother came to visit. He said her son was doing very well at school. Her husband had been taken to a meeting and shot the day after she left. He was the only land-lord in the area to have been executed, probably because he was one of the oldest and was sick in bed. People said the work team had wracked their brains to work out a plan that would fulfill their assignment. His execution spared the rest....

Xiuzhen had no idea what the assignment meant. In any case,

her husband was dead, and if his death meant the rest were spared then he hadn't altogether died in vain. Moreover, without his opium supply, she knew he wouldn't have survived anyway.

In the evenings she rolled up comfortably in her small bed. She really felt that her life had changed for the better. However, she still couldn't rid herself of the horrors of the past, and was often haunted by the memory of her sisters killed in the waterhole.

Life in the doctors' home was peaceful. Though she herself had never had a happy childhood, the years with the doctors' family made up for the loss.

When she was forty she even fell in love.

Once a month a man came to clean the windows and carpets and wax the floor. He was a jolly fellow who was always telling jokes. Everybody called him Old Tie. Each time he came Doctor Huang told Xiuzhen to give him some Shaoxing liquor. After a few glasses the man would be unstoppably chatty. He didn't care whether anyone was listening, and as he chatted, what would normally have been a simple lunch extended into a long meal. When the weather was cold, Xiuzhen was obliged to heat and then reheat the food and the wine. As the doctors' children took their lunch boxes to school, nobody else would be at home. Bustling around him, Xiuzhen often felt as though she was behaving like his wife.

He was a great eater, each time consuming two big bowls of rice. Xiuzhen knew this, and each time she filled his bowl she made sure she piled it high.

"Your dishes are so appetizing," he mumbled sheepishly one day as he took yet another big bowlful.

Xiuzhen cast him an affectionate look. "You must have tape-worms to be so greedy."

"True! There are probably enough worms in my belly to devour a mountain." Old Tie crinkled his eyes mischievously.

Old Tie was a native of northern Jiangsu, and had been a widower for many years. In his youth he had been a coolie, but now that he was getting on he made his living by cleaning houses and waxing floors. He had a list of regular customers and had no trouble supporting himself.

Even though he was approaching fifty, he was still a strong worker, able to move a mahogany cabinet with little more than a few firm pushes and pulls. Xiuzhen enjoyed watching him exert himself—his muscles rippling and flexing under his skin. She felt the urge to touch them.

Sexually speaking, Xiuzhen didn't know much about men, in spite of the fact that she had given birth to a son. Tailor Long had lacked virility, and her dead husband was no more than an opium addict. Only Old Tie was a real man. As his eyes fell on her well-developed breasts, Xiuzhen felt, for the first time, genuine desire.

She began to look forward to his coming. Once a month seemed too long to wait. Evidently Old Tie felt this too, for he began to come more often, at first once every few days, then every day.

Xiuzhen was honest. When Old Tie didn't come to work she paid for his food and wine out of her own pocket, never putting the expenses on her employer's bill.

Old Tie was a great drinker. One day, after he had had a glass of wine, he blushed suddenly and blurted out: "Live with me." He set his glass down in front of him. "You can't live between the kitchen and the stairs for the rest of your life."

Xiuzhen didn't utter a sound.

Old Tie pushed her bowl away. He stroked her crimson face and pale neck with his rough hand. When he saw that she didn't resist, his hand moved down to her breast, then further down still. But before his hand had reached her waist, Xiuzhen violently pushed him away and pulled her dress tightly around her.

Old Tie was startled. A disappointed look appeared in his face.

"Old Tie," Xiuzhen stammered, "I'm sorry, but I have difficulties...."

Old Tie sat stiffly for a while, then turned and left.

That evening, Xiuzhen lay in bed turning over what had happened during the day. But the moment she touched the cold bars around her waist her excitement turned to sadness.

"Old Tie seems an honest person; should I marry him?" she thought. "People say banks are buying in gold at ninety-six yuan per ounce. A couple of gold bars would be enough to rent a room and buy some furniture. I'm over forty; it's time to settle down. But will I be safe if anyone else knows about my savings? Besides, I'm not pretty, my ex-husband was executed and I have a son back in the countryside. Will he mind? Without my savings things may be easier."

A week later, on the day Old Tie was scheduled to come and clean, Xiuzhen was on tenderhooks. Would he come? Here he was, looking as though nothing had happened. He stepped inside and handed Xiuzhen a greasy paper bag.

"Sauced pork from the Duliu Store," he said. Then, in the manner a husband might use with his wife, he added, "Shall we heat it with the rice for lunch?"

Xiuzhen emptied the pork into a bowl. Then she threw away the bag, which was made from an old newspaper. If she could have read she would have seen that it contained a notice from her old master saying he was looking for someone called Xiuzhen, who had worked years before in the He residence close to the new city-god temple. He had been jailed at the end of the Anti-Japanese War, and released after Liberation. His current address was somewhere in Qinghai.

Xiuzhen brought out the appetizing sauced pork for lunch and heated some rice wine.

"I must be getting old," said Old Tie suddenly. Xiuzhen's heart missed a beat. Old Tie cut in half a big piece of pork with his chopsticks and dropped the lean piece into Xiuzhen's bowl before continuing: "Last week when I was working at the Lius, I almost broke a purple pottery teapot in the cupboard. If I had I wouldn't have been able to pay for it even if I lived to be a hundred. That kind of accident has never happened to me before. My eyesight must be getting worse."

"What sort of teapot is it that costs so much?" As Xiuzhen feigned ignorance of the subject, her mind went back to those early years when she had carefully cleaned the Hes' priceless teapots on the shelf in that cozy living room. How young and dynamic she had been! All of a sudden Tailor Long's fair-skinned face rose before her. She was too deep in memories to catch what Old Tie was saying. He had been chatting away with gusto.

"Don't you think it might be an object created by supernatural beings?"

The question dragged Xiuzhen out of her reverie. "What did you say?" She asked absent-mindedly, her voice hoarse.

Old Tie patiently repeated his story. "It was just six or seven inches tall." He described it with his chopsticks. "But the strange thing is, as you pour tea into it, it turns from dark brown to fresh green...."

"What?" Xiuzhen burst out in fright. "Did you see it?"

"How could I?" Old Tie gave a faint smile. "I only saw picture of it. It's not for us mortal beings. Anyone who keeps it is dogged by misfortune; it's just like the piece of jade hanging from Jia Baoyu's neck*. Mr Liu—he was a lawyer with a bad name before Liberation—said its owner was called a traitor because of this teapot, and had his house sealed and everything confiscated. What a money grabber to stay in jail rather than give it away. It isn't worth it; you can't take it with you into the next world anyway!"

Xiuzhen felt a chill run down her spine. *He must have found out my secret, perhaps even the place where I keep it; he is trying to draw me out with this story...*

"Why do you look so pale?" asked Old Tie. He pushed back the sweaty hair pasted to her forehead with his chopsticks, then laughed. "Why am I harping on about other people's problems? I'd rather talk about us. Were you mad with me the other day? I didn't mean anything bad; I was sincere...."

"Old Tie," Xiuzhen began cautiously, "I have to tell you the truth. My husband is still alive, farming back in the countryside. For some time I didn't get along with him, but now...."

Even she was surprised at this story and her acting.

Old Tie was dumbstruck. He was completely at a loss.

"This...is no good!" he said, finally squeezing out the words

---

* Hero in the classic novel *A Dream of Red Mansions*.

after a long silence. Then he swung around, picked up a mop and cleaned the floor with all his might. He was venting his anger.

After that he still came once a month; he couldn't afford to lose the job; but he no longer joked with Xiuzhen. At mealtimes he took his food and sat on the balcony, and he no longer asked for a refill. He no longer drank wine. Even the doctors were surprised at the change.

Xiuzhen's small room was filled with sadness. Several times she took out the teapot and wished she could smash it. Then one day, as she was sitting in a bus on her way to Wanyouquan Meat Store to buy some ham, she suddenly saw a familiar figure walking along the pavement. He was dressed like anybody else in a "people's suit". She rushed to the window and cried out at the top of her lungs, "Master! Master!" The other passengers laughed at this outdated form of address but she didn't care. The master stopped and looked around in surprise, but the trolley bus had turned the corner. At the next stop Xiuzhen hurried off the bus and rushed back, only to find he had disappeared. For a while she pushed her way back and forth amongst the crowd but failed. To Xiuzhen the master embodied the period in her life when she was young, capable and in favour. She had taken care of all the silk padding for the family's winter clothes, working with ease on that mahogany board, her bracelets tinkling as her hands moved swiftly through her work. And the mistress' keys, fur coats and silverware—all were entrusted to her. No wonder people had been anxious to please her. Even the Hes' three married daughters had treated her differently, to say nothing of the servants... But those years had disappeared like a dream, just as the glimpse of the master had a moment ago! The only proof of her youth was the treasure around her waist, cold and solid.

After he finished high school, Xiuzhen's son was accepted by an ordinary college in Hangzhou. His grades were good enough for medical school, but because of his family background the medical college closed its doors to him. Anyway, working as a doctor or a teacher would make no difference to his salary, which would be a mere fifty-eight yuan and fifty cents a month. He decided to leave the countryside for good and start life in the city. This was important.

Either due to her estrangement with the Zhous or to the fact that her son hadn't grown up beside her, Xiuzhen behaved coldly towards him, unlike Sister Hu who put her child first in everything. Xiuzhen wouldn't be that silly!

7

Year in, year out, each day passed like the one before it.

But the world was no calmer.

Sometimes Xiuzhen thought her life was just like Gong Chun's Teapot—her past years, like the tea inside, bittersweet. Yet life was not exactly like the teapot, which could change completely and then revert to its original form; human beings could never recover the past, and one could never retrieve one's youth. Life was endlessly troubling.

That year chaos broke out. Everything went wrong; even the honest doctors had a hard time.

Teenage "red guards" came to search their home. They put dunce caps on the couple's heads and made them kneel on broken pieces of china. The couple almost died of fright.

The "red guards" adopted Xiuzhen, however, as their class sister. "Look," they said to her indignantly. "Look how they have treated you! They have a nice room, a nice spring bed, but have put you between the kitchen and the stairs. You must switch places with them tonight."

They searched everywhere for any gold the doctors might have hidden. They even searched Xiuzhen's room. Xiuzhen was scared to death.

After a while they found several bank certificates, but when they discovered that they were Xiuzhen's savings they gave them back to her. As for Gong Chun's Teapot, they didn't even give it a second glance.

"But my savings are the result of hard work, too," Mrs Huang said, grief stricken. "I have worked as a doctor since I graduated from college. My husband ran a hospital, not me..."

"You shut up!" The "red guards" brandished leather belts. "Who is to distinguish you from your husband?"

"I can!" Xiuzhen protested.

The "red guards" were not prepared for this. They fixed their eyes on Xiuzhen, who continued, "The mister is male and the mistress female—that's easy!"

"You!" One of the guards rushed at her, but hastily turned away holding his nose. It was the height of summer, and throughout those chaotic days Xiuzhen hadn't had a bath or changed her clothes. Her old dress was stained and stank of sweat. The odour was more than the "red guards" could bear.

"What a low level of class consciousness—that's peasant ideology for you!" They left, grumbling. This was the beginning of the "cultural revolution". The "red guards" hadn't learned how to distinguish different classes. If they had they wouldn't have let Xiuzhen off so easily.

With the continuation of the "cultural revolution" Doctor

Huang's family was done for. Doctor Huang was jailed and his wife hung herself in a detention room. Of their two children, one went to Heilongjiang and one to Anhui. Xiuzhen bought them mosquito nets, bedding and blankets out of her own money, and on the floor of her room she made each of them a floss-padded jacket. She had planned to make floss-padded quilts for them as well but gave up the idea because of the high price of floss. She tearfully saw them off.

For some reason Xiuzhen was nicer to her employers' children than to her own. The fact that she hadn't brought her own child up was certainly one reason, and there were probably others.

So the Huangs were done for.

The moment their apartment was empty the head of the "rebels" moved in.

Xiuzhen had no place to go. Fortunately she was on good terms with her neighbours—she had often helped them buy groceries and clean the public stairs in the building—and they allowed her to stay with them.

Few people engaged amahs during the "cultural revolution"; nobody wanted a stranger in their home at a time like that.

As Xiuzhen had no regular employer she did odd jobs; doing laundry, fetching milk for the neighbours and sweeping the lane. She made a dozen or so yuan a month, and received another ten from her son. She had no Shanghai residents permit, so was unable to collect grain and cooking oil rations. Nobody knew how she managed. Each morning, the sound of her sweeping could be heard as regularly as clockwork: weary but persistent; and the lane was always clean.

Her son, Baiqi, came to see her once or twice. He had done very well at school, and as a result of his good behaviour he had only spent a short time farming before being transferred back. Now he was back at the college, teaching the children of workers, peasants and soldiers.

"They said my behaviour is good," he said proudly, "and that I am educable. I'm the only one to be given a teaching job at the college." Xiuzhen had little interest in this. She had seen the world. Nothing could impress her any more.

Baiqi was dressed in a clean, well ironed "people's suit", and had three fountain pens tucked in his upper pocket. Though intellectuals were no longer respectable, he was proud of himself. "He has grown up and is doing quite well for himself," thought Xiuzhen. "But look at me—possessing only a dress left by a dead woman and a pair of patched trousers. I look half human and half ghost. Why didn't I have Baiqi's luck in having a capable mother like me? That opium addict begot his son, then left me to take care of everything. I have almost worked myself to death for others, but who cares about me?"

"Kissinger came to China and the relationship between China and the U.S. is normalized." Baiqi blabbed on and on. "English will probably come back into fashion. Don't you think?" In a roundabout way he began to tell her he had a girlfriend.

"Enough!" Xiuzhen stopped him. "I have to rise very early in the morning to clean the lane. You'd better go."

If the He residence marked the high-point in her life, Baiqi was a reminder of all her hardships. Each time he came he aroused painful memories which left her moody for several days after. "He's even won the heart of a girl!" she exclaimed indignantly to herself. "What a lucky girl to get the man she loves. Why didn't I have such luck instead of being lumbered either with feeble Tailor Long or stout Old Tie?"

Baiqi became increasingly successful. He got married and moved into a new apartment. He wrote to Xiuzhen asking her to quit her job and move to Hangzhou and live with them. Xiuzhen ignored the letter. She didn't even go to the wedding or her grandson's month-old celebration.

Xiuzhen was old; her back was bent and her steps unsteady. Apart from sweeping the lane and helping the neighbours with a few groceries, she had fewer and fewer jobs to do. People were scared of her slovenly appearance.

Sister Hu was old too, and came less frequently. Her small lodgings were given to her daughter on her marriage, and she herself went to nurse a paralyzed old woman, taking care of her every need, even changing the filthy sheets. Still, at least she had a place to sleep. But after the old woman's death?... Sister Hu was worried.

"I told you before," sneered Xiuzhen when Sister Hu complained. "There is no sense in raising daughters when you're hard up. You should have dumped her in the well!"

Sister Hu gave a sigh. "People say her father is doing quite well in Taiwan, that he owns an accountancy firm." She rubbed her bleary eyes with her chilblained hands. "I have asked somebody to take him my address."

"So," Xiuzhen mocked, "you expect him to come back and claim his wife, do you?"

"No." Sister Hu gave a sad smile. "He has got a family over there. As long as he remembers me and gives me some money so I won't have to work. That's all I can hope for. If he can send my daughter's family abroad, so much the better."

Xiuzhen put her hands on her hips, as was her wont, and sneered again. "Can't you ever forget about your daughter? She got married and kicked you out!"

Sister Hu gave a hopeless smile, making her eyes sink even deeper into their sockets. "What else could I do? She is my daughter no matter what." She changed the subject. "How can you be so slovenly, Xiuzhen? And how can you live in such a pigsty?"

Indeed, a sickening odour emanated from the room, and even more strongly from Xiuzhen herself.

But Xiuzhen laughed it off. "I toil from morning to night. I haven't the time to clean it. Nobody ever comes here, so what difference does it make? Why don't you mind your own business?"

Sister Hu was cut off. "Xiuzhen really is getting on," she thought. After that she dropped in less often.

8

Xiuzhen's back was bent even lower. If someone called her from behind she had to slowly turn her entire body. Now, except for a few old acquaintances, no one asked her to do anything. It was nerve-wracking to watch her work.

Then, one day, the lane suddenly became filled with young girls, all with Shaoxing accents, all perfumed and all fashionably dressed. Nowadays country girls were coming in droves to Shanghai, just as Xiuzhen had done in her youth. They were no longer called "amahs" but "nursemaids".

The family now living in Doctor Huang's apartment engaged one too. The girls often gathered together in the living room to chat. They ate melon seeds, watched television and gossiped about their employers; even making jokes about what they did in bed. Their voices could even be heard from behind the kitchen door.

"How ill-mannered! They don't behave like hired helpers, but more like arrogant princesses!" thought Xiuzhen.

On summer evenings the girls created an even bigger rumpus. They either went to the cinema in threes or fours or sat on the steps singing and laughing. Their merry laughter drifted across on the evening breeze; the shadows of their slim figures danced in the moonlight.

Xiuzhen wept for her lost youth. Suddenly she rushed to the window and shouted down angrily into the street: "Stop your noise, you stupid girls! You are disturbing other people's sleep!"

Her shout was greeted by another gale of laughter, louder and more insolent than ever.

"You filthy old witch! You're nothing more than a bag of trash!"

That day Xiuzhen went to work at the Zhangs who lived opposite. She went there three times a week to clean and do the laundry, coming back after lunch.

Old woman Zhang was about the same age as Xiuzhen, and since she believed that washing machines ruined clothes she always gave the laundry to Xiuzhen to do. That day, as Xiuzhen carried a basketful of laundry out of the bathroom, she was sitting at the table shelling peas.

"Why don't you join your son and daughter-in-law and let them support you?" asked the old lady. "You are no longer young."

Xiuzhen couldn't reach the clothes line on the balcony. She climbed onto a stool and leaned out.

"Be careful. Let me help you..." The old lady stood up. But before she had finished her sentence the stool collapsed with a crash and Xiuzhen was gone.

9

Trolley buses in Shanghai were always crowded.

Sister Hu, in a brand-new woolen overcoat, struggled into the bus helped by her daughter and son-in-law. These days few people offered to give up their seats to the elderly. A sudden lurch threw Sister Hu forward and she trod on a girl's fashionable stockings.

"You walking corpse!" spat out the girl, cocking her head to deliver the insult. "Why bother going out before you die?"

Sister Hu's daughter responded in kind. "You won't even live to my mom's age. Better watch out you don't get knocked over by a bus, or fall down some stairs or choke to death on your beancurd..." The stream of abuse effectively silenced the girl.

Sister Hu had regained contact with her man in Taiwan, and he was due in Shanghai at the end of the month. Since she had re-established contact, her daughter and son-in-law had become pleasant to her again. Her son-in-law had ordered a suit from a very reputable tailor and they were on their way to try it on. "You must look at shoulders first. A good suit must have well-fitting shoulders." Having worked at the Hes, Sister Hu knew something about suits.

A sharp female voice came from the middle of the bus. "My sister's hospital just received an old woman who had fallen from the second floor. She was alive when she got to the hospital but died the next day."

"A fall from the second floor wouldn't necessarily kill someone," remarked her listener.

"True, and she landed on the ground buttocks first. It

wouldn't have been fatal except that she had gold bars tied around her waist..."

At this all ears pricked up.

"Twelve bars, four bracelets, six rings and three ingots..."

"She must have been a self-employed merchant!" someone guessed.

"No, she used to work as an amah."

Sister Hu was so engrossed in the story that she overshot her stop. "It's unbelievable," she thought, "this world has too many unbelievable things. I must tell Xiuzhen. How could that amah make so much money, while we end up with nothing."

10

The small room housing Xiuzhen's bed was eventually vacated, and the gold given to Baiqi. Overjoyed at the windfall, he couldn't be bothered with the old clothes in the soap box. Whoever wanted them could take them, he said. But none of the fashionably dressed young nurses were interested. It so happened that a garbage collector was passing the door and picked up the unwanted belongings.

Baiqi's wife was dismissive of that dull-looking teapot. With a thermos-flask available, what was the point of keeping this filthy thing? The dustman picked it up and threw it into his back-pack.

11

One day an evening newspaper ran the following article:

Among the teaware made by the famous pottery mas-

ter Gong Chun of Yixing was a teapot possessing a u-
nique feature bestowed by a secret kilning process: it
changes colour from brown to jade green as it is filled
with tea, then reverts slowly back to dark brown as it is
emptied. It is a miracle of heavenly engineering rather
than mere craftsmanship. The world seems full of such
wonders we still don't know about. And nobody seems
to know whether the teapot is still in existence....

Translated by Li Guoqing

Row, Row, Row: Row to Grandma's Home

Row, row, row: row to Grandma's home.
She calls me a lovely child
And offers me crackers and sweets.
I eat to my heart's content,
And then I feel much pleased.

THIS ancient nursery rhyme has been sung to many generations of children. Every time I sing it, it reminds me of my childhood world. That world, as the song says, was a world full of love.

Every summer, according to our traditional custom, married daughters who had left home would come back to their parents' bringing their children. All the visitors were treated like distinguished guests, but the grandchildren were especially pampered—they were treated like "little emperors".

When I was a child my mother had to work, and my brother had reached the age where, though still a boy, he had begun to think of himself as a man. He regarded going to Grandma's as kid's stuff. So, to keep the custom, I went alone.

Grandma's house was only a penny bus ride away. But every summer vacation, my grandpa would come to take me. Carrying a bundle of clothes, I would ride with him in a pedicab. As I left, Mom and Dad exhorted: "Be good," as if I were going off on a long journey.

The lane where Grandma lived was built in 1930. The word "1930" was formed by small blue porcelain tiles on the white ceramic bricks of the entrance way. All the houses in the lane were commodious and had modern drainage systems, gas and bathrooms, but on the outside they kept to the traditional Shanghai style—stone walls and small courtyards.

At the entrance of the lane was a cobbler's stall. Rain or shine, the old shoemaker was always at his post. While I was growing up, all my cloth shoes were shaped by his hands.

"Oh, here you are." He would look up and greet me, then go back to his work. He knew everyone in the lane, and everyone knew him.

At the end of the lane stood three houses which harmoniously combined Chinese and Western styles. Each had a small garden in front and an iron gate which was seldom closed.

Grandma's house was the middle one, the one with wisteria vines climbing the gate. You could see the flowers as soon as you entered the lane. They spread gracefully over the wall, creating an atmosphere of fragrant tranquility. Later, when I myself had a daughter, I once read her a riddle: "There is a bowl in front of Grandma's door, which catches the rain but never is full." It reminded me of the bowl-shaped wisteria climbing the gate.

Four or five families were crowded into the three-story building, but I remember that neighbours would almost never quarrel—let alone come to blows—over trivial matters like dividing up water and electricity fees or keeping the landings clear.

For many years before the so-called "cultural revolution," simple customs and courtesies were still honoured. My grandparents lived on the ground floor in two rooms, a living room and a bedroom. The iron bars on the windows were installed later for security. In those days the windows—almost as tall as a man—were always open, but Grandma never lost as much as a sewing needle. Outside her door was a corridor, so people often passed by. They would tap on the open door and ask: "Sister Pan, I am going shopping. Can I get you anything?"

As was often the case with close neighbours, the guest of one was the guest of all. Every summer when I went to Grandma's, all the neighbours would come downstairs to greet me. The elderly grannies would say: "Oh, here is the young miss." For them "young miss" was not in the least sarcastic or bourgeois.

On the first day of my visit the dining table was always covered with dishes: steamed lotus with glutinous rice, steamed pork wrapped in lotus-leaf, tender corn and other delicious things. All were prepared by those grannies and aunties especially for me. My playmates were always there too. As soon as summer vacation began they would ask Grandma over and over: "When is Naishan coming?"

Grandpa was well-educated. His Chinese and English were both excellent. He did at one time have a successful career, but unfortunately he wasn't permitted to use his talents, so he retired early.

Grandpa was also quite handsome. Grandma, on the other hand, was plain-looking, old-fashioned and illiterate, but they deeply loved each other.

When Grandpa died he left us a private autobiography. Until then I didn't know he had been lashed by painful emotions. During the Anti-Japanese War, Grandpa lived alone in Chongqing*. He was young and dashing. A female colleague

---

* The wartime capital.

who had studied in France fell in love with him, and he was attracted to her as well. But in the end, with much regret, Grandpa made his choice—he left her.

After V-J day he came back to Shanghai, which he had left eight years earlier. When he stepped off the ramp of the plane he looked up, and there was Grandma along with my mother and the grandson he had never seen—my brother.

The regret buried in Grandpa's heart at last flew away. As he wrote in his autobiography: "Eight years I was away from home. You couldn't say I had returned with fame and fortune, but my conscience was clear."

Memories are forever preserved in one's heart. Some of them are never divulged. In Grandpa's life there was one such memory. Once on the train from Shanghai to Hangzhou he was sitting opposite a young lady wearing a close-fitting cheongsam. To conceal his timidity in front of this graceful and pretty woman, he opened the newspaper to block the view between them. But in doing so he knocked over a tea cup on the side table, spilling the tea on the front of her dress. It was hot, and her dress was thin. He was terribly flustered. He hurriedly gave her his handkerchief, though he knew it was useless.

"It's nothing," she said with a smile. She took his newspaper, folded it, and carefully slipped it under the wet spot on her dress. Then she struck up a friendly conversation with him, so that he wouldn't feel too awkward and to show that she was not angry. It was the hot season, so in a short time her dress was dry. When the train reached the station she removed the paper and gave it back to him.

"Good-bye," she said. They never saw each other again. They didn't even know each other's names. But the woman on that train was engraved on Grandpa's memory until the day he died. I don't know if that nameless woman is still alive, or if she knew her image was forever sealed in another's heart.

In my memory, Grandpa was very meticulous, honourable, and well-educated. He had great talent but no opportunity to use it. All he could do was to take English books and translate them into Chinese, then translate them back into English. He did it over and over again. If his political background had been acceptable, Grandpa would have been an excellent civil servant. He filed everything in perfect order, from family letters to eggs laid by the hens to rags used in the kitchen. Needless to say, he was even more careful with his books and old photo albums.

Often you could hear the click-clack of the abacus when you were passing by his room. He was doing the family accounts. Though the amounts were small, his dignified and careful manner gave him the air of a cashier in a bank. So even though he didn't have a job, he was always busy at home. He sat down at his desk early every morning. Neatly arranged on the desk were glue, a paper knife, blotting paper and an inkpad. Like a bank manager, he would sit there all day long.

Occasionally he would chat with one or two old neighbourhood friends in the living room. They would talk idly about the hard times of the Anti-Japanese War, their gains and losses in the pre-Liberation stock market or well-known figures in Shanghai.

One of these old men spoke the Suzhou dialect, which was pleasing to the ear. I never got tired of his lively story-telling. Unfortunately, during the "cultural revolution", when people were shouting slogans, this old man, because of his poor hearing, misheard "Long live Chairman Mao" as "salted beancurd milk", because the two phrases sound nearly identical in Suzhou dialect. When he innocently shouted the "salted beancurd milk" he was immediately seized as a counterrevolutionary criminal and died without being cleared of this false accusation.

Grandma's daily life was quite different from Grandpa's. Morning was the busiest time for her. Even during the many years when she had a maid she always did the cooking herself, because she was a wonderful cook, and she knew what Grandpa liked. While Grandpa and his friends were chatting volubly in the living room, several grannies and aunties were preparing food and enjoying the cool air at the kitchen door. Naturally they liked to gossip about the fortunes and misfortunes of this or that family, but never in a hurtful or malicious way. I was interested in both conversations, so as soon as I ran to the kitchen, I would want to run back to the living room and hear what I was missing. I never expected such idle conversation would stimulate me to take the road toward a writing career and provide me with the raw material for my literature.

Grandma wasn't pretty, but she had a wonderful sense of humour. She liked to make fun of Grandpa. Once he was talking about the old days when country people seldom wore cotton stockings and considered them a treasured possession. It wasn't easy, but Grandpa finally obtained a pair. He begrudged wearing them until his wedding day. As he was recalling this story, Grandma interrupted him and laughed. "Now I remember. At the wedding people were whispering and giggling because there was a hole in your stocking. I heard someone say, 'Look at the hole. Maybe he was too careful for his own good. He thought his fancy stockings were safe in a hiding place, but that just made it easier for the rats to get to them.'" That gave Grandpa and me a good hearty laugh.

Grandma was over seventy then, and according to the traditional custom she began to prepare her grave clothes. The sleeves should be cut long enough to cover the fingers. When the tailor was taking measurements, Grandma told her jokingly, "Don't cut the sleeves too long. That way I can also wear it *before* I die."

But unfortunately, after the Red Guards went rampaging through her house there was nothing left. She died wearing only her pyjamas, without even a pair of decent shoes.

Grandma was old-fashioned, but Grandpa was not ashamed to take her out. Once on an airplane they found the lady next to Grandma was the wife of a high-ranking Kuomintang official. This made Grandpa a little nervous, so he tried to change Grandma's seat, but she said, "Don't worry about it. She just married rank. I'll be polite. If she wants to get up on her high horse, that's her problem."

To Grandpa's surprise, the two women—one cosmopolitan and the other unsophisticated—chatted merrily the whole trip. Afterwards Grandpa asked: "How could you find so much to talk about?" She replied, "We're both women, so naturally we have a lot to chat about—family, children and things."

It was late at night. When I went into my bedroom yawning, Grandma had already lighted the mosquito coil. My pillow and straw mat were suffused with a delicate fragrance. Peering through the darkness, I could discern the tiny red spot silently glowing in the dark. A wisp of smoke formed ever-changing figures which reminded me of Andersen's "Little Match Girl." I was very contented. This childhood world was so wonderful, and so many people loved me!

Was I too young to know? Was the world really as good as I thought? It seemed so beautiful, and the people were so kind-hearted. Though Shanghai was a flourishing metropolis, it retained the humanity of its simple folk customs.

August of 1965 was the happiest time for my grandparents. It was the first time in my life that I received a salary—I had been assigned to a middle school to teach English. To show my filial piety, I bought them some soya-sauce-flavoured pork and soft Suzhou candy, which they liked better than anything. They kept it in a tin. When guests came, they would offer them some and say, "Try it. This is from my granddaughter."

"Oh, you have a filial granddaughter. How lucky you are!" the guests would say enviously. My grandparents would smile contentedly.

Gradually, things changed in the neighbourhood. New neighbours moved in, installed fences and lived their own lives. Nobody bothered anybody else. Some of them started to quarrel over trivialities. They didn't talk much, and their conversations were limited to stock phrases about the weather.

Then in 1966, the Red Guards came and searched Grandma and Grandpa's house. They smashed and confiscated possessions. My dear grandma, who was always so open-minded and magnanimous, was sad and angry. She threw all her jewelry into the toilet. But the Red Guards caught her in the act and spat insults at her. This was more than she could bear. She died of a sudden heart attack that night.

The only consolation for me was that she had shared the happiness of my first salary.

Grandpa was deeply grieved. In memory of her, he wrote a poem. The last lines were:

I understand that everyone has this eternal regret .

Loving couples can't finish life's journey together .

Grandpa lived another ten lonely years . He witnessed the downfall of the "Gang of Four", but it's a pity that he didn't live long enough to read my short stories .

When I was a schoolgirl I never knew how to start a composition . So I always started with "Time flies by just like a galloping horse". Only now, after decades have passed in flash, do I realize how true it is .

For several decades the old cobbler at the end of the lane was always engrossed in his work . He seemed not to notice the street life in front of him . I thought he must be unfeeling . He just busied himself with day-to-day survival . But actually his mind was quite sharp, and nothing escaped his attention .

On the day when Grandma's house was looted of almost everything, as the Red Guards went away cockily with their spoils, the old cobbler suddenly strode forward to block the way and said, "You shouldn't do that . It's getting cold . At least you should leave some winter clothes for those old people ."

The old man's bravery startled the Red Guards . They stopped and threw down a suitcase . He called over his son to help carry the case to Grandma's home .

My dear old cobbler has passed away, and his stall has become a public phone booth . But he remains in my memory . He reminds me of the old man in the opening shot of a Soviet movie . This weather-beaten old man was playing a stringed instrument . His face was a blank, but the music he coaxed from the strings reflected the ebb and flow of human life .

The elder generation has passed away silently, and I myself have entered middle age . Many former Red Guards have gone abroad to make money. But some must still feel guilty for what they have done. They viciously persecuted their elders by making them kneel on broken glass, slapping them in the face, even putting them to death.

I visited the United States last spring and finally met my uncle, whom I had never seen. He is my mother's only brother and is over sixty now. Seeing him was like seeing my Grandpa come back to life. It reminded me of an old saying: "May the tree of human life remain ever green."

On the wall at my uncle's home a picture of my grandparents smiles down at me. The wall is covered with group photos of my greatgrandparents, grandparents, mother and uncle when they were young. As I was looking at the photos my uncle said to me: "I want to let the kids know they are Chinese." His two sons are "ABCs" (American-Born Chinese). They are American born and reared and cannot speak Chinese. But according to our custom they are still descendants of the dragon—China.

"Row, row, row: row to Grandma's home." The wisteria vines at Grandma's gate still bloom every year, but the faces inside the house are different now.

Every grave-sweeping festival, I got to see my grandparents. They eternally sleep on Lingyan Mountain in Suzhou. On their grave bloom bunches of white roses. Seeing the roses as I approach from a distance reminds me of the wisteria I used to see as I approached their house. Perhaps the roses are a blessing from my dear grandparents.

Before the "cultural revolution", every Spring Festival Eve my grandparents held a memorial ceremony for our ancestors. Later, because of the changed political climate, they stopped hanging the pictures of our ancestors, but they still used joss sticks and candles when offering sacrifices. Four cups of wine were put on a square table. Then rice and dishes were solemnly present-ed. My grandparents, although they were proud of rejecting all kinds of superstition, would pay their respects devoutly. They loved me dearly but at that moment of devotion insisted I behave respectfully. For me, the whole ceremony just meant a good meal. I would laugh at them for their old-fashioned ways. Now I realize that my grandparents were setting an example. They were showing the young generation how to respect their ances-tors. They believed that if only those who loved their family and friends had cherished the memory of their ancestors, the tragedy of young people abusing their elders would not have happened. I think in this period of reform and openness we must not forget our roots—traditional Chinese culture.

My dear grandparents, I'm lucky enough to see China today and to be able to write this article in memory of you. I have also seen your only son, whom you said goodbye so long ago and nev-er saw again.

Grandpa, like all other honest and plain-living Chinese intel-lectuals, you didn't leave me a fortune. You left me only your biography, which was a great help to my career. You also gave me boundless love and taught me how to be a simple and honest person.

How nice it is that as I go my own way you keep on blessing me from another world.

Translated by Zhang Zhenzhong
and William R . Palmer

图书在版编目（CIP）数据

蓝屋/程乃珊著；李国庆等译.－北京：外文出版社，2003.9
（熊猫丛书）
ISBN 7-119-03359-X

Ⅰ．蓝...　Ⅱ．①程...②李...　Ⅲ．①中篇小说-作品集-中国-当代-英
文②短篇小说-作品集-中国-当代-英文　Ⅳ．I247.7

中国版本图书馆 CIP 数据核字（2003）第 059887 号

外文出版社网址：
　http://www.flp.com.cn
外文出版社电子信箱：
　info@flp.com.cn
　sales@flp.com.cn

熊猫丛书
蓝屋

作　　者	程乃珊
译　　者	李国庆等
责任编辑	陈海燕　李　芳
封面设计	唐少文
印刷监制	张国祥
出版发行	外文出版社
社　　址	北京市百万庄大街 24 号　　邮政编码　100037
电　　话	（010）68320579（总编室）
	（010）68329514/68327211（推广发行部）
印　　刷	北京市密云春雷印刷厂
经　　销	新华书店/外文书店
开　　本	大 32 开
印　　数	0001—5000 册　　　　　　印　张　10.25
版　　次	2005 年第 1 版第 1 次印刷
装　　别	平
书　　号	ISBN 7-119-03359-X
	10－E－3570P
定　　价	16.00 元